─ THE ─
FEBRUARY 23RD COUP

Chaitram Singh

iUniverse, Inc.
Bloomington

The February 23rd Coup

Copyright © 2011 Chaitram Singh

This is a work of fiction. All of the characters, names, incidents, organizations, and dialogue in this novel are either the products of the author's imagination or are used fictitiously.

iUniverse books may be ordered through booksellers or by contacting:

iUniverse
1663 Liberty Drive
Bloomington, IN 47403
www.iuniverse.com
1-800-Authors (1-800-288-4677)

Because of the dynamic nature of the Internet, any Web addresses or links contained in this book may have changed since publication and may no longer be valid. The views expressed in this work are solely those of the author and do not necessarily reflect the views of the publisher, and the publisher hereby disclaims any responsibility for them.

Any people depicted in stock imagery provided by Thinkstock are models, and such images are being used for illustrative purposes only.

Certain stock imagery © Thinkstock.

ISBN: 978-1-4620-2054-6 (sc)
ISBN: 978-1-4620-2053-9 (hc)
ISBN: 978-1-4620-2052-2 (e)

Library of Congress Control Number: 2011908297

Printed in the United States of America

iUniverse rev. date: 7/1/2011

To
My West Point Classmates
Company D-2, Class of 1973
"Proud and Free"

Special thanks:

To my many military and paramilitary friends who were willing to share reminiscences with me and to offer technical advice; among them, Tom Stanford, Doug MacIntyre, Tom Fitzsimmons, Paul Murtha, Dyal (Zab) Panday, Jack Mangra, Jonathan Graves, and Ken Mullis.

To Maureen Morgan, for her assistance in manuscript preparation and proofreading; Chris Diller, for line editing; and to Anna Miles, Darla Fox, and Joan Christian, for additional proofreading.

To Berry College, for travel and research grants and for a sabbatical in spring 2009 to allow me to complete the first draft of the manuscript.

May 8, 2010
Kaieteur Restaurant, Queens, New York

My name is Ralph Godfrey Rambarran. I am Anglo-Indian. Light complexioned, I have some of the features of my maternal grandmother, Susan Spooner, who is white. However, my grandfather, Daniel Spooner, is of mixed ethnicity. All of his relations were East Indian, except for his paternal grandmother, who was black. The only hint of that in my immediate family is the slightly wavy hair of my mother, Maria Elena, a veterinarian in Queens, New York, where we live. My mother grew up on a beautiful plantation her parents owned in Guyana, but we rarely talk about it when she is around because it upsets her dreadfully.

My father practices internal medicine in the Queens area, though, at an earlier stage in his life, he had been a military officer. Like my mother, he emigrated from Guyana but traces his lineage entirely to India, from where some of his forebears had been taken as indentured laborers to work on the sugar plantations that dot the Guyanese coastline. My paternal great grandfather was an exception to that pattern of settlement. A Rajput, born in Nainital at the foothills of the Himalayas, he had enlisted in the British army and served in Europe during World War I. When the war ended, he settled in Guyana and started a family. Innumerable recounting of the Rajput traditions and obligations propelled my father into military service, first as a cadet in the United States Military Academy before being commissioned as an officer in the Guyanese army.

My father and his friends have gathered here at the Kaieteur Restaurant for a commemorative dinner for Asad Ali Shah, my father's very close friend. Two days ago, Uncle Asad was struck by a passing car as he was crossing Liberty Avenue. His funeral was yesterday. Stephen Erikson, who was a Captain in the U.S. Army, is also present, as are several former officers who had served with my father in the army in Guyana. Erikson and my father were classmates at West Point and had roomed together at various points during their four-year stay. The other two older gentlemen are Colonel Tom Stanford and Colonel John Wesfall. They are now retired and work for defense contractors, but my father insisted I address each by his rank. The presence of the Colonels explains why I and my friend, Altaf, Uncle Asad's son, are here this evening. I was assigned to pick up Colonel Stanford at JFK earlier this afternoon and to attend him as a military aide would; Colonel Wesfall was Altaf's assignment.

The plan is for them all to go after dinner to the wake at Altaf's home on 111th Street in Richmond Hill. Indo-Guyanese wakes can go into the wee hours of the morning, continuing each day for a couple of weeks as friends and relatives, especially those in the New York area, return again and again to be with the family of the deceased.

The Kaieteur Restaurant is on Lefferts Boulevard and Jamaica Avenue, a popular dining spot for West Indians, but Guyanese and Trinidadians especially. The dining area is a large rectangular space with a wall separating it from the octagonal sports bar fronting Lefferts. Large paintings depicting scenes from Guyana adorn the walls. The painting on the far left wall close to the kitchen is a depiction of Orinduik Falls; the large painting on the back wall directly in my line of sight is the Canje Creek Bridge and a part of Sheet Anchor Village.

It is Saturday evening, and the restaurant is filling up. Three tables have been joined together to accommodate our group. Altaf sits facing the front entrance, and I am directly across from him facing the Canje Creek Bridge. Glasses clank at our tables as these older gentlemen welcome one another. Steve Erikson and my father begin by catching up the Colonels on what they had been doing the past couple of years. When the second round of drinks comes, my father proposes a toast to their departed friend, Asad Shah, to whom he said they owed their lives. My father asks that they remember the others as well, especially Captain Ralph Godfrey Spooner, Colonel Franchette Taylor, Captain Malcolm Felix, and Lieutenant Anil Rampersaud. There is a moment of silence, then my father says, "Gosh, who would have thought things would have turned out the way they did?"

This is the story those gentlemen proceeded to tell.

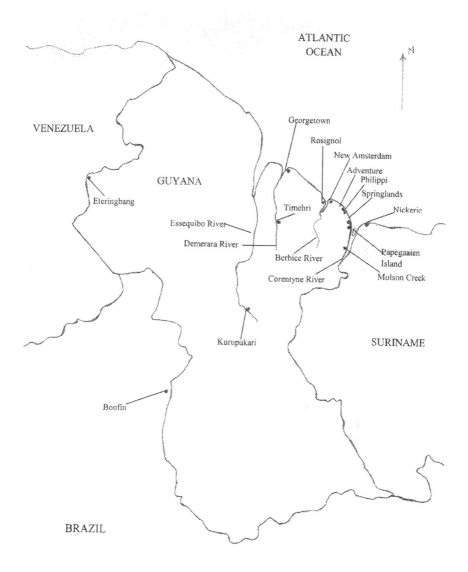

ATLANTIC
OCEAN

N

VENEZUELA

GUYANA

Eteringbang

Georgetown

Rosignol

New Amsterdam

Adventure
Philippi

Springlands

Timehri

Nickerie

Essequibo River

Demerara River

Berbice River

Corentyne River

Papegaaien
Island

Molson Creek

Kurupukari

SURINAME

Bonfin

BRAZIL

ONE

Guyana, 1979

It was not the best of times, nor might it have been the worst of times, though many thought so; and an exodus began. A nation of immigrants started to migrate again. But the work day still began at 05:30 with Indian film music from Radio Demerara; death announcements still occurred at the same times; and the Kabaka Party still ruled the land.

They say that when the Dutch first encountered the Guyana coast land in the early 1600s, they fell in love with the place because it reminded them of home. The land was below sea level, like the old country, and they set about building a seawall running about three hundred miles from the northwest, along the coastline, all the way to the eastern border. They drained the swamp and introduced sugarcane. Then, the story lost its sweetness. The Dutch brought slaves from Africa to work their sugar plantations, housing them in ten-by-eight *logies*, made of wood scraps, with a roof, a door, and one wooden window, hinged to the ceiling above. What followed were whippings, revolts, and the roasting of captured rebels over slow fires.

Except for a brief period of French control, the Dutch stayed for close to two centuries; then in 1814, the British finally took over. They kept the sugar culture, the plantations, the slaves and the whip, the seawall and the Dutch place names, though they added many of their own, including the capital's, and they introduced breadfruit and salted codfish into the colonial diet. A century elapsed before the British developed a bad conscience about slavery, or was it that slavery was bad for business? But they ended slavery only to reintroduce it in the form of indentured workers, mainly from India. Back into the old slave *logies* they went, with the same tasks; resistance met with jailings, collective protests with shootings, and official inquiries exonerated the plantation owners. These are all part of the national collective memory, but the emerging ethnic polyglot had no choice but to forgive and continue to bring in the sugar crop.

After emancipation, black people had moved from the sugar plantations to set up cooperative farming communities, but farming on inhospitable remnants of land discouraged many, and a new internal migration began. Some went into the interior and became *pork-knockers,* mining for gold; others went into the handful of towns, taking menial jobs at first, then gradually moving into the civil service, the police, and teaching. After the Second World War, many black people moved to the bauxite mining towns on the Demerara and Berbice Rivers. The Indians remained in agriculture after the indenture system ended. Many moved off the sugar plantations into rice cultivation and into business, and educated their children for the professions.

Along the narrow swath of coast land that the Dutch cleared out and the British ruled for a century and a half, black villages alternate with Indian villages. History had brought them to the coast, and family ties have kept them there. A small community, they wake up at 05:30 every day to the sounds of Indian film music from Radio Demerara, a half-hour of Christian worship, then the slow, deep organ music preparing everyone for death announcements. The young man who comes on afterwards must surely not have listened to the death announcements because he promptly declares what a wonderful day it is and drums out any lingering sound of the organ with a melange of American pop and West Indian music. Curry flavors and Indian film music in the evening mark the end of the work day.

From the northwest corner of the colony to Crabwood Creek on the eastern frontier, the Dutch laid out a dirt road paralleling the seawall, interrupted only by the mouths of the three almost evenly-spaced internal rivers that part the coastline and empty into the Atlantic. The only diversions from this main road are perpendicular dirt roads that run along the banks of the three rivers, and shorter ones into the sugar plantations.

As independence neared, the British graded the coastal dirt road but left it unpaved, except at the outskirts of the capital. The donkey carts gave way to trucks, not that these were always faster. Stuck in muddy roads, trucks carrying bags of flower, potatoes, split peas, and onions could remain in place for hours before tractors arrived to pull them out. Nevertheless, the day of the motorized vehicle had arrived. All along the coast, large colored buses, with diamond-shaped luggage compartments on top, hauled clerks and their bicycles, market vendors with their fish, fruit, and vegetable baskets, and students with their book and lunch bags.

After independence, American money helped to pave the coastal roads, but the pitch had not long dried when the Kabaka Party introduced a new creed, which promised to make "the small man into a real man," sustained by cassava bread and milk, and secured by the simple concession of trusting the Kabakans to lead them to the promised land. But the small men soon realized that the real men carried swagger sticks, wore heavy leather boots, and called each other "comrade." Soon, flour and potatoes disappeared from the grocery shelves, then cheese, split peas, and canned goods of all kinds. Still, the cassava bread and milk did not come. The water taps sputtered; electricity deserted the transmission wires; and, late at night, the small men of this kerosene-lamp culture listened intently in their dark, shuttered houses for the "clop, clop" from the heavy leather boots of the comrades carrying swagger sticks.

Then, dissension broke out among the comrades who wore leather boots and carried swagger sticks.

Two

August 8, 1979
Officers' Club, Timehri, Guyana

"Why now, Colonel?" Captain Spooner asked, sitting across from Colonel Franchette Taylor at the square card table, butted against the back wall of the lounge at the southern end of the Club. Spooner was well turned out in garrison uniform: dark green fatigues with three shining pips on each epaulette, a blue lanyard over his left shoulder, and his green beret neatly folded and fashionably tucked under the right epaulette with the brigade emblem facing forward. The son of a *dougla* veterinarian and an American mother, Spooner was a strikingly handsome, twenty-seven year old man, who might have passed for Frankie Avalon except for his yellow complexion and his wavy, light brown hair, cropped low to meet army regulations. Born on the family's farm in Philippi, he was a country boy at heart even though secondary schooling at Queen's College in Georgetown and Officer Cadet training in the England had made him perfectly comfortable in urban settings.

Captain Spooner commanded B-Company, currently deployed at three separate locations along the Venezuelan border. Following the practice of company commanders with interior deployments, Spooner had set up his command post at Camp Stevenson, Timehri, from where he flew in once a week to visit each of his platoons. Until the end of its border deployment, B-Company was one of three companies which constituted the Border Operations Command, under Colonel Llewelyn Ovid LaFleur, headquartered at Camp Stevenson. Spooner's Company was scheduled for rotation to the coast in the middle of the month, at which time he would be serving with the Internal Operations Command.

Colonel Franchette Taylor was in mufti: a gaberdene shirtjac and matching trousers, proper formal attire for a traveling official from a socialist state, where Western-style suits were seen as relics of imperialism. At five feet ten, he sat at eye-level with Captain Spooner.

A squared jaw, dark brown man, his sinewy frame appeared to have defied years of garrison duty and extended hours at the Officers' Clubs. His slightly sunken eyes and a hint of gray on the sides of his head were the clearest indications of the ten-year age difference he had over his junior colleague.

Taylor was a man of the city. A descendant of emancipated slaves who had hurried away from the plantation life, he was born and educated in Georgetown and had been one of the first cadets sent for officer training at Mons in the UK. After the British officers turned over the army following independence in 1966, Taylor and other black officers rose rapidly in rank. How times had changed though! Wanting to perpetuate itself in power, the Kabaka government, like its counterparts in Africa, was now worried about its Colonels.

Franchette Taylor was in charge of Internal Operations Command, headquartered at Camp Ayanganna, the main army base located at the northeastern edge of Georgetown, at the intersection of Vlissengen and Thomas Roads. The three infantry companies in his command were on three-month deployment along the Atlantic coast and would soon be redeployed to border locations. Taylor was scheduled to take the 11:00 a.m. Carib Air flight outbound from Timehri International Airport to Port-of-Spain, where he would change planes to travel on to Washington, D.C. The Colonel was representing his government at a conference on hemispheric security at the U.S. National War College. The late breakfast meeting with Spooner was his idea.

"The short answer," Colonel Taylor replied, "is that the situation has never been clearer than it is right now and never more threatening." Palms wrapped around his coffee cup, he was sitting upright and looking directly at his younger colleague. Spooner shook his head and looked down. When Spooner made eye contact again, Colonel Taylor braced for the recriminations; none came. "Look, Ralph," Taylor continued, "I know you don't like this government."

"Never did," Spooner insisted.

"Okay, and you thought something should have been done before. But you just can't overthrow a government every time it does something you don't like."

"You are oversimplifying my position, Colonel," Spooner said. "I first spoke to you about this five years ago. The President had rigged two elections."

It was common knowledge that the Kabaka Party had rigged both the 1968 and 1973 elections. The British media had run documentaries exposing the fraudulent voter registration and conduct of both elections, and the Opposition People's Party never ceased reminding people of these through their newspaper and their pamphlets. However, the Opposition People's Party seemed to have accommodated itself to the Kabakans being in power indefinitely and had modified its tactics by calling for a national unity government in which it would participate. The fact that both parties were committed to the socialist transformation of the country would serve as the cement holding such a coalition together. So far, the Kabakans had not found any appeal in that proposal especially since they controlled the means to retain power without the inconvenience of a coalition partner.

"Ralph," Colonel Tayor responded, "you must remember that the Kabaka party had a lot of support in 1968. People were worried about communism, which the Opposition People's Party embraced. Remember too that the army was only two years old; British officers held the top positions; I was a Captain, and you weren't even in it. Most important, though, a majority of the local officers supported this government."

"Alright, how about 1973?" Spooner asked. "The Comrade Leader, as he likes to be called, shamelessly rigged that election, declared the Kabaka Party socialist and paramount over the state. And what did the army leadership do? It collaborated with the rigging and pledged its allegiance to the Party."

"I'm glad you've brought this up," Colonel Taylor said. "The people who made those decisions were the Chief of Staff and the Brigade Commander. I was a Battalion Commander at the time."

"Those people are still in charge, Colonel, and you're still a Battalion Commander. So, I'll ask again, why now?"

"Because the situation in the country has changed dramatically. Everyone is suffering under this government; even black people who staunchly backed the Kabaka Party in the past are today protesting outside of Parliament. But, most important, we have a core of army officers who might be persuaded to act."

"Toward what end?" Spooner asked.

"What do you mean: 'Toward what end?'"

"Well," replied Captain Spooner, "when I used to talk about the need to change this government, people would say that was the same as turning over the government to the Indians. What's changed?"

"A lot, Ralph; a lot. Look, we now have a new party on the scene."

"Yes, Colonel, the Workers' Party. Its leader, Dr. Nelson, is a committed socialist. So you want to remove one socialist and put in another? Colonel, I don't plan to risk my neck for that."

Colonel Taylor looked at his watch. "I have a flight to catch, but I think you are missing a few ways in which the political landscape has changed. Donald Nelson is a socialist, true, but he went into predominantly black areas and told black people that this government was exploiting their fear of Indians solely to stay in power. And he has succeeded in changing a lot of minds. Also, he and his university colleagues have shown that a multi-ethnic party draws crowds, that the black-Indian divide was created by the Kabaka and the Opposition parties because it suited their ends, not because it was foreordained."

"You sound like a political commentator," Spooner said, smirking.

"No, I'm a pragmatist. You're worried about socialism? Don't be. No one has done more to discredit socialism than this government. People are flocking to the Workers' Party meetings because they yearn for change, not for socialism."

"And military intervention? Please, close the loop for me, Colonel."

"Military intervention will give them breathing space. It will allow us to re-shuffle the deck, to push out the extremes and allow moderates to emerge."

"How long will the army play ombudsman?"

"As long as it takes."

"Well, Colonel, you have a plane to catch," Spooner said, rising. "Let me think some more about this, though I must admit I like what you've said."

"Sit, sit," Colonel Taylor implored, "I'm not in that much of a hurry. Besides, you know I don't have to join any of those lines at the airport."

"In that case, Colonel, what size of force will you need?"

"Well, Ralph, you've given this a lot of thought. What size of force do you think we'd need?"

"Minimum? Four companies, Colonel. Which, of course, makes the situation interesting."

"How so?" Colonel Taylor asked.

"As Commander of the Internal Ops, you only have three companies after each rotation. Where will you get the fourth? Unless Colonel LaFleur is on board?" Colonel Taylor nodded without looking directly at Spooner. "In that case," Captain Spooner continued, "I'd like to know if Captain Rambarran is on board as well."

"You're the third Company Commander I've talked to, Ralph," Colonel Taylor replied. "I haven't yet raised this with Captain Rambarran. As you know, he is in the interior right now and should be out by the time I get back. I know you're very close, you and he—"

"That's not important here, Colonel," Captain Spooner replied. "As you know, Andrew Rambarran is the only American-trained officer in the Brigade. It would help us greatly with the Americans if he were with us. Anyway, I think so, and I believe the other company commanders might feel the same way, too."

"I agree, and I plan to raise it with him after I get back."

"Very well, Colonel, I'd like to think this over. I don't like the direction this country is going. I haven't for a while. But I'd like to think on this some more. I'll let you know when you get back from the US."

"I understand," Colonel Taylor said.

"By the way, Colonel, why do you suppose the President is sending you to this Conference on Hemispheric Security?"

"The senior officers have been talking about this," Colonel Taylor replied. "We believe that the Americans want to gauge our thinking about developments in Central America, and the President for his part is trying to figure out what their designs might be for Guyana. That, of course, is one angle."

"And the other?" Captain Spooner asked.

"This has not been talked about openly, but you've surely guessed that the President is going to rig the constitutional referendum."

"Of course; the man is already seeing himself as another Papa Doc.

Do you know he consults with an *obeah-man* to help him commune with the spirits?"

"So, I've heard," Colonel Taylor replied with a chuckle. "Well, anyway, I think the President is doing the old ideological two-step."

"What's that, Colonel?"

"Well, he is one of only three Caribbean leaders who's accepted the American invitation. I think he is showing the Americans some accommodation to get them to be quiet when he tightens his grip here at home. It's what he has always done. Show he is not as much of a communist as the Opposition and buy himself some elbow room."

"Stick with the devil you know?"

"Exactly," Colonel Taylor replied.

"Will it work this time, after all the stuff he has said about them?"

"I think so," Colonel Taylor replied. "The Americans have a problem in Iran, and a serious one in Central America. Guyana is an irritation they can deal with at anytime. They can afford to just watch the Comrade Leader for a little while longer. The question is: can we?"

Their eyes met and they studied each other for a few moments, then Captain Spooner rose. "Would you like me to accompany you to the airport, Colonel?"

"That won't be necessary, Ralph, but you could get my driver out of the kitchen."

Spooner laughed. "Is he getting some nourishment or going after the cook?"

"Both would be my guess," Colonel Taylor replied, emptying his cup.

"Well, have a good trip, Colonel," Captain Spooner said, taking leave.

Colonel Taylor nodded his thanks and watched Captain Spooner wend his way around the furniture in the lounge, wondering whether he could meet Spooner's condition about recruiting Captain Rambarran. Spooner was the third Company Commander who had asked about Rambarran.

Captain Rambarran was an enigma. From four years of working with him, Colonel Taylor had come to admire his competence. He was a good planner and tactician. His performance against the Surinamese, after their incursion into the New River triangle, had earned him a medal. Unfortunately, try as he could to fit in, he continued to stick out. He pronounced words differently; the music out of his room was different, more rock than reggae. He was the only Officer who wore high-top, American boots, instead of the standard issue, low-cut army boots and puttees. He rarely used the word, "Comrade," and sometimes addressed senior officers as "sir." West Point seemed to hang around his neck like a neon sign. It was what the officers called him when he wasn't around, and it was precisely why the other company commanders wanted him on board. With him, the chances of successfully removing the government would be greatly enhanced. On the other hand, if the attempt failed, American concern for Rambarran might very well save them all from the worst.

Colonel Taylor looked at his watch and rose abruptly. He might not have to join lines at the airport, but they surely were not going to hold the plane just for him.

THREE

August 11, 1979
Eteringbang, Guyana Hinterland

Andrew Rambarran sat on the mound by the landing place at the river's edge, looking across the Cuyuni. He had started another letter to Lena, fulfilling a promise that he would write often whenever he was in the interior. That promise was made shortly after his first stint in the Guyanese hinterland, as a freshly minted Second Lieutenant. Some Colonel at Camp Ayanganna had evidently thought border deployment was the best way to break in junior officers, and Rambarran had drawn Eteringbang, a rifle shot from Ankoko Island, still under Venezuelan occupation.

Eteringbang is a solitary observation post on the southern bank of the Cuyuni River, about a mile downstream from its confluence with the Wenamu and on the fringe of the region Arthur Conan Doyle fictionalized in *The Lost World*. So many species of plant and tree life inhabit the banks and forests inland, a botanist could spend a lifetime trying to catalog them. All of them remain unnamed to the transient dwellers of Eteringbang, except for the wallaba and the mora, which are distinguishable by their height and the size of their trunks.

At Eteringbang, the river is not much wider than one of the internal drainage canals of Black Bush Polder. The water is black but provides a refreshing bath if you can avoid an encounter with an electric eel. At the lower course, by Bartica, the Cuyuni widens and joins the Mazaruni and Potaro Rivers, and all three rivers have drawn mining companies, and *pork-knockers* with their sifting pans, to the alluvial riches hidden below.

Manning an observation post especially at a remote border location was a peculiar duty especially when the orders did not permit a return of fire in the event of an attack. The routines at the post resembled a concentration camp: daytime patrols, perimeter security at night, volleyball and soccer to keep the men active, cards and dominoes for recreation, and nights in bunkers. Breakfast consisted of eggs and a slab of meat; no bread, *roti*, or *bakes* because of the ban on wheat flour. The weekly supply of chicken and beef was barely adequate, but fish was plentiful. Soldiers learned from the Amerindians that all you needed was a flashlight and a cutlass by the rapids a mile up-river. At night, when the *luckanani* sailed over the rocks into the shallow water below, the massacre began.

Rambarran remembered how dreadfully lonely his first tour of duty was at Eteringbang. When he returned to coastal duties, Lena made him promise to write as often as possible. It helped. The letters went out once a week, and her letters diverted his senses from the practice common among the soldiers to seek comfort in the seclusion of the bush with a girlie magazine. However, Lena had another reason for her insistence on the letters. Remarking that on his return he behaved like a sailor from a year-long voyage, she said the letters were the only way in which he communicated his affections for her. He spoke of love more in his letters, she said, than when he was, as she put it, rifling under her skirt like a *pork-knocker* who had dropped a large nugget under the Cuyuni. He remembered being amused by the expression but undeterred in his quest.

What should have been a one-week site inspection on this occasion became extended to two weeks because engine problems had caused the Air Wing to reshuffle its schedule. Colonel LaFleur had sent him to check on the camp after the Venezuelans blew up a Guyanese mining rig in the Cuyuni River. The *pork-knockers* were allowed off the vessel before the charges were laid, but the detonation had been in Guyanese waters. The Venoes claimed the *pork-knockers* were prospecting in their side of the Wenamu River, and that they were in hot pursuit. Except for the diplomatic sparing which continued, things had calmed down along the river. Every day that week he had waited for word from Air Wing. They had now confirmed his extraction, and now he waited for the welcome sounds of the Twin Otter's approach. At the end of that plane ride, Maria Elena Spooner would be waiting.

The eruptions of laughter in the camp made Rambarran turn around. "What's going on back there?" he asked Lieutenant Shah, who was approaching in his gym shorts, towel and soap in hand.

"The game crew shot a baboon," Lieutenant Shah replied.

"What are they going to do with it?" Rambarran asked.

"Cook it," Shah replied. "Some of the soldiers said baboon stew is great. It should be ready before you leave."

"No thanks," Rambarran said. "It's one thing when it's a matter of survival; it's quite another when you still have chicken and beef rations in the storeroom. How was your patrol?"

"The Venoes came across the river about three miles downriver."

"Surely not while you were on patrol out there?" Rambarran asked.

"No, but recently," Lieutenant Shah replied. "It's by the large clearing where the river bends. You know the spot?" Rambarran nodded. "Well," Shah continued, "we found beer and soft drink bottles, cigarette butts, and a crunched up cigarette pack."

"How do you know they weren't left there by *pork-knockers?*" Rambarran asked.

"*Cerveza Polar? Frescolita? Consul* cigarettes? Banks Beer and Bristol cigarettes would be what our miners carry."

"But the *pork-knockers* trade in the Venezuelan village across the Wenamu," Rambarran noted.

"Come on, Captain, the *pork-knockers* aren't the types to stock up on rations in La Boca on the Venezulean side and then have a picnic on this side."

"True," Rambarran said. "And the litter was just lying there?"

"Yes," Lieutenant Shah replied, "scattered, but just lying there."

"Well, they're trying to rattle our cage; it's clear they wanted us to find that stuff. Send a signal to Camp Ayanganna. And you'll need to extend the daytime patrols further down and up river." Lieutenant Shah nodded. "Have the next patrol take a shotgun and discharge a few rounds near that clearing." Lieutenant Shah smiled. "Also," Rambarran continued, "take some of the spent cartridges we have and drop them at various sites along the bank. They should get the message: if they want to come over, fine, but if they collide with buckshot while we're hunting, that's their problem."

"What time are you leaving?" Lieutenant Shah asked.

"I don't know, whenever the Twin Otter gets here."

"Can you get us out by the end of next week?" Shah asked.

"I'll try. The first squad will go out with me. Unless Ayanganna interferes, Air Wing assured me that second squad would be out on Monday. That'll leave you and third squad for the latter part of the week."

"Please try," Lieutenant Shah pleaded. "Three months out here can drive a man to bestiality."

"Yeah, the next baboon they bring in might be alive!" Rambarran said and watched Lieutenant Shah walk down to the river, laughing.

It was just after 16:00 when Lieutenant Shah awakened Captain Rambarran in the command bunker to tell him that the Twin Otter was landing. By the time Rambarran and Shah reached the plane, the weekly supplies had been offloaded and the replacements for Shah's departing First Squad had reported to the platoon sergeant. With Rambarran and First Squad on board, the plane departed Eteringbang at 16:22, and twenty-five minutes or so later, landed at Bartica to offload supplies for the army transit station there.

At 17:35, Rambarran disembarked from the Twin Otter at Ogle, where a 3-ton truck from F-Company was waiting for him and Lieutenant Shah's First Squad. The corporal supervised the boarding of the soldiers, and Rambarran climbed into the cab beside the driver. Twenty minutes later, the truck was being logged in at the Main Gate at Camp Ayanganna. Once inside the base, the truck proceeded to the barracks area where everyone disembarked. Rambarran hurried with his haversack to the bachelor officers' bungalow, ascending the external stairway and looking at his faded white Mini Minor parked between two sets of stilts supporting the building. The front door was unlocked. He walked down the corridor to the second room on the left and used his key to gain entrance. The room, with its sole window facing Vlissingen Road and Kitty, the eastern suburb of Georgetown, was a modest rectangular space with a cot, a wooden wardrobe in front of which he had hung a small mirror, and a table on which rested his stereo equipment. He dropped his haversack on the cot, removed his boots, divested himself of his fatigues which he tossed onto the cot, then went out with a towel draped around his waist to the shower stall.

Returning to the room, Rambarran caught sight of the framed picture of the Comrade President hanging precariously on the two-inch nail, which was all but pulled out of the enlarged hole in the cardboard wall. The picture was already in the room when he was assigned to it on his return from a staff course in Brazil back in May, and he figured it prudent to let it remain even though officers' rooms were typically adorned only with personal items. He unhooked the picture and placed it on the floor with the top leaning against the cardboard wall, before dressing quickly in a dark pair of slacks, white shirtjac, and his tan desert boots. Then, he tackled the question of where he should take Lena for dinner. On a normal Saturday when he wasn't traveling back to town from some out of the way place, he would already have been en route to the Timehri Officers' Club, whose seclusiveness made it the perfect site for seduction. But Lena had already been waiting for hours and was no doubt as hungry as he. If, on the other hand, most of the officers were up at Timehri, then the Club at Ayanganna should be empty. He walked across the street, entering the Club by the main entrance on the ground floor and was immediately greeted by the drums of Babatude Olatungi. The front of the lounge and the bar area were empty, but just when he thought he and Lena might be comfortable there, he caught sight of the Chief of Staff, the Padre, and a Kabaka Party man with a goatee and a dashiki, gaudily embroidered around the open neck and chest. They sat in the north side of the lounge facing three wide-hipped women, with their backs to the entrance. When his eyes met the Chief's, Rambarran braced to attention; the Chief nodded his acknowledgment; and the three women in the Chief's company turned laboriously around to take a look at the intruder. The thought of bringing Lena here within view of this group was not at all appealing to Rambarran. He walked upstairs to the dining area and used the hall phone to call Lena; then, he left by the outside stairway for his bungalow. Retrieving his keys, he opened the door to his faded white Mini Minor and dropped into the driver's seat. With some apprehension, he tried the ignition and got the car started on the second try. Reversing onto the main artery of Camp Ayanganna, he straightened up quickly and sped to the entrance, where the guard waved him through.

Lena had tried to hide her impatience when he called. It was quite understandable, he thought, since she had been dressed and waiting on him for a couple of hours. He had offered his apologies and explanations, hoping that getting these out early would salvage their evening from any unpleasantness. Lena had appeared relieved to finally hear from him and the excitement in her voice just before she hung up assured him there was no need to dwell on his lateness. From Thomas Road he turned onto Vlissingen Road, then traveled along the seawall to Kitty Public Road, which took him into Subryanville.

When he pulled off the street onto the embankment in front of the house, Lena was standing with her aunt on the landing. She wore a light green blouse with some yellow specks and frilly sleeves, and a black wrap-around skirt with a belt around her narrow waist. She descended the stairway and followed the concrete footpath to the metal double gate. Once through, she turned around to latch the gate, then walked across the bridge over the drainage ditch to the passenger side where Rambarran was holding the door. The yellow-specks on her blouse turned out to be butterflies. Her skirt extended below her knees and a pair of tan leather sandals exposed her white feet. How differently she looked away from the family farm at Philippi, where her slender, sinewy frame usually presented itself in long-sleeved shirts rolled up to her elbows and shirt-tails tied in front of her stomach, blue jeans that appeared welded on from her waist to her calf before disappearing into a pair of mackintoshes, and her auburn hair pulled back into a pony tail.

With her aunt still in view, they greeted each other with a smile before she took her seat, then Rambarran turned the car around and took the Seawall road to the Pegasus Hotel. He escorted her through the main entrance and the dining area across from the lounge into the partially sheltered courtyard. At 19:00, the sun was going down, but it was still light, and the gentle breeze from the Atlantic added to the exhilaration Rambarran felt at seeing Lena again.

"It feels like an evening on my veranda at Adventure," Rambarran said, holding the chair for Lena.

"You know I prefer the veranda at Adventure," Lena said.

"I do too," Rambarran said, "but this is heaven compared to Eteringbang."

The waiter came back with a wine cooler for Lena and a tall glass of Guiness for Rambarran. The waiter explained that it was a

16

buffet dinner, and while he detailed the items on the buffet for Lena, Rambarran downed the Guiness, and accepted the waiter's offer to get him another.

"You need to take it easy," Lena cautioned.

"I just came out of the bush, you know."

"I know," Lena replied, "and it worries me."

"Well, don't worry," Rambarran assured her, "the first one, they say, always goes down fast."

The waiter returned with the second Guiness. Rambarran took a sip, then escorted Lena to the buffet table, where he followed her, selecting from containers of curried shrimp, curried chicken, fried *banga-mary*, chicken chow-mein, fried rice, and a salad mix of lettuce and cucumber. Only a year ago, *dal pooris* would have been a standard offering at a buffet table; now, flour was available only on the black market. Still, this was decadent living, Rambarran thought, compared to Eteringbang, where at the time of his departure, his soldiers were sampling baboon stew.

"How are your parents?" Rambarran asked, as they ate.

"Not well," Lena replied.

"Someone sick?"

Lena shook her head. "Nothing like that," Lena replied. "Daddy thinks the government is trying to force him off the farm."

"What?" Rambarran exclaimed. "They can't do that."

"Well, Daddy thinks that's what the government is trying to do."

"How?" Rambarran asked.

"By taxing the property," Lena replied. "Last year, the tax assessment was so large, Daddy had to go to court to challenge it. He won because Mother had records for everything. But this year, it's different."

"How so?"

"Last year, they taxed the rice lands and the fruit orchard. You know, we have some of the land under cultivation and we lease some. Well, we had records for those. This year, they taxed the savannahs not under cultivation."

"But that's swamp land," Rambarran said.

"Exactly. On both sides of the dam leading to the house are the savannahs that are completely under water when it rains heavily. That's why, years ago, Daddy had the system of drainage canals dug. As you know, they provide good fishing, but they spill over during the rainy season. Anyway, the new tax assessment on the savannahs is at a rate comparable to the rice lands."

"That's outrageous," Rambarran said, signaling the waiter to bring another Guiness.

"That's what my parents said, but the government controls the judges. You know how things are in this country."

"So what's your father going to do?" Rambarran asked.

"Well, the matter is in court right now. Daddy thinks they are punishing him for criticisms he made of the government a couple of years ago. Someone told him the harassment would stop if he joined the Party."

"So, is he going to join?"

"My father? Become a socialist?"

"Lots of business people play that game. They join the Party to keep the government off their backs."

"And look at where it's gotten them," Lena said. "Store shelves are bare. The country is on the fast track to ruin."

"I know," Rambarran said, "but the choices are limited. The Opposition Party is also socialist."

"Some Party man asked Daddy why he didn't take his American wife and go to America."

"Really? What did your father say?"

"Daddy said that the man had been drinking, and Daddy didn't want to get into a brawl. But he is quick to point out that he is more Guyanese than the Comrade Leader."

"In what way?" Rambarran asked.

"Because he is mixed with every race here, except Amerindian and Chinese."

"It's really a shame how badly things have gotten in this country," Rambarran said.

"I know," Lena said, "but let's talk about us."

"Okay," Rambarran agreed, quickly adding, "I really, really missed you these past two weeks."

"I missed you too, and I can't wait for your army contract to end."

"It won't be long now. I'll send in my letter requesting discharge from the Brigade next June and, of course, my contract ends in August."

Lena smiled. "It can't happen too soon for me. Do you know, Mother said we can have the house in Orlando?"

"What good will that do? We'll be in school in Gainesville."

"The house is rented, so we'll get to use the rent to defray some of our expenses while we're finishing up graduate school."

"That's very generous of your parents," Rambarran said.

"Well, they're sort of dividing up the assets. Ralph is keener on staying on the farm. My parents think it might not be safe for me here after a while."

"I haven't seen Ralph in a couple of months. How are things between him and that Indian girl he was seeing?"

"Not good," Lena replied. "She dropped out of university. The family didn't want her to do the compulsory National Service stint. They had heard horrible things. They said the safest place for an Indian girl nowadays is overseas."

"How's Ralph taking it?"

"He's broken up about it, but what can he do? He wants to stay here; she wants to go overseas with her family. It's what's happening everywhere. You know that. Look at us. Everyone is fleeing this socialist paradise."

"I know," Rambarran said. "When I left this country for West Point, the President spoke about setting up a consultative democracy. When I came back, the same fellow was a declared Marxist-Leninist."

"Daddy thinks it will eventually collapse."

"It's collapsing right now," Rambarran said. "A bunch of thieves are running the country and offering socialist phrases to paper over the misery they are inflicting on people. The problem with societal collapse, though, is that there is no definite endpoint and no formula for bringing it back. Just look at Haiti."

"Can we talk about something else?" Lena asked. "I'm feeling depressed."

"I'm sorry. How about dessert? I think they have cassava pone and pineapple tarts."

"I'd like to try the cassava pone," Lena said.

"I'll get them," Rambarran said. Walking over to the buffet table, he crossed paths with the waiter whom he asked for two cups of coffee and the check, but moments after he had parted company with the waiter, he called after him and added a brandy to the original request. The waiter was confused about whether he was substituting the brandy for the coffee, and with others monitoring the exchange, Rambarran, with a wave of his hand and a slight slur in his speech told the waiter to bring them all.

The cassava pone sat at the table in large sheets, which had been crisscrossed with a cutting instrument into generously large, rectangular servings. Placing one piece on each of the two plates he had picked up, he proceeded back to where Lena sat, frowning at the unsteadiness of his gait. The waiter was quite prompt with the coffee, and through dessert, Rambarran explained how the deployment of his three platoons would work. What pleased Lena most was the assurance that he would be spending most evenings at his house in Adventure, which meant that they would be able to see each other every day. Midway through dessert, the brandy arrived at the table, and Andrew Rambarran found himself under a quizzical glare from his companion, who relaxed somewhat when he raised the glass and said, "To my one true love."

"I wish you'd say that more often," Lena said, "especially when you haven't been drinking."

"Well, it's true, always," he said by way of reply and elicited a smile from Lena.

"Maybe, you should drink some more of that coffee before we go," Lena said, and Rambarran dutifully complied, but only after he polished off the brandy he had kept within sniffing distance. When the waiter rechecked with them, Rambarran settled the bill and, noticing that Lena had picked up her handbag, he rose to leave.

With his arm around Lena's waist, Rambarran retraced the way out of the dining area and through the entrance of the Pegasus Hotel, but coming off the steps onto the sidewalk, he swayed to the right.

"Would you like me to drive?" Lena asked.

"No, I'm okay," Rambarran replied. "It's just a short ride." And, indeed, it was. He took the Seawall Road to Camp Street, then turned by the YMCA onto Thomas Road and, in no time, he was back at Camp Ayanganna, slowing to allow the guard to open the gate. He directed the car between the stilts under his bungalow with just the park lights on, then with some effort, pulled himself out.

"You know I don't like this hide-and-seek stuff," Lena said softly, getting out of the car.

"Don't worry," Rambarran said. "It'll end soon."

Walking up the stairs, he swayed sideways but grabbed the side rail just as Lena reached around his waist to support him. Once steadied, he draped his arm over her shoulder while she continued to support him by the waist to the top of the stairs. He opened his room door but did not turn on the light. Instead, he reached around Lena's waist, pulling her toward him and kissing her on her lips. Then, as if in the first move of the foxtrot, he moved her backwards towards the cot. She lowered herself to an almost seated position before bouncing directly up.

"Oh my God, what is that?" she asked.

"Sorry," he replied. "That's my haversack and stuff. I forgot to put them away."

"Maybe we should wait," she said.

"No, no," he said, "we could do something else, you know ..." He kissed her again, rotating her away from the cot, his hands undoing first her belt then the button holding up the wraparound skirt. She helped him with his shirt while he reached into her panties, massaging her cheeks and pudenda in semicircular motions of his hands from back to front and back again. Then he reached under her blouse, undid her bra strap and pressed his mouth on her right breast, unaware that his unsteady frame had acquired forward momentum and had caused Lena to lose her footing. She lurched backward, pulling him with her, and rendering a body slam to the cardboard wall, which was followed by the cracking of glass from the blow of one of his advancing boots onto the picture frame resting against the base of the wall.

"What's that?" Lena asked.

"Just a stupid picture frame I left on the floor."

She stood there breathing heavily while he shed his shoes and trousers. When he stood before her again in dishabille, he smiled sheepishly and kissed her, running his hands up and down her slender, sinewy frame. Then he lifted her right leg to its highest extremity.

"Andrew," she said. "This is going to be uncomfortable ... Oh God!"

The cardboard wall bowed and straightened in harmonic motion as the two bodies fused and unfused; then, the motion stopped. Andrew

Rambarran had another idea. Raising Lena's left leg, he supported her entire body on his forearms, with his open palms pressed against the cardboard wall. Her torso was now much higher than he intended and, despite his best efforts, he appeared unable to calibrate its elevation for optimal penetration. Pronouncement on the futility of this exercise in acrobatics came from Lena, who, very firmly but without reproach, said, "Andrew!" He was ready to tell her he could make it work, but his palms began to slip on the cardboard wall. He quickly lowered her legs, one at a time, and, taking her by the hand, led her over to the cot. In a sweeping motion with his right hand, he cleared the cot of all impediments, sending them scattering on the floor and against the wall, then lowered Lena onto the bed. Approaching from the foot of the bed, he picked up her legs and pressed them forward, and with eyes now fully adjusted to the darkness, he superimposed himself on her. "Gosh, I can't wait until we're finally together," she said.

"Soon," he said. "I promise. Soon." His voice trailed. He lowered her legs and moved his hands to her face, kissing her repeatedly. Grasping his shoulders, Lena bucked and swayed her roundly sculpted behind. The cot creaked in rebellion, but neither of its occupants seemed to care. His heartbeat now racing, Andrew Rambarran became more purposeful. Like the jockey, Banduk, riding the thoroughbred, *Bush-Cook,* in the eight-furlong at the Port Mourant Race Course, he felt the rush of adrenaline on the home stretch, and with the skill of Banduk and the intensity of *Bush-Cook*, he crossed the finish line. A sweet stillness settled on their two intertwined bodies.

FOUR

August 13, 1979
National War College, Ft. McNair, Washington, D.C.

Looking across the table through the oversized convex window, Colonel Franchette Taylor wondered how they ever managed to keep student interest in that seminar room. Located on the 4th floor in the southwest corner of Roosevelt Hall, the window was centered on the other long side of the Hill Conference Room, rising from the floor to ceiling and accounting for at least one-third of the total wall space. What a view it presented of the Washington Channel and the Potomac River, where sailboats and speedboats crossed paths in tantalizing proximity!

Colonel Taylor's choice position at the seminar table had been the accident of an alphabetical placement of the ten countries represented there. The Air Force Colonel, who was moderating the seminar, sat at the western head of the long conference table dominating the room. On his right, and backing the window, were the officers from Argentina, Bolivia, Brazil, Chile, and El Salvador. Directly across from them were the officers from Guatemala, Guyana, Honduras, Jamaica, and Uruguay. The rest of the seats at the table were taken up by field grade officers in civilian clothes, as well as State Department personnel, most of whom were students at the National War College, which had officially sponsored the conference. The attendee overflow were seated on chairs hugging the wall behind Taylor and also at the eastern end of the room, to his left.

In his opening presentation, the moderator acknowledged that the conference's main emphasis was the situation in Central America, the discussion of which would be deferred to the fuller session after lunch. This more truncated morning session, which began at 10:00 hours following the coffee and pastry reception in the rotunda, appeared to be the warm-up before the real show. Officers from the countries represented were invited to highlight security issues facing their respective armed forces.

The presentations from the officers representing Argentina, Brazil, and Uruguay took up the entire morning session. All three officers struck strongly anti-communist notes, defending their individual militaries against the notoriety they had achieved overseas for human rights abuses. They all spoke about the obligation they felt to protect their countries from the chaos communist terrorists threatened, and all three condemned the termination of U.S. aid to their countries by the Carter administration. The questions to the presenters were quite politely delivered, Taylor thought, but the responses were lengthy and discursive and, at one of the long pauses, the moderator thanked the officers who had presented and terminated the session.

As he walked out of the conference room, Colonel Taylor watched a tour boat executing a wide turn out of the Washington Channel into the Potomac River. He kept the boat in view as he walked by the window, troubled that he did not share the intensity of hatred for socialist regimes. Perhaps it was because he had heard socialist expressions from the political parties at home for much of his adult life and had learned to disregard them. Of course, he did not like his own government because it was a failing regime bent on perpetuating itself in power, but he knew that he could not engage in the scale of killing for which the Argentine, Brazilian, and Uruguayan military regimes had become known. He knew he was not the anti-communist zealot the Latin American officers appeared to be, and wondered why he was at this conference at all.

*   *   *

The afternoon session began with a twenty-minute briefing by a State Department official on the types of contact the U.S. government had had with the Sandinista regime in Nicaragua and on the U.S. offer of aid to that government. That was followed by the presentation from the Salvadoran Colonel sitting diagonally across from Colonel Taylor. It sounded to Taylor as if the Salvadoran military was the last bulwark in the defense of the Western hemisphere from communism. The Salvadoran Colonel accused Nicaragua and Cuba of shipping arms to the communist guerrillas in his country and decried the frequent sermons from the U.S. Congress to the Salvadoran military about human rights violations. It was a highly impassioned presentation, and

Taylor was impressed with the fact that the Salvadoran did not allow his struggle with the English language to water down the intensity and zeal with which he presented the hemispheric threat from communism that the Salvadoran military was attempting to stem.

Taylor heard the approaching footsteps on the hard wood floor before he felt the tap on his left shoulder.

"Colonel Taylor, telephone call from Georgetown, Guyana," the secretary whispered. "You can take it in the office across the hall. I'll show you."

"Thank you," Taylor replied, rising from his chair. He followed the secretary out of the conference room, turning right into an alcove with several cubicles.

"You can use this one," the secretary said, pointing to the third cubicle. "It's a bit more private," she added.

Picking up the phone, he said, "This is Colonel Taylor." He heard a female operator on the line tell someone to go ahead.

"Franchette, this is Clive Agrippa."

"Yes, General." Colonel Taylor heard his voice echo. In the few moments before the voice came back, Taylor wondered what could be so bloody urgent for the Chief of Staff to interrupt him at a foreign conference.

"Sorry to bother you, Franchette, I'll come to the point," General Agrippa said. "The President has decided he wants a new Chief of Staff."

"What?" Colonel Taylor exclaimed. "Did something happen, Chief? I thought you'd just been renewed for another term."

"Yes, I was renewed," Agrippa replied, his voice sounding weaker. "I was."

"What's going on down there, General?" Taylor asked.

"The officers are asking the same question," Agrippa replied. "I'm still in shock, especially since the new Chief of Staff will be a policeman, Tony Downs."

"You can't be serious!" Taylor exclaimed.

"I couldn't believe it myself," Agrippa replied, "but it's a fact. You should have been in the Officers' Club today—the officers were hopping mad."

"My God, what an insult to the army," Taylor said, wheeling the chair backward to check the hallway.

"Yes, it's what they would call here a real *eye-pass.*"

"Has the President gone mad?" Taylor asked. "Does he expect military officers to take their orders from a policeman? And what about Colonel Cadogan? As Force Commander, he was next in line to be Chief of Staff."

"Colonel Cadogan has resigned."

"This is unbelievable," Taylor said. "What's happening, General? You must know something."

"I really don't," Agrippa said. "And, to tell the truth, some of the things I hear are not flattering, like I've outlived my usefulness."

"I'm sorry," Taylor said, trying to sound sincere but acutely aware of how unpopular the Chief of Staff had become with the officers.

"It's alright," Agrippa said, "maybe it's time for me to go."

"So, where does that leave us?" Taylor asked. "What about the chain of command?"

"That's something you all will have to sort out now," Agrippa said, adding, "it's a new day."

"I still don't get this, General," Taylor said. "Why would the President want to antagonize the army? Is he insane?"

"Who knows the mind of the Comrade Leader!" Agrippa laughed. "Whatever he is though, he isn't insane. My guess is that he wants to re-fashion the army, move it away from its British traditions. If that is true, this is a trial balloon."

"How far do you think he'll go?"

"With Cuban advisors, who knows?" Agrippa replied. "A complete dismantling of the army? A revolutionary army?"

"Well, we'll just have to put an end to this nonsense," Taylor declared.

"There's been a lot of talk about that recently."

"What do you make of it?" Taylor asked.

"At any other time, I would have called it a far-fetched idea; now, the conditions might be just right. I wish I could help, but after Friday I will have no official duties until the handover."

"Why Friday?" Taylor asked.

"That's when the visiting Indian officers leave. As you know, I arranged the visit. The Indian government is expected to provide engineers and equipment for the Madhia road-building project. It's a big grant, and I don't think the President wants to screw that up."

"I see," Taylor said. "Well, best wishes to you, Clive."

"Thanks, Franchette. I'll be okay. I'm feeling a bit isolated right now. It's good you're overseas; it made it easier to contact you. If you were here, we probably wouldn't be having this conversation at all. Anyway, watch yourself."

Colonel Taylor rose slowly from the plush swivel chair, shaking his head. He wondered whether the President had approved his two-week seminar at the National War College Defense University just to get him out of the way. This seminar on hemispheric security just three weeks after the Sandinista takeover in Nicaragua was a way of gauging American designs on Guyana, so he was told. Now he wondered whether the President did not have an ulterior motive—to get one of the two Battalion Commanders out of the country while he reorganized the army. If a police officer is to be the army Chief of Staff, who will be the Brigade Commander? Christ! He should have asked Agrippa. What else is likely to happen before he got back? Would he be relieved of his command?

The Chilean officer was speaking when Franchette Taylor took his seat at the conference table. The Chilean Colonel had evidently used the developments in Nicaragua to revisit the achievements of the Chilean military in dealing with the institutional threats the Allende regime had posed to the Chilean armed forces. Allende's model, the officer asserted, was Cuba, and his plan was to supplant the Chilean armed forces with a people's militia. He pointed to Nicaragua as another example where the regular army had been supplanted by a guerrilla army and ended his comments by noting the urgency of stopping the communist threat in El Salvador, which was teetering on becoming another Nicaragua. This theme was also picked up by the Guatemalan, whose presentation followed.

It was now Colonel Taylor's turn to address the security concerns facing his country. With no communists to lambast, he started out feeling like the joker in the deck. Striking a matter-of-fact tone, he spoke of the perennial worry to his army posed by the prospect of a Venezuelan invasion. He briefly outlined the history of the claim

Venezuela had made to Guyanese territory and the periodic bullying with which his country had had to cope. Border defense by the army was intended to show the flag in the disputed area and to engage in holding action against a Venezuelan incursion while diplomatic efforts were engaged in bringing about a cessation of hostilities. There was also a border dispute at the southeastern corner of the country, where Suriname had laid claim to an area called the New River Triangle. This was a more manageable affair, partly because Guyana had the edge in so far as military capabilities were concerned, but largely because the governments of the two countries were more disposed to a peaceful settlement. Taylor concluded by acknowledging a long-standing internal security role for the army, one which was a major source of controversy at home.

The presentation was brief and lacked the passionate anti-communist ranting of the earlier speakers. The officers listened politely, Taylor thought, and he was glad when it was over. Nevertheless, for a few minutes into the presentation by the Lieutenant Commander from the Jamaican Coast Guard, Taylor sat evaluating the adequacy of his security outline before his mind returned to developments at home. A tugboat pushing a sand barge up river on the Potomac had just come into view at the side of the window. Taylor watched the steady, monotonous drift of the solitary barge-and-tug in the middle of the Potomac under the glaring mid-afternoon sun and contemplated his options should he be asked to resign his commission on his return home. Much of the question-and-answer period focused on Central America, leaving Colonel Taylor to conclude that he was probably off the hook. However, as the session neared the end, the moderator asked if there were any other questions and, to Colonel Taylor's surprise, the question which followed was directed at him.

The questioner was a young, uniformed officer with twin silver bars on his right collar, sitting in one of the chairs to Taylor's left. He appeared to be in his late twenties and the black name tag above his left pocket advertized his last name as Erikson. The blond hair of his Viking forebears had been sheared and neatly parted on the left. His finely chiseled nose projected forward of his slender face, illuminated by a pair of light brown eyes, which appeared to Taylor to be not only intelligent but kind. Sitting in a regally upright position, he was at least two inches taller than Taylor, and his khaki shirt dropped crisply down from his wide shoulders like a plumbob.

"Colonel Taylor, Guyana has a People's Militia, does it not?" Captain Erikson asked. The Colonel nodded. "Well, sir," Erikson continued, "I was wondering how your army feels about the Militia."

Colonel Taylor felt trapped. The security changes at home were worrisome but, as his country's representative here, he was uncomfortable showing disloyalty to outsiders. Still, after the comments of the Chilean officer regarding President Allende's attempt to use a people's militia to replace the regular army, he did not want to appear naive.

"We do have a People's Militia," Taylor replied, "but it's more of an organized reserve. It's like your National Guard here."

"May I ask, sir, what the size of the militia is?" Captain Erikson asked.

"Well, it's scattered throughout the country—small units here and there," Taylor replied. "Platoon strength in some towns like Georgetown and Linden. I'd say one battalion altogether."

"But your army is brigade strength, as you said in your presentation?"

"I know that the People's Militia appears proportionally large," Taylor acknowledged, "but that's because of a simple addition of everyone who has attended military training. They have never been convened together or trained together. Let me assure you, the army doesn't see them as a threat."

"How about your National Service units, sir? Aren't these parts of your reserve as well?"

Colonel Taylor smiled. "I am impressed by your knowledge of our security forces," he said, "and, yes, the National Service is a part of our reserve."

"Can you tell us, sir, what the size of that unit is?"

"About two battalions, but again, the National Service units don't hardly compare to the regular army in terms of training, military proficiency, and general combat readiness."

"But they do draw down the security budget, don't they?"

"To some extent, yes, they do." Colonel Taylor felt it would be pointless to deny the obvious. He hoped the admission would end the line of questioning.

"Colonel, judging from the literature the National Service puts out, it appears to be a very ideologically indoctrinated organization," Captain Erikson observed.

"Well, the government of Guyana has chosen a socialist developmental path. It wants to ensure that the security forces understand what it is doing."

"Are you saying, sir, that the army is also subjected to political indoctrination?"

"I wouldn't use the term indoctrination. Let's say that the soldiers are periodically given political education, mostly about governmental policies."

"Officers and men, sir?"

"The officers are required to avail their soldiers. But the officers are much more independent. They play the game just as much as they have to." The audience laughed.

Colonel Taylor was relieved when another questioner shifted the discussion to Nicaragua. However, he felt sure, based on the questions and answers, that most in the room probably reached the conclusion that the Guyana army had been defanged. It was getting there, no question. He'd know for sure in a few days.

*   *   *

The Officers' Club, Ft. McNair

The attendant at the drinks table ladled a generous serving of the orange concoction he called Artillery Punch for Franchette Taylor and delighted in detailing the recipe of the firewater and its legendary power. Even for one who was accustomed to repeated rounds of rum and Coke, Taylor found the first sip exhilaratingly explosive. With the Latin American officers unapologetically speaking in Spanish, Taylor decided to seek out the Jamaican officer. Sipping the colorful firewater in his glass as he moved through the lounge, Colonel Taylor drifted to the Commandant of the War College and host of the evening banquet, who was chatting with Captain Erikson.

"I appreciated your comments at the seminar this afternoon, Colonel Taylor," the Commandant said.

"Thank you, General," Taylor replied, "and thank you for attending."

"I am sorry I was not able to be there for all of the presentations," the Commandant said, "but I managed to make it for the Chilean officer's presentation and, of course, yours."

"I'm glad, General, and thank you again."

"By the way, Colonel, this here is Captain Erikson," the Commandant said. Colonel Taylor and Captain Erikson shook hands. "Colonel," the Commandant continued, "may I make an observation?"

"Of course, General."

"I have met many officers from socialist countries before—Eastern bloc mostly, but Cuban ones too. You don't speak like a socialist, Colonel. Not once did you talk of the imperialist forces or make charges about destabilization, though your government does."

"Well, General, I leave ideology to others. As I explained in my presentation at the opening session, the Guyana army is primarily concerned with defending the borders with Venezuela and Suriname, and as far as I am aware, Karl Marx did not produce a primer that would assist us in coping with those threats."

The Commandant laughed. "I like how you put that, Colonel, and I quite agree."

The General's conversation with Taylor ended when they were joined by the officers from El Salvador, Guatemala, Chile, and Argentina, all of whom seemed eager to get the Commandant's ear. The Commandant was fluent in Spanish but switched to English from time to time to accommodate others who had now joined the group. Colonel Taylor resigned himself to being just another member of the audience, politely nodding to those parts of conversation conducted in English. He wondered whether the Commandant knew yet of the appointment of a police officer to head the Guyanese army. He wondered too why the Commandant had made such a point of recognizing that this Colonel did not appear to share the socialist passion of his own government.

FIVE

August 14, 1979
Miami International Airport

Carib Air announces the departure of Flight 431 to Port-of-Spain, Trinidad, and Georgetown, Guyana. Passengers who have not yet checked in are kindly asked to do so at the Carib Air counter.

"Thank God!" Captain Steve Erikson said. Rising from the plastic chair and slinging his small, soft-shelled carry-on over his shoulder, he picked up his briefcase and walked over to the trash can with his half-filled styrofoam cup. He had eaten a large slice of pepperoni pizza, an apple, and a Snickers bar during the six-hour layover. The cup he tossed was his fourth cup of coffee. His stomach gurgled in protest.

With no one needing special assistance, the Carib Air representatives at the gate invited all passengers to board, regardless of seat or row numbers. In a few minutes, Erikson arrived at Row 27 and put his carry-on in the empty overhead compartment. He pulled out a writing tablet and some briefing papers before lodging his briefcase under the seat in front of him. Sitting down in his aisle seat, he dutifully buckled his seat belt and waited for things to settle down. Arriving so quickly at his seat and finding an empty overhead compartment to stow his luggage had temporarily persuaded him that the West Indian approach to seating might be preferable to the American way of seating by row numbers. The disadvantages, however, soon became apparent. Flight attendants were being called to arbitrate seat occupation because early entrants into the plane had taken whatever seats they fancied. At several rows, standing passengers were insisting that they be allowed to sit at the seat designated on their passes but confiscated by the earlier arrivals. The matter having been settled in favor of the correct seat holder, there was now the question of repositioning of luggage from overhead compartments. The negotiation over seats and the commotions over repositioning gave the inside of the plane the appearance of a West Indian market in full swing.

It must have been about thirty-five minutes before the DC-10 left the gate and another ten before they were airborne. When the plane leveled off at thirty-three thousand feet, as reported by the pilot, Erikson began leafing through the briefing papers resting in his lap. He felt ridiculous to have had a classmate from Guyana for four years at West Point and to have known so little about the place, until recently. Of course, Academy days had been hectic, and with so much else to learn, questions about Guyana tended to be mostly cultural. Besides, for the most part, few of the cadets thought of Andrew Rambarran as foreign—he wore the same uniform, performed the same duties, used the same slangs, with a bit of an accent, and he seemed no different in his behavior from anyone else. Still, it was the fact of this being his former roommate's home country that made the Guyana assignment so exciting to Erikson, certainly much more so than going to Bolivia or Belize.

That Guyana had the distinction of being the only English speaking country in South America, he had long known. Its population of just over eight hundred thousand people, descendants of slaves and indentured laborers, mostly resided on the narrow Atlantic coastline, where the Dutch and the British had laid out sugar plantations. Three rivers running roughly perpendicular to this coastline divided the country into thirds. Guyana was in a state of cold war with Venezuela, which had laid claim to a huge chunk of its territory. It had friendlier relations with Suriname, its western neighbor, even though it also had an unresolved territorial dispute with them. Its capital, Georgetown, also the seat of government, was located on the coast, at the mouth of the Demerara River. Looking at it on the map, Erikson thought of how easily the city could be isolated in a country where communication and transportation systems were so underdeveloped.

Political developments in Guyana seemed the most troublesome for Washington insofar as the circum-Caribbean region was concerned. Whereas ethnic confrontation between the country's blacks and Indians had shaped the political context in the 1960's, Marxism-Leninism was now the ideology of choice of the major political parties. The Opposition People's Party had long established its Marxist-Leninist credentials but it was the Kabaka Party, catapulted to power with American assistance in the mid-60s, which was now asserting itself as the country's vanguard socialist party. An ideological bidding war had begun, with the centrists being squeezed out. Worse still, the Workers' Party, a more radical Marxist group with a university base, was gaining in popularity at the expense of the older parties.

Erikson recalled that Colonel Taylor in his presentations at the National War College had sidestepped ideological matters in his country, choosing to take shelter behind a military professionalism that obligated the soldier to carry out the orders of the duly constituted civilian authority. But Colonel Taylor had shown irritation with the encroachments by the various militias on the military's exclusive right to bear arms in the defense of his country. The reports from Colonel Stanford, the Military Attaché in Guyana, had suggested that Colonel Taylor was very distressed by political developments there and about the security changes likely to diminish the role of the army. Taylor had been careful not to show his hand while he was at the War College, but he did convey the impression that he was not passionate about Karl Marx. That Taylor was troubled by developments at home was apparent, but was he likely to do anything about it?

Steve Erikson understood that if elements of the army in Guyana were planning a coup, he needed to find out and track the coup development. Critical to his task was to get an insider's view of the army's thinking, which was probably why he was chosen for the Guyana assignment. He had long indicated his preference to be a Foreign Area Officer. His tour as a Battery Commander in Germany having ended, he was heading for language training when he received the appointment as Assistant Military Attaché. The expectation was that he would establish contact with his West Point classmate and former roommate. He had long since moved beyond the initial pangs of conscience about using his friend, convinced that in attempting to change the political course Guyana was set on, he was not only helping Washington achieve a desired goal but was at the same time helping his friend and the people he served.

The economic profile of the country was simple enough: cane sugar, rice, and bauxite were the country's main exports. Both the sugar and bauxite industries were unionized and prone to strikes, which opposition parties used to apply pressure on the government. However, it was the Public Service Union which had the greatest disruptive power in Georgetown. In the 1960s, with CIA funding, strikes by this union had crippled the Marxist government and paved the way for the

Kabaka Party to take power. Having learned from that experience, the Kabaka Party had since ensured control of the union leadership. Now, however, that leadership was being challenged from within by people who appeared to be more pro-American than the government. Were they to succeed in taking over the union and going on strike, they could render Georgetown ungovernable and, as Yogi Berra said, it would be "déjà vu all over again."

The flight attendants were rolling the drinks cart up the aisle and taking drink orders. Erikson tapped the papers on his lap to square off the corners, then replaced them in his briefcase. When the cart arrived by Row 27, Erikson learned that the wine choices were a chardonnay and a merlot of a brand he did not recognize. A regular beef eater, he chose the merlot, which he expected to nurse until dinner was served. From his neighbor in the middle seat, whose tongue had been loosened by a Carib beer, he learned that most of the passengers were Trinidadians, who had come to Miami on vacation and to shop. Tiny Trinidad had become wealthy after the OPEC oil embargo, and now, money was flowing through the island like a dose of castor oil, so the man said. In the plane, however, it seemed like alcohol was flowing like castor oil. From his vantage point in the rear third of the plane, Erikson observed that the "Call" button was alight in several rows, and stewardesses hurried bearing mixed drinks or bottles of Carib beer, for which they were handsomely tipped by semi-inebriated men from the calypso island, loud in their expression but joyous in their mood. The coach section of the plane was like a bar at happy hour on a Friday afternoon. But, there was a temporary hush when a black stewardess stood in the aisle in the vicinity of Row 20 and yelled above the din, "Who ordered a rum and Coke?" And, hearing no claimant, she said, "Somebody ordered a rum and Coke!" The matter remained unresolved, the stewardess retreated with the drink, and the bacchanal resumed.

Dinner was the usual airline service: a rectangular plastic tray with a small bed of rice, a few pieces of chicken in a sauce that hinted of curry, some overcooked pieces of baby carrots and green beans. Dessert was a square piece of brownie imprisoned in a plastic casing, which required considerable pulling power to liberate. The decibel level had dropped noticeably while passengers ate, and after the trays and scraps had been picked up, Erikson ordered another merlot to sedate himself for the rest of the trip.

The announcement that they were descending into Piarco Airport awoke Erikson, and in a semi-dazed state, he watched most of the passengers disembark. Carib Air, Erikson had been told, had acquired notoriety for losing luggage. He hoped that would prove wrong when he arrived at Timehri; right then, he was grateful the airline was sticking to schedule and that the stop at Piarco was a brief one. He remained awake for the flight to Timehri International Airport, and at about 21:15 hours, disembarked from the plane and walked on the tarmac to the terminal building. At Immigration, he was delayed because there was no one at the desk for diplomatic personnel. Once that was remedied, he passed through and was greeted in the baggage area by Colonel Tom Stanford, the Military Attaché at the U.S. Embassy, Georgetown. Like Erikson, he was a West Point graduate, who had been the Tactical Officer for Erikson's cadet company at the Military Academy. They were both artillery officers, and Stanford had been aware that Erikson was interested in being a Foreign Area Officer. When developments in Central America and the Caribbean created openings for assistant attaches in a handful of countries, Stanford alerted Erikson, who was finishing up his tour of duty in West Germany.

Carib Air, it turned out, had not lost any of Erikson's luggage, and with assistance from Colonel Stanford, all of his three suitcases were taken through Customs to the Colonel's Toyota Celica in the unsheltered parking lot in front of the airport terminal. Colonel Stanford drove out of the lot, down the hill and stopped before making the left turn onto the East-bank road leading to Georgetown.

"This is the second largest military base in the country," Colonel Stanford said. "Most of the military base, Camp Stevenson, is straight ahead in a six-acre, enclosed compound." Erikson nodded. Stanford pointed to the two parallel single-storied barracks as they executed the turn, noting that they housed rifle companies. The two-storied building next to the barracks, from which loud reggae music was coming, was the Sergeants' Mess.

"It's 21:45," Erikson said, "and there are no guards at those buildings."

Colonel Stanford chuckled. "Actually, there is usually a guard below the Mess. You can't see him because of the columns. But out here, I don't think they see a threat to those buildings. And civilians tend to stay away."

The car made a right turn in front of the Motor Transport compound. "Now, on the left there," the Colonel said, pointing, "that's the Officers' Club, and the other buildings up from it are Officers' quarters. On the right's where the Women Army Corps is billeted." Steve Erikson nodded. "What you can't see from this road," Stanford continued, "is the enclosed camp. That's where the base HQ is located."

"Could we drive by it?" Steve Erikson asked.

"Yes, but I'd prefer we did that during the daytime. An incident at night out there could put us in an awkward position."

"I understand," Erikson said.

"The HQ building used to be the American military hospital during World War Two. When we had this, during the days of Lend-Lease, it was called Atkinson Air Base."

"I understand from the briefing I received that this is where their Border Operations is headquartered," Captain Erikson said.

"Yes, but that might not accurately describe what's going on here. As you probably know, the army here consists of two infantry battalions, an Engineer Squadron, and support personnel. One battalion is deployed along the coast and has its HQ at Camp Ayanganna in Georgetown, the other is the Border Operations battalion. They rotate the companies every three months so that those on the border next serve on the coast under Internal Ops. And yes, the full Colonel, who is in command of Border Ops, has an office here at Camp Stevenson. They retain one company here and then deploy platoons from the other two along the border with Venezuela. They are not so much for border defense as for border monitoring."

"How about the Air Wing and Maritime Command?" Erikson asked.

"The Air Wing," Colonel Stanford replied, "has two Islanders and two Twin-Otters. They're used to transport troops to the border or to hinterland locations, usually one squad at a time. They also do weekly resupply runs."

"I don't suppose they're armed?"

"No," Colonel Stanford replied. "Too much trouble for little benefit.

However, they do have two MI-24 Hind attack helicopters and two observation helicopters, which have side-mounted machine guns."

"Hinds? They have Hinds? How?"

"From the Russians, of course," Colonel Stanford replied, "via the Cubans."

"What kind of armaments do they carry?" Erikson asked.

"One Yak-B machine gun and four rocket pods, each containing S-5, 57-millimeter rockets. The Yak is essentially a 4-barrel Gatling gun, firing 12.7 millimeter rounds."

"Wow!" Erikson exclaimed. "Are their pilots trained to handle all of that?"

"They are trained," Colonel Stanford replied. "How well? That's a different question."

"How about their Maritime Command?"

"Not much there. Two small Vosper craft for river patrolling and two 105-foot Vosper coastal patrol boats, with 20-millimeter cannons. They are called *Peccari One* and *Peccari Two.*"

"*Peccari?* They named a patrol boat after a wild pig?"

Stanford laughed. "They sure did. But then their Comrade Leader is a peculiar fella. His Kabaka Party's symbol is a cayman, a bloody crocodile."

"Altogether, this doesn't sound like a formidable military presence," Erikson observed.

"They're not meant to be. They couldn't withstand a Venezuelan attack. Their purpose is simply to notify the government of any Venezuela incursion so that they can scream bloody murder at the United Nations." Colonel Stanford laughed and looked over at Erikson, who was smiling. "Mind you," the Colonel continued, "soldier per soldier and officer per officer, I believe that Guyanese are better trained. They just don't have the numbers or the equipment to match the Venezuelans."

"What kinds of weapons do they have?"

"The standard issue for the infantry is the semi-automatic SLR, the British version of the Belgian FAL. Some of their soldiers also carry sub-machine guns. These are British SMGs, updated versions of the Sten. They also have a General Purpose Machine Gun, a belt-fed machine gun, similar to our M-60."

"Any heavy weapons?" Erikson asked.

"Nothing much. They have a Mortar platoon with mostly 81mm mortars and two Russian-made anti-aircraft guns that the Cubans gave them."

"Seems pretty rudimentary," Erikson observed. "Not much of an army."

"No, but then you have to consider what the army is for. When you have neighbors like Brazil and Venezuela, you don't go out there picking a fight. What the army does is monitor the borders. You don't need much to do that. The rest of the force is really directed toward internal security, basically to keep this government in power."

"That's risky for the government, isn't it? Relying on the army to prop them up?"

"Ah, that's why the government has built up the National Service, as a counterweight to the army. It is more ideologically grounded and more loyal to the Kabaka Party."

"Didn't the army see that coming?"

"Some officers did, but they were too junior. The army leadership was in the hands of former civil servants-turned-soldiers, giddy with power and dissolute by habit. Besides, the government launched the National Service as a way to break into the hinterland. Who could argue with the desire to expand into the remaining ninety percent of the country? Then gradually the National Service grew."

"So, is it too late for the army to reassert its premier security role?"

"Until ten days ago, I would have said 'yes.' But the appointment of a police officer to head the army might be the straw that breaks the camel's back."

Six

August 15, 1979
Georgetown, Guyana

Steve Erikson took the pedestrian footpath centered between the two one-way drives of Main Street, his natural inclination to brisk walking slowed by a compulsion to look up at the flame-red flowers on the flamboyant trees lining both sides of the pathway, and by the slowness of the people ahead of him. He crossed over Main to the sidewalk in front of the Tower Hotel, skirted around the Public Library and, when the lights allowed, made his way over to the sidewalk along High Street. The Victoria Law Court was within view when he turned into Regent Street, taking the right sidewalk beside City Hall. Indian film music drew his attention to Regent Street's other landmark on the opposite side. Not as stately looking as City Hall, but even in its bustling squalor, *Sangam*, Georgetown's notorious whorehouse, functioned with greater efficiency than the Kabaka government; that, at least, was the judgment Colonel Stanford had rendered. Erikson smirked.

After the King Street intersection, both pedestrian and motor traffic were brisker, Erikson walked past pavement beggars, teenagers in school uniform, office workers on lunch break, and others who looked eerily at him. At the Camp Street intersection, he was obliged to wait on the lights and watch the rush of uniformed students on bicycles intermingled with car traffic. Standing near to him were students who had just crossed over Camp Street, debating whether to go into the snackette at Kwang Hing or continue on to Demico House.

About midway up the block from the intersection was the store Erikson was looking for. It occupied the lower half of the two-storied building on the opposite side of the street. The awning from the mid-section of the building covered part of the sidewalk in front of it and, on the horizontal sign above the awning was the red lettering, *Rambarran's Variety Store*. Like most of the structures on Regent Street, the upper-level appeared to be living quarters, and the lower-level dedicated to business.

With jaywalkers making their way from one side of the street to the other, cars were moving slowly. Erikson crossed the street directly in front of the store, hastening his steps over the second half of the road to avoid a car heading toward him. Beads of perspiration running down his face, Erikson left the bright mid-day sun for the darker but cooler inside of the store. He used his handkerchief to sop up the perspiration and looked around the store for someone to assist him. A roughly three-foot wide wooden counter ran along the right and left sides of the store and along the back wall in a horseshoe formation. The store seemed evenly divided between men's and women's apparel. The men's section on the right seemed devoid of customers. The two salesgirls on the right, who had been conversing, parted and one moved along the counter closer to where Erikson stood. Behind the salespeople on shelves against the wall were bolts of cloth and shirts in cellophane wrapping stacked on top of each other. There were also bolts of cloth in lateral piles at intervals across the counter. Shirts in wrappers also sat in piles at various places along the counter. In the center of the horseshoe, bolts of cloth stood in clumps on the wooden floor, and on the men's side, were a couple of racks with shirts of different colors. At the rear of the horseshoe was a wire cage which housed the cash register, and perched on a stool behind it, was a plump light-complexioned, round-faced Indian woman with short black hair. Four-foot fluorescent lights hung from the ceilings, but they were meant to supplement the daylight that came into the store through the large showcases on either side of the wide store entrance. The inside was cooled by a window-unit air conditioner, the hum from which was the dominant sound in the store.

Erikson walked up to the salesgirl at the counter on his right. She seemed curious about his presence in the store but hadn't said anything.

"I am looking for a couple of shirtjacs," he said.

"Over there," she said, pointing to the racks and, lifting a hinged portion of the counter, she came over to join him at one of the racks.

"What size?" she asked.

"How about extra large?"

"No, no, no," she laughed. "That's fat people size."

"Really?" Erikson was at once surprised and amused by the candor in the salesgirl's declaration. "And you don't think I'm fat enough?"

"No, you're just tall," the girl replied. "Large would work."

Erikson took the white shirtjac from the salesgirl, holding it a shoulder width up against his body.

"You can try it on," the girl said.

Erikson glanced around for a fitting room, but there appeared to be none.

"You can wear it over what you have on," the girl advised.

Erikson unbuttoned the shirtjac and slipped it on over his polo shirt. The polo shirt made the shoulders a bit snug, but the length seemed fine since it was meant to be worn over the trousers. "I'll take this white one and that light blue," he said pointing to the rack. The salesgirl reached for the blue shirtjac while Erickson slipped the other shirt off. "By the way, is the proprietor here?" he asked.

"You'll have to ask her," the salesgirl said, pointing to the plump cashier in the wire cage at the center rear of the store.

The salesgirl took the shirtjacs over to where the cashier sat, showing them to her before passing the shirts to her assistant who bagged them and handed them to Erikson. The cashier tapped on the keys of the cash register and a piece of paper receipt emerged. Erikson took out a hundred-dollar note from his billfold, glanced at it, and handed it to the lady. Odd, he thought, how beautiful the currency looked but how worthless it had become in that economy. The cashier gave him change, tore the piece of paper tape, and handed it to him.

"Say, is the store proprietor on the premises?" he asked.

"No," the cashier replied. "Something I can help you with?"

"Well, it's sort of personal."

"His daughter usually comes in at about this time," the cashier said. "If you want to wait, she should be here anytime."

"Thanks, but I'd like to take a quick look at the Bourda Market down the street."

Erikson picked his way around the bolts of cloth, out of the store and onto the pavement, where he stood looking in the direction of Alexander Street. Just then, he became aware he was blocking the way of a very well dressed woman who had turned into the store. "Oh, I'm sorry," he said to the woman, stepping aside to allow her easier access to the store entrance. She hesitated. A slender woman of about five-foot-six and light-brown complexion, she looked him over briefly as if to discern a purpose, then walked into the store. Erikson cast a quick glance behind him and left for the Bourda Market. He must have gone about fifty feet in the direction of the market when he heard someone behind him shouting, "Mister! Mister!" Erikson turned around to see the salesgirl who had waited on him.

"She's here," the salesgirl said, adding for clarification, "the owner's daughter."

Erikson retraced his steps into the store where the neatly dressed woman, with whom he had only moments before crossed paths, stood facing him.

"Hi," he said, and she nodded. "My name is Steve Erikson, and I'm a classmate of Andrew Rambarran from the Military Academy. I gather he is a relative of yours."

She nodded. "Yes, he is my cousin. I'm Anita."

"Is there a place where we could talk in private?"

"Yes," Anita replied. "Why don't we go inside?"

She led him to the back counter where she lifted a hinged horizontal section of the counter, allowing them to pass. A door in the back wall led into a hallway, on the left of which was an office, then what appeared to be a toilet and, beyond that, a kitchen. On the right side was a stairway, enclosed but for the first two steps, which led to a closed door. Anita took a bunch of keys out of her handbag and inserted one into the lock. She invited him to precede her up the stairs, then pulled the door shut behind them.

Erikson emerged from the stairway onto a cappuccino colored hardwood floor with a high gloss. Turning around, he saw that Anita had taken her shoes off at the foot of the stairway, so he took his off, set them close to the wall at the top of the stairway and waited for her. To his right was an open kitchen where a middle-aged woman cast a curious glance away from the large, black wok she was stirring. The scent of freshly prepared food was unmistakable, though Erikson wasn't quite sure if it was a curry of some sort. Anita showed him to the left of the stairway into the living room and invited him to sit on the sectional sofa, which arched around the windows fronting Regent Street and backed against the rail enclosing the stairway they had just ascended.

Erikson noticed metal bars outside the front windows, a common form of burglar proofing in the more affluent areas of Georgetown.

Anita excused herself and went into the center bedroom, directly across from the living room, returning with a picture frame in hand. She set it down on the coffee table in front of Erikson, positioning it so that it was visible to both of them. It was the class photo taken on the porch of the MacArthur building during Erikson's final year at West Point.

"So, Mr. Erikson?" Anita asked, sitting on the solitary morris chair across the table from Erikson.

"Steve, please," Erikson interjected, reaching to retrieve the photo.

"So, Steve," Anita said, "you and Andrew were classmates?"

"Yes," he replied, rising and moving around the coffee table to where Anita sat. Bending over near to her, he pointed to a figure on the far left of the picture with his right leg over the porch rail. "That's me," he said, "and that, of course, is Andrew." Andrew Rambarran was on the opposite side of the porch steps, leaning forward with his hands resting on the rail. "We were in the same company and we actually roomed together twice."

"And he doesn't know you're here?" she asked. Erikson shook his head from side to side. "Well, this would be quite a surprise to him," she declared.

The fragrance from Anita's perfume suffused his nostrils and made him reluctant to relinquish his position, but he walked back to the sofa, replacing the photo on the coffee table.

"May I ask what brings you here?" Anita asked.

"I've been posted here as the Assistant Military Attaché," Erikson replied. "It was a vacancy that developed rather quickly; I didn't have time to notify too many people. To tell the truth, the situation in your country right now makes it a little awkward for me to contact an old classmate serving in the military here, but I thought I could do it on the sly."

"I'd be happy to let Andrew know you are in the country. I'm sure he'd want to know."

When he stood beside her in the store downstairs, Erikson had thought Anita Rambarran a shapely woman. Now, sitting across from her, he was struck by her facial beauty. Light complexioned, with a slender face, pointed nose, small mouth, and intelligent eyes, she blushed as he stared into her face not saying anything. "Do you run the store?" he finally asked.

"No," she replied. "I'm an attorney, but I know the business. And when my father is away, I look after things. I generally come home for lunch. Most people here tend to eat at home or in their offices. Have you had lunch?"

"No, but I wouldn't want to impose on you."

"No imposition at all. Andrew would be upset with me if I let you leave on an empty stomach. Besides, you're a new arrival and you might want to start adjusting to the local cuisine." She rose. "Shall we?"

The dining table was visible from where they stood, just beyond the inside stairway they had just ascended, and in the neck connecting the main body of the house to the kitchen on the far right side. Anita invited Erikson to wash his hands at a pedestal sink on the bedroom side across from the dining table, while she gave instructions to the woman she had identified to Erikson as a domestic. Next to the sink was the door to the toilet, the plumbing above partially visible since the internal walls of the house did not rise from the floor to the ceiling. Instead, there was a four inch ventilation space between the floor and the wall. The wall itself rose up to within about two feet of the ceiling, and a floral lattice filled the space between the wall and the ceiling, as was also the case with the bedroom walls. The shower occupied a separate room next to the toilet. Beyond it was the kitchen where a refrigerator and a stove dominated the far wall. The counter was devoid of the usual appliances in American homes; the space was instead taken up by bottles of pickled peppers, pickled limes, and mango chutney.

Anita briefly introduced the housekeeper when she came to the table with two plates. She greeted Erikson and proceeded with her duties. After a couple of quick trips, the housekeeper retired from view. Resting before Erikson on the plate was a heaping bed of rice, at the side of which was a light salad of leaf lettuce, cucumbers, and tomatoes, evidently tossed in a vinegar and pepper dressing. In a large shallow dish were two whole fishes in a tomato, green onion, and pepper sauce. Erikson tapped one of the fishes with his knife. The texture and the brown color indicated it had been fried. It had clearly been gutted and cleaned, and the two deep slashes across its body were probably to facilitate cooking, but there it rested in its full length, head and all.

Anita laughed. "I know you are accustomed to your fish filleted. Out here, that ritual is performed at the dining table."

"What's the bit with the head?" Erikson asked.

"People eat that," she replied. "When I was a child, I was told that eating fish-head made you smart."

"It evidently worked," Erikson said.

"I don't know!" Anita said. "I used to wonder: if fish were so smart, how come they got caught?"

Erikson smiled. Severing the head from one of the fishes, he shoved it to one end of the dish.

"Don't worry," Anita said, "You don't have to eat the heads."

"Thank you, though God knows I probably need the smarts."

Erikson watched as Anita filleted and deboned her fish with the efficiency of a surgeon, taking bits of fish and rice on her fork. Imitating her, he shoveled his first fork-full of fish and rice into his mouth. It didn't take long to feel the sting of hot pepper on his tongue and palette. Eyes watering, he reached for the glass of lemonade after he swallowed his first mouthful of food.

"Too hot?" Anita asked.

"Just a bit," he admitted, "But the sauce is actually very tasty. What type of fish is this?"

"I'm not sure about the correct zoological name, but we call it *hoori*."

A light banter ensued. Erikson learned that Anita Rambarran was an attorney in her second year of practice in Georgetown. She had attended Bishop's High School and had done her undergraduate and legal training at the University of the West Indies. Her older brother was a physician in Toronto, Canada. Her parents, who, like her, had permanent residence status in Canada, were interested in migrating to Canada as soon as her father could sell the business. Her mother spent most of the year in Canada, her father making several ten-day visits a year. When he was away, Anita looked after the business.

Her father was the fourth in a family of eight; Andrew's deceased father had been the eldest. A couple of aunts had passed away, the others had migrated to the U.S. or Canada. Andrew was the third in a family of six boys, all of whom were living or studying overseas. Her family was very close to Andrew and his three younger brothers, all of whom resided with her family at Regent Street when they studied for their A-levels at Queen's College. Andrew himself had been thinking of returning to graduate school in the United States. He and Lena Spooner, whose brother was also a Captain in the army, intended to get married after he resigned his commission.

Erikson told Anita that he came from a small family. His only sister was a high school teacher in Cartersville, Georgia, where the family owned a furniture store. He had not contemplated anything other than a military career, though he hoped to pick up a second career after twenty years of service, which was the term of service required in order to earn a pension from the army. He had been married until a year ago; divorced, he had no children.

In the span of a half hour or so, Erikson did carve through both fishes, not as deftly as Anita, which meant that at times he had to rescue himself from thin rib bones that entered his mouth. Anita was amused at his travails, but he was gratified by her attention as he tried to adjust to the spiciness of the sauce. Dessert was a freshly prepared custard, a welcome dousing to his slightly inflamed tongue and pallette. More comforting, however, was the sweetness of this accented voice and the compelling composure presented across the table. What had started as a quest to get information about a former classmate had become transformed into an unquenchable desire to get closer to his cousin. Anita glanced at her watch and began stacking the dishes in from of her.

"I'm sorry," Erikson said, "I hope I didn't make you late."

"No, no," Anita replied, "I'm not late, but I do need to be getting back to the office."

"I guess I do too," Erikson said, standing up. "Shall I walk you over to your office?"

Anita Rambarran stood holding the dishes in front of her with both hands seemingly neutralized. It was the longest pause since they had met. She seemed to be deep in thought, only he couldn't figure what so perplexed her. When, finally, she spoke, her tone was almost apologetic. "Perhaps some other time."

"I'm sorry, I didn't mean—"

"No, no," she said, "it's really nice of you. It's just that what might seem to you to be an act of courtesy could lead to unnecessary gossip.

It's the nature of the society. I'm an unmarried woman from a Hindu family. I must bow to some traditions even though I may not like them."

"I understand," Erikson said. "I hope I see you again."

"I'm sure I'll see you with Andrew sometime."

Anita walked into the kitchen with the dishes, and Erikson went over to the sectional to retrieve his package. She returned to show him out, allowing him to precede her down the internal stairway.

"I'll tell Andrew I saw you," she said while he slipped on his loafers. "How can he get in touch with you?"

"I usually go for coffee at Guyana Stores. I'm there from ten. Until I see him, I'll linger there until ten-thirty."

"Goodbye, Mr. Erikson," Anita said.

"Steve, please," he said, taking her outstretched hand.

"Steve," she corrected herself, and smiled.

SEVEN

August 15, 1979
Office of the Chief of Staff
Camp Ayanganna, Georgetown

"Captain Rambarran, you are charged with conduct unbecoming an officer in violation of Section 75 of the Defense Act, in that on or about Saturday, August 9, you did vandalize a portrait of the Comrade President and Commander-in-Chief." General Agrippa looked up from the charge sheet at Captain Andrew Rambarran standing at attention beside the Brigade Adjutant. At five feet eight, Andrew Rambarran was even shouldered with the Adjutant, but his light brown complexion and wiry frame contrasted sharply with the jet black, portly Adjutant, who had escorted him in to answer the charge.

"General," Rambarran began, "the damage to the picture frame was an unfortunate accident."

"The glass was shattered, Andrew," General Agrippa interjected, holding up the large frame on the right side of his desk so that both he and Rambarran could see it. The black-and-white photograph of the Comrade President with his neatly trimmed goatee seemed intact except for an indentation in the center breast part of his white shirtjac. The photo was rimmed out by jagged pieces of plain glass clinging precariously to the frame. "How did that happen?"

"General," Rambarran replied, "the photograph had been hanging in the room for some time. The wall separators are made of thin cardboard and the picture frame is heavy, so the nail was being pulled out. I took the photo down and leaned it against the base of the wall to prevent it from falling on the floor."

"Then what? Did you kick it?"

"Not deliberately, General. Last Saturday night, I accidentally struck it as I moved in the dark."

"I see," General Agrippa said, leaning back in his chair. "Did you have a female companion in your room that night?"

"Yes, General, but—"

"That's the problem, Captain. The word out there is that you kicked the photograph of the Comrade President to impress your lady friend."

"Nothing could be further from the truth, General. It was an accident, plain and simple. I intended to have the glass replaced during the week, but the MPs came in on Monday morning and impounded the picture."

"Look at the picture, Andrew," General Agrippa, again holding up the frame. "The glass is shattered. That had to be quite a blow."

"It really was an accident, General," Captain Rambarran repeated.

"The cardboard walls are made of thin cardboard, you said?"

"You know they are, General."

"Too frail to hold up such a large picture frame?" General Agrippa asked.

"Over a long period of time? Yes, General."

"Well, one of your neighbors said you had been slamming against that wall for about ten minutes on Saturday night. Were you testing the resilience of the cardboard, Captain?" General Agrippa leaned back in his chair, touching his cheek with his thumb and fingers.

"No, General," Captain Rambarran replied quietly, face flushed.

"You are aware that women are not permitted in bachelor officers' quarters on this post?"

"Yes, General, but most—"

"I know, most of the officers break that rule. But I am wondering whether the damage to the Comrade President's photo did not occur during all that wall slamming."

Captain Rambarran remained silent, looking directly in front of him.

"You've put yourself in a very tricky position, Andrew," General Agrippa said, leaning forward and resting his chin on the back of his hands. "There are people in the Party who would like me to give them your head on a platter. They are not going to be happy with me, but I'll be out of here shortly anyway. So, to hell with them. I'll accept your explanation that the damage to the picture was an accident."

"Thank you, General."

"Oh, I am not through, Captain. You are to replace the photograph and hang it securely in that room. Do you understand?"

"Yes, General," Rambarran replied.

"The Adjutant will give your name to the Base Commander. You will serve as Duty Officer for the next four weekends. That should damper your social activities a bit. Now, do you have anything you'd like to say?"

"No, General."

"Very well, the Adjutant will escort you out. You are returned to duty, but I'd be careful if I were you."

"Yes, General." Captain Rambarran saluted, about-faced and marched out with the Adjutant.

Seating his beret on his head, Captain Rambarran walked down the short hall and then down the flight of stairs onto the first floor veranda facing the drill square. His driver, McCurchin, was standing on the square by their quarter-ton talking to the Chief of Staff's driver.

"Okay, Mac," Rambarran said, climbing into the jeep, "let's head out to Rosignol."

$*$ $*$ $*$

The pontoon and tugboat were already moored to the wharf when the jeep pulled into the holding area at the Rosignol ferry station. Cars were already on the pontoon and others were rolling along the ramp, one at a time. When Captain Rambarran presented his priority pass to the police constable, the constable stopped the loading of additional vehicles to allow the jeep to the front of the line before embarkation resumed. After all the vehicles were on board, pedestrian passengers were allowed to board, winding their way around the vehicles to positions on the periphery of the pontoon and in the open glare of the sun, now almost directly overhead. The ramp was winched up, and the tugboat slowly eased the pontoon away from the wharf and then opened its throttle. A few minutes into the ride, Rambarran saw the ferry at the New Amsterdam station in the distance pulling away from the wharf there and executing the wide turn to re-commence another run to Rosignol.

The two vessels crossed paths at about midway on the familiar diagonal course which they continually plied from the crowing of the first cock to early evening. Nearing the New Amsterdam ferry station, the tugboat went past the wharf in a wide turn, then edged its way back alongside the wharf where ready hands waited to help with the mooring. The exit from the pontoon was considerably faster than would have been the case with the ferry, and the jeep was soon out on the quarter-mile stretch of harbor road. It turned left onto Strand and proceeded to Esplanade Park, where Lieutenant Shah's platoon was encamped, pulling up to the bandstand at the center of the park.

Lieutenant Shah rose up from the hammock he had rigged up across the bandstand to greet the Company Commander. "Just in time for lunch, Captain," Shah said.

"What's on?" Rambarran asked.

"I think they are just about done with the *cook-up*."

"Good," Rambarran said. "I'm hungry." Instructing McCurchin to be ready to leave after lunch, Rambarran seated himself on the bench that circled the bandstand and stretched his legs out.

"How did it go with the Chief of Staff?" Shah asked.

"Administrative punishment," Rambarran replied. "I'll be the Duty Officer at Camp Ayanganna for the next four weekends."

"That's not too bad," Shah said.

"No," Rambarran replied, "but not too convenient. I was hoping to spend those at home, with Lena."

"Still beats me that somebody would have reported a thing like that," Shah said.

"Beats me too," Rambarran agreed, "but we are talking about a picture of the Comrade Leader!"

Lieutenant Shah laughed. "Have you seen this?" he asked, walking over with *The Guardian*. The headline read, "*Sugar Union Announces One-day Strike*." Rambarran glanced down the article to learn that the strike was in sympathy with the bauxite workers, who were on strike in Linden. A one-day strike was probably the best the sugar union could offer since it was not grinding season at the sugar factories and most sugar workers were in seasonal unemployment.

"You'll have to do some night patrolling at both the Rose Hall and Blairmont sugar estates," Rambarran said.

"I plan to," Lieutenant Shah replied.

McCurchin walked close to the bandstand to invite the two officers to lunch. With two plates laden with a *cook-up* of rice, black-eyed peas, beef, chicken, and spinach, the two officers returned to the bandstand, where McCurchin had deposited two bottles of Pepsi from the platoon canteen. Over lunch, Rambarran informed Lieutenant Shah of the command post location and the weekly routines, including a visit of Shah's platoon three times a week. He shared his concern about the possibility of higher incidence of unauthorized absence by soldiers in the New Amsterdam area, indicating that penalties would be severe. He himself would be overnighting at the family home at Adventure, where he was heading after setting up an office at the Albion Police Station and visiting with Lieutenant Duncan Clark.

"There used to be a donkey tied here," Rambarran said.

"It still is," Shah said, smiling. "Mr. Sackiechand, the owner, took *Eveready* this morning. I imagine he's pulling a cart somewhere in town."

"I hope it doesn't become too much of a distraction. But God knows, with a name like *Eveready*?"

They both laughed.

"Will you be visiting Third Platoon in Springlands?" Shah asked.

"No," Rambarran replied. "I think I'll just stop by and see Second Platoon at Albion; then, I'll retire for the day. I can use some emotional sustenance. Which reminds me, I'd better call Lena. I hope I can use the phone next door at Central Police Station. Getting an outside line there can be such a pain."

"Does Lena know about the trial?"

"No, I didn't want to upset her unnecessarily. She'll cope better after the fact."

* * *

Central Police Station, New Amsterdam

Rambarran dialed the Spooner residence. The housekeeper, who picked up the phone, put Rambarran on hold. Lena Spooner was helping her mother in the vegetable garden. Andrew knew it was going to be a long wait. Ten minutes later, a breathless voice said, "Hello."

"Sorry to pull you away," Andrew said.

"It's okay," Lena replied, "I was just helping Mother gather up some vegetables for dinner. You are coming, aren't you?"

"I'm not sure I'm up for too much company this evening."

"What's wrong?" she asked.

"Well, it's just one of those days when I feel so buffeted by life, I just need a warm and welcoming bosom on which to rest my weary head."

"You always sound so dramatic, but I like it."

"Thank you."

"But dinner first," Lena insisted, "welcoming bosom later. Besides, Mother wants to see you. With Ralph's Company posted to the interior, she hardly sees him. When you are here, it's almost like he's home. Please come."

"Okay, I'll be there."

"I love you, Andrew." A few moments of silence passed. "And you say?" Lena prompted.

"I'm sorry," Andrew replied, "of course, I love you too."

"You need to work on that," Lena admonished.

EIGHT

August 23, 1979
Piarco International Airport, Trinidad

Colonel Taylor's plane lifted off at 08:15, as scheduled. Once the plane had leveled off to cruising speed, breakfast service began in the first class cabin. Taylor downed the small glass of orange juice on his tray but declined a refill from the vigilant stewardess standing beside him with a can of Trout Hall. With coffee came a copy of the *Trinidad Express*, which Taylor unfolded to find that Guyana had made the front page. The headline read, "*Guyana Signs Standby Agreement with IMF*." The writer remarked that after extensive negotiation and great vacillation, the Guyana government had bowed to the inevitable and accepted the draconian conditions for the IMF loan it desperately needed. Reflecting on the experiences of other countries, the article projected drastic cuts in government spending, which would likely result in massive retrenchment in the Guyana Public Service, a major source of employment for blacks, the traditional supporters of the Kabaka Party. It described how the Guyanese standard of living had plummeted, conservatively estimating unemployment at thirty percent and a consumer price index increase of over two hundred percent over the past five years. There were shortages of virtually everything, and a thriving black market.

Franchette Taylor felt depressed. He paused to sip his coffee, then resumed reading. A strike by the bauxite workers, supported by the sugar union, presaged greater industrial unrest in the days ahead. It was unlikely that the Public Service Union, which represented government employees, could keep the lid on dissatisfaction once its members began losing jobs in larger numbers. The article reminded readers that, in the early 1960s, the public service workers had made Georgetown ungovernable and paved the way for the Kabaka Party to take power.

Remarking that elections in Guyana were "*a sensitive matter*," the article noted that Guyana was preparing for a national referendum on a new constitution which would greatly strengthen the power of the president. Given the outcomes in previous elections, the Kabaka Party was certain to carry the day again, but the IMF agreement was likely to produce tectonic shifts in the political landscape. The writer discussed Trinidad's Black Power riots against the government of Eric Williams and questioned whether the Kabaka Party could withstand similar protests by urban blacks, who had until now acquiesced in the electioneering chicanery of the Party. Complicating matters for the Kabaka Party was the fact that a new gravitational pull had emerged in the form of the Workers' Party, led by the black sociology professor, Donald Nelson, and it was already siphoning off urban blacks from the Kabaka Party. The article ended by remarking that Guyana was entering interesting but turbulent times.

Taylor folded the newspaper and glanced down at a clump of eggs still steaming from its recent microwave blast and at the marble-sized roll resting beside a slab of cheese. On another day, perhaps he might have found this breakfast appealing; right then, he just needed to think and, on his signal, the stewardess refilled his coffee cup.

Clearly the change in army leadership, which had so preoccupied him, was not the only game in town, but unions and political parties were not his cup of tea. Even if he could muster the support of enough troop commanders to push the government aside, there was the question of running a bankrupt country. Would the army really be up to the task? What if the Public Service Union went on strike, could the army cope? How much force would be required to keep things quiet, and for how long? And what if things didn't improve after an army takeover?

There would be a need for alliances, surely; but with whom? The Opposition People's Party was more socialist than the Kabaka Party, and the very idea of the army forming an alliance with an Indian-dominated party would be anathema to black officers. Then, of course, there was Donald Nelson, another socialist, but his was the only fresh face on the political scene and his Workers' Party was a multiethnic coalition. Its leaders were mostly university professors with the types of skills to staff a government and, more importantly, it was drawing support from both blacks and Indians. If the party could be persuaded to moderate its positions, an arrangement could be worked out. Nelson, after all, was not a stranger to Taylor. They had been classmates at Queen's College through the Sixth Form. He had not spoken to Nelson in years, but then their paths simply had not crossed. Perhaps the time had come for a meeting.

All of that assumed, of course, that Taylor himself would retain his position in the army. So far, only the Chief of Staff was to be replaced. The Brigade Commander had resigned, but that was his decision entirely. How that position was filled would really give Taylor a good read on where the President intended to take the army. And, there wasn't much time to lose.

*   *   *

Timehri Airport, Guyana

The DC-10 touched down at 09:05 and taxied to a stop in front of the terminal building. Colonel Taylor unbelted himself from his first class seat, rested his beret on his head, and reached into the overhead bin for his attache case. He was the first passenger out of the door, walking down the scaffolded stairs onto the tarmac and into the terminal building, where Captain Spooner was waiting for him by the immigration checkpoints. The Immigration Officer stamped Taylor's passport and returned it to him, well ahead of other passengers, who were just then queuing up at the other immigration stations.

"Well, what's new here?" Colonel Taylor asked Captain Spooner as they walked over to the baggage area.

"Colonel LaFleur is the acting Brigade Commander," Spooner replied.

"I have seniority over him," Colonel Taylor matter-of-factly, trying not to sound surprised or despondent.

"I know, Colonel, but you were out of the country. Anyway, it's just a temporary appointment to give General Downs time to choose his own man."

"General Downs? The man's a Police Superintendent."

"Not anymore, Colonel," Captain Spooner replied. "The man is now the army Chief of Staff. We're in new territory."

They entered the baggage area, empty except for the drivers of the jeeps of Taylor and Spooner. Both drivers snapped to attention when the officers approached. Walking away from the drivers to the edge of the baggage platform, Colonel Taylor asked, "Who's likely to be the new Brigade Commander?"

"No one knows for sure, Colonel; rumors are flying wild. The bet is on Lieutenant Colonel Ulric Fields from the National Service," Spooner replied. "He used to be the head of the Kabaka Youth Movement."

"Christ!" Colonel Taylor sucked his teeth. "Another Party man."

The baggage area was filling up with passengers, and people were positioning themselves to retrieve their luggage. The two army drivers came over and stood besides the two officers, waiting for instructions. Colonel Taylor assured them he only had two suitcases, which he pointed out in the first baggage truck pulling up to the platform. No sooner were the bags off-loaded than the drivers scooped them up and the four military figures made their way to one of the customs stations where the officer on duty waved them on. The suitcases were placed at the back of Colonel Taylor's jeep, parked in front of Captain Spooner's along the curb in front of the airport building.

"Ralph," Colonel Taylor said, "I'd like to stop by the Club and get something to eat. Why don't you join me?"

"If you like, Colonel," Spooner replied. "Sure."

Within a few minutes, the jeeps pulled into the compound of the Officers' Club and parked. Colonel Taylor and Captain Spooner got out and walked up the outside stairway into the Club.

"Let's go in the lounge," Colonel Taylor said.

"Very well, Colonel. Shall I order you something?"

"A couple of egg sandwiches and coffee, please."

Colonel Taylor chose a booth on the eastern side of the lounge, far enough away from the entrance and from the bar. Captain Spooner returned, followed by a Mess attendant with a tray, containing a jar of instant coffee, a milk decanter, a large thermos, and cups on saucers, which she placed on the table before the Colonel.

"Your sandwiches will be out in a few minutes, Colonel," the attendant said.

"Thank you, Private Griffiths." Colonel Taylor watched Private Griffiths walk off, then began spooning out some coffee into the cup. "How has Colonel LaFleur been behaving since he took charge of the Brigade?" he asked Spooner, pouring hot water into the cup.

"I don't know, Colonel," Spooner replied. "He's now based in Georgetown at Camp Ayanganna. I haven't seen him recently."

"I see," said the Colonel, sipping his coffee and watching Spooner fixing himself a cup. "Haven't you talked to any of the officers at Ayanganna?"

"No, Colonel, but my impression from the officers here is that no one is taking LaFleur's appointment seriously. There is a feeling though that it was meant as a sop to neutralize his opposition to the changes in the army structure."

"Is the sop working?"

"That, we won't know for some time, but I've told you before, Colonel, I personally don't trust Colonel LaFleur."

"Yes, I remember that, but that may not matter now that he has relinquished command of Border Operations."

"Well, Colonel, let's assess where we're at. We have a new Chief of Staff, an acting Brigade Commander and, soon, a new commander of Border Ops. Events are moving fast. So I'd be inclined to say, forget it."

"Ralph, nothing's fundamentally changed," Colonel Taylor insisted. "If anything, things are likely to get worse. If the new constitution is passed, and it will be, because you can bet the Comrade Leader will rig the referendum, he will become President for life, with absolute power."

"I agree with that, Colonel. I was simply reflecting on the current disposition of forces."

"But you also know of two other Company Commanders who are strongly opposed to what's going on. The leadership changes within the army, I am sure, will be the last straw."

"Maybe, Colonel, but the betting among the officers is that you will be pushed out next, and then it will be all over. Officers will leave en masse, and the government will re-make the army."

"Have you made up your mind firmly or would you let me raise this again with you after I've talked with others."

"You can talk with me again, Colonel, but—"

"Don't worry, I'll talk with Captain Rambarran soon."

*   *   *

Camp Ayanganna, Georgetown

Colonel LaFleur rose from behind the large polished desk to greet Colonel Taylor when he walked into the Brigade Commander's office on the west wing of the Headquarters Building. Inviting Colonel Taylor to sit, after shaking his hand, LaFleur asked, "How was the conference?"

"Short," Colonel Taylor replied. "Of the two weeks, only three days were actually spent at the National War College. The rest of the time they had us on a bus tour of various military sites, including one whole day at West Point."

"What did you do at the War College?"

"The Americans are clever," Colonel Taylor said. "You might recall that the invitation was for us to participate in a Conference on Hemispheric Security. It turns out that this was the focus of one of their courses at the War College, and officers from the region, like myself, were invited to discuss the threats from their country's perspective."

"Ah! So what did you tell them?" LaFleur asked.

"I spoke about the border problems with Suriname and Venezuela," Taylor replied.

"Did you get a sense of how they feel about things here, the socialist trend, I mean?"

"I don't think they like it, but at the moment they have bigger fish to fry in Central America."

Colonel LaFleur did not appear to have any additional questions about the trip; he had picked up a rubber band and was stretching it with the fingers of both hands around which it was placed. Taylor thought LaFleur was getting ready to say something or was expecting him to say something. Finally, Taylor broke the awkward silence. "Oh, congratulations on this appointment, Ovid."

"Thank you, Franchette, but it's just a temporary appointment."

"I know, but still I am glad you got it instead of an outsider," Taylor said.

"Thank you, Franchette. I think they did it because you were away. I mean you have seniority." LaFleur spoke falteringly, his eyes focused on Colonel Taylor.

"Don't worry about that," Taylor reassured him. "Better you than a National Service man. In fact, I hope they confirm you as Brigade Commander. I would support that."

Colonel LaFleur's eyes lit up. "You know that would mean a lot if the other officers knew your position."

"I would prefer you to an outsider, Ovid," Taylor repeated, "and I would tell that to anyone. We've been working together for a long time, you and I."

"Yes, that's true, Franchette."

"I think we could make this work," Taylor said. "The Chief of Staff is just a liaison person. You would be in operational command." Colonel Taylor paused. "You know I was angry when they appointed a policeman as Chief of Staff because I also thought they'd put one of their henchmen in operational command. But with you in charge, I'm okay again."

"To tell the truth," LaFleur said, "I was feeling the same way but, as you said, we can make it work. Only thing, Franchette, this is a temporary appointment."

"Well, only the Chief of Staff and the President can make the appointment permanent, but I'll let them know I support you."

"Thank you, Franchette," Colonel LaFleur said, rising from his chair and walking around his desk with his hand extended.

*   *   *

Kitty, Greater Georgetown

Colonel Taylor had just finished dinner when he first heard the loudspeaker. It sounded as if a political meeting had started at the Kitty marketplace on Alexander Street, the main artery through Kitty, Georgetown's eastern suburb. These days, only the Opposition People's Party and the Workers' Party kept open air meetings to rant against the government, but the Kitty marketplace used to be a popular spot for the Kabaka Party as well. A decade and a half of control over the government changed that. The Comrade Leader didn't see a need to appear there anymore; he preferred grander venues like the Square of the Revolution. At times, some of his underlings did hold public meetings at the Kitty marketplace, but those meetings tended to be closer to election times to rally enough of their supporters and to prepare them to counter protests after the Kabaka Party's likely referendum victory.

Taylor seated himself in a rocking chair on the verandah on the eastern side of his two-storied stucco house at the intersection of Vlissengen Road and Sandy Babb Street, and waited for his wife, who was clearing the dishes. The sound from the public address system only a block over was coming in clearly, and Taylor realized that the meeting had been called by the Public Service Union. The first speaker was telling people of the number of civil service jobs that had been lost and questioned why they had to bear the burden for the entire country. He blamed the union leadership, and he said that the time had come to move aside those people who had been bought off and stood impotently by while jobs were being lost. Then, he introduced the man who would be the new leader of the union, Joe Henry. That was when Franchette Taylor realized that it was the union rebels who had called the meeting. His wife had now joined him, and they sipped the coffee she had brought. The pause between the change of speakers at the Kitty Marketplace allowed Taylor to tell his wife what appeared to be going on out there. Then, the second speaker began.

Joe Henry, whose full-time position was with the Ministry of Education, began with the IMF Agreement the government had signed, telling his listeners that, everywhere the IMF had intervened, public sector employees were the first to get the axe. The government was trying to sell the retrenchment as only the first stage in a scheme to redeploy workers but that, to date, no one had been redeployed. Public sector workers needed to unite now and take action before those who had jobs lost them. Then he launched a broadside into the Public Service Union's leadership, which he said was toeing the government's line. They had used their executive positions to feather their own nests. They lived in big houses; they took lots of trips overseas; and they had spoken as invited guests at the Kabaka Party congresses. But what had they done for civil servants? Inflation had eaten away at wages, and now even those paltry wages might be lost, unless they voted out the union leadership in the upcoming election. Clapping and cheering erupted.

Taylor's wife was more interested in what was going on in the army: a conversation they had been having over dinner. Taylor assured her again that having a police officer at the head might take some getting used to, but that the new Chief would need regular army officers to advise him, which was why he thought his own position secure. He had an understanding with Colonel LaFleur, he felt, and the next day's handover ceremony should bring some more clarification as the President or the new Chief of Staff might indicate additional personnel changes. Taylor felt guilty. Everything he said was true. What he couldn't tell his wife was what he was planning with other officers. He did worry though about what might happen to her if he failed.

The Taylors' conversation was interrupted several times by cheering and clapping as from a dense mass of people at a soccer rally. Then the loudspeakers became quiet. A babel of voices followed. Screams of panic brought Taylor to his feet. Leaning against the rail, he tried to figure out what might be happening. The loudspeakers were alive again. Joe Henry shouted that they had secured police permission, but that did not stop the scattered shrieks and the sounds of stampeding feet on the pitched roads. There were some scratching sounds from the loudspeakers suggesting a tussle over the microphone, then the loudspeakers fell silent. People funneled out of Alexander Street onto both sides of Sandy Babb Street, seeking safety from policemen charging with batons. Heads popped out of open windows from homes at the end of Alexander Street and from those on Sandy Babb. People scaled private fences; the pursuing policemen pounded the concrete pavement. Then the electricity sputtered out; Kitty was in darkness. The stampede had dissipated; the police gave up chase. Sandy Babb Street was empty again, and quiet.

NINE

August 24, 1979
Guyana Stores, Main Street

On Captain Rambarran's instruction, Private McCurchin pulled off Main Street onto the concrete apron on the eastern side of Guyana Stores, and parked. This was not legal parking space, but what police constable would challenge the presence in that location of a jeep carrying an army Captain? The northern section of the apron was meant to accommodate three executive vehicles, but those were the days when white people ran the business. Then, of course, Guyana Stores used to be owned by the sugar company, Booker Brothers, McConnell and Company Limited. When the sugar industry was nationalized, the multipurpose stores were part of the assets acquired and now run by the Kabaka Party. The Guyana Stores building stretched from Main to Water Street. The eastern wing fronting Main Street housed the apparel division, the gift shop, and the snackette, the western wing with its semi-bare shelves bore a faded resemblance to the supermarket Booker Brothers operated. The concrete apron, where the jeep was parked, led around to the front of the building, narrowing into a pavement, which ended around the western side on Water Street.

Leaving McCurchin with the jeep, Captain Rambarran entered the store, walking along the wide central aisle past the men's apparel sections. Toward the end of the eastern wing of the store, on the right side of the central aisle, a large, aged Coca-Cola crown, affixed to an awning, hung over the counter and seating of the snackette, much of which lay hidden behind rows of handicraft in the gift shop. On the two side walls, hammocks of multicolored cotton and Amerindian hammocks of *tibisiri* hung aloft, as did woven hats and baskets. Rambarran turned into a narrow aisle displaying postcards and beaded necklaces with pendants of highly lacquered pieces of coconut shell, on one side, and serving trays and coasters, with postcard pictures displayed below the glass surfaces, and napkin holders of polished kabakali, on the other side, emerging to find a solitary figure seated on a stool at the counter.

"How's the cow?" Rambarran asked.

With a loud laugh, Steve Erikson swung around and hopped off the stool to display the full length of his six-foot frame, grasping the outstretched hand and embracing his friend. "Wow, look at you," he said, stepping back and scanning Rambarran from head to toe. This was the first time they had seen each other since graduation, and the first time Erikson had seen his former room-mate in a uniform different from his own. Andrew Rambarran was wearing green fatigues with his shirt sleeves rolled up above his elbow and his trousers neatly tucked into his high-top airborne boots. A three-inch wide stable belt was tightly wrapped around his waist and secured on the right side by three leather straps in small buckles. A blue lanyard looped over his left shoulder and hooked into his left breast pocket. Three shiny pips adorned the epaulette on each side of his shoulder, and a green beret with a silver-colored Brigade badge at the front was seated neatly on his head.

"You look great, Andrew," Erikson said, motioning Rambarran to sit. "How have you been?"

"Fine," Rambarran replied, "except for the weekends. This is my second weekend as duty officer."

"Punishment?"

"Yes," Rambarran replied. "I collided with a picture of the President in my room."

"Shall I guess how it happened?"

"No," Rambarran replied. "You'd probably be right. So, how have you been? How did you draw this assignment?"

Erikson related how he had been alerted to the vacancy by Colonel Stanford when his duty tour ended in Germany.

"How is the Colonel these days?" Rambarran asked. "I used to see him once a year when I visited the Ambassador at the Embassy. Last year was different. No Ambassador."

"I served briefly with Colonel Stanford after graduation," Erikson said. "We kept in touch afterwards, of course, which eventually led here. He's fine though. Same old fellow."

"How's Gail?" Rambarran asked.

"We got divorced a year ago," Erikson replied. "It didn't work out. She decided she didn't want an army life after all."

"I'm sorry to hear that."

"Understand you're still single," Erikson said.

"Yes," Rambarran replied. "You remember Lena?" Erikson nodded. "Well, she came back to Guyana when I did. But she still had two years of course work to get her degree. So we held off. She attended university intermittently. She's now finished. We're planning to get married next year."

"That's great," Erikson said. "I'm glad I'll be here for that. How does one get to see you in the meantime?"

"Well, my Company is deployed in Berbice County. The problem is that after this weekend, I'll have two more tours as duty officer, before I'll be free to have you down for the weekends."

"I'll look forward to that," Erikson said.

"In the meantime," Rambarran continued, "I usually come to Georgetown on Fridays, overnight at Regent Street, and assume duties at Camp Ayanganna on Saturday morning. Maybe we could have dinner on Fridays."

"That sounds good," Erikson said. "Give me a call, would you?"

"Sure," Rambarran replied, "but I have to tell you that I don't have a phone at the house. I usually use the phone at the police stations. You have to go through an operator and wait for an external line. It's a pain. Not to worry though. You'll hear from me or from Anita, my cousin."

"She's something, your cousin," Erikson said.

"I'll take your word for it," Rambarran said.

"Mind if I ask something about her?"

"Not at all," Rambarran replied.

"How come an attractive woman like that is unmarried?"

"Well, she plans to emigrate after my uncle sells the store, but they've arranged for her to marry a physician in Canada."

"Arranged? She didn't have a choice?"

"Oh, she did," Rambarran replied. "The parents arranged it; she met the fellow and agreed to the match."

"These things still happen?" Erikson asked.

"Yes, it's very commonplace in Indian families," Rambarran replied.

"So, is this an immutable contract?" Erikson asked.

"I wouldn't characterize it as such," Rambarran replied. "People have been known to change their minds."

"How old is she?" Erikson asked.

"Three years younger than us," Rambarran said, adding, "twenty-four."

"Has she interacted extensively with the doctor?" Erikson asked.

"No, not really," Rambarran replied. "They met at my uncle's house. I believe she and her parents visited the doctor and some of his family on one occasion. Then the parents acted as go-betweens, and she agreed to the match."

Erikson sipped his coffee. "She is a remarkable woman."

"I agree," Rambarran said, "but, of course, I'm very biased."

"I must confess, I have developed something more than a mere curiosity in her."

"That fact has not escaped me, Steve," Rambarran said.

"Final question, then," Erikson said. Rambarran nodded. "How steep a climb would it be for me?"

"Oh, boy," Rambarran said. "I don't know quite what to say."

"Come on, Andrew, you know the culture here!"

"And I thought you came to see me," Rambarran remonstrated, smiling.

"I did," Erikson said, "I did. Except life intervened."

"Well," Rambarran said, "the biggest strike against you is that you're divorced."

"Why is that such a big deal?" Erikson asked.

"Divorce is sort of anathema among Indian families. A well-to-do family marrying their daughter to a divorced man is rare."

"Is there anything in my favor?" Erikson asked.

"Two, maybe," Rambarran said, taking a sip his coffee and swirling it as if to fully savor the flavor of the brew. "You are here, and the good doctor isn't."

"Can you help, Andrew?"

"Not directly. My uncle would kill me, if I messed up the arrangement. If, on the other hand, she chose freely, why that would be a different matter altogether."

"You said there were two things in my favor?"

"Did I?" Rambarran said.

"Damn it, Rambarran, you did. I heard you distinctly. And you know it."

Andrew Rambarran looked down into the cup, aware that Erikson was staring expectantly at him. He raised his head, bit his lower lip, then spoke slowly. "When she called to tell me about your visit, she seemed quite animated."

"What the hell does that mean, 'animated?'" Erikson protested.

"What do you think it means?"

"Quit playing games, man. What are you trying to say?"

"I don't know exactly," Rambarran replied. "I don't want to speak out of turn here. I'm not usually around when they discuss the marriage business; it's just that I detected a liveliness in her description of your meeting that I had not heard whenever she and I have talked about the fellow in Canada."

"How does she talk about him? I mean, what kind of intonation does she use?"

"It's been more matter-of-fact." Rambarran paused. "It's like, the marriage is something that will happen. There's a sense of resignation, I'd say."

Steve Erikson smiled. "Well, as Alexander the Great probably said at the Battle of Gaugamela, there might an opening in the Persian lines, after all."

As they nursed a second cup of coffee, Andrew Rambarran described the political situation in the country. The narrative was close to what Erikson had read in his briefing notes but more authentic because it came from someone on the scene in whom he had great confidence. Rambarran shared his plan to resign his commission at the end of his contract and to return to graduate school in the US, and Erikson offered to help in any way possible, including facilitating processing of his visa application.

Rambarran explained that he had come to Georgetown earlier than usual, not only to see Erikson, but also to attend the changeover ceremony at Camp Ayanganna. What did he think of the new Chief of Staff? He didn't know very much about him, except that he was a policeman and he had close ties to the Party. Both of those were strikes against him, but most officers found the fact of his police background more objectionable. Would officers take any type of action in protest? Not likely. There was coup talk, but that would soon dissipate, he was sure.

With the surge of caffeine and the spirit of brotherliness, the conversation drifted to the familiar days at the Academy. They rambled about classmates and interwove stories about Plebe year, summer at Camp Buckner, Airborne School at Fort Benning, getting drunk after the Army-Navy games, wine-tasting at the Brotherhood Winery, and picking up women at the Saturday night hops. Then, it was time to go.

"I'm sort of badly parked," Rambarran said, rising from his stool, "and I'll have to buy off my driver for such a long wait. But it's been great to see you, Steve."

"Same here," Erikson said.

"We'll have more time when you come to see me. You'll love it on the Corentyne Coast."

"I can't wait to see where you grew up," Erikson said. "Just let me know when."

"I'll give you a call or get a message to you."

"Okay, man," Erikson said, standing with his hand outstretched. "Of course, I wouldn't mind at all if you directed your messages through Anita."

"I believe I'm losing a friend," Rambarran said, and they both laughed.

$$* \qquad * \qquad *$$

Camp Ayanganna

At 14:45 hours, the Brigade Band, in ceremonial dress, marched to a low drum beat onto the drill square directly in front of the Headquarters Building and positioned themselves at the southern edge, backing Thomas Road but facing the HQ building. The sky was a clear blue and, through a breach in the cirrus clouds, the sun shone like a freshly minted shilling. Cars began pulling off Thomas Road and parking on the embankment; pedal cyclists and pedestrians also stopped to observe.

Seated on the lower-level veranda of the HQ building were the President, behind whom stood two burly black bodyguards, and the heads of the Police Force, the National Service, and the Peoples' Militia. At the upper-level veranda, staff officers and other ranks at HQ were joined by the three company commanders: Captain Andrew Rambarran, Captain Malcolm Felix, and Captain A. C. McGowan.

At 15:00 hours, the official commencement of the handover ceremony, the Band struck a British marching tune. Behind the HQ building, Captain Spooner's voice rang out, "By the left, quick … march!" In a minute, Captain Spooner appeared, sabre drawn and shouldered, rounding the building ahead of his three platoons. To his right was a solitary color guard carrying the green Brigade flag. The three platoon leaders marched ahead of their respective units, the first one directly behind Spooner and the color guard.

"Right wheel," Spooner ordered and, one by one, the platoons turned off the road onto the drill square. Another "Right wheel" oriented the platoons due west. When the second platoon was centered on the HQ building, Spooner halted the company. With the color guard following, he repositioned himself in front of the second platoon.

"Company will advance!" Spooner ordered. "Right … turn!" The entire company pivoted on their right feet and, with a sharp thunderclap, brought their left heels, in unison, down on the concrete. The entire company now faced the HQ building. The platoon leaders repositioned themselves at the center of their respective units. The officers and men were in ceremonial dress: white tunics, green trousers with black side stripes, and scarlet berets. The officers, with their sabers drawn, had scarlet sashes around their waists, and scarlet lanyards over their left shoulders.

Colonel LaFleur, the acting Brigade Commander, entered the square ahead of the Brigade Adjutant, General Agrippa, and General Tony Downs, the Chief of Staff designate. Colonel LaFleur came to a halt about six paces ahead of Captain Spooner. General Downs took his position facing the formation, several paces behind LaFleur, two paces in front of General Agrippa, who faced the HQ Building. The Brigade Adjutant stood between them to the side and faced inward.

"Report!" Colonel LaFleur ordered.

"Colonel, the Company is all present or accounted for," Captain Spooner replied, saluting with his sabre.

Colonel LaFleur returned the salute.

70

"Present the flag!" he ordered.

"Color guard," Spooner called out, "front and center!"

The color guard advanced with the Brigade flag past Colonel LaFleur and stood beside the Adjutant, who read the order appointing General Tony Downs Chief of Staff effective 15:00 hours, August 24, 1979. The color guard presented the flag to the Adjutant, who handed it to General Agrippa, who presented the flag to General Downs, saying, "General, the command is yours." General Agrippa then marched off the square. General Downs returned the flag to the Adjutant, who passed it back to the color guard.

"Color guard, post!" Captain Spooner ordered, and the color guard returned to his position beside Spooner. The Band began to play the national anthem. "Present ... arms!" Spooner ordered, raising his sabre to salute. When the anthem ended, he commanded, "Order ... arms!"

"Dismiss the formation!" General Downs ordered Colonel LaFleur, who relayed the order to Captain Spooner.

Spooner about-faced. "Officers," he ordered, "return sabers." Spooner and his three platoon leaders returned their drawn sabres to their scabbards. "Officers, dismissed." The company sergeant major marched up to Captain Spooner and saluted. "Permission to carry on, Captain."

"Carry on," Spooner replied, saluting. Then he walked off the drill square, leaving the sergeant major to dismiss the rest of the company.

*   *   *

Officers' Club, Camp Ayanganna

Captain Rambarran entered the Club trailing behind the Brigade Adjutant and three staff officers. Seated on the inside right of the entrance at the head table were the President, behind whom were the two bodyguards, Chief of Staff Tony Downs, Colonel LaFleur, Colonel Taylor, and the heads of the Police, National Service, and the People's Militia. The occupants at the other tables seemed to have seated themselves by rank except in the right corner, two tables over from the head table, where Captain Spooner sat in ceremonial dress with his three lieutenants. Bracing to attention as he passed the head table, Rambarran walked to the table in the far corner, diagonally across from the head table. There, he took the seat against the window which faced out to the seawall. Next to him was Captain Malcolm Felix, and sitting directly across was Captain A. C. McGowan.

When Colonel LaFleur stood up, the Club fell silent. He welcomed the guests at the head table, especially the President, whom he thanked for taking time to join in celebrating the appointment of General Tony Downs as the new Chief of Staff, and he pledged the support of the officers and men to General Downs. The new Chief of Staff spoke next. Standing in his new uniform, General Downs thanked Colonel LaFleur for his pledge of support. He said he was very proud of the achievements and traditions of the army and that he looked forward to working with the officers and men to support the President and the goals he set out for the nation. Last to speak was the President, who praised the army for its role in securing the borders and in preserving internal order. He said that in choosing a successor to General Agrippa as Chief of Staff, he had thought long and hard and ended up choosing General Tony Downs because Downs had demonstrated the administrative skills and loyalty, which should serve the army well. He said he felt certain he could count on the officers to give maximum cooperation to General Downs.

Two attendants served the head table; the officers at the other tables were obliged to fetch their own drinks from the bar. Those going to the bar to fetch drinks crossed paths with attendants carrying trays of fried chicken, cheese straws, minced meat patties, and black pudding, a sausage made of seasoned rice and cow's blood stuffed into cow intestines. From the furthest table in the lounge, Captain Felix went to the bar and fetched three bottles of Guiness.

"Did you ever think you'd see this day?" Captain A. C. McGowan asked in a hushed voice.

"Which part, A. C.?" Captain Rambarran asked.

"A clown parading as the army Chief of Staff," Captain McGowan replied.

"Well, A. C., my friend," Rambarran said, "I hate to tell you this, but we've had a clown parading as Chief of Staff for several years."

Captain Felix laughed; McGowan remained somber. "It's bad enough to have a Party man as Chief of Staff, but a policeman?" he muttered.

"Wasn't Agrippa a Party man?" Rambarran asked.

"Yes," Captain Felix interjected, "and, A. C., I didn't hear you object when General Agrippa pledged the loyalty of the army to the Party."

"I didn't have anything to do with that," McGowan said. "That was Agrippa's doing."

"But you yourself used to sing the praises of the Kabaka Party," Captain Felix noted.

"Well, the scales have fallen from my eyes," McGowan replied. "I didn't think things would ever come to this."

"So, what do you expect us to do about it?" Captain Felix asked.

"I don't know about you," McGowan replied, "but I think the time has come to change course."

"Easier said than done," Malcolm Felix said.

"Not if we all act together," McGowan asserted.

"Are you serious?" Andrew Rambarran asked.

"Absolutely," McGowan replied. Captain Rambarran, who had the widest field of view stood up first; the others followed suit. The President had gotten up from the head table and was taking leave of General Downs. When he left with his bodyguards, the officers took their seats again. "I have to drive up to Timehri," McGowan continued. "One of my platoons is flying out tomorrow to Kamarang. But I think the answer lies with the army. And I think it's now or never." He rose, retrieved his green beret from under his right epaulette, and made his way out of the Club.

"Was he baiting us?" Andrew Rambarran asked Malcolm Felix.

"I don't think so," Felix replied. "His family has fallen out with the Party."

"Really?" Rambarran asked, furrowing his eyebrows. "He hasn't done anything."

"No," Felix replied, "but his brother has."

"Who's his brother?" Rambarran asked.

"Joe Henry," Felix replied, "Public Service Union."

"How can he be McGowan's brother?"

"Henry is their mother's maiden name," Felix replied. "Their parents weren't married when Joe came along."

Rambarran was incredulous. "I would never have guessed that," he said. "I can understand why McGowan is singing a different tune. His brother was arrested yesterday, wasn't he?"

Malcolm Felix nodded. "Actually, Andrew, that's something I want to talk with you about," Felix said, leaning forward. "It's best done here, sort of in public. It wouldn't look good for Company Commanders to be meeting in private."

"Are you heading where I think you're heading?" Rambarran asked.

"Yes," Felix replied. "I've been approached, as have a couple of other Company Commanders."

"Not here, please," Rambarran said.

"Can we talk later then?" Felix asked.

"If you like," Rambarran replied, "but you might not like my response."

An uncomfortable silence fell between them, and Malcolm Felix looked away to hide his disappointment. Meanwhile, the lounge had acquired a festive atmosphere; the attendants were spinning records on the phonograph behind the bar; and the loud talk and laughter from the tables around the lounge had erased the formal aura, which had blanketed the lounge at the beginning of the reception. It was well past 16:00 hours; officers coming off duty were now joining the celebration in the Club, and people were circulating more freely around the lounge. At Rambarran's table, the mood relaxed somewhat when Captain Spooner came over to join them, taking the chair vacated by Captain McGowan.

"You looked good out there, squaddie," Malcolm Felix said.

"What a farce!" Spooner hissed, looking around.

"You did your job well," Malcolm Felix said. "That's the important thing."

"Like an army officer," Rambarran added, patting Spooner on his upper arm.

"A dying breed," Spooner retorted caustically, checking around to make sure he wasn't overheard.

Chief of Staff Tony Downs was moving around the lounge, introducing himself to junior officers and inquiring about their deployments. When he walked up to the corner table where the three company commanders sat, they stood up. "Sit, sit," General Downs said, motioning with his hand. "That was very impressive today," he said to Captain Spooner, "very impressive."

"Thank you, General," Spooner replied. "Welcome aboard."

"Thank you," General Downs said, then turned to Captain Rambarran. "I bet you are enjoying your deployment in Berbice County."

"I am, General," Rambarran said. "It's good to be close to home again."

"Sorry you have to interrupt your weekends to travel up here," Downs said smiling. "Agrippa said you had a minor accident. Well, we're all starting on a new slate as of today. I'll see what I can do about a reprieve."

"Thank you, General," Rambarran said. The entry of more officers into the lounge momentarily distracted General Downs. "It's the dinner crowd," Rambarran explained. "I'd say they're crashing the reception."

Downs laughed. "You're also deployed close to home this go-around, aren't you, Malcolm?" Downs asked Captain Felix.

"In a way, General. My parents still live in Vergenoegen, but I took up permanent residence in Kitty after I got married. So, yes, West Demerara is still my old stomping ground."

"Malcolm and I served on a Joint Operations Command a few years ago," General Downs told Spooner and Rambarran. "That makes us old squaddies," Downs continued, looking around the lounge. "Well, gentlemen, I'd better go over and greet the newcomers. Don't forget though, if you ever have a problem, come and see me."

The three officers watched until General Downs was a safe distance from the table. "I didn't know you and Tony Downs were squaddies," Spooner said to Malcolm Felix.

"That's not how I would put it," Felix responded. "What the General didn't say was that it was a squad from my second platoon that broke into the Bartica jail to free one of their comrades. The Police Commissioner sent Downs to investigate. It wasn't pleasant."

"How did it turn out?" Rambarran asked.

"Well, Agrippa got involved; the President got involved; and they tried to hush it up. The company had to do a punishment march from Linden to Timehri."

"The same thing happened to F-Company last year," Rambarran noted. "Alan Moore was the company commander. What happened was

75

a handful of soldiers broke into the jail at the New Amsterdam Police Headquarters to free one of their squaddies. F-Company had to do a punishment march from Springlands to New Amsterdam."

"Just goes to show," Spooner interjected, "soldiers don't like policemen. And soldiers hate policemen who pretend to be soldiers." The three officers looked at each other. What remained unsaid was that when all the ceremonies were over, they would end up with a policeman in their midst. Captain Spooner broke the silence. "As the Trinidadians would say, the President appointed a policeman to *mamaguy*, to mock us. So, gentlemen, I'd say we have a *mamaguy* for a Chief of Staff."

Captain Felix smirked. "Well, fellas, I have a wife and two children to go home to; so, if you don't mind." Felix rose and walked over to the bar, where he retrieved his revolver then left the Club.

"Are you staying for dinner?" Spooner asked. Rambarran nodded. "I'd like to get out of this uniform," Spooner added. "Would you mind walking out with me?"

They navigated through the full lounge onto the main road through Camp Ayanganna. Because the road ended at the Officers' Club, there was no traffic there. When they had walked a safe distance from the Club entrance, Spooner stopped them on the side of the road. "Did Felix talk to you about what some of us have been considering?"

"You mean the change business?" Rambarran asked. Spooner nodded. "He tried, but I stopped him. It wasn't safe in there, and I was not interested. Are you a part of this?"

"Yes," Spooner replied.

"I see," Rambarran said. "May I ask who's heading this venture?"

"Colonel Taylor," Spooner said quietly.

Andrew Rambarran was pensive. He knew Spooner was waiting for him to declare his position. "Why didn't you tell me about this before?" he asked.

"This is all very recent," Spooner replied. "I've passed by your house two weekends in a row. You were back here pulling Duty Officer."

"I don't know what to say, Ralph," Rambarran said. "At another time, probably; but I've got some other plans for my life."

"Look, Andrew, I know how you feel. I know the plans you and Lena have. But you should know this: Lena is leaving partly because you want her to and partly because my parents think it would be better for her to." Spooner paused. "My family loves this country, Andrew. I don't want to leave it, and I don't think Lena wants to leave it, not permanently anyway."

"Ralph, Lena and I have gone over this, time and time again," Rambarran said. "Our minds are made up."

"If Lena were convinced things could be changed for the better, she would stay. And we could change it. Heck, you used to talk about this way back when."

"Rum talk, Ralph," Rambarran remarked, "just rum talk."

"No, not from you, Andrew," Spooner insisted. "You made a good argument then. So, what happened?"

"I got tired waiting," Rambarran said, "and I made other plans."

"But the conditions are just right," Spooner insisted. "We'll never get this chance again. What did Shakespeare say? 'There's a tide in the affairs of men, which taken at the flood, leads on to success.'"

"Funny," Rambarran said, "that was precisely the quotation I cited when Lena and I made our plans."

"Would you please think about what I said?" Spooner pleaded.

"I will," Rambarran replied, "I will, but I have a feeling you are not going to be happy with my decision."

TEN

August 27, 1979
Embassy of the United States, Georgetown, Guyana

Ambassador Hales began the Monday morning meeting by thanking everyone for the grand reception and welcome they had accorded him and his wife. He also extended his own welcome to Captain Stephen Erikson, who was joining the Embassy staff as Assistant Military Attaché. Flanked by the Deputy Chief of Mission and the Political Officer, Ambassador Hales said that the decision to reappoint someone of ambassadorial rank at this mission was reflective of general concern in Washington with developments in the Caribbean. The overthrow of the Somoza regime in Nicaragua and the possibility of further radicalization of the Sandinista regime needed to be dealt with but, equally worrisome, was the likely spillover effects into El Salvador and beyond, and the spreading influence of Cuba. This, of course, was where Guyana came in.

As he understood it from his readings and from all of the briefings he had received, Guyana was a de facto one-party state. The regime maintained some of the trappings of a democracy, such as periodic elections, a parliament, and a partially free press. But, as was common in many Third World countries, the elections were rigged to perpetuate the ruling party's hold on power, and one was left to hold one's nose while dealing with that regime because the alternative might be worse. This appeared to be the situation in Guyana, with one significant difference which was that, whether from a sense of ideological fraternity, economic desperation or border insecurity, this regime seemed to be rolling out the welcome mat to Cuba, the Soviet Union, and China.

He did not want to exaggerate the strategic significance of this country or of these developments. After all, it was hemmed in by Venezuela and Brazil, both of which were concerned about spreading communist influence in general, and Cuban influence in particular. The view in Washington was that the situation in Guyana was an irritation, which warranted close monitoring. However, he was interested in hearing from personnel here on the ground. With that, Ambassador Hales invited the Political Officer to briefly sketch out the current domestic political situation and to anticipate as best he could any major development he thought would have consequences for the United States.

The Political Officer began by noting that the country was due for a referendum to approve a new constitution which would institutionalize the ruling Kabaka Party as paramount over all state institutions, in essence creating a one-party state and conferring dictatorial powers on the President, commonly referred to by the Party faithful as the Comrade Leader. The Comrade Leader had created the National Service to break into the country's hinterland, but the main body of the National Service had received military training and was now armed in a manner no different from the army. A highly indoctrinated organization, it was being shaped as the strike arm of the Party and as a counterweight to the regular army, which was a brigade-sized force with two infantry battalions and ancillary units such as a construction squadron and an agricultural corps. Army officers were not happy with the existence of an armed organization of equal strength but had not been able to do anything. The Comrade Leader was able to defang the army by catering to the corruption of General Agrippa and the senior officers, and by timing the establishment of the National Service after the last tumultuous election when the army was preoccupied with maintaining internal order. The removal of General Agrippa and the appointment of a police officer as Chief of Staff presented a completely new challenge to the army. The individual to watch was Colonel Franchette Taylor, recently returned from a senior staff course at Camberley in the UK. He seemed to have the respect of the junior officers for being untainted by the corruption in the senior ranks.

The CIA Station Chief Fred Hitchcock, sitting on the Ambassador's right, after the Deputy Chief of Mission and the Consular General, cleared his throat and shifted his position in his chair as the Political Officer spoke. It struck Erikson, sitting diagonally across from Hitchcock, as if the Station Chief was trying to alert the Ambassador to the existence of a position different from the Political Officer. A small-headed, bespectacled man in his late fifties, Hitchcock sat with his fingers interlaced in front of his chest, his chair pushed away from the table to make room for his enlarged stomach. He had evidently made food and drink an integral part of spycraft, which he began practicing after service in the Korean War. He crinkled his upper lip and moustache intermittently as if the movement would push up the black-rimmed spectacle riding low on his oversized nose. He reminded Erikson of a large rat with shortened whiskers.

The question, the Political Officer continued, was whether the Kabaka regime really posed a threat to American interests. He believed that it did not. It was at best an irritation, as the Ambassador had said, but otherwise posed no serious threat. Guyana was hemmed in by Brazil, whose military regime regarded communism as anathema, and Venezuela, which had laid claim to five-eights of Guyana, giving it the ability to apply pressure on the borders virtually at will. Domestically, socialism was an intra-elite rhetorical contest. The so-called masses, having endured enormous privations, had been voting with their feet. The economy was in tatters. Sugar was heavily dependent on European concessionary access; rice was floundering under various administrative disincentives; and the bauxite industry, plagued by strikes and a dearth of capital investment, had been losing market share. Foreign exchange holdings had been depleted, and, to get essential goods, the Kabaka government had been forced to engage in barter trade with the Eastern bloc. In short, socialism was leading Guyana on a path to nowhere. If the United States could put up with the recitation of socialist rhetoric, which had become such an integral part of the political dialogue in the country, its patience would be rewarded with an eventual collapse. Guyana could be the anti-paradigm, the model that showed other developing countries that socialism led to economic ruin not development.

At the Ambassador's invitation for other views, Colonel Stanford said that he did not think that the political situation was as static as the Political Officer had sketched it. Recent developments, such as the impending constitutional referendum and the prospect of a president-for-life, plus changes in the army leadership structure, had made regular army officers restive. Station Chief Hitchcock nodded his approval, as though Stanford was articulating a position they had previously agreed on.

The Political Officer then offered his rebuttal. The recent appointment of a police officer to head the army reflected the ruling party's confidence it had subordinated the army, having counterbalanced it with a much more thoroughly indoctrinated force, the National Service. Indeed, the new appointment would lead to even further domestication of the military.

Station Chief Hitchcock shifted position in his seat, crinkling his upper lip and moustache. "I tend to agree with Colonel Stanford that there is considerable room for maneuver in this domestic situation, and we should try to figure out how to take advantage of it. I also want to take issue with the notion that, because Guyana is supposedly hemmed in, it poses no strategic threat to U.S. interests. I suppose it depends on what you regard as strategic interests, but that type of a position makes a mockery of four decades of American policy of wanting to contain communism. The fact is that this government has adroitly used its position in the Non-Aligned Movement to isolate Venezuela and to advocate socialism. A country hurtling without obstruction toward communism emboldens others and undercuts our efforts."

The Political Officer acknowledged Guyana's visibility in the Non-Aligned Movement but reasserted his assessment that a socialist Guyana posed no urgent threat to the United States compared to the threat posed by others such as Nicaragua. Furthermore, he pointed out that the Guyana government was careful not to directly confront the United States, and various ministers have asserted that they played the socialist game to outflank the more doctrinaire Marxist-Leninists in the Opposition People's Party. Various re-statements of positions followed between Station Chief Hitchcock and the Political Officer before Ambassador Hales thanked them for this initial installment, which he called very useful, and brought the meeting to an end.

Everyone but the Ambassador and the Station Chief rose to leave. Then, with a tinge of amusement, Erikson watched the Station Chief press down on the side arms of his chair to elevate his stuffed frame up. Ambassador Hales saved him the full effort when he invited the Chief to remain behind, along with Colonel Stanford and Captain Erikson.

"I gather both of you have a different take on the domestic situation here than our Political Officer," Ambassador Hales said to Hitchcock and Colonel Stanford, when the others had left the conference room. "I'd like us to pursue this some more, if you don't mind. And, Chief, could we start with you?"

Station Chief Hitchcock rested his arms on the table, fingers interlaced, and crinkled his upper lip and moustache a couple of times before he began. "The situation is more dynamic and could be more menacing than it has been in a long time."

"How so?" the Ambassador asked.

"Well, the traditional analysis holds that what we have here is a racial contest, the ruling Kabaka Party and the Opposition representing the blacks and the Indians respectively, with the Kabaka Party neutralizing the numerical superiority of the Indians by rigging the elections. This is how it has worked since 1968, and is likely to continue indefinitely. The ideological convergence between the two parties has helped the ruling party assert its socialist credentials internationally and to enlist the support from the opposition for its domestic socialist programs."

"That's pretty much as the Political Officer laid it out," Ambassador Hales noted.

"Yes, Ambassador," Hitchcock replied, "but where we part company is in regards to the Workers' Party, the third major socialist force here. The party is centered at the university and led by a dissident sociology professor, who appears to be a combination of Malcolm X and Lenin. The party is drawing its support from blacks and Indians. The Political Officer believes that the Workers' Party will never be able to demonstrate its numerical support because of rigged elections."

"It seems like a reasonable conclusion, given the trend," Ambassador Hales suggested.

"Yes, Ambassador, except that Donald Nelson, leader of the Workers' Party, advocates the removal of this government by any means possible. Therein lies the appeal of the party. We could end up with a revolutionary socialist transformation. This is probably the worse likely scenario."

"What's the better one?"

"I'll defer to Colonel Stanford."

"Colonel?" Ambassador Hales asked, turning to Colonel Stanford, sitting on his left.

"We believe the senior officers in the military might be considering a coup against this government."

"What's the basis of this position?"

"Well, sir, earlier this month, the President retired the army Chief of Staff and appointed in his place a police officer. This is a tremendous affront to the military as a whole and to the officer corps in particular. When added to existing disgruntlement over pay, I believe it spells trouble for this government."

"Huh," Ambassador Hales grunted pinching his lower lip with his right thumb and fingers. "And you, Captain Erikson, do you have a view on this?"

"As a matter of fact I do, sir. An affront to the professionalism of the Officer Corps has triggered coups in many countries, but I was also present at the Conference on Hemispheric Security in Washington earlier this month and listened to Colonel Franchette Taylor, who appeared to be quite disenchanted with the socialist direction his country was taking."

"I see."

"Also, Ambassador," Erikson continued, "although I didn't know it at the time, the Colonel took an international call on an unsecured phone. According to the transcript, when he was told that a police officer had been appointed Chief of Staff, he talked about removing the country's president from power."

"Well, so that I am honest with you all, I was briefed on that phone call," Ambassador Hales said. "But isn't that simply someone just lashing out from the initial disappointment from being passed over?"

"It could be," Colonel Stanford replied. "It could also be that they attempt a coup and fail. But when senior officers engage in coup talk, I'd say we ought to pay attention."

"I quite agree," Ambassador Hales said. "Are there any other considerations?"

"As a matter of fact," Station Chief Hitchcock said, pushing his upper lip and moustache up toward his glasses. "There are some significant changes taking place in the trade union movement. There's been a young Turks revolt in the Public Service Union, previously a bulwark of support for this government."

"Cause?" Ambassador Hales asked.

"Massive retrenchment in the predominantly black public service."

"Short and long term significance?" Ambassador Hales asked.

"Long term, who knows? But as you are aware, I am sure, it was the Public Service Union that rendered the country ungovernable in the early 1960s, paving the way for the rise to power of the Comrade Leader. History could repeat itself."

"I'm not sure I follow," Ambassador Hales said.

"Well, Ambassador, strikes by the Public Service Union could provide the anvil against which the hammer of a military coup strikes. Many officers are from Georgetown and have close relatives who are civil servants and, therefore, members of the Public Service Union."

"Is this the only likely outcome of public service dissatisfaction?" Ambassador Hales asked.

"No, Ambassador," Station Chief Hitchcock replied. "It could be that the Political Officer is right and that the military does not act. Strikes and demonstrations by the Public Service Union could immobilize Georgetown and create the circumstances for the Workers' Party to remove the government by any means possible, as its leader, Donald Nelson, so often says."

"Are you recommending we support a military coup?" the Ambassador asked.

"I'm not sure I'm ready to make that recommendation yet, but what I feel strongly about is this: a military government brought to power under the current circumstances would be more conservative and would likely provide us with the time we need to work through the situation in Central America. We could deal with the question of returning civilian rule later, under terms that would prevent the emergence of a socialist regime."

"Colonel Stanford?"

"Ambassador, I agree that in this current hemispheric climate a conservative military government would serve American interests infinitely more than any other alternative."

"Well, gentlemen, this has been a most enlightening session. I would like you to monitor coup planning in the military as best you can."

"Ambassador," Colonel Stanford said, "the government goes to great pains to insulate its officers from contact with American personnel. Monitoring coup plans might require more aggressive efforts."

"As long as you do not violate our laws," Ambassador Hales responded, "and try not to violate theirs. Remember too I said to monitor, not promote, coup planning."

"Ambassador, I feel obliged to acquaint you with one possible outcome one might regard as the outcome from hell," Hitchcock said.

"What's that, Chief?"

"It's where the military stages a coup and turns over power to the Workers' Party."

"How likely is that?" the Ambassador asked.

"Not at all likely, Ambassador," Hitchcock replied, "but it is theoretically possible."

"Well, let's hope, that doesn't happen." Ambassador Hales stood up. "Thank you, gentlemen."

*   *   *

Steve Erikson sat in his office on the western side of the first floor of the Embassy, digesting the views the Station Chief had expressed to the Ambassador. Colonel Stanford had not tasked him much his first week, encouraging him to travel when he wasn't unpacking or otherwise settling in. He had gone up the West Demerara Coast and traveled to Springlands in Berbice County, electing on both occasions to forego private transportation in order to experience the hazards of local day-to-day travel. Now, it seemed there was a greater urgency about the Guyanese military, and he would need to stay in Georgetown. He had already read a mimeographed history of the army written by one of its officers, as well as many of the pamphlets of the National Service, most of which read like tracts for the Soviet Komsomol. Now, he felt he needed to bone up on trade union history. He swiveled around to look out of the window only to be reminded that the view was of the concrete security wall. He swung back in response to the knock on his door. Colonel Stanford was standing in his office, coffee mug in hand.

"Well, what did you think?" Stanford asked. "Of the meeting, of course?"

"Very interesting," Erikson replied, motioning him to one of the two empty chairs. "If I didn't know better, I'd say that the Station Chief was running things here."

"It depends on what you mean by 'running things,' but he's probably the most powerful individual here."

"Gross bastard," Erikson observed.

Stanford laughed. "He's not spit and polish, that's for sure. But, mind you don't cross him. Hitchcock can be very helpful if he likes you, and he has a big expense account."

"His reporting procedures are different from ours, aren't they?"

"Yes," Colonel Stanford replied, "but he has provided quite a bit of competition. He and his case officer work the trade unions. But Hitchcock has a Napoleon complex. He wants to call all the shots. And he seems to have tapped into the military. I'm not sure how."

"Why do you think so?" Erikson asked.

"Well, when I'd brief the Charge d'Affaires about the military here, he's butted in with info that proved to be accurate."

"Huh," Erikson uttered. "Does he have a military background?"

"Yes, Korea. He was a sergeant. Saw lots of his platoon killed. Hates communists with a passion."

"I gathered so," Erikson said.

"Anyway, I should let you know that both Hitchcock and the Ambassador are aware that Andrew Rambarran was your classmate at West Point. I think there'll be an expectation that you work this link."

"You mean, you want me to make him into a spy?" Erikson asked.

"No, no. Nothing like that. Look, I know Rambarran, too. The problem is that our meetings have been rare. You, on the other hand, have a good reason for more frequent contacts."

"I just can't out and ask him to give me a summary of every officer meeting he attends," Erikson said.

"No," Stanford replied, "but look, he's not happy with the way things have been going. He's told me so. He's very open with us. In fact, he is thinking of resigning his commission and returning to graduate school."

"Well, there you go," Erikson said.

"Yes, 'there you go,'" Stanford repeated. "But our interactions have not been lengthy. Yours can be. And if there's going to be a coup, he's likely to tell you that."

"I see."

"Look, Steve," Stanford said, "we're all on the same side, Rambarran and us. Rambarran no more wants communism or authoritarianism than you or I. Just talk to him, okay?"

"I was planning to."

"Gentlemen, may I join you?" Station Chief Hitchcock stood blocking most of the width of the door he had pushed fully open.

"Sure," Erikson and Stanford said, almost simultaneously.

Hitchcock closed the door behind him and took the vacant chair. He took a sip from a large mug, then sat it down on the desk. Interlacing his fingers on his flat chest, he pushed up on his glasses with his mustachioed upper lip and nostrils. "I think we have a real window here," he said.

"To do what?" Erikson asked.

"To see a military government in place," Hitchcock replied.

The room was silent. Erikson was not quite sure what to say or whether it was his place to respond, but from the way Stanford and Hitchcock were looking at him, he guessed they both had some expectation that he would react.

"It might happen," Erikson finally said. "The Colonels don't seem to have taken too kindly to having a police officer assuming command over the army."

"That's just the problem," Hitchcock said.

"What is?" Erikson asked.

"You said 'it might happen,'" Hitchcock replied.

"Yes," Erikson said.

"Look," said Hitchcock, "the anger and frustration are there. We all agree that a conservative military government would be preferable to the current one-party socialist government or, worse still, to one run by the Workers' Party. It would give us the room to reshuffle the deck and allow more moderate forces to emerge."

"So?" Erikson asked.

"So, why not give them a nod and a wink?" Hitchcock suggested.

"Chief, you heard the Ambassador say we should 'monitor' not 'encourage.'"

"The Ambassador is new, Captain. By the time he gets around to doing anything, that window would have closed."

"But it is the policy of the current American government not to promote military overthrows," Erikson reminded them.

"What American government?" Hitchcock asked. "The American government, son, is a collection of disparate agencies all working to promote the interests of the United States as they define them! In this particular context and, given the hemispheric difficulties confronting us, a military government here would best serve our needs." The Station Chief turned to Stanford.

"I'm inclined to agree with Fred," Stanford said. "The army here is poised to do it anyway. Why not nudge them a bit? The threat from the Workers' Party is growing."

"So, what should we be doing?" Erikson asked Stanford.

Hitchcock responded instead. "See how far along they are in their planning. Find out when a coup is planned for and how they plan to execute it, and what if anything, they need."

The room was silent again. Hitchcock took his cup and sipped, but Erikson was aware Hitchcock's eyes were still on him.

"You have a West Point classmate in the army here," Hitchcock continued. "Get his help."

"You want me to make him a stoolie?" Erikson asked.

"No, Captain, I'd like you to act in the interests of the United States," Hitchcock replied. "I think, Captain, that your loyalties are misplaced." Hitchcock pushed himself up to a standing position and retrieved his mug. Tapping Colonel Stanford on his shoulder, Hitchcock delivered his parting shot. "Tom, you need to give your young whipper-snapper the facts of life here."

Flushed and seething, Erikson watched the wide back exit the room, pulling the door closed.

"He's right, you know," Stanford said calmly.

"You know, if that grotesque bastard calls me 'son' or 'whipper-snapper' again, I'm going to punch him out."

"Be careful, Steve, he can be a formidable foe. He is also a zealot who doesn't care for the usual rules of decency. What matters to him is the outcome. On the other hand, he could be a good ally and, as I've said before, he has access to considerable resources."

"Thanks for the warning, Colonel."

ELEVEN

August 28, 1979
Guyana Stores, Main Street, Georgetown

The female voice which said "Coffee, please" sounded so familiar, Steve Erikson instinctively glanced over his right shoulder. Seated on the next stool was Anita Rambarran, her elbows leaning on the counter and her shoulder-length hair partially covering her face. She wore a white blouse and dark gray skirt; the black handbag she brought was resting beside her on the counter.

"This is quite a surprise," Erikson said, rotating on his stool in her direction. "How are you?"

She turned and smiled when their eyes met. "I'm fine, thank you, and I hope you are," she replied. "I'm actually here with a message. Andrew asked me to invite you to his place next weekend."

"I thought he was going to be the duty officer that weekend," Erikson observed.

The attendant served Anita her coffee, and she reached into her handbag for her coin purse. Erikson stopped her. "No, please, let me," he said, paying the attendant from the change which sat in front of him.

"Thank you," Anita said, adding sugar and milk to the cup and stirring. "The new Chief of Staff excused Andrew from the two remaining weekends. Andrew wanted to have you down this weekend, but he has to be in Georgetown on Saturday."

"What's happening on Saturday?" Erikson asked.

"We're commemorating *Janamasthmi*," she replied, rotating on the stool to face him.

"Which is?"

"The birthday of Lord Krishna," she replied.

"Ah, from the *Bhagavad Gita*," Erikson said.

"You've read it?" Anita asked, looking intently at him.

"Yes," Erikson replied, "it was required reading for a philosophy class I took my senior year."

"I'm impressed," Anita said, raising her neatly shaped eyebrows and reaching for her coffee cup. Except for a trace of mauve lipstick on her small mouth, her light bronze face showed no evidence of make-up.

"How do you plan to celebrate it?" Erikson asked.

"Well," Anita replied, "my father is back and he plans to have a religious ceremony — what we call a *pooja.*"

"I see," Erikson said, his mind conjuring images of fire and incense, and people in white robes. He was about to redirect the conversation to the prospective trip to see Andrew Rambarran when Anita spoke again.

"It's a long service, and you have to sit cross-legged on the floor," she said, looking at him as if to assess his reaction.

"Are you inviting me?" Erikson asked, sensing an opening.

"Andrew would be there," Anita continued.

"Are you inviting me?" Erikson asked again, fairly sure now that, however hesitant the approach, she wanted him to attend.

"If you'd like to come," she replied, "you'd be very welcome."

"I'd like to come," Erikson said.

"Okay, it starts at 7 p.m."

"Should I wear anything in particular?" Erikson asked.

"Do you have a *kurta* and a *dhoti?*" Anita turned her head away laughing.

"I have seen enough *Hare Krishnas* in New York City to know what those are," Erikson replied, smiling, "but no, I don't have any of those."

"Then just wear a white shirtjac," she advised, "I know you have one of those." Then she rose to go.

"Aren't you going to finish your coffee?" Erikson asked.

"Actually, I'm not much of a coffee drinker," she replied. "I came because I had to deliver a message and I wanted to catch you while you were still here."

"Couldn't you nurse that coffee a little longer?" Erikson asked. "You could tell me how to get to Adventure since I was planning to drive."

"I'm sorry," she admitted, "that slipped my mind." She reseated herself and, in the brief extension of her stay, outlined the directions to her cousin's house at Adventure on the Corentyne Coast.

*   *   *

September 1, 1979
Georgetown

Steve Erikson drove slowly past *Rambarran's Variety Store* on Regent Street and found a parking space for his green Mitsubishi Lancer a few car lengths from the store's entrance which, at 18:30 hours, was closed. Both halves of the gate on the east side of the property had been pulled open, and Erikson followed the concrete driveway to the back, walking alongside three cars parked one behind the other. At the end of the driveway, an external stairway led up to a four-by-four landing a few feet above the ground before ascending to a covered porch off the kitchen on the second story. With a brief greeting, Erikson walked past a couple of men on the landing, dressed as he was in white shirtjacs and smoking cigarettes. The kitchen porch at the next level was inhabited by several children, whose chattering stopped when Erikson reached them. They cleared a path to the open kitchen door, giggling when he said "Hello."

There was no doorbell or greeter, so Erikson stepped into the kitchen. On the floor on the right inside of the doorway, a litter of shoes persuaded him to shed his. Several women in white dresses were arranging large basins with cooked food on the kitchen counters. One contained rice, another had a steaming mash of pumpkin, and a third was filled with curried potatoes. There were also others with food items which Erikson could not identify. Further in the kitchen, two women were draping a white cotton sheet over an assortment of containers on the dining table. The largest, a white basin, contained a dark brown pudding; the smaller containers each had slices of different fruits. As Erikson stood awkwardly looking from container to container, the woman at the far end of the dining table noticed him and walked over to invite him into the living room.

"Do you know if Andrew or Anita is here?" Erikson asked.

"Andrew isn't here as yet," she replied, "but Anita is inside. I'm her aunt, her *mousii*." She led the way into the living room calling out, "Anita." Anita came out of her bedroom looking more like a bride than a congregant at a religious function. She wore a white cotton dress and, draped around her neck and shoulders, was a short, white, embroidered shawl, the ends of which rested on her bosom.

"Hi," she said by way of a greeting to Erikson, then turned to her aunt. "Aunt Savi, this is Steve Erikson, Andrew's friend."

Aunt Savi smiled as though she had been let in on a secret and excused herself.

"Not your friend?" Erikson asked quietly.

"I'm sorry," Anita replied, "it was easier that way."

The furniture in the living room had been pushed to the outermost perimeter of the room, and the large open space created was now covered with white linen sheets with an under layer of blankets, the edges of which were visible at various points along the perimeter. At the center of the room was the *kund*, a small, rectangular, concrete fire pit, reminding Erikson of the centrality of fire in Hindi religious services. Folded blankets for seating lay at the four compass points around the *kund*. Close to the *kund* on the southern side was a heaping pile of aromatic pine sticks, roughly split and unevenly cut, but none longer than six inches, and a few goblets and plates, all made of brass. On the northern side, was a garlanded picture frame, depicting a bluish image of Lord Krishna playing the flute.

There was no assigned seating, but it appeared to Erikson that women and children sat closest to the center of the ceremony and men on the periphery. Older women, who were already seated, had their white *urnees* (shawls) draped over their heads; the younger ones kept theirs around their necks. A couple of women seated at the southern side of the *kund* area were warming up with their musical instruments. One woman was playing some notes on the harmonium, another held an iron rod which she tapped rhythmically with a horseshoe iron bow that reminded Erikson of a large tuning fork. A small, dark-complexioned, Indian man was tapping both ends of a cylindrical goat skin drum, tightly cradled across his lap.

Anita led Erikson to the southern side of the living room looking out to Regent Street, where three men stood conversing. She tapped gently on the shoulder of the tallest, whom she called "Daddy." The elder Rambarran, who had evidently been told that his nephew's American classmate would be attending the *pooja,* turned and welcomed Erikson, then introduced him to his friends. He apologized for Andrew not already being there, explaining that his lateness was on account of the distance from the Corentyne. Someone announced that the pandit had arrived, and Mr. Rambarran excused himself to go and greet the officiating priest.

With the commencement of the service imminent, Anita invited Erikson to choose a seat, speculating that Andrew would likely remain in the kitchen area when he arrived. Erikson elected to sit at the southwestern rear to allow himself some stretch room for his legs, should the Buddha position prove too stressful over the course of the hour-long service. From where he sat, he had a diagonal view of the *kund* and part of the kitchen in the distance. Men began to file into the living room, taking seats around him, as Anita's father escorted the pandit to his seat at the southern side of the *kund* and seating himself on the pandit's left, facing east. A young boy, who accompanied the pandit, sat on the latter's right to assist with the ceremony.

Anita, who had been moving barefooted back and forth in the kitchen area, finally returned to the living room to choose a seat, smiling with Erikson when their eyes met. She sat down on the white cotton sheet a couple of rows behind the musicians, her profile directly in Erikson's line of sight. Shortly after, she saw Andrew coming through the kitchen and squatting down on the outer perimeter of the guests already seated in that section of the living room.

The pandit said something to the musicians and the chanting began of a prayer to Lord Krishna. One woman led off, then the others repeated the line. Soon, it became obvious to Erikson that most of the lips around the room, including Anita's, were engaged in the chant. The *bhajan*, as it was called, turned out to be very long, but it was lyrical and entrancingly melodious. By the time the lead singer had returned to the chorus for the third time, Erikson, who had sung in the Protestant choir as a cadet, picked up the tune and was singing with the others:

Aarti kunj bihari ki
shri giridhara, Krishna morari ki

Several people nearby looked over at Erikson and nodded approvingly, and from a few rows ahead and slightly to the right, Anita, with her eyes wide open, pressed her lips together to suppress laughter. He shrugged his shoulder when their eyes met and continued with the chorus. She herself had stopped singing but glanced over intermittently to reconfirm that he was and used the end of the shawl over her mouth to hide her amusement. The *bhajan* ended; Anita lowered the shawl from her mouth, unveiling a broad smile on her face.

The lights in the living room were turned off. Softly uttering an incantation, the Pandit inserted a piece of camphor in the *kund* and lit it with a match, adding pieces of pine onto the flame. With a mango leaf curved by his fingers into the shape of a spoon, he made offerings to the Hindu deities by adding melted ghee to the fire, terminating each offering by saying "*swaha.*" The fire crackled; the flames shot up each time. Finally, the pandit began his adoration of Lord Krishna, chanting:

Om vasudevam sutam devam, kansa chanura mardanam
devakie parma nandam, krishnam devam jagat gurum

The aroma from the burning pine and ghee melded with the scent from a lighted incense stick to suffuse the senses with a powerful yet calming sweetness inspiring devotees to worship. Except for the voice of the priest above the soft cackle from the burning pine and ghee, the room was absolutely still. From his position, Erikson could see the *kund,* but mostly he looked at Anita, whose face brightened every time the pandit added melted ghee into the fire. She appeared focused on the ceremony, but glanced over at Erikson intermittently, and they held each other's gaze through a corridor of silhouetted heads for a couple of moments each time before she looked away, blushing as she did so. Erikson, who had dreaded sitting in the Buddha position for an hour, now wished the ceremony would go on and on, but his thoughts were interrupted when everyone stood up and began singing "*Om jai jagdish hare,*" as the Pandit blew a conch shell and his young assistant, armed with a wooden mallet, energetically whacked a small brass gong, hanging from a cord in his left hand, one stroke each time the conch shell was blown.

The singing of this final *aarti* (prayer) concluded the ceremony. Several of the men sitting around Erikson rose and went into the kitchen, as did Anita. The Pandit remained seated beside Anita's father and attended to the petitions of women who approached him. With more space available for treading, Andrew Rambarran moved from his position near the kitchen and sat next to Erikson, explaining that the men who went to the kitchen would be distributing the *prasad,* a sampling of the food offerings to the gods. Indeed, the men returned with trays of small brown paper bags, which they passed out to the guests seated on the floor.

Erikson looked into the paper bag he received and found a third of a banana, a slice of mango, a piece of pineapple, a tiny wedge of watermelon, and a lump of flour-based pudding with raisins, resting on a grainy, cream powder.

"Try some," Rambarran said.

"What's the pudding?" Erikson asked.

"It's called *mohanbhoog* or food offering to Krishna," Rambarran replied. "Mohan is another name for Krishna, and *bhoog* is a food offering to a Hindu deity. But it is a flour-based pudding, as you correctly identified it."

"It's very good," Erikson said, digesting a pinch of the *mohanbhoog*. "So, do I eat all of this now?"

"If you like," Rambarran replied. "Normally, the distribution of the *prasad* ends the service. However, in some cases, like today, the guests are going to be fed a vegetarian meal."

"Isn't this like serving the dessert before the meal?" Erikson asked, holding up the brown paper bag.

Rambarran laughed. "That would be imposing a Western meal sequence on a Hindu religious service. With the *mohanbhoog*, you are sharing in a food offering to the gods. The vegetarian meal is simply a devotee's hospitality to his guests. Talking about which, I'd better see if I can help."

"Can I do something?" Erikson asked.

"No, no, just relax and enjoy."

"Actually, it's kind of lonely back here," Erikson said. "I'd feel more involved if I did something."

"Okay, come with me. This should be interesting."

Erikson followed Rambarran as he picked his way around the guests sitting on the floor. The kitchen was crowded with middle-aged women uncovering containers of food. A few of the men, who had served the *prasad*, had returned to the kitchen to help with serving the food, which was being directed by Anita's aunt. Erikson's appearance in the kitchen surprised everyone there, including Anita. Her aunt thought he should sit and be served since he was a guest, but Andrew Rambarran interceded. "He wants to help serve the food," Rambarran said. "It'll be okay. He'll just follow me."

Anita looked at Erikson, laughed and continued laughing as she turned back to sorting out the food trays. Andrew Rambarran gave Steve Erikson a large saucepan with *dal* and a ladle. "I'll serve the rice," he said, "then you pour the *dal* on top of the rice in their plates."

Anita laughed out loud, as did the others in the kitchen. Erikson himself was amused by the assigned task and the attention it had drawn. He couldn't wait to see how it would work out in practice. He followed Rambarran, who spooned out the rice into the paper plates the guests on the floor had been provided. Erikson waited for each guest to make a hole in the pile of rice, into which he ladled the *dal*. They were followed by other men carrying containers of pumpkin, curried potatoes, spinach, curried *kattahar*, and mango chutney. In about ten minutes, they had served all of the seated guests, and returned to the kitchen to refill the containers.

"We need to make another pass," Rambarran said, "just to see if anyone would like some more." And, sure enough, several of the guests accepted a second serving.

"Aunt Savi said that you and Steve should sit down and eat," Anita said to Andrew, when he and Steve returned to the kitchen after their second trip out. She handed them each a paper plate with rice and dal, and around the periphery of the plate were dollops of pumpkin, curried *kattahar*, and spinach.

"I put some mango achar in yours," Anita said. "I didn't know about Steve."

"What's that?" Erikson asked.

"It's a chutney made of mango, but it is hot," Rambarran cautioned. "Why don't you try it, for the experience?"

With their loaded plates and plastic forks, they went into the living room and sat below the windows facing Regent Street. Erikson ate all of what was on his plate save the dollop of mango chutney. They leaned against the wall, stretching their legs out into the space vacated by some of the guests.

"That was rather good," Erikson said.

"Not quite a dinner outing at the Steak-and-Brew in New York

City," Rambarran replied. "Remember those days? I've never put down so much beer in my life."

"Who cared then, eh? It flowed and flowed."

Anita's aunt came in and retrieved the empty paper plates. Behind her was Anita with two plates laden with other food items. She handed one to each of them, then returned with her aunt to the kitchen.

"What's this?" Erikson asked.

"Dessert," Rambarran replied. "The white stuff is *keer*, white rice boiled in milk, to which raisins and sugar have been added."

"And this jam-like stuff?" Erikson asked.

"That's mango koorma, a syrupy jam made of mango pieces," Rambarran explained. "The flat bread is *puri*, a deep fried *roti*."

"Oh, roti, I know. But how did they get the flour for the *roti* and the *mohanbhoog*? I thought flour was banned."

"It is," Rambarran admitted, "but people are allowed to bring in small amounts each time they enter the country. Anita's parents travel a fair amount and they saved up for this ceremony."

"Do you remember what you used to say about us?" Erikson asked.

"No, as I'm sure you'll recall I said a lot of things."

"Well, you said you thought Americans ate a lot."

"They do," Rambarran asserted.

"Well, what do you call this? They'll have to roll me out of here when I'm done."

"Don't worry, it's only once in a while. The rest of the time the government has us on a starvation diet. And don't forget, you were eating food for the gods."

"Right."

By 21:30 hours, about a third of the guests had left. The musicians re-commenced chanting, but it was a smaller group, and the guests didn't appear to be participating. Most in fact were on their feet appearing to be saying farewell to someone or other. One woman was picking up the linen from the floor. Andrew Rambarran rose to help.

"Can I give a hand with anything?" Erikson asked.

"As a matter of fact, you can," Rambarran replied. "We need to move the sofa back into position."

The task completed, Erikson indicated he was ready to leave and wanted to thank Anita and her father. They walked over to where the elder Rambarran was speaking to the pandit and a couple of women. Erikson thanked Anita's father for having him at the *pooja,* adding that it was the first time he had attended a *pooja* and was very impressed by the way it had been conducted. The pandit nodded his satisfaction, and Anita's father invited Erikson to visit his home again. Heading into the kitchen for Erikson to retrieve his shoes, they crossed paths with Anita.

"Steve's leaving," Rambarran said to his cousin.

"I'll show him out," Anita replied. "Auntie Savi wants to talk with you."

Rambarran shook hands with Erikson, inviting him to visit the Corentyne coast the following weekend, then left to see his aunt. Anita led Erikson to the kitchen entrance where he put on his shoes. The guests on the kitchen porch opened a path for them to walk down the stairs to the concrete driveway. When they had turned the corner of the house and were facing the gate, Anita stopped.

"Thanks for coming," she said.

"Thanks for inviting me," Steve Erikson said. "It was really interesting, and I had a good time. Now I can chant the *aarti* chorus."

She pressed her lips together to suppress her amusement, and looked away. When she looked back at him, he was standing directly in front of her. Perhaps sensing something imminent, she stopped smiling and appeared apprehensive.

"I'd like to see you again," he said. She looked down for a moment, then back at him. The pause was lengthy. She appeared in deep thought but conflicted. He waited.

"If you are prepared to come here," she finally said.

"I am," he replied.

She smiled, then extended her right hand. He took it with his left hand, reaching for her right, he lifted both to his lips. The upward tug, and the difference in their heights, unbalanced her slightly causing her to shift forward. They now stood close to each other, his face looking down on hers. He kissed the back of her hands again, and as he lowered them, reached forward and kissed her lightly on her lips.

TWELVE

September 5, 1979
Adventure Village, Berbice County

Andrew Rambarran sat on a rocking chair on the second-level back porch, sipping a cup of instant coffee. The covered veranda, which ran almost the full width of the house, was sheltered from the morning sun by a large breadfruit tree adjacent to the scaffolded water tower at the northeastern corner of the house. The mango tree on the western side of the property shaded the veranda in the afternoons. It helped, too, that the house was built on a northwesterly axis, a consequence of orienting the house front parallel to the bend in the Corentyne coastal road, only several feet away, to facilitate access to the grocery store on the lower left side of the building. The back veranda was the only modification he had made to the house after his father died and his mother emigrated. She was not too happy to learn he had cut down the tamarind and *jamoon* trees which obstructed his view of the Atlantic shoreline, but she enjoyed the porch whenever she visited. He was glad he didn't cut any of the coconut palms in the backyard; when cooking oil became scarce, Gyalie, the housekeeper, harvested the dried coconuts to make coconut oil.

Rambarran loved the back porch, which commanded a view of the Atlantic shoreline and the channel leading up to the Lesbeholden sluice. Beyond the back fence of the property, small shrubs had asserted a firm, if scattered, existence on the sandy soil. The mangroves, which used to line the Atlantic shoreline only a mile away, had long since been cut down to fuel the wood-fire stoves so common on the Atlantic coast and, on a clear day, Rambarran could see small figures pulling seines in the shallow edge of the ocean. But the best view by far was of the fishing boats turning into the channel after a night out and slowing to a crawl toward the Lesbeholden sluice to be moored and to have their catch unloaded. In the early evening, some of these boats retraced this path leaving the Lesbeholden sluice for the channel to fish along the

Atlantic coast or in the Corentyne River. Not long ago, these fishermen crowded the shop downstairs from mid-morning to early afternoon to quench their thirst after enduring the privations of a night at sea. Later, they would return to buy supplies for the outbound trip. But the shop closed after Rambarran's father died and his mother had emigrated to be closer to the rest of the family in New York.

Living so close to the Lesbeholden sluice meant enjoying a daily fresh fish diet. From Atlantic fishing came *gilbakka*, *queriman* and snapper, while *basha*, butterfish, and *banga-mary* made up the catch from the Corentyne River. Very often, the fish, especially the smaller species, were still alive at the time of sale, and it was up to Gyalie to carry out the execution before dressing them for a curry or a stew in the cast iron *karahee*.

The basic house structure had remained unchanged though the furniture had been modernized. The three bedrooms were on the western side with the windows of the front bedroom facing the coastal road. The living room occupied most of the eastern side except for an enclave, in the northeastern side close to the water tower, where the upstairs toilet and bath depended on the rainwater collected in the cisterns from the corrugated zinc sheets lining the rooftop. The door on the eastern side of the living room opened onto a landing and an external stairway pointed downward to the gated entrance of the property.

On the first floor, directly below the bedrooms, was a large kitchen with a huge cast iron stove from which rose a chimney to exhaust the smoke from the wood in the side fire pit. Adjacent to the kitchen, on the eastern side was the main dining room and, from the passageway between the two rooms, an internal stairway led directly up into the living room. The front door of the kitchen led onto a small porch with surround seating, but the rest of the bottom house on the eastern side was open and there sat Rambarran's white Mini Minor, parked between the stilts supporting the house.

For Andrew Rambarran, leaving that house was going to be difficult. Not only had he grown up here, but he loved country living. In the old days, the bottom house was alive from the time the shop opened until early evening and, after market each day, entering the kitchen through the porch meant negotiating a gauntlet of chattering women who only paused to observe each detail of his bearing and manner and to compliment his mother as he made his way up the internal stairway. These days this porch did not get much use except when his platoon leaders visited, but they too preferred retiring to the privacy and the view afforded by the upper-level veranda. There, he napped in the hammock slung between the upper rails, when he was not sharing it with Lena in bouts of mid-morning love-making and again in the early evenings.

Did he really want to leave this place forever? Was Ralph Spooner right that, those who could, should change the suffocating circumstances of life imposed on so many? Could he really disassociate himself from Ralph Spooner while he was engaged to his sister? And what if Ralph and the others embarked on a coup attempt while his own company was deployed along the coast? Would he really obey orders directed against them? Would Lena forgive him if Ralph failed and was incarcerated or killed? He shook his head and reached over to the card table for *The Guardian*. The headline read, *"Unity talks between the President and the Opposition Leader."* He ignored the article and glanced over the piece about the hurricane bearing down on Jamaica. Unity talks between the President and the Opposition Leader had first begun a few years earlier when the Opposition Leader had called for a national front government to work for the socialist transformation of the country. Nothing tangible ever came out. That, however, did not stop the President from resurrecting the talks every time his government was in a tight spot. Venezuelan troop movement near the border was the cause of the latest alarm.

McCurchin came out to the porch laying a couple of plates on the card table, then returned to the kitchen downstairs to fetch the remaining breakfast items. Rambarran sat facing the plate with three poached eggs and two bread slices McCurchin had toasted on the *tawa*. McCurchin's plate had scrambled eggs and toast. Between them rested a plate with slices of Dutch gouda Rambarran had purchased in Springlands. Setting the newspaper aside, Rambarran, to McCurchin's amusement, began performing surgery on his eggs, carefully cutting around the edges of the yolks.

"Why don't you let me poach just the egg whites, Captain?" McCurchin asked. "You never eat the yolks."

"It gives me something to do instead of just feeding my face," Rambarran replied. "Are we out of marmalade?"

"No, Captain," McCurchin said, rising from his chair. "I'll get it." The sound of someone outside on the road shouting "Captain" caused McCurchin to make a bee-line to the front windows. Standing by the gate was a constable from the Adventure Police Station.

"Mac," the police constable called out. "Tell the Captain I got a message for him."

McCurchin turned to relay this, but Rambarran had heard and was already making his way to the external stairway. "Captain," the constable said when Rambarran had arrived by the gate, "Colonel Taylor called. He wants you to contact him by radio as soon as you can."

"Thanks," Rambarran replied, "I'll do that. And please tell your sergeant I might be over in a little while to use the telephone."

After breakfast, Rambarran got Colonel Taylor on the radio. Colonel Taylor was on his way to Berbice for a meeting at 11:00 with senior management at the Rose Hall Sugar Estate and wanted confirmation that Rambarran could attend. When Colonel Taylor asked if they could have dinner together, Rambarran invited him to his house. That issue settled, Rambarran tried to get Lieutenant Shah in New Amsterdam to let him know that the Colonel would be in the area and would likely visit his platoon on his way to Rose Hall, but Shah's radio was not turned on, nor was Lieutenant Peters' at Albion. He decided to phone the nearby police stations to get a message to both officers.

At 08:30, Rambarran left for the Adventure Police Station with McCurchin in the quarter-ton jeep. While he was on the phone with Lieutenant Shah in the sergeant's office upstairs, rain fell. It began like pellets riveting the corrugated zinc roofing just a few feet overhead, then the steady downpour produced a loud gushing sound as though a giant hose was spraying the rooftop. The overflow from the gutters cascaded steadily onto the bare earth below with the flatness of an untuned bass drum. Sprays from the overflow blew in through the two louvers on the eastern side, and Rambarran adjusted the glass vanes before leaving the office. It was then 08:45.

McCurchin had pulled the jeep close to the lower-level exit, but by the time Rambarran had entered the vehicle, his arms were wet and his fatigues were speckled by raindrops. The downpour thinned down to a drizzle as they moved westward and when they reached Bloomfield, the asphalt road was wet but the sun shone brightly.

"Like somebody dead, Captain," McCurchin said. Rambarran glanced over at McCurchin. "That's what they say," McCurchin insisted, "sun and rain means somebody dead."

"People die every day, McCurchin."

"But you know that's what they say when you got sun and rain at the same time."

"I know that's what they say," Rambarran conceded.

"Is September, Captain, we ain't supposed to get any rain."

"McCurchin, I don't think nature follows statistical predictions."

"What you mean?"

"I mean if it's going to rain, it will rain, whether it's August or September."

"I agree with that," McCurchin said. "You can't tell God what to do."

Rambarran decided to let that pontification go unchallenged. Then, as if to validate McCurchin's pronouncement, a light drizzle began as they passed the Port Mourant Train Line, swelling gradually into torrents by the time they reached the Apollo Cinema in Rose Hall Town and remaining with them all the way to Albion. When the jeep pulled into the back of the Albion Police compound, Captain Rambarran got out and made a dash to the recreational bungalow where Lieutenant Peters had said he'd be.

Rambarran found him in front of a small portable blackboard on an easel and stand, his corporals sitting with their respective squads on the floor. Peters braced to attention to acknowledge his Company Commander then resumed his presentation. Garrison duties can be very boring, and Rambarran was glad that his platoon leaders spent the mornings, especially a rainy one, on military education, which the soldiers preferred to close order drill. Peters, who, like the other Lieutenants in F-Company had done the officer's short course at Sandhurst, was sharing some of his recent experiences with coastal patrolling. When he was through, he released the men to their respective squad leaders to ready their weapons and kit for a possible inspection by Colonel Taylor, the Battalion Commander, and then joined Captain Rambarran.

"Anything new to report?" Rambarran asked.

"Just some disagreements with local Party officials," Ron Peters replied. "They wanted me to conduct search-and-seizure raids against some local members of the Opposition."

"What did you tell them?"

"I told them I would do that when the situation warranted it and when I had cleared it with my Company Commander." Rambarran nodded his approval. "Between you and me, Captain, there is nothing going on to warrant searches," Peters continued. "The last thing we want to do is to provoke a backlash against the army, and against the government, for that matter. This is a predominantly Indian area, and Opposition support here is very strong."

"I agree with you," Rambarran said. "Unfortunately, those guys don't give up. They really do believe that the army is here to do all of the Party's bullying work."

"Don't worry, I can handle them," Peters said. "Captain, we're out of mosquito coils."

"How are you coping?" Rambarran asked.

"The usual way in these parts," Peters replied, "we burn coconut husks. The problem is that the smoke gets into the tents, and the men can't sleep."

"I'll let the Supply Sergeant know," Rambarran said. "I'm sure we can get you some by tomorrow."

Accompanied by Lieutenant Peters, Captain Rambarran left the recreation hall for the Police Station in the front of the compound. The sun was shining but there was a light drizzle.

"Looks like somebody died," Peters said.

"You too?" Rambarran asked, not breaking his stride.

"That's what they say," Peters asserted.

"I know that's what they say. It's what McCurchin's been saying on the way out here." Rambarran shook his head, and Peters laughed.

They went up to the second floor where Rambarran had an office, courtesy of the Police Inspector in charge of the Albion Police Station. The company Sergeant Major was down the hall in a loud conversation in the police sergeant's office. Rambarran called the operator and requested an outside line, which he secured a few minutes later. He tried to reach the company Supply Sergeant at Camp Ayanganna without success. When the Sergeant Major came into his office, Rambarran asked him to chase down the Supply Sergeant and rush mosquito coils to the three platoons.

At 10:15, Captain Rambarran and Private McCurchin left the Albion Police Station for the Rose Hall Sugar Estate. The rain had stopped completely; the sun shone; and a brilliant rainbow arced the sky. In a few minutes, they went past the Borlum Turn and settled in for the straightaway to No. 19 Village. Soon, a stench from the right-side savanna suffused the cab of the jeep, and McCurchin quickly rolled up the window on the windward side. Rambarran looked over at the ring of carrion crows around two bovine carcasses lying in the savanna, casualties no doubt of the August drought. Another set of crows sat on the side of the road, patiently waiting their turn or already surfeited from the feast. A safe distance away, McCurchin lowered the window, and they relaxed with the incoming breeze from the Atlantic. At 10:30, they rounded Seawell Turn, and a few minutes later, turned at the center of Sheet Anchor onto the Canje Road for the final three miles to the Rose Hall Sugar Estate.

Captain Rambarran arrived to find Colonel Taylor's jeep already parked along the driveway of the Senior Staff Club, a white colonial bungalow at the center of the managers' compound on the eastern side of the Canje Road. Dispatching McCurchin back to Adventure with dinner instructions for his housekeeper, Rambarran entered the Club by the external stairway and was greeted at the entrance by an Indian attendant, who pointed him to the lounge. Colonel Taylor was having a Coke with the Administrative Manager, Colin Gilchrist, flanked by the Factory and Field Managers of Rose Hall Sugar Estate, all of whom Rambarran had met before. They were all expatriate short-timers, who were more willing to give a candid assessment of the industrial situation in the sugar industry than their local counterparts at the Albion or Skeldon Sugar Estates. Rambarran shook hands with them all and accepted the offer of a Coke, which he took with him when they retired to the adjacent conference room.

Once seated around the rectangular table, Colin Gilchrist, the Administrative Manager, proceeded to outline the state of industrial relations in the sugar industry. He pointed out that the Rose Hall and Albion Sugar Estates were the bell weather stations for predicting strikes owing to their proximity to the sugar union's headquarters in

New Amsterdam and the fact that the union leader lived there. The major issue centered on what the assured minimum daily wage should be for sugar workers, a wage that should suffice, in the union's view, to tide the workers through the off season. The government, on the other hand, which now owned the industry and wanted to maximize profit, was unwilling to concede what amounted to a hundred-percent increase in pay for laborers. A strike was almost certain; the question was simply when. Gilchrist believed that if a strike did not occur within the next few weeks, it would then be in the early part of the new year. The union would not want the workers to go without pay during the Christmas-New Year holiday period; they would continue talks to buy time.

Rambarran asked why management was so resistant to the wage demands of the sugar union, considering that sugar was the largest foreign exchange earner in the country now that the bauxite industry was plagued by market factors and industrial unrest, and the sugar workers were the lowest paid. It wasn't simply the off season they were concerned about; it was also trying to make ends meet in an economy plagued by scarcities and high prices.

Gilchrist prefaced his response to the question by noting that, since the government's nationalization of the sugar industry, expatriate managers were being eased out, and that he expected to be leaving in a year or so. The question of wage increases for sugar workers was not simply an industrial relations issue; it was also a political issue. The sugar workers were predominantly Indian and supporters of the Opposition People's Party. The government was disinclined to make wage concessions to them, much less wage increases of the magnitude being demanded, regardless of where the sugar workers ranked relative to unskilled workers in other industries. Beyond that, the government, as everyone knew, was in desperate financial straits, and wanted to gather up as much as it could from what had become the golden goose of the economy and, even though sugar prices were currently high because of concessionary rates negotiated with Britain, there was no assurance they would continue at that level. World market prices fluctuate for sugar as well as other agricultural products. In a future situation of low world prices, the industry would be stuck with high wage rates, if wage concessions were now made to the sugar union. Then there was the ripple effect in other industries; if sugar workers succeeded through their union in achieving significantly higher wage rates, one could predict labor agitation in virtually every other sector of the economy, including the public service, for similar percentage increases, which the government could not afford to make. The sugar union understood this but would not be deterred from pressing the issue, and the sporadic fires in the sugar cane fields were a reminder of the seriousness with which they viewed the matter. In sum, the industry was heading for a major strike by the sugar workers, and Gilchrist believed it would come in late January or early February once the workers have made it through the holidays.

"What about these fires?" Colonel Taylor asked, looking over at Captain Rambarran.

"Colonel," Gilchrist said, preempting Rambarran, "we have thousands of acres under cultivation. It's not possible to predict where a fire would be started. The sugar union, which always denies blame, uses the fires to apply pressure. That's our view anyway."

"So, your best guess is that the sugar workers will likely be called out on strike in the early part of next year?" Colonel Taylor asked Gilchrist.

"If it doesn't happen by mid-October, yes. I'd say late January or early February."

"Thank you very much for your candor," Colonel Taylor said to Gilchrist. "I assume this assessment has been shared with the government."

"Not exactly, Colonel," Gilchrist responded. "This is what I think based on my discussions with the local union officials and with the Managing Director, who, as you know is a Guyanese. He, of course, advises the government on all matters pertaining to the sugar industry, but I can't imagine his assessment to be very different."

"Can the strike not be averted?" Captain Rambarran asked. "Isn't there room for compromise? It seems to me that the sugar workers have a legitimate claim. If you can't grant a hundred-percent increase, how about a significant fraction of that to avert the disruptions to the economy a strike would cause?"

"Well, Captain, Bookers' no longer owns the sugar industry; the government does, through the Nationalization Act. It's their call. Unfortunately, there is very little separation between what is a purely industrial matter and what is a political matter. The government's starting position is always that strikes in the sugar industry are politically motivated."

"So the government's intransigence will make a strike inevitable?" Rambarran asked.

"I'm a foreigner," Gilchrist replied, "but I'd say your comment is on the mark."

The session concluded, Gilchrist invited the officers to have a drink at the bar, but when both declined, he pressed a buzzer at the table to have lunch served. The Indian attendant knocked and, at Gilchrist's invitation, entered with a tray of sandwiches, which he identified by clusters as chicken, cheese, and cucumber sandwiches. A second attendant followed bearing a tray with a coffee decanter and cups. What followed was a couple more trips by the attendants with plates, a pitcher of water, and one of lemonade, all of which were laid on the side table against the near wall. Gilchrist invited the officers to precede him and, Rambarran, who followed Colonel Taylor, carefully avoided the cucumber sandwiches.

All three managers had served as officers in the British army during World War II. Gilchrist, who was a Flight Lieutenant in the RAF, wore his hair long to cover a bullet wound at the back of his neck which he had sustained during the Battle of Britain. The Factory Manager was a sapper in the British Engineers, and the Field Manager had been an infantry platoon leader. Both of them had seen action during and after the Normandy invasion. During the extended lunch session, the three managers narrated episodes from their wartime experiences. Rambarran was impressed by how relaxed the managers were with local military officers, perhaps because the uniforms so closely resembled what they themselves had worn. Nevertheless, what really lingered with him was the prediction that the sugar industry would likely face a strike beginning in late January or early February.

At 13:30, Captain Rambarran, riding in the rear of Colonel Taylor's 3/4-ton jeep, left with the Colonel for a visit with Lieutenant Shah's platoon in New Amsterdam. The visit with Shah's First Platoon was unremarkable since Shah reported only routine patrolling in his area of responsibility. It was the same when Taylor and Rambarran later stopped at Albion to see Lieutenant Ron Peters. Nevertheless, the Colonel, who enjoyed light bantering with his junior officers, propped his feet on Lieutenant Peter's desk and spoke of his visit to West Point. He, and the Latin American officers attending the conference at the National War College, had arrived during what his cadet escort called "Reorganization Week," when all of the cadets reconvened at the Academy for the academic year. The seniors had been training the new cadets that summer; the juniors were returning from assignments at various army posts; and the sophomores had spent the summer in training at Camp Buckner. He described the concrete apron in front of the Eisenhower and MacArthur barracks as a madhouse where the new cadets, carrying duffel bags with books or clothing, were being randomly stopped and hazed by upperclassmen. The hazing continued at lunch. He was seated at a table for ten in the Second Regiment area of mess hall and, during the entire meal, it seemed, the new cadets at different tables were yelling out bits of information in response to questions from the upperclassmen. Colonel Taylor, who, like Ron Peters, had been commissioned after completing the six-month officer training course at Mons in the UK, wondered how on earth anyone could survive four years of that stuff.

"Of course, only one year was like that," Andrew Rambarran said, standing near to Taylor with his back against the wall.

"Tell me the truth, Andrew," Taylor said, rising from his chair, "could you see yourself doing that all over again?"

"Hell no," Rambarran replied, straightening himself in preparation for departing.

"I don't know," Colonel Taylor said, shaking his head. "Somehow, I think you would. Anyway, I suppose we'd better go. It'll be dinner time when we get to Adventure Village. We'll visit Third Platoon tomorrow."

Thirteen

September 5, 1979
Adventure Village

At 17:30, Captain Rambarran walked down the embankment with
Colonel Taylor, who seemed chained to his attache case, through the
open gate and around Captain Rambarran's parked jeep onto the
kitchen porch, where McCurchin was eating dinner. With a wave of
his hand, Colonel Taylor discouraged McCurchin from standing up and
followed Andrew Rambarran into the kitchen. While Colonel Taylor
greeted Gyalie, the housekeeper, Rambarran retrieved a tray of ice and
a Bass Ale from the refrigerator, which he took with them when he and
Taylor retired upstairs. He fixed a Scotch and soda for Colonel Taylor,
emptied the Bass Ale into a glass, and led the way out onto the veranda,
where they each took a rocking chair.

"How long's Gyalie been your housekeeper?" Colonel Taylor
asked.

"She assisted my mother for a very long time until my mother
emigrated. I kept her on because it was the only way I could have the
house taken care of and, of course, she needed the money. But she'd be
offended if she were referred to as the housekeeper. She thinks of herself,
and we think of her, as family."

"You're lucky. As I recall from the last time, she's a damned good
cook."

"She is," Rambarran agreed. "I really couldn't manage without her
and her family looking after the place when I'm away."

"By the way, where did you get the Scotch?" Colonel Taylor
asked.

"Springlands," Rambarran replied, "from our friend, Inspector
Pollard."

Gyalie came out to the veranda with a tray, which she laid on the
card table and invited the officers to help themselves. Two large bowls,

one with boiled chickpeas and another with a heap of *phulourie,* sat next to a small, deep dish of tamarind chutney.

"Let's see," Colonel Taylor said, laughing. "Scotch, split peas, chickpeas, flour: these are all banned items, my friend."

"Colonel," Rambarran replied, "you can get all of these in Springlands. The border with Suriname is a sieve. I just let Inspector Pollard know what I need and I pick it up when I go up to check on Third Platoon."

Colonel Taylor dipped a *phulourie* into the tamarind chutney and bit into it. "Oh my, this is the real stuff," he exclaimed after he had chewed and swallowed the mix. "I could get spoiled down here."

Both officers helped themselves to some of the chickpeas and *phulourie,* then sat down again in the rocking chairs.

"I had originally planned to see Lieutenant DeFreitas in Springlands today," Colonel Taylor said, spooning some of the chickpeas into his mouth, "but this opportunity with the Admin Manager at Rose Hall came up."

"That was a very interesting meeting," Rambarran said. "Surprisingly candid, those managers."

"Yes, they were," Colonel Taylor agreed. "Anyway, about Michael DeFreitas, what do you think of him?"

"Michael is a very competent officer," Rambarran replied.

"What does he think of the recent changes?"

"None of the officers in this company like the idea of a policeman running the army, Colonel, but they are too junior. What can they do about it?"

"How do they feel about the general direction the country is going in?"

"Colonel, that's a tricky area," Rambarran replied. "I can't speak about the political views of my officers; that they'll have to do themselves."

"You're right, and the rebuke is justified," Colonel Taylor admitted. "To be perfectly frank, I don't like the direction this country is going and I don't like this government."

"Your position is understandable, given what has happened recently to the chain of command," Rambarran said.

"Oh, come on Andrew, I think you know better. I have not liked the direction of things for some time, though I must admit the appointment of a policeman to head the army has infuriated me further."

It was dusk; the sun had barely disappeared below the horizon, and Rambarran knew that Gyalie would be anxious about getting home. "Colonel, how about dinner? I could fix you another drink if you like."

Colonel Taylor declined the drink but rose to indicate he was ready for dinner. They walked into the house, down the stairway and turned into the dining room. The large rectangular table, which normally accommodated six, had two chairs removed from the longer sides to give them greater room as they sat across from each other. A small bowl of *dal* sat next to each plate and, at the center of the table, a large serving dish displayed multiple chunks of *gilbakka* in a curried sauce with traces of tomatoes and green mango. On one side of this serving dish was a large bowl of rice and, on the other, freshly prepared *roti* lay on a plate. Another bowl had a dense heaping of *sijan baagie*, which McCurchin had harvested from the *sijan* tree behind the house. Gyalie explained to Colonel Taylor that she had cooked the *baagie* in coconut milk. The last two containers were covered with a napkin which Colonel Taylor lifted to peek at slices of cassava pone on a flat sheet and a larger bowl with freshly made *mohanbhoog*.

"Oh, my favorite!" Colonel Taylor exclaimed. "You really shouldn't have gone to so much trouble."

"It wasn't much trouble," Gyalie said. "It's easy to make, and I know how much you liked it the last time you came."

"Well, thank you," Colonel Taylor said. "Andrew is lucky to have you helping him. He lives like a maharajah out here."

Gyalie laughed, watched them seat themselves, then retreated to the kitchen. As the two officers served themselves, McCurchin came in to tell Captain Rambarran he was leaving. Rambarran reminded him to be back by 21:00 to take the Colonel to the Government's Guest House at No. 63 Village.

"What arrangements do you have for him?" Colonel Taylor asked when they heard the slam of the jeep's door.

"McCurchin parks the jeep overnight at the Adventure Police Station. They've also provided sleeping quarters for him there, but he has a sweet-woman just up the road at Limlear."

"So, what's your guess? Is he heading for the Police Station or Limlear?"

"I'd place my money on Limlear," Rambarran replied.

Refocusing on his plate and on the array of dishes on the table, Colonel Taylor exclaimed, "This is a bloody feast. I'd say you live damn well out here, you know?"

"Colonel, the Corentyne is the breadbasket of Berbice County," Rambarran replied. "Besides, what we don't have, the Surinamese next door can supply."

"To tell the truth," Colonel Taylor said, "I brought a shopping list from my wife. My driver's supposed to pick up the stuff from Inspector Pollard. By the way, this is great curry."

"Gyalie is a good cook, no question," Rambarran said.

"I meant to ask you," Colonel Taylor continued, "why did you assign Asad Shah to New Amsterdam? His family lives in Albion."

"It's what he wanted, Colonel."

"Why?"

"He's freer when he's away from home. His father is the *moulvi* for the Guava Bush-Sand Reef area. Which means he can't drink." Rambarran leaned back in his chair and looked directly at Colonel Taylor. "About a year ago, I was in Springlands for a meeting with the Police Superintendent. It was a Saturday, and the meeting dragged on, and the Supe took me out to lunch at *Sabsook's Restaurant*. In the meantime, Asad Shah and Michael DeFreitas had been drinking with Inspector Pollard at *Samaroo's Beer Garden*. When I was leaving Springlands, Shah asked me for a ride home. I didn't realize how much he had had to drink until we arrived at his parents' house. He had just passed through the gate, when he swung around, grabbed the fence and started throwing up, in the full view of his parents and some people, who were consulting with the *moulvi*. I'll never forget the look his mother gave me, and I had nothing to do with it."

"Have you been back?" Colonel Taylor asked, laughing.

"Oh yes, I went back on Monday morning to get him. His parents invited me in to have breakfast. I had already eaten, but his mother was so insistent, I had a half of a *roti* with *dal* and a cup of tea. Evidently, Asad explained he had gone out drinking on his own. We still laugh about the episode, he and I. And his parents are really wonderful people; I've known them a very long time."

Gyalie, who kept a watch from a distance, saw they were through with the main course and came in to clear away the plates. While the officers served themselves some *mohanbhooj*, she fixed them some coffee. Rambarran was aware that it was getting dark outside and Gyalie would want to leave so he invited Colonel Taylor to have coffee on the veranda upstairs. They had hardly seated themselves down on the two rocking chairs, when the electricity went off.

"A regular feature out here," Rambarran said.

"Unfortunately, it's the same everywhere," Taylor observed. "The timing of the blackout is different at other areas — that's all."

Gyalie came up with a kerosene lamp which she laid on the table, telling Rambarran she had placed the other on the dining table. The officers thanked her for the meal, and she left pulling the kitchen door shut behind her.

"This has the feel of being out in the bush," Colonel Taylor observed, "except in greater luxury."

"I must say I like the tranquility," Rambarran said, slapping a mosquito on his right arm. "Colonel, I could light a couple of mosquito coils or we could keep the mosquitoes away with the smoke from a couple of cigars."

"I prefer the cigar approach," Colonel Taylor said.

Rambarran retrieved the cigars from his room, and they both lit up. Because of the stillness of the air, the smoke lingered like a fog which had rolled onto the porch and had been stopped by the outside wall of the house. The puffing slowed as the officers sipped their coffee, and the smoke gradually drifted around the leeward edge of the house. Nevertheless, the impending mosquito invasion had been checked. For a while, both officers just sat rocking gently, sipping coffee and taking occasional puffs on their cigars. Then, the smoke began clearing away more quickly than before, the tree tops swayed audibly, and the kerosene lamp on the card table flickered. The Atlantic tide was coming in.

Colonel Taylor took another deep draw on his cigar before setting it down on the ashtray on the card table. He arched his head back and blew out a steady stream of smoke, which blew back into his face and quickly dissipated above his head. "Where'd you get the cigars?" he asked. "I bet those didn't come from Suriname."

"Actually, Colonel, I got those from a Cuban trawler captain I met way back at the Ayanganna Officers' Club. Whenever they put in at Georgetown, he'd call me up."

"I didn't think you cared about socialism," Colonel Taylor said.

"I don't, and neither does he, for that matter. In any case, one can appreciate a good cigar without trading in one's political beliefs."

"That's what I wanted to talk to you about," Colonel Taylor said.

"What's that?"

"Your political beliefs," Colonel Taylor replied.

"I have a feeling, Colonel, you're about to ruin my evening."

"No, seriously, Andrew, you used to say that what this country needed was a government of national unity." Colonel Taylor had stopped rocking. He reoriented his chair to face Rambarran; his feet were firmly planted on the flooring.

"I was naive, Colonel," Rambarran replied. "Alan Moore, Ralph Spooner and I had a vision of a younger generation of leaders, not jaded by the racial animosities conjured up by two major parties, asserting themselves on the basis of common historical suffering of slavery and indentureship and moving this country forward in a more enlightened fashion. But, look at what happened to Alan Moore. I was overseas on a Company Commander's course and you were in the UK on a Senior Staff course when they shoved him out of the army. I've quit dreaming, Colonel."

"It might still be possible, Andrew."

"Be serious, Colonel. I know the caliber of officers we have. Most of them are technically competent, but they don't have the idealism, the breath of vision, or the courage to act on those as an Alan Moore or a Ralph Spooner for that matter."

"Perhaps, but there was also the question of opportunity, of timing. Have you thought of that?"

"Very well, Colonel, timing is important. So, what's your point?"

"Aspirations are one thing, finding the right time to act is quite another. I think the time is now right. I think we should shove this government aside. We could reshuffle the deck and allow new leadership to emerge that would take us beyond the racial divide created by the Kabaka Party and the Opposition."

"How, Colonel? With what?"

"That's what I want to talk with you about, Andrew. I would like you to join me and three other Company Commanders to take out this government. It's why I wanted to get together with you."

Andrew Rambarran got up from the rocking chair and backed himself against the upper rail. He looked directly at Colonel Taylor.

"Colonel, I thank you for thinking so highly of me, but the answer is no. I should tell you that Captain Spooner spoke to me about this enterprise, evidently with your blessing. Not only did I decline participation, but I discouraged him from participation."

"Why did you do that?"

"Because, Colonel, I don't think it would succeed."

"And why not?"

"First off, Colonel, the government must surely be aware that you are not happy with the appointment of a police officer as Chief of Staff. They are going to watch you like a hawk before they cut you loose."

"Why don't you let me worry about that, Captain?"

"I'm sorry, Colonel, but this is a matter of concern to everyone even tangentially involved in this project. You are asking officers to risk their lives!"

"Andrew, I can't believe your decision is based entirely on my short-term survival in the service, which would be a moot point, if the enterprise were successful."

"You're right, Colonel, it isn't."

"We've been together a long time, Andrew. Level with me, please."

"Colonel, I don't know all of the Company Commanders you approached; but I do know about Spooner, Captain Felix, and Captain McGowan. Spooner's motivation, I understand. His family owns a lot of land at Philippi, and the government is trying to force them out. Felix is a very fine officer, very principled. He's Catholic and he started disliking the government when it took over the Catholic schools."

"Well, there you go," Colonel Taylor interjected. "You'd be in excellent company."

"Ah, but there is Captain McGowan, Anthony Cassius McGowan,

the joker in the deck. He can't be trusted; you told me so a long time ago."

"Conditions in the country have changed, Andrew, and so has he."

"He's an opportunist, you mean."

"Aren't we all, to some extent?" Colonel Taylor asked.

"I suppose, Colonel," Rambarran replied, "but this guy was a Party man. He spied on other officers. When Alan Moore was pushed out of the army and I took over F-Company, Lieutenant Beharry was transferred to McGowan's company so that he could keep an eye on Beharry."

"True," Colonel Taylor said, "but things have changed. McGowan's brother is now the head of the Public Service Union, and the union has been fighting against the government since."

"I still don't trust him, Colonel. Just look at his name. Anthony and Cassius were on opposite sides in the Roman civil war. So, which side is he really on?"

Colonel Taylor laughed. "You're reading too much in his name, Andrew. What I was told was that his father played Marc Anthony in the Theater Guild's production of *Julius Caesar*. He was also an avid fan of boxer Cassius Clay."

"I'm sorry, Colonel. In these parts, people are superstitious, and some of that has rubbed off on me. I don't trust McGowan. I'd never know if he's running with the hare or hunting with the hounds."

"Well, we could sideline him after the coup," Colonel Taylor said.

"If he doesn't betray you first, you mean."

"Don't be so cynical, Andrew."

Rambarran returned to his chair and pushed his feet against the siding of the veranda to regulate his rocking; Colonel Taylor rocked from flat-footed position. It had now darkened considerably outside, and the flickering kerosene lamp on the table projected their elongated silhouettes against the fruit trees swaying aback. The moisture-laden breeze from the incoming tide brought a chill which, however, did nothing to douse the intensity of contemplation of the two solitary figures. After a few minutes of silence, Rambarran spoke again, calmly but definitely. "Colonel, so that you don't leave believing I can still be persuaded, please know that I will not join you in this project."

"Very well, Andrew, I respect your decision," Colonel Taylor said, "but there is something I'd like you to do for me. How about it?"

"If I can, I will, Colonel," Rambarran replied. "However, before we get to that, how about a brandy?"

"That would be nice," Colonel Taylor replied. "The Atlantic breeze is refreshing, but it sure penetrates the bone."

"Especially at night," Rambarran added, picking up the lamp and walking back into the house with Colonel Taylor following. "Take the sofa," he said to Colonel Taylor.

"How about if we sit at the dining table downstairs?" Colonel Taylor asked.

"That's fine," Rambarran replied, taking the brandy out of the cabinet and pouring liberally into the two inhalers before passing one to Colonel Taylor. Leading the way with the kerosene lamp, Rambarran walked down the stairway into the dining room, where he took the chair Colonel Taylor pulled out for him at the head of the table. Rambarran touched glasses with Colonel Taylor, who sat on his right, and took his first sip. "Okay, Colonel, the favor?"

"Andrew, you're the best military planner I know," Colonel Taylor began.

"Oh, come on, Franchette," Rambarran protested.

"No, I really mean it," Taylor asserted. "Most of the officers I know went through a basic course and then shorter courses later. You were more thoroughly prepared."

"Okay, Franchette. So, what is it you want me to do, other than join the revolution?"

"Outline for me an operational plan for the overthrow of this government." They looked at each other. Colonel Taylor took a sip of the brandy. "How would you do it?" he asked Rambarran again.

"That's serious business, Colonel," Rambarran said, lifting the glass to his lips.

"These are serious times," Taylor replied.

"Well, the first thing I would tell you is not to accept a plan from someone who won't himself participate in its implementation."

"Noted," Taylor said, "but humor me, please. If you were involved, how would you do it?"

"Planning with you gets me involved, Colonel," Rambarran pointed out.

"I won't tell anyone, nor would you, Andrew. Look, you don't like this government anymore than me. You don't want to join for personal reasons. Okay. But some very good people will. We can't meet to plan. Help us think this through, please."

Rambarran leaned forward, his interlaced fingers supporting his chin. He was aware Colonel Taylor was looking expectantly at him. He thought of Ralph Spooner and Malcolm Felix. Yes, these were very good people. "Well, Colonel," Rambarran said slowly, "some of this is fairly obvious. Georgetown is the seat of government. Isolate it."

"Okay," Taylor said. "Go on, lay it all out." He reached for his attaché case and pulled out a notepad, which he set in front of himself, and other papers, which he gave to Rambarran. "Here, I brought some maps."

"You need to control all air, land, and water routes to Georgetown, which means taking the International Airport and the Army Air Wing at Timehri, the Ogle Airport, the Vreed-en-Hoop ferry to Georgetown, the Berbice ferry to Rosignol, and the Maritime Command bases at South Ruimveldt and at Crabb Island at the mouth of the Canje Creek."

Colonel Taylor nodded as he wrote.

"Set up roadblocks at the two overland routes into the city, the East Coast road and the East Bank road from Timehri. I would recommend the Sheriff Street junction for the East Coast road and the turn by the Rahaman Soda Factory for the East Bank road."

Rambarran paused. Colonel Taylor took a moment to complete what he was writing then looked up.

"Take the two radio stations, Radio Demerara on High Street and the Guyana Broadcasting Service on Durban Street; and, of course, take the newspapers, *The Guardian* and the two party mouthpieces—the *Cayman News* and the *Red Star*."

"What size of force?" Colonel Taylor asked.

"It is imperative you control Camp Ayanganna in Georgetown and Camp Stevenson at Timehri. You'll need a company at each location to do that. They'll need to secure the ammunition dump and the armories at those locations. The Company at Camp Stevenson can shut down the international airport and the Army Air Wing. They'll need to set up a road block on the Linden Highway and a back-up at the Soesdyke Junction. Company Commanders at Ayanganna and Camp Stevenson should set up free-fire zones along the East Coast road close to the city and along the Linden Highway close to the Soesdyke Junction."

"Very thorough," Colonel Taylor commented.

"For all of that, you'd need at least three companies," Rambarran said, then sipped on his brandy.

"Where would the resistance come from?" Colonel Taylor asked.

"The only organized resistance would likely come from the National Service units located at Kimbia. One way out of Kimbia would be by trail to Linden and then along the Linden Highway. If you can present them with a fait accompli, they would be unsure what to do and would stay put."

"What if they don't?"

"It would take twenty-four hours to get to the Soesdyke Junction if they left on notice, but they would be without food and other supplies and would be ill-prepared to take on the rifle company holding the Linden Highway."

"How about if they come up the Berbice River?"

"That's a problem. You need a company to protect that flank. At any time, you only have three companies under your command. How do you get the fourth, and how do you keep them quiet about these plans?"

"Well, Andrew, no one said this would be easy. I'll just have to work on that one."

"Shall we talk about the big one?"

"I was wondering when you'd get to that," Colonel Taylor replied. "What do we do with the Comrade Leader?"

"You're going to have to pick him up," Rambarran said. "What do you plan to do with him?"

"We'll put him on a Cessna and fly him out to Trinidad," Taylor replied.

"Colonel, it's one thing to take the government, it's quite another to hold it."

"Meaning what?" Taylor asked.

"Colonel, you are attempting a coup with the minimum amount of forces. You are counting, not only on the obedience of the soldiers under your command, but also on the acquiescence of the non-participating units in the army. The National Service contingents and Kabaka Party supporters across the country are likely to oppose you. If you ship out the Comrade Leader too early, he could use radio broadcasts to produce dissension in your own ranks and rally some or all of those other elements to create problems for you."

"What do you suggest we do with him?" Taylor asked.

"Hold him incommunicado for a few days while you consolidate control. Convince the other army units and the Police that there is no alternative to military rule. Get the Police to maintain law and order, thereby freeing up your forces for other duties."

"Then what?" Taylor asked.

"Negotiate asylum for the Comrade Leader someplace in Africa where he has friends. A threat to execute him should produce a quick arrangement."

"Any other consideration you might care to share?"

"Just one, Colonel," Rambarran replied. "The officers, I presume, will be taken into confidence, but the other ranks will follow by habit. Any glitch that allows them to question what they are doing could lead to an unraveling of the entire scheme. In the circumstances, any breach of discipline must be dealt with swiftly and summarily."

Colonel Taylor nodded. "This has been very helpful, Andrew," he said. "Wouldn't you please reconsider your position?"

"Colonel, I have thought hard on this since Ralph Spooner raised it with me, but my mind is made up. I have been accepted into a graduate program in the U.S. I have just sent in my application for a visa."

"And Lena?"

"She's going as well. She has dual citizenship; her mother is American as you know."

"Marriage?"

"Yes, and she will be attending vet school."

"Well, I wish you all the luck, Andrew," Taylor said, raising his brandy glass.

"And I you, Franchette," Rambarran said, lightly touching glasses.

The sound of the jeep's horn alerted them to McCurchin's presence outside. Colonel Taylor began stuffing his papers back into his attache case. "Can I ask you one final question, Andrew?" Franchette Taylor asked.

"Sure, Franchette."

"If your company is on a coastal deployment, as you are now, and you are ordered to move against us, would you?"

Andrew Rambarran looked at his friend; his eyes moistened; and he looked downward. When he raised his head again to respond, his hands were on his hips. "Let's hope it never comes to that, Franchette."

September 5, 1979
Greater Georgetown

At 13:15, as promised, Anita Rambarran arrived in her white Toyota Celica at Erikson's Bel Air Park house and sounded the horn. She had offered to drive instead of having Erikson pick her up at Regent Street because she said it would cause fewer complications with her father who only knew that she was going to visit Andrew and Lena, a trip she had made numerous times before. She kept the car running and watched Erikson descend the concrete stairway under the house where his green Lancer was parked. As he walked through the metal gate, she unlatched the trunk for him to put in his overnight bag and rucksack. When he entered the passenger side, she greeted him with a smile, then backed onto the bridge over the drainage ditch in front of his house and retraced her way back to the East-Coast road in the direction of Rosignol.

Traffic in and out of Georgetown on a Friday afternoon was very heavy from Sheriff Street well past the University at Turkeyen. At Buxton, Erikson's stomach growled.

"Have you had lunch?" Anita asked.

"No," Erikson replied. "Since I was taking the afternoon off, I stayed at the Embassy through lunch."

"I have some sandwiches in the basket on the back seat," Anita said. "Also, there are soft drinks in the cooler."

"What kind of sandwiches are they?" Erikson asked, as he reached for the basket.

"A couple with cheese and a couple with chicken," she replied. "Be careful with the cheese sandwiches. They have pepper in them."

"What kind of cheese?" Erikson asked, lifting the towel from the basket, which he had seated in his lap.

"Dutch gouda."

"Isn't that banned?" Erikson asked.

"Yes," she replied, "but it is available for sale in Springlands. People bring it across from Suriname, and Andrew buys it."

"I see," Erikson said. "You're very close, are you? You and Andrew, I mean."

"Yes," she replied. "He's just a few years older than me. I used to be the go-between for him and Lena."

"What did you do as the go-between?"

"I carried the love notes from one to the other."

Erikson nodded. "What type of sandwich would you like?"

"You go ahead," she said, "I don't like to eat when I'm driving."

"Have one," he said, "I'll help keep an eye on the road."

"Okay," she said, "I'll take a cheese sandwich."

Erikson handed her half of a cheese sandwich and, while she ate, he reached for the cooler and took out a bottle of Coke. Using his Swiss army knife, he opened the drink and handed it to her after she was through with the sandwich. He helped himself to half of a chicken sandwich, which he ate as they drove by the LBI Sugar Estate.

"What's LBI?" he asked.

"La Bonne Intencion," she replied.

"For a former slave plantation?"

"Yes, it is odd," Anita replied, "but I'm sure to the people back in France it sounded like they were doing God's work out here."

"I'm sure," Erikson agreed, as he reached again into the basket. "Would you like the other half of the sandwich?" She looked at the Coke bottle in her left hand. "Here," he said, retrieving the bottle and handing her the sandwich.

As she bit into the sandwich, Erikson took a swig from the bottle, then another. Anita was looking over, her eyes opened wide.

"What?" he asked. She shook her head, smirking. "You wouldn't do that, would you?" he asked. "Drink after someone else, I mean?"

"It depends," she replied, "if it were my parents, or Andrew, or Lena. But I couldn't drink after—"

"A stranger?" Erikson asked. She tucked in her lips and looked straight ahead. "That's what you were going to say, wasn't it? The truth now."

"Yes," she replied, "but I didn't mean like a stranger. I meant someone other than my immediate family."

"Okay," Erikson said, "that's better, I think." He took another swig while she finished the sandwich. "I can open another bottle for you, if you like,"

"No, there's no need," she replied. "I'll drink from that one."

"Are you sure?" he asked, passing the bottle to her.

"Yes," she replied, "but don't look."

For the rest of the trip, Anita played cassettes Erikson had selected from the case she had in the car. They started with Neil Diamond but, at Erikson's request for some local music, switched to Sparrow, followed by Sundar Popo. By the time the Sundar Popo cassette was half-finished, they were pulling in behind the line of vehicles waiting to cross with the ferry. The wait turned out to be a short one, and loading began immediately after the *Kurtuka* had docked and disgorged its passengers and vehicles. When the *Kurtuka* finally swung out for its return trip to New Amsterdam, Anita led Erikson to the upper deck, via the stern stairway. They walked through the sheltered passenger seating area to the open bow end of the vessel, where they stood against the rail to enjoy the view up river and the cool breeze tempering the heat from the afternoon sun. But it was a brief respite. A steady stream of beggars and proximity to the New Amsterdam ferry station made them retreat to the car, around which swirled vendors of boiled chickpeas, *salt sav,* and plantain chips, from whom Anita purchased four packets each of the *salt sav* and plantain chips.

The grating chimes of the reverse engines made the other drivers on the lower deck return to their cars and trucks and, as the *Kurtuka* eased in to be moored, the lower deck was suffused with fumes from these vehicles, which had been started in anticipation of disembarkation. When the gang plank was lowered, a sailor on the lower deck directed the vehicles, one by one, off the vessel. At 15:40, Anita's white Toyota Celica left the ferry station by the harbor road. Turning left on Strand, she bypassed New Amsterdam for the thirty-five mile run to Adventure.

"Have you ever had *salt sav?*" Anita asked, pointing to the packet as they passed Seawell Turn.

"No," Erikson replied, glancing at the packet. "They look like pretzels."

"Oh, they're much better," Anita asserted. "Why don't you open a packet?"

Erikson ripped open the plastic bag and offered it to Anita. She chose one and waited on him to munch on his.

"This is very good," he said. "What's in it?"

"It's a mix of split peas and flour," she replied, "fried, of course."

On the rest of the drive to Borlum Turn, they shared the rest of the packet and a bottle of Coke, and listened to the rest of the Sundar Popo cassette.

At 16:15, they arrived at Andrew Rambarran's house. Anita drove down the embankment to the gate and stopped. Erikson retrieved his luggage, and Anita led the way to the kitchen porch where Andrew greeted them. Anita left them talking on the porch and went into the kitchen to see Gyalie, who was stirring a black semi-circular *karahee*, from which emanated a loud sizzle and the pungent fragrance of masala. Gyalie briefly relinquished the stirring to hug Anita then resumed her stirring, and Anita returned to the porch.

"Smells like you had a curry bath," Erikson said, smiling.

"I did," Anita replied. "It's what's for dinner." She then excused herself to allow Andrew to show Steve around, promising to be back with Lena for dinner by 18:00.

Reversing the car up the embankment, she straightened up on the public road and accelerated to cruising speed. In a few minutes she was in Kildonan, having passed through Limlear, Friendship, and Nurney, each of which spanned about a quarter of a mile roadway. In Kildonan, young girls with buckets were making treks to the stand-pipe on the leeward side of the road while *Bluebird*, the multicolored bus, passed by on its final run to New Amsterdam.

At Bush Lot, Anita slowed down. The *Odeon* Cinema had a predominantly male crowd in the courtyard awaiting ticket sales for the 5 p.m. double feature: *Operation Daybreak* and *Enter the Dragon*. The large billboard above the heads of the waiting patrons advertized Saturday night's Indian double-feature: *Kati Patang* and *Sholay*.

The villages of Maida and Kilmonark went by quickly, and Anita had finally reached Phillipi. Like the other villages, there was no sign bearing the village name or distinguishable lines of demarcation separating it from the adjacent ones, at least none that an unwary traveler could recognize. Anita slowed as she drove by the western front of the Spooner property located on the leeward side of the Corentyne coastal road. A wide drainage canal ran parallel to the public road, and a barbed wire fence on the inside bank of the canal kept the cows on the grassy savanna from crossing the road.

The Spooners' residence was visible from the road, its three-stories towering above neighboring houses like one of the administrative managers' houses on the sugar estates except that its corrugated zinc roof was painted green. A metal gate and a watch-house on the right side controlled the half-mile gravel road leading to the house. Magenta bougainvillea covered the left and right poles supporting the gate with some of the vines riding along the top string of the barbed wire on both sides. The road to the house was lined with dwarf flamboyant trees, watered by canals on both sides of the road, which ran up to about a hundred feet or so of the house lot before turning east and west for some distance then angling due south and reconverging on the back side of the house.

Anita turned right into the open gate, idling the vehicle while she greeted the watchman, then slowly negotiated the top layer of crushed, red clay bricks, which covered the road. By the time she reached the concrete apron skirting the house, Lena was downstairs to greet her. With her were *Bess*, her black-and-tan Alsatian, and *Pip*, Andrew Rambarran's reddish brown Corgi, which she kept while he was away. Anita parked under the house, whose reinforced brick columns had been surrounded by white lattice and served as a garage and game room. With Lena helping with her luggage, they ascended the short flight of stairs into the living room, walking through to the bedrooms on the western side, one of which Lena occupied whenever Anita came and stayed over. Once Anita had freshened up, she rejoined Lena in the living room, and they went to the kitchen in the southwestern corner of the house where Mrs. Spooner was supervising dinner preparation. A brief hug for Mrs. Spooner, whose hands had been kneading dough, then the women left through the outside kitchen stairs for the back of the house to allow Anita to get reacquainted with *Bluebell*, Lena's white mare.

A one-storied trailer, close to the back of the house, served as Dr. Spooner's office, and adjacent to the trailer were coops for the chickens and turkeys, which the Spooners reared. A huge pavilion covered the Spooners' farm implements, which included a Massey-Ferguson tractor, a harvester combine, a tractor-drawn mower, and ploughs. A waist-high enclosed corner of the pavilion served as the watch-house at nights, and, beyond those on the right was the barn, where the horses were kept. A barbed wire enclosure further back secured the milking cows and their calves. *Bluebell* whinnied when Lena approached with Anita and the dogs, and extended its head over the half-open Dutch door. Lena gave *Bluebell* a hug, and the mare stood still as Anita stroked its face.

"Would you like to go for a ride?" Lena asked. "I could have the gelding saddled up for you."

"Thanks," Anita replied, "but I promised Andrew we'd get back to his place for dinner at six."

"Andrew?" Lena asked with a mischievous grin.

Anita blushed. "Well, Andrew and Steve," she replied, looking into Lena's inquisitive face. "What?" Anita asked. Lena smiled and shook her head. "I'd love for us to walk to the back canal."

"Okay," Lena said, and off they went with the dogs following.

From the concrete apron at the back of the house, a wide, unpaved road ran south all the way to the back canal, about quarter of a mile way. Drainage canals on both sides of the road emptied into the back canal and were joined to the canals which ran along the front road to the house and around both sides of the house. It was as if the house was surrounded by a moat, whose waters drained into canals running due north and south of the house.

Along the sides of the unpaved road were flamboyant trees but, further away from the house, mango trees alternated with *jamoon* trees and coconut palms. There was even a *sankoker* tree on the right side near the back canal. The dam behind the canal separated the residential section of the property from the rice lands beyond the back canal. The Spooners owned over two hundred acres, some of which they planted themselves; the rest they leased to local farmers. A high green-heart bridge over the back canal connected the unpaved road to the rice lands, allowing farm machinery access over it and canoe passage underneath.

On the eastern side of the back road, just inside of the back canal, was the fruit orchard. A row of mango trees formed the outermost boundary, but there were multiple rows of banana and plantain suckers, and a row of mixed fruit trees including star apples, sapodillas, and sour-sops. Another green-heart bridge connected the back road to the fruit orchard.

Closer to the house, on the eastern side as well, the Spooners kept a vegetable garden. There were several rows of cassava, sweet potato, and eddo tubers, eggplant and okra, lettuce and spinach of all kinds. A wide footbridge spanned the canal from the back road to the dam on the other side. The network of canals provided irrigation and water borne transportation for produce but were also laden with fresh water fish, which made poaching by locals a perennial nuisance since the Spooners never prosecuted them.

At 17:30 hours, Anita and Lena left in the Toyota Celica for Adventure. Gyalie had completed all of her cooking by the time they arrived at Rambarran's house and, after showing the women where everything was, Gyalie left for the day. Anita and Lena took two bowls with the appetizers Gyalie had prepared and went upstairs to the back veranda where Rambarran and Erikson were each sipping a Heineken. They set down the containers on the card table and invited Erikson, the newcomer, to sample the dishes.

"What's this?" Steve asked pointing to the bowl containing what appeared to him as elbow macaroni done up in a dried curry sauce.

"That's *pachownie*," Andrew replied. "Try it."

Erikson forked a few pieces and put them in his mouth. "It's a bit rubbery, sort of like curried octopus."

"Actually, it's the entrails of a sheep, washed and scrubbed, and cooked dry in a curry sauce; what's called a *bhoonjal*."

"It's quite flavorful," Erikson remarked. "A bit hot, but flavorful. Sure gives your jaws a workout." He chewed and swallowed, then turned his attention to the second container. "And, what's this?" he asked. "It looks like another *bhoonjal* of some sort."

"It is," Rambarran replied. "It's *bhoonjal* sheep liver."

Erikson tried a piece of the liver; everyone else waited for his response. "This is very good," he said. "It has a nutty texture and flavor. You really can't tell it's liver. It certainly doesn't have the strong taste of beef liver, which I am not too fond of."

With this declaration, everyone relaxed, and the party began. Lena offered to get Anita a glass of wine, and Andrew got up to help. He retrieved a bottle of red wine and uncorked it for Lena, then he went downstairs to the refrigerator to retrieve a couple of Heinekens for himself and Erikson. When he returned to the veranda, Lena had pulled out a chair for herself and placed it next to his rocking chair. Anita was already seated next to Erikson.

"That's a Portuguese wine you have there," Erikson said, pointing to the bottle on the card table. "I thought there was a ban on those luxury items."

"There is," Andrew replied. "I get a few bottles once in a while from the local parish priest. He's a very good friend. Lena's Catholic, you know."

"You mean that is communion wine?" Erikson asked.

"It's part of the stock that's used for communion," Andrew pointed out.

"I'm happy for you," Erikson said. "You don't seem to suffer the privations of ordinary folk."

"We have a saying among a small group of friends: cooperate and survive."

"It's more like cooperate and celebrate," Erikson observed.

"No harm in that, is there?" Andrew asked.

"I suppose not," Erikson replied. "If you can beat the system, why not? From what I hear, this government of yours lives in luxury while the people suffer."

"Isn't that the truth?" Andrew declared. "But let's leave that discussion for another time, shall we? Cheers."

When the sky darkened and the first wave of mosquitoes struck, the group retired to the dining table, where over a dinner of *dal puri*, curried chicken, and chicken chow-mein, they went over the plans for the next day. Andrew was taking Steve on a tour of the area, after which they would join the women on the Spooner property for a fishing expedition in the canals. Lena insisted that Andrew return with Steve in time for lunch, which she offered to prepare. No one seemed keen on dessert of any kind, and after coffee, Anita and Lena left for the Spooners'. The electricity was still on, but Andrew lit a kerosene lamp, which he took upstairs, setting it on the card table on the veranda. Then with a glass of brandy and a Cuban cigar each, he and Steve retired to the rocking chairs.

"How do you like being an attaché?" Andrew asked.

"It's okay, I guess," Erikson replied. "The best part is being here, getting to see you."

They sipped their brandy and blew thick puffs of cigar smoke, which swirled around them, protecting them from the mosquitoes. "Of course, you know that military attachés are declared spies," Erikson continued.

"I sort of figured that," Andrew said, "but there's not much going on here. We are as poor as North Korea and we have an idiot pretending to be Kim Il Sung. Other than that, it's sort of boring."

"I wouldn't say that," Erikson said. "For instance, I'm aware that a coup attempt was being contemplated, but it seems to be fizzling out." Andrew offered no response. "I gather you don't think it would succeed," Erikson continued.

"What makes you say that?" Andrew asked.

"Well, the word is that you refused to join."

"You are well informed," Andrew said, as the electricity went off. "On the other hand, at times like these, I feel that this government ought to go."

"But you are not involved in the current venture?" Erikson asked.

"No," Andrew replied, rising to retrieve the kerosene lamp, which he placed on the card table.

"You don't think a coup attempt would succeed?"

Andrew took a deep draw on the cigar and blew out slowly. "No, I don't think so," he replied.

"This is like picking teeth, Andrew, but can you tell me why not?"

"Sure," Andrew replied. "To move this government out, you need four companies minimum. I mean, absolute minimum. They have three Company Commanders on board. They'd like me to be the fourth. The problem is I just don't trust one of those Company Commanders."

"Does he have a name?" Erikson asked.

"You'd love this: he's Anthony Cassius McGowan. AC, for short."

"That *is* peculiar," Erikson declared. "Anthony Cassius? Sounds like his daddy couldn't decide which side he was on."

"Exactly! But here's something else. The entire coup attempt is premised on the assumption that soldiers will follow orders. They would not know that they're actually overthrowing the government until it is over or close to being over. Any hiccup along the way that gives those soldiers room to question what they are doing and the entire enterprise will unravel."

"But isn't that always the case in coup attempts? No one consults the enlisted ranks."

"True," Andrew conceded, "but most of those have involved larger military contingents where breaking ranks is more difficult and, if it happens, it can be easily dealt with. When you have a bare minimum of forces to do all the tasks necessary, dealing with rebellion in the ranks, however small, becomes problematic."

"I see your point," Erikson said.

"There's also the question of governing," Andrew continued. "Most of the non-socialist intelligentsia have fled the country, and this army *does not* have the ability to keep order and govern simultaneously."

"Would there be a big problem with public order?"

"There could be," Andrew replied. "In the immediate aftermath of a coup, there would be an internal problem of selling the coup to the army units that did not participate. That can be easily managed. However, forces that did not come into play during the coup, such as the National Service and Kabaka Party militants, would have to be demobilized. One of the things the Kabaka Party has been good at has been its ability to provoke racial tensions by selective attacks on non-blacks. The Party networks would still be operating. What happens if they instigate racial violence and the army, which is predominantly black, has to arbitrate? Loyalties would be heavily stressed; let me put it that way."

"What if we supported the removal of this government in terms of rapid recognition and massive infusion of advisors and aid in the aftermath? Would you change your position?"

"Are you speaking on authority or is this a hypothetical question?" Andrew asked.

"Hypothetical, let's say."

"That would change things quite a bit, and I would be more inclined to participate. But the suspicions I have of Captain McGowan would remain. Your promise to provide material support afterwards would be worthless if the coup failed."

"Can I ask you something else I've been trying to figure out?" Erikson asked. Andrew looked over in anticipation. "Is there anyone in the upper ranks who has a connection with any of the labor unions?"

"Funny you'd ask that," Andrew remarked, "that's Captain McGowan."

"What's the connection?"

"His brother, Joe Henry, is the new head of the Public Service Union."

"What's with the names?"

"Henry is the mother's maiden name. The parents weren't married when he came along. I didn't know this until a week or so ago."

"I see," Erikson said, "thanks." He took a sip from the brandy inhaler and leaned back with a slight rocking motion. "This is really nice out here, you know. It feels like old times."

"It does," Andrew responded, "and I'm glad you're here."

FIFTEEN

September 6, 1979
Adventure

Following breakfast, Rambarran and Erikson left in his Mini Minor for Springlands, taking the indirect route through the Black Bush Polder. Near the Lesbeholden sluice separating Adventure from Hog Sty, Andrew turned onto the Black Bush Polder road, which followed the drainage canal through the rice-farming villages of Lesbeholden, Mibikuri, Johanna, and Yakusari, and emerged by the No. 43 Village sluice to rejoin the coastal road. The entire empoldering effort, including the canal system and sluices, had been a Dutch aid project of the early 1960s. Taming the rattle-snake infested bush became the task of Indian homesteaders lured into the area by grants of fifteen-acre plots for rice and vegetable cultivation. And, what a successful agricultural enterprise it became! Small, independent farmers transformed the area into a veritable rice bowl, providing a ready export and fresh produce for coastal villages and giving their children the educational foundation which catapulted them into the professional classes.

The drive along the horseshoe road, from the Lesbeholden sluice through the entire polder to the No. 43 Village sluice at the other end, had changed little over the years, revealing a placid but monotonous repetition of footbridges across the canal linking the road to the houses on the other side, many of which were partially hidden behind decades-old mango or genip trees. With the windows on both sides of the Mini Minor lowered for ventilation, road noise, including the loud hum of the engine, permeated the cab and compelled conversation at a higher than normal decibel.

"How often do you travel this way?" Erikson asked.

"Once every two weeks or so," Andrew replied. "Third Platoon, which is located at Springlands, patrols it once a week. Most of the people in the Black Bush Polder are Indian and they tend to view the army as an instrument of the Kabaka Party. Lieutenant DeFreitas is aware of that, so he sends through a patrol in the evenings for genuine security purposes. Residents might be too intimidated by a daytime presence."

"Are all troop commanders as sensitive?"

"I'd say they are sensible enough and responsible enough not to want an ethnic incident on their hands. To tell the truth, many Black officers are just not comfortable with the relationship between the army top brass and the Kabaka Party."

"I can't imagine the appointment of a policeman to head the army was helpful in that regard."

"No, it wasn't. The problem is that there's too much suspicion in the army for cohesive action. And the Kabaka leadership knows that."

"The Comrade Leader, huh?" Steve Erikson chuckled.

"Yeah, isn't that a laugh? A dictator with a Kim Il Sung complex. You haven't been here long enough. Wait till you see the North Korean-style mass games."

"How do you stand it?" Steve asked.

"Well, the truth is that we're insulated from that nonsense. Much of the social life of the officers center on the clubs at Ayanganna and Timehri. The drinks are cheap; food is free. Even banned items like flour and cheese are available at the Officers' messes. On the other hand, we face no imminent external threat, so we have a lot of thinking time. That's really when you ponder the role of the army and the direction the country is going. And you get mad. At least, some of us."

"I can't presume to speak for you, of course, but if I estimated a reasonable chance of success in doing so, I'd take this type of government out."

Andrew looked over at Steve Erikson and, for a few moments, they held each other's eyes in silence. Farms gave way to other farms, and the houses differed in sizes, but there was no need for commentary. When they rejoined the Corentyne coastal road at the edge of No. 43 Village, fishing boats with their night's catch were pulling in on the Atlantic side of the sluice.

"Judging from the size of those boats, I'd guess they don't do much deep sea fishing out here," Erikson observed.

"True," Andrew replied. "Those boats ply the Atlantic coast and the Corentyne River. Some of the larger ones fish off the coast of Suriname and French Guiana, but that's poaching, and we've had problems with the impounding of their boats in Suriname."

"I understand the Surinamese own the Corentyne River," Erikson said.

"They do. In fact, the border is at the high water mark on our side."

"That's odd," Erikson remarked. "Right down the middle of the river would have been a more reasonable settlement."

"You would think so, but that issue was settled long before we got independence. I'm sure there's a better diplomatic explanation for what actually happened, but the story is that the border between the two colonies was settled by the British and Dutch governors over a bottle of rum. Evidently, the Dutch governor held his liquor better than his British counterpart." They both laughed.

"I suppose that's the cause of the border dispute between the two countries today, eh?" Erikson asked.

"Not really," Andrew replied. "The dispute has to do with the course of the Corentyne River. The Surinamese claim that the New River, which flows through Guyana and merges with the Corentyne River, is the western tributary of the Corentyne River, and that would put the international border further west than historically designated on the map. This would mean that the triangle between the New River and the Corentyne River, currently held by Guyana, belongs to them."

"But you can use the Corentyne River?"

"Oh yes, we are allowed to patrol it."

"Can we go up river sometime?" Erikson asked.

"Sure. I'll arrange it with the Springlands Police. They have a patrol boat. It'll have to be on another of your trips down here."

At Springlands, Andrew introduced Erikson to Assistant Superintendent Cabot, Officer in Charge at Springlands Police Station, and to Inspector Pollard. Cabot, whose daughter was a nurse at Jamaica Hospital in New York and had visited the United States several times, lamented the fact that he was about to leave for New Amsterdam and could not spend more time with Erikson but invited him to stop by anytime he was in the area. Inspector Pollard was also very hospitable, offering to take them to a popular watering hole in Springlands, but Andrew declined on account of prior commitments.

Andrew's meeting with Lieutenant Michael DeFreitas was brief and perfunctory. After being introduced to Steve Erikson, DeFreitas reminded Andrew that he was off for the weekend. He was heading home to Georgetown and was getting a ride to the New Amsterdam ferry station with Superintendent Cabot, for which reason he asked and received Rambarran's permission to leave a couple of hours early.

Rambarran left with Erikson, driving past the Skeldon Sugar Estate and turning around in Crabwood Creek. "People sometimes refer to Crabwood Creek as 'road end' because it's the last stop the buses make, and it's literally the end of the paved coastal road. But there is an unpaved road running further along the bank of the Corentyne River past Molson Creek."

"What type of interactions do people have with one another, across the Corentyne River?" Erikson asked.

"Lots. There are intermarriages between Surinamese Indians from Nickerie and Indians on this side, so the communities are very close. There are frequent daily river crossings. Technically, they are not legal, but it's hard to stop them; and no one tries, except to prevent smuggling of big-ticket items."

"But there is an official crossing point, I assume?"

"Yes," Rambarran replied, "the ferry station is in Springlands. The access road is across from the police station. I'll point it out on the way back."

At 10:45, they crossed the Molson Creek bridge, and Rambarran turned around. In Springlands, he pointed out the access road to the ferry, which plied the mouth of the Corentyne River taking passengers to Nickerie and back. People in cars and on foot so congested the road that Erikson declined Rambarran's offer of a ride to the ferry terminal. Instead, they remained on the coastal road for the return trip.

They arrived in Adventure well before noon. Andrew changed out of his field uniform into a pair of weathered khaki trousers and a blue long-sleeved shirt. He gave a poncho to Erikson in case it rained and placed one for himself in his haversack. Then, after holding up his holstered Ruger pistol for Erikson to see, he seated it on top of the poncho and secured the cover of his pack. With a smirk, Erikson revealed the .45 caliber he had brought and placed it in his rucksack. With their back packs and a cooler of beer in the trunk of the car, they left for the

Spooner farm, each wearing a cap displaying the Atlanta Braves logo, compliments of Steve Erikson.

On entering the Spooner property, Rambarran and Erikson observed Lena and Anita waiting by two canoes beached on the inside bank of the canal close to the concrete apron in front of the house. The two women walked over to the vehicle when it came to a stop on the apron. Lena wore a white, long-sleeved shirt rolled up to her elbows, a pair of faded blue jeans, and a pair of Adidas. Anita was dressed in a white and cherry-red floral sun-dress with side slits below the knees, and a pair of white sandals. Both women had on sunglasses and each carried a wide-brimmed straw hat by the elastic chin-strap.

"Aren't you going to put that on," Erikson asked Anita when he got out of the car. When she made a face, he handed her his Atlanta Braves baseball cap. "Here, take mine," he said. She seated it on her head, and he went behind her to adjust the back strap for a comfortable fit. "There," he said when he was finished, and she smiled.

Erikson helped Andrew with the cooler from the trunk and they all walked over to the canoes. The fishing rods and the earthenware bowls with the worms were already in the canoes. Andrew swapped some of the beer for soft drinks in Lena's cooler, then loaded one in his canoe while Erikson put the other in the second. Once the sandwich baskets were loaded, one to each canoe, and the boats ready to be pushed off, the group walked back to the house to introduce Steve Erikson to Lena's parents.

Susan Spooner, Lena's mother, who was paying the farmhands in the trailer, stopped to welcome Steve Erikson and to invite him and Andrew to dinner. They found Dr. Daniel Spooner further back on the property giving directions to some of the farmhands who were working over the weekend. He excused himself from the farmhands to welcome Steve Erikson, expressing the hope that they would be able to visit longer in the evening. He also advised that they concentrate their efforts on the canals on the eastern and western perimeter because they were not as heavily traversed by canoes and the lily pads provided shelter for the fish. A final handshake between Dr. Spooner and Steve Erikson, and the group made off to the canoes.

Rambarran took the lead canoe, steering from the rear seat with Lena paddling at the mid-section. Steve Erikson and Anita Rambarran were similarly positioned in the second canoe, following a couple of boat-lengths behind. The canoes moved at a leisurely pace in the placid light-brown canal water, traversing the front savanna to the western perimeter of the property. At the junction, Rambarran turned the canoe southward, away from the coastal road, and stopped at the base of the flamboyant tree overhanging the water. Steve maneuvered the second canoe to a parallel position so that the broadside of the boats butted against each other.

"This is really nice," Steve remarked, looking up at the mature branches shading that section of the canal from the mid-day sun. "Someone here really loves flamboyant trees."

"That'll be my mother," Lena said. "Thirty years ago, when she came to this country, she was very impressed by the flamboyant trees lining Main Street in Georgetown. So, when she did the landscaping for this property, she lined the driveway with them and made sure that there was one at the four compass points of the property, on the inside banks like this one. The trees really flourish if they are close to a water source which is why the ones on the perimeter are so large. Of course, she has the ones on the driveway pruned regularly to keep the sizes fairly uniform."

"It is truly a work of art," Erikson said. "I've never really thought of owning a farm, but I'd kill for one like this." He took out his field glasses from his haversack and trained them downstream. As Lena said, there was another flamboyant tree where the canal turned eastward. He then fanned over to the distant part of the levee which came all the way up to the front of the property and formed the outside bank of the canal.

"The trees on the other side of the levee are mostly *sankoker*," Lena said, anticipating Erikson. "My father left those for privacy when they were clearing the property. Our fence runs just beyond that line of trees."

"Okay," Andrew interjected, "let's eat."

Lunch consisted of *bhoonjal* chicken rolled up in half-sections of *dal puris*. The women washed theirs down with Cokes; the men preferred beer. Dessert was a thick sour-sop shake, which everyone decided to forego until later in the expedition. Erikson pushed against the other canoe, then paddled mid-stream to allow Rambarran to move away from the base of the flamboyant tree and to reassume the lead. The canoes moved slowly up the canal while the women baited the hooks on their bamboo fishing poles. Close to the water's edge on both banks, clumps of *carrion crow* bush with long yellow blooms alternated with black sage, and berry-laden *bulbuloo* bush, and further away from the junction, the lily pads were denser on the water surface and lotus flowers in full bloom protruded upward on their erect vertical stems like pink periscopes. Following Dr. Spooner's advice, Rambarran stopped the lead canoe in an area dense with lily pads, positioning it across the canal so that he could join Lena on the center seat and fish on opposite sides of the boat. Erikson had already stopped his canoe several boat-lengths behind and was using a rod-and-reel at the back while Anita used a bamboo rod at the front.

When Lena reached out with her rod to drop her baited hook between the lily pads, Andrew lit a cigar then dropped his hook on the opposite side of the boat. The silence that ensued was shattered by an exultant yell from the second canoe. Anita's bamboo rod was partially bent by a fish on her line and Erikson had moved up with the net to help her.

"What the heck is that?" Erikson asked when he saw the eight-inch long black fish.

"It's a *hassar*," she replied.

"People eat that?" he asked.

"Of course," she said laughing. "It's very good. It's a fresh-water crustacean."

"Okay," he said, reaching into the net to retrieve the *hassar*.

"Be careful," she warned, "the dorsal fins can really sting."

The *hassar* was dropped into a bucket, half-filled with canal water, then the fishing resumed with Erikson casting toward the rear getting frustrated each time the hook fell on top of lily pads. After several "Oh hecks," he got the baited hook to settle in the water between the lily pads, lit a cigar, and watched the float. But the silence was again interrupted by the thudding hooves of a black gelding. The rider, one of the Spooner farmhands, stopped closest to Rambarran's canoe and dismounted, retaining the reins in one hand.

"Captain," he said, addressing Rambarran, "there's a policeman at the house. He said that a fire broke out at your New Amsterdam camp."

"A fire?" Rambarran asked. "How on earth could a fire—?" He stopped himself, realizing that this man would have no clue about what might have happened. Paddling to the inside bank, Rambarran stepped out, then held the bow for Lena to get out.

"Would you like me to come with you?" Erikson shouted.

"No need," Rambarran replied. "Why don't you enjoy the outing? We'll join you as soon as we can."

Rambarran accepted the messenger's offer to ride the gelding back and to leave the canoe with him. With Lena behind him on the gelding, Rambarran returned to the house at a slow trot and, at 13:35, he and Lena left for New Amsterdam in the Mini Minor.

Erikson and Anita continued fishing the western perimeter canal, where Anita had added a brim to her catch. Steve Erikson, whose use of superior technology had not produced much, except a handful of brim, switched from using the rod-and-reel to one of the bamboo poles he had taken from Andrew's canoe before the farmhand had left. He lowered the baited hook between the lily pads at the edge of canal where the *sankoker* trees were casting short reflections from the two o'clock sun. Nursing a beer, he watched the float with increasing impatience, and then, bingo! The float went under swiftly, and the line moved from side to side. He pulled the rod upward, reaching forward with the net to scoop the dangling fish. Anita pulled in her line and joined him.

"It looks like a sunfish," he observed, reaching into the net and squeezing behind the head of the fish to extricate the hook.

"It's actually a *hoori*," Anita said.

"Wow, look at those serrated teeth!" Erikson exclaimed.

"They are a bit boney," Anita said, "but they are very delicious."

Erikson held up the fish, still maintaining his choke. "About a pound, you think?"

"At least," Anita replied, watching him drop the fish into the bucket.

By the time they reached the back canal, Erikson had added several *hassars* and *hooris* to the total catch. Because the back canal was completely unsheltered from the afternoon sun, and the water surface was clear of vegetation, they decided to paddle to the eastern perimeter and fish out there for a little while before returning to the Spooners' residence. Just before they reached the eastern canal, the sky broke open, and the rain came down. They paddled vigorously to the corner where a huge flamboyant tree sat on the causeway, with Erikson steering the boat under the tree branches. Anita got out and Erikson, with his haversack in one hand, stepped out and pulled the canoe up the bank. He reached into his rucksack for the poncho, with which he covered Anita, and then pulled out a T-shirt and dried her arms and shoulders. Anita was about to sit on a grassy patch under the flamboyant when Erikson stopped her.

"Here," he said, taking his field blanket out of his rucksack and spreading it on the grass. He watched her sit, then he lowered himself next to her. "I suppose we can just sit out the rain. I can't imagine it will go on for long, not with the sun still out as it is."

"We can share the poncho too, you know," Anita said, extending the upraised poncho for him to get under. He placed his left arm around her shoulder and wrapped the other half of the poncho around himself. For a while, they watched the raindrops rippling the water surface of the back canal. But the sheer proximity of their bodies compelled mutual glances. Each time, Anita blushed and turned her head away. When he finally squeezed gently on her shoulder, she looked over anxiously to find his face only inches away from hers. He kissed her lightly on her lips, then extending his other arm around her and holding her more firmly, he kissed her again, gradually lowering her onto the field blanket. And, with the poncho covering them and an occasional drop of water slipping through the branches to tap on the plastic poncho, they became lovers.

*　　*　　*

At about 14:10 hours, Rambarran pulled into Esplanade Park and stopped by the bandstand. Lieutenant Shah, the camp commander, and his platoon sergeant were at the northwestern edge of the camp with the firemen from the New Amsterdam Fire Brigade. As Rambarran and Lena walked out to meet them, the acrid smell of wet ash from burned grass and shrubs was unmistakable. They could see from the perimeter of the aborted burn that the fire had threatened the businesses near the intersection of the Harbor Road and Strand. Lieutenant Shah and his sergeant braced to attention when Rambarran approached with Lena.

"What happened?" Rambarran asked.

"As you know, we've been burning coconut husks to keep mosquitoes away," Lieutenant Shah began. Rambarran nodded. "Well," Shah continued, "the buckets with the husks were on the windward perimeter. Around 12:00, something spooked *Eveready*, and he ran everywhere braying and kicking. Eventually, he knocked one of the buckets into the air, scattering the lighted husks. That started the fire, and it spread very quickly."

"But coconuts husks burn very slowly," Rambarran asserted. "Why didn't someone put it out?"

"It appears that some of the husks in the bucket had the dry coconut shell in them, and you know how quickly those burn. Some of them fell into the brush on that far side." Shah pointed in the direction of the Berbice River.

"Well, thank God, there was no serious damage," Rambarran said. "Asad, you need to get rid of that donkey. A military camp is no place for somebody else's jackass."

"We took care of that, Captain," Lieutenant Shah said. "*Eveready* is now tethered outside of the camp."

Rambarran thanked the firemen, who were preparing to leave, then walked back with Lieutenant Shah and Lena to the bandstand, where he left Lena before continuing on a walking inspection of the camp. But for the mishap with the smoke bucket, everything seemed to be in order; the excitement over the fire had subsided. Two squads were away on weekend passes; members of the remaining squad were playing cards or dominoes under the flamboyant trees that lined the leeward edge of the park along Strand. When they walked back to the bandstand, Lieutenant Shah, who was going to see his parents at Albion and had asked for a ride, picked up an overnight bag and crawled into the back seat of the car. Rambarran reversed the car in the compound and drove out of the park, stopping to merge left on Strand; then it began to rain.

"Looks like somebody died," Asad Shad said. Lena glanced over at Andrew and suppressed what started out as a loud laugh with her hand over her mouth. "That's what they say," Asad insisted, smiling. "Of course, we could have used this rain a little while ago."

*   *   *

When Rambarran and Erikson arrived for dinner at the Spooners, they were met by Dr. Dan Spooner, who escorted them up to the living room and offered them drinks. Both gentlemen elected to have beer while Dr. Spooner poured himself a glass of cabernet from the stock he said his wife had brought back from her last US trip. With Lena and Anita helping in the kitchen, Dr. Spooner offered to take Rambarran and Erikson up to "the Observatory."

From the western side of the living room, they ascended a flight of stairs to the second floor at the center of which was a circular rail from which radiated four wide passage-ways, each to a separate bedroom. Within the railed area, a winding staircase led up to a large octagonal study, which Dr. Spooner called the Observatory. Large, plain-glass windows with screens were centered on each side of the octagon, and the section of seating below each window was hinged so that it could be lowered to facilitate observation of the property. Framed landscapes in watercolor hung on the walls adjacent to the windows, some depicting sections of the Spooner farm, including one from the coastal road, and others of the Corentyne coast, including one of the Lesbeholden sluice and the channel to the Atlantic. Against the rest of the available wall space were bookshelves displaying works of fiction, philosophy, agriculture, and a large collection on animal husbandry. There were a couple of binoculars on the seating, and a Nikon camera mounted on a tripod near one of the windows. A five-blade ceiling fan with lights hung from above and two floor lamps provided additional lighting for the small writing desk at the center of the Observatory.

It was 17:45, and the afternoon sun was still well above the horizon. Dr. Spooner invited Erikson to take a pair of binoculars and experience the farm from above ground level. Erikson began at the western window and moved around, finally settling at the southeastern window and training the glasses on the flamboyant tree in full bloom, a detail he had missed earlier in the day when he took shelter there. Lowering the glasses, he turned to Dr. Spooner. "Do you think I could get a photograph from this angle?"

"Sure," Dr. Spooner replied, setting down his drink and moving the camera and tripod to the window. "Here, I'll let you take it, and I'll take another for you tomorrow around mid-morning."

Erikson stepped behind the camera, zoomed in and clicked twice.

"It'll take a little while to have those developed," Dr. Spooner said, "but I should be able to get them to you in a couple of weeks."

Erikson thanked him, and they retraced their steps down to the living room, where Susan Spooner invited them to the dinner table adjacent to the living room. It was located in a large open space, above which hung a circular, cast-iron chandelier powered by an outside Lister generator. The center sleeve of the mahogany table had been removed for a more intimate accommodation of the company. At the head of the table sat Dr. Spooner, who invited Erikson to sit on his left. Rambarran sat at the end, directly across from Dr. Spooner, and when Susan Spooner finally came in, she took her place next to her husband. Lena and Anita paired themselves with Rambarran and Erikson, and, as Rambarran looked to his right, he was surprised at how natural it had become to see Anita and Erikson together.

Dr. Spooner poured from the carafe of cabernet for his wife and Steve, then passed it around the table. When it was returned back to the head, Dr. Spooner said grace and, raising his glass in a toast, he welcomed Erikson on behalf of his family, adding that he regarded Andrew and Anita as a part of that family. While Dr. Spooner carved generous portions of the two golden brown, oven-roasted ducks and passed the plates around, Susan Spooner described for Erikson the rest of the spread, including the rice pilaf, stir-fried *bora*, spinach, roasted eggplant, and boiled pumpkin. All of the vegetables, Susan Spooner noted, had been grown on the farm. She spoke of her admiration for the farmers on the Corentyne Coast, lamenting the way rice farmers were being treated by the Kabaka government. She said that the government had no appreciation of the toil which went into farming. It was true that Dr. Spooner's grandfather had inherited a good deal of land, but every generation of Spooners had toiled to make the farm what it had become.

As knives and forks cut and scraped on bone china, Dr. Spooner asked Erikson about his Academy days with Rambarran. Erikson related how he and Rambarran met at Beast Barracks, as their first summer of induction and basic training was called. When the entire Cadet Corps reassembled for classes that fall, they were assigned to the same company in the Second Regiment of the Cadet Brigade. They went through Airborne training at Fort Benning together, and they spent numerous weekends together in New York City. He mentioned that he met Lena for the first time when she came up for Ring Hop toward the end of their junior year.

After the wine carafe had made the circuit the second time, Dr. Spooner, with an air of lightheartedness and a slight slurring that comes from incipient inebriation, requested anecdotes of some of their extracurricular activities, perhaps a funny one, or even one that might be embarrassing to the two gentlemen. Over Rambarran's objections, Erikson related their visit to the Brotherhood Winery. It was mid-spring of their junior year. With very little money and the recommendations of other classmates that it was a cheap way of getting drunk, they had, that Saturday after lunch, gone up for the wine tasting which Brotherhood generously opened to the public in the hope of generating sales. By the time they had reached the last station, they were completely sloshed. Young and unaccustomed to so much alcohol in such a short time, they disgorged much of it before the trip back to the West Point reservation. The story made Dr. Spooner chuckle, and Susan Spooner smiled at Rambarran's apparent discomfiture and said, "Those poor boys!"

Lena joined in the conversation, relating how they had, on several evenings during Steve and Andrew's senior year, driven up to Saratoga Springs to bet on the trotters. Under the vigilant eye of Anita, who had remained silent during most of the dinner, Lena omitted any mention that Steve, in those days, was accompanied by the girl he eventually married.

Dessert was a mixed fruit compote, topped by freshly churned mango ice cream. Steve remarked on what was for him a delightful change to enjoy such a wide array of tropical fruits as he had in the short time he had been in Guyana. He was especially fond of the sapodillas and star-apples and had become addicted to sour-sop shakes in the mid-afternoon.

While Lena and Anita helped Susan Spooner clear away the dishes, Dr. Spooner led the others to the front veranda, off of the living room, but their stay outside turned out to be short on account of sandflies. They rejoined the women in the living room for coffee and tea, which Lena and Anita preferred. Susan Spooner, who had grown up in Florida, asked Steve about his hometown in neighboring Georgia, an inquiry which produced a confession from Steve that he had not been home to

Cartersville except once a year. Three years at a duty station in West Germany, a year and a half at Fort Sill, Oklahoma, and various issues of life had all intervened to reduce the frequency of his visits to his parents. However, he did note that people in Georgia were still proud to have one of their own as President, and a huge billboard with a picture of Jimmy Carter towered over the pine trees along I-75, just outside of Valdosta. Susan Spooner said that she was actually born in North Carolina, but the family had moved to Florida after she finished high school. Thirty years of living in Guyana, however, had validated her claim to being Guyanese, not simply by citizenship but also by depth of affection. Of course, she admitted, one never lost the love of one's place of birth, and she and her husband had, as a hedge against political uncertainty, kept a house in Orlando for their children.

For much of the rest of the evening, Susan and Dan Spooner related anecdotes from their farming experience in Philippi. When Anita fell asleep on the sofa, Andrew and Steve decided to take their leave. Dr. Spooner showed Andrew and Steve out to the Mini Minor, parked on the concrete apron in front of the house. With the windows lowered for ventilation, Andrew drove out slowly, crunching the gravel up to the coastal road. They did not speak much on the short drive back to Adventure, though Steve admitted that he was filled to the gill and declared that the hospitality meted out to him thus far had been extraordinary in a country so badly run and so plagued by shortages.

Back at the house, Andrew and Steve retired to the back porch, each with a cigar and a tot of brandy. For a couple of minutes they simply sipped their brandy and puffed on their cigars. It was a still night, and the smoke lingered on the veranda insulating them from mosquitoes and sandflies.

"I sensed great anxiety in Susan Spooner's voice," Steve observed.

"She has good reason, wouldn't you say, given the way things are going?" Andrew asked.

"I suppose," Steve replied. "What I can't understand is why people put up with it."

"Partly it's based on an assessment of the odds, which overwhelmingly favor the government. Also, politics in this country are not simply framed in ideological terms but more importantly in racial terms. Indians believe that all blacks support the Kabaka Party, which isn't true, and blacks believe that all Indians support the Opposition. It's been difficult to build a cross-racial coalition. The Workers' Party with its university roots seems to be making inroads."

"Still, it strikes me odd that people would just roll over for a government that has rigged its way to power for what, fifteen years?"

"I don't think you're being charitable to these people, Steve," Andrew said. "Americans don't appreciate what it's like to be in a situation where being in the opposition risks losing everything, including your life. Let's face it, opposition in the US does not carry those risks."

"You're right, Andrew," Steve replied. "I guess I was just venting my own anger based on what I've seen."

"They are angry here, no question," Andrew said. "It's just that they've found an outlet in emigration. Just look at the lines outside of the US and Canadian Embassies. People simply bide their time until they can get a visa out of here, and this complicates mobilization against the government."

They rocked and puffed in silence for a while, then Andrew asked. "How's it going with you and Anita?"

"Actually, I want to ask your advice about that. Do you mind?"

"Not at all," Andrew replied.

"Well, I'd like to ask her father for her hand in marriage."

"I wouldn't do that if I were you," Andrew said.

"Why not?" Steve asked. "It's the honorable thing to do, isn't it?"

"It may be, but it won't work."

"Why not?" Steve asked. He had stopped rocking. His feet were firmly planted on the floor, and he was looking intently at Andrew.

"Her father will tell you 'no,' politely, of course, but firmly. As far as he is concerned, she is pledged to be married to a doctor in Canada, and you are just an interloper."

"You are not very encouraging, are you?" Steve declared.

"Look, I know my uncle. He's given his word. Everyone's been notified. That's it."

"So what the hell do I do?" Steve asked.

"Have you asked her to marry you?"

"No," Steve replied. "I thought you had to ask the father first. Isn't that how the doctor did it?"

"You aren't the doctor!" Andrew laughed. "You are an outsider who wants that man to break his word. What's worse? You are a divorced fella. He's going to throw you out of the house."

"Then what do you suppose I do?" Steve sounded dejected.

"The first thing in siege warfare," Andrew replied, "is to consolidate your own ranks. Make sure Anita's on your side. Ask her."

"*Then* do I approach her father?"

"No, let her do that."

"But that's not honorable," Steve asserted.

"Would you stop with that honorable crap? Go with what will work. She is the only one who can make her father change his mind."

"I don't know," Steve muttered. "I feel uncomfortable, almost cowardly, hiding behind Anita."

"I'm just telling you what I think will work," Andrew said. "My uncle will not let his youngest daughter marry someone she doesn't want to. Of course, it won't be easy. She will say she's changed her mind; he'll get mad and insist she has to go through with it. She'll stand her ground; he'll get madder. There'll be a cold war in that house for a couple of days and then his position will soften. I've seen that happen over and over. She's strong willed and, on matters of her welfare, she usually prevails."

"So, what do I do? Just wait?"

"Yes, when he has relented, he'll want to see you."

"How about the divorce bit?" Steve asked.

"At that point, that would just be a detail, an important one, on which you will have to provide reassurance, but you'd be pretty much across the finish line. That's my view anyway, but, Mr. Erikson, if you want to take the honorable approach …"

"Okay, okay. I can do without the sarcasm."

Sixteen

September 12, 1979
Officers' Club, Camp Ayanganna

At 09:15, Andrew Rambarran entered the Officers' Club through the road entrance, leaving McCurchin to park the jeep. Walking upstairs, he found the dining area empty, but the loud chatter in the kitchen reassured him that breakfast was still possible. He pushed the pile of newspapers along the table to the center, where he sat and rang the bell. The headline on the front page of *The Guardian* read "*Part II of National Security Act Activated.*" He glanced down the first two paragraphs. In preparation for the constitutional referendum, the government had reactivated Part II of the National Security Act, which would give the security forces enhanced powers to maintain order, including arresting anyone whose behavior "*could potentially disrupt the democratic process.*" What a crock! he thought, shaking his head. It was clear that the real violators of democracy were about to use the entire security apparatus to rig another vote and were going to use the National Security Act to incarcerate anyone who got in the way. He was now sure that he was about to receive his marching orders at the 10:00 meeting.

"Bascom," he said to the kitchen attendant, who came out, "can you fix some breakfast for Private McCurchin when he comes by the kitchen? We just got in from Berbice, and he hasn't eaten anything."

"Yes, Captain," Private Bascom replied. "How about you? Would you like your usual?"

"Sure, but let's start with some coffee, please."

Private Bascom left and returned with a tray, which she seated in front of Captain Rambarran. "Private McCurchin is in the kitchen, Captain," she said.

"Good, make sure he gets a good breakfast," he replied, adding "and he's limited to only one chocolate bar on my tab."

Private Bascom chuckled, as she walked away.

Rambarran reached for the kettle on the tray and poured some hot water into a cup, adding instant coffee from the Nescafe jar, followed by milk and sugar. Sipping the coffee, he looked over the comic section of the newspaper, reading through *Andy Capp* and *Beetle Bailey* before setting *The Guardian* aside. He scanned the front page of the *Red Star*, where the constitutional referendum issue was the main focus. The paper reported what had already been publicly pronounced by various Opposition figures that the People's Party and the Workers' Party were going to boycott the referendum, alleging that the fix was already in. The article outlined those new provisions in the Constitution granting what amounted to dictatorial powers to the President, including immunity from prosecution for anything he did in his public or private life. When Private Bascom brought out his breakfast of poached eggs, toast, and cheese, Rambarran set aside the paper to eat.

*   *   *

Headquarters, Internal Operations Command

"Captain Rambarran is on the base," Colonel Taylor said to Captains Spooner and Felix. "I believe he's at the Club. We still have some time before the meeting, so let's go over a few things before he gets here."

"Is Andrew still not on board?" Captain Felix asked.

"He's very sympathetic," Ralph Spooner replied, preempting Colonel Taylor.

"That's not good enough," Felix protested. "We need him involved."

"No, we don't," Spooner said. "Not right away."

"What do you mean 'we don't'?" Felix asked. "We need that eastern flank protected."

"It will be," Spooner asserted. "Andrew will be there with F-Company. He won't act against us; I am sure."

"That's a hell of an assumption to make," Malcolm Felix said, looking at Colonel Taylor, whose raised eyebrows and nodding head seemed to indicate agreement with Spooner.

"I hadn't thought about that angle," Taylor said, "but as I think about it, I'm inclined to agree that Andrew Rambarran will not act against us. The mere presence of F-Company in the east will be a deterrent to any prospective threat. They will assume he's with us."

"Is that fair to him?" Felix asked.

No one responded for a few moments. Finally, Colonel Taylor said, "Don't worry, we still have time; we'll work on him."

"Colonel," Felix said firmly, "I have three Lieutenants I have to convince to come along. They will want to know who else is involved. If Rambarran is involved, they will assume we'll get American backing. If he's not involved, they'll want to know why not, and I can tell you they'll back away."

"Tell them he's with us," Colonel Taylor said. "You too, Ralph. They'll never know the difference. Once we've removed the government, it wouldn't matter too much. I expect the army will unite behind us."

"Colonel," Captain Felix said, "things never work out as smoothly as planned and, if we have to make mid-course corrections, we would need one of the best minds we have as well as one of the best companies in the brigade. What's his objection anyway? Does anybody really know?"

"It boils down to this," Colonel Taylor replied, "he does not trust Captain McGowan. He believes McGowan will sell us out. If I had another Company Commander, I wouldn't use McGowan, but I don't have that luxury."

"What if we keep McGowan on the periphery of the operation?" Felix asked. Both Colonel Taylor and Captain Spooner looked at him with deep interest. "The two critical phases of the operation are isolating Georgetown and taking the President into custody. Ralph Spooner and I can do that. Just let McGowan secure Camp Stevenson and the airport at Timehri."

"That would work," Taylor said. "I'll pitch that to Rambarran at the appropriate time." Both Company Commanders seemed satisfied with the proposal, and Taylor himself felt he was inching closer to getting Captain Rambarran on board. "There's one other thing I wanted to mention," Taylor said. "I met with the leader of the Workers' Party over the weekend. Donald Nelson and I were high school classmates. The meeting was a social one, arranged by a mutual friend, a high school classmate of mine and Nelson's, as a matter of fact."

"Colonel, Nelson is a socialist," Spooner interjected tersely, and with some irritation.

"I know," Taylor responded, "but we will need civilian allies in the aftermath. We met as former classmates. I wanted to get a sense of his estimate of his own political strength. You've seen the crowds at his public meetings. Anyway, Nelson was glad of the contact to plead that the army not assist the Kabaka Party from closing off the electoral process. That was the extent of it."

"I just don't like this, Colonel," Spooner said. "I'm being frank."

"I appreciate that," Taylor replied. "I told him that I was there to listen. My only concern was the army, and the army did not have a monolithic position."

"Will you be seeing him again?" Spooner asked.

"He expressed the hope that we meet again," Taylor replied. "I'd like to do that, with your permission. Nelson and his Workers' Party are more popular in Georgetown than the President. That could be very useful in maintaining order after we remove this government."

"I'd like to think about this," Spooner said.

There was a knock on the door, and the battalion Executive Officer popped his head in. "Colonel, Captain Rambarran is here."

"Good," Taylor said. "Show him in and let's start the meeting."

Captain Rambarran entered with the Exec, saluted, and took a seat, then Colonel Taylor began his briefing.

Taylor pointed out that even with expanded powers for all of the security forces, only the police could make arrests. Army units were expected to conduct search-and-seizure operations in their areas of deployment. However, if the referendum were boycotted by the supporters of the People's Party and the Workers' Party, and if their supporters did not obstruct the transportation of referendum ballots, there was no need for the employment of coercive measures. Company Commanders were expected to conduct saturated patrolling before referendum day and after. Company Commanders should designate one three-ton truck to transport ballots. Captain Rambarran was responsible for all of Berbice up to the Mahaicony River, Captain Felix West Demerara and the Canal Polders, and Captain Spooner for Georgetown and the East Coast. Captain Spooner would have the assistance of the "clerks and jerks" of Headquarters Company. The ballots from the interior and Essequibo would be flown in, but Essequibo will be patrolled by a draw-down of troops from the border locations.

There being no questions, Colonel Taylor continued. Responsibility for the New Amsterdam-Rosignol ferry was Rambarran's; the Georgetown-Vreed-en-Hoop ferry was Felix's responsibility. Captain

Spooner was to secure the Ogle airport, to which ballots would be flown in. He was also responsible for putting up roadblocks at the junction of Sheriff Street and the East-Coast road, by Rahaman's Soda Factory on the southern edge of the city, and to maintain two roving patrols in clockwise, counter-clockwise directions around the perimeter of the city. He was also expected to do intermittent checks at the two radio stations and at Telecoms. Captain McGowan would be operating out of Camp Stevenson at Timehri and would be responsible for the international airport and the Army Air Wing. He would be setting up roadblocks at the Soesdyke junction and up the Linden Highway, just in case supporters of the Workers' Party in Linden decide to come out to protest. Any further instructions would be given by Colonel Taylor himself during his weekly inspections. If there were no disturbances following the referendum, troop rotations to the interior would follow shortly, starting in mid-October, with coastal redeployments in mid-January.

As Captain Rambarran listened, he realized that Colonel Taylor planned to use the referendum to conduct a dry run for the coup. "Why not finish the job?" he wondered. A coup at the moment of a rigged referendum would receive popular support. Oh, but would the soldiers prove reliable? A trial run would show up any glitches and, once the soldiers had become habituated to these tasks, they would perform them on the second go-around, without question. A clever man, Colonel Taylor.

SEVENTEEN

October 6, 1979
Embassy of the United States, Georgetown

Ambassador Hales took his place at the head of the conference table and glanced quickly around as if taking a silent roll of the attendees. "I've read the individual reports you've submitted," Hales began, "but I thought we should get together for a reassessment of the situation facing us here. Whether the referendum was rigged or not, and there is considerable evidence that it was, the reality is that we have a leader with considerably strengthened constitutional powers, and his party is unmovable. The question then is this: Does any of this pose a threat to US interests?"

"I'd be inclined to say not," the Political Officer said, "no more than it did before the referendum anyway." He explained that the basic facts had not changed. The economy was in tatters, the socialist rhetoric notwithstanding, and the country was vulnerable to pressure from Brazil and Venezuela. The President had merely codified powers he was exercising anyway. Cooperative socialism was a failure. Who would want to imitate a country which had become destitute by nationalizations and socialist bombast? The President was an opportunist whose only concern was to maintain himself in power.

"So all this socialist rhetoric, the rituals, the nationalizations, their foreign policy—all of these are just a part of a game played by an opportunist to stay in power?" Ambassador Hales asked.

Station Chief Hitchcock chuckled loudly.

"Not exactly," the Political Officer replied. "Politics in this country was shaped by the struggle for independence which employed anti-imperialist, anti-Western rhetoric. The form of socialism the President represents is a mere form of nationalism."

"Are you saying that the roots of Marxism-Leninism are shallow here?" Hales asked.

"Not really," the Political Officer replied.

"You don't appear to be confident about this," Hales said. "What's the problem?"

"To be frank," the Political Officer said, "I am concerned by the number of Marxist ideologues who have left the Opposition Party to join the ruling Kabaka Party, authenticating its credentials as a socialist party."

"Let me sum up," Ambassador Hales said. "We have an authentic Marxist party in power here and likely to remain there indefinitely, but it lacks the economic or other resources to extend itself and thus poses no threat to us." Ambassador Hales looked at the Political Officer with raised eyebrows.

"Ambassador, this country has become dirt poor," the Political Officer replied. "I don't see how it could threaten us. And I have to say candidly that any exaggeration of the threat from poor countries such as this invites intervention which only adds to their misery and tarnishes our image."

Station Chief Hitchcock cleared his throat loudly, attracting the Ambassador's attention. "I think," he began, "that our Political Officer is missing the nature of American interests, certainly as it has been broadly conceived since the late 1940s, and that's to prevent the spread of communism. What we are hearing is that this country is moving inexorably into the communist camp while the Comrade Leader presents himself to us as more moderate than the Opposition Leader. He is playing us for suckers, if you ask me."

With his elbows on the table and his hands supporting his chin and his eyes peering over his glasses, Ambassador Hales listened silently. Station Chief Hitchcock leaned back in the chair, which was pushed back from the table to accommodate his distended belly. He crinkled his upper lip a couple of times before resuming. "From an American point of view, I'd say the situation is actually getting worse."

"How so?" Ambassador Hales asked.

"Well," said Hitchcock, "let's look at the labor situation, shall we?" Hitchcock then proceeded to describe the implications of changes in the Public Service Union leadership. He noted that during the early 1960s, the Kabaka Party's two sources of power were its virtual control over the black vote in the country and its control over the Public Service Union, which gave it the ability to make the cities, especially Georgetown, ungovernable. After it gained control of the government, the Party added the predominantly black security forces to its power base. These and rigged elections allowed it to hold on to power for a decade and a half. However, a couple of the tectonic plates had begun to shift under the Comrade Leader.

The ouster of the leadership of the Public Service Union by a more progressive group linked to the University crowd and Donald Nelson, in particular, meant that for the first time in the Comrade Leader's political career, the Public Service Union would no longer do his bidding. Instead, the Comrade Leader has lost the union to his arch-nemesis, Donald Nelson. The massive retrenchment of public service employees produced that result, but it also had other effects. More urban blacks were attending the political rallies of the Workers' Party. Also, loyalties in the military might be shifting because many of the black army officers were from the urban middle class and their parents or relatives had been affected by the retrenchment.

The silence accompanying each pause Hitchcock made was the clearest indication of the interest he had generated in the analysis he was providing. Erikson noticed that Ambassador Hales' eyes never left Hitchcock. Hitchcock crinkled his upper lip before he spoke again. The Trades Union Council, the umbrella organization for labor unions in the country, had traditionally been controlled by the sugar union, which was the largest in the country. After the nationalization of the sugar industry and the Opposition take-over of the sugar union, the TUC executive created a weighted system of voting to prevent a single union from taking control. Food shortages and problems of pay in both the bauxite and sugar industries had brought both of those unions together. Add the Public Service Union into that coalition and you had a situation where the direction of the country would be dictated by this coalition. Strikes in the sugar and bauxite industry would lead to economic paralysis. If the Public Service Union joined them, the country could become ungovernable without a heavy application of force, and in those circumstances, the security forces might prove unreliable, at least from the Comrade Leader's point of view.

Hitchcock acknowledged that the Comrade Leader was no fool; so, what was he likely to do? What he had always done in tight spots: engage the Opposition leader in talks about a coalition government.

This time, it might happen. If it did, the government would be more firmly in the communist camp. Even if a coalition did not eventuate, pressures from the Opposition Party and the progressive unions would propel the Kabaka Party in a more orthodox socialist direction. Either way, the United States would lose.

"What do you recommend we do?" Ambassador Hales asked.

"Well," replied Hitchcock, "we sure as heck shouldn't be passively looking on. I say we throw a monkey wrench into the whole business."

"Can you be more specific?" Ambassador Hales asked.

"Not at this time," Hitchcock replied, "but I do think we should work on several fronts. We still have leverage with some union leaders dating back from the 1960s. Perhaps you can put some pressure on this government by making some statements critical of the conduct of the referendum."

"I plan to," Ambassador Hales said. "As you know, the Chinese have the largest embassy here and, like us, both Brazil and Venezuela are concerned about the Cuban presence here."

"Perhaps we can get some more detailed information about the military and about Cuban or Chinese advisers," Hitchcock said, looking over his glasses directly at Steve Erikson.

"Captain?" Ambassador Hales turned to Erikson. However, while Erikson repositioned himself in his chair in preparation to respond, Hales spoke again. "Whatever happened to all of the talk about a coup?" he asked. "Was that just talk or has some type of planning been underway?"

"Ambassador," Erikson replied, "some of it was just anger over the appointment of a policeman as Chief of Staff. On the other hand, Colonel Franchette Taylor explored the possibilities with several Company Commanders. My impression is that he has given up on the idea."

"Based on what factors?" Ambassador Hales asked.

"Ambassador, what they have here is a brigade-sized unit with six infantry companies, an engineer squadron, and support units. The companies are organized into two battalions. The Border Operations Command has three of those companies which are deployed at various border locations on three-month tours of duty. The Internal Operations

Command has the other three companies, which are deployed along the coast to guard against internal subversion. Colonel Taylor is in command of Internal Ops, and the problem he has is that the rotations put sympathetic Company Commanders at border locations when he would need them internally."

"Are you telling me that a mere scheduling problem has derailed an enterprise of such import?" Ambassador Hales asked.

"Not entirely," Erikson replied. "Colonel Taylor does not have the commitment of enough Company Commanders."

"I see." Ambassador Hales' curtness hinted of irritation, though Erikson was not sure whether it was with the general state of affairs or with him. "I'd like to follow up with you on this in a day or so. At that time, I would like a more detailed profile of those six Company Commanders."

"Yes, Ambassador," Erikson replied. "I'll make an appointment with your secretary."

"One other thing," Ambassador Hales said. "I understand that my predecessor met at least once a year with American-educated officers, except for last year when we did not have an ambassador in residence."

"That was what Colonel Stanford told me as well, Ambassador," Erikson said. "However, we only have one such officer. Captain Rambarran."

"I would like to meet him," Hales said. "Please set it up."

"Yes, Ambassador," Erikson said, before glancing over at the Station Chief.

"Is there a problem, Captain?" Ambassador Hales asked.

"Well, Ambassador, I understand that there's been a virtual ban on interactions between army officers and American diplomatic personnel. I wonder whether such a meeting might not compromise Captain Rambarran too much."

"Look, Steve," Ambassador Hales said, "Captain Rambarran is a West Point-educated officer. We know it; they know it. Nothing we do will change that fact. We educated him, and we are entitled to a courtesy visit. Besides, I'd like them to know we do have an interest in him and in how they treat him. I should think that's a form of protection for him right there."

"Sorry, Ambassador," Erikson said. "I hadn't quite thought through that one."

"Let's not play the game of this government," Hales said. "Their officers meet with the Cubans all the time. Let's get in on this when we can. I plan to invite army officers, Colonels and above, to Embassy functions."

The meeting ended and everyone filed past Ambassador Hales in silence. It was clear to Erikson and to everyone else, he was sure, that Ambassador Hales intended to assume a more aggressive posture in his dealing with the government. On his way out, Erikson stopped at the secretary's desk to set up the appointment with the Ambassador. However, on returning to his office to retrieve his coffee cup, he found the Station Chief seated in the guest chair.

"What are you doing here?" the Chief asked as Erikson walked around the desk to his chair.

"I should ask you that, Chief," Erikson replied. "After all, you are in my office."

"Don't get smart with me," Hitchcock said. "You know exactly what I am talking about."

"No, I don't, Chief," Erikson replied. "Now, either you get to the point or leave."

"Okay, what are you doing in this country, Captain? You deliberately withheld information from Ambassador Hales. I'd like to know why."

"What the hell are you talking about?" Erikson asked.

"Hales asked you for an update on the coup planning, and what did you say? It's all but fizzled out."

"That's my assessment," Erikson replied.

"You withheld an important piece of information," Hitchcock said.

"Namely?"

"Namely that the only holdout is your pal, Captain Rambarran," Hitchcock replied.

"Andrew Rambarran's reluctance is based on a better assessment of the reliability of his fellow Company Commanders than you or I can offer."

"And I think your loyalties are misplaced, Captain," Hitchcock said.

"I don't know what you are talking about," Erikson said, "nor do I care to know. So, why don't you get the fuck out of here before I throw you out."

"We are trying to prevent the consolidation of communist regime in this country," Hitchcock said, standing up, "and you are in the way!"

"What the hell do you want from me, Hitchcock?" Erikson asked.

"I want you to nudge Captain Rambarran to join the coup effort."

"And why should I do that? My job is to monitor, not engage in coup promotion."

"Look, I know Captain Rambarran," Hitchcock replied. "He no more wants a communist regime here than you or me. I can understand that he's made other plans, given what's been going on. But if you give him a hint that we're more than a little interested this time ..."

Erikson stared up at the Station Chief. "You want us to use him?"

"There you go again," Hitchcock said. "We share the same philosophical positions, he and us. How is acting in concert using him? It's his country, for Christ's sake!"

"And what happens if a coup attempt fails?" Erikson asked.

"Give him every assurance we'll get him out."

EIGHTEEN

October 20, 1979
Officers' Club, Timehri

"This is quite a hideaway you have here," Steve Erikson remarked, taking a seat across from Andrew Rambarran at the center booth on the western side of the lounge.

"It is," Rambarran acknowledged, glancing around at its sheer emptiness. "As they say, so far from Georgetown, so close to nirvana! By mid-afternoon, this place would be full of senior officers with their *sweet women*."

"No kidding? And they get away with it?"

"Of course. At Timehri, no one talks. Well, that's not quite true. No one reports back to the wives, I should say. At Camp Ayanganna, the wives are nearby. Now, there have been some raucous confrontations, one involving the last Chief of Staff and his wife. But the practice goes on. It's part of the subculture."

"Really?"

"Oh, yes," Rambarran replied. "Every top official in government, and even some not so top, feels it's his privilege to have a woman on the side."

"Well, you'll just have to settle for my company for the moment," Erikson said, laughing.

"That's fine," Rambarran said. "I gather from your call you had something to ask or to transmit. I wasn't quite sure which."

"Both, actually," Erikson replied.

"Well, before we get started, let me at least show you some hospitality. I ordered some sandwiches and coffee, a sort of late breakfast that counted on your punctuality."

"Did I come through?"

"You most certainly did," Rambarran replied.

"Say, it's awfully quiet in here," Erikson observed.

"It's Sunday," Rambarran replied. "The lounge doesn't officially open until noon. I asked Private Jones, the bar attendant, to open for me. It's not an uncommon request when officers have guests. There's an 11:00 hours Carib Air flight every Sunday, and people, en route to and from the airport, do stop by."

Private Jones and another attendant came in with trays and placed them on the table. One had a jar of instant coffee, milk and sugar containers, and an open thermos with hot water. The other tray had plates and silverware, and two cheese and two egg sandwiches. Rambarran poured hot water into the cups and invited his friend to help himself.

"I want to thank you for your advice about approaching Anita's father," Erikson said. "It worked out rather well."

"I'm glad," Rambarran said. "And I'm happy for both of you."

"Is it safe to talk here?" Erikson asked, fixing himself a cup of instant coffee.

"Sure," Rambarran replied, "at least for the next hour or so. This place gets hopping closer to lunch time. But, if you prefer, we could go and sit under the *benab* outside."

"This is fine," Erikson said. "We could always move if we had to."

Andrew sipped from his cup and glanced over at his friend, who seemed preoccupied with stirring his cup. Looking up slowly, Erikson asked, "How goes the revolution?"

"It's on, I'm pretty sure," Rambarran replied, matter-of-factly.

"Our side would look favorably on a change of government here," Erikson said. "I know the reservations you have *but*, if you think the chances of success would be improved by joining the effort, significant people on our side would be very pleased." Steve Erikson took a sip of coffee. "Odd," he said, "how quickly I've adjusted to instant coffee. This Brazilian blend is especially flavorful."

Andrew Rambarran leaned forward looking directly at his friend, seemingly weighing what was said. "And what role, if any, would your side play?"

"We would monitor the operation and provide advice. Afterwards, we would recognize the new government and provide more aid than the Kabaka government had ever seen."

"What happens if the effort does not succeed, Steve?"

"Before I answer that, Andrew, please know that I am here to represent our interests, but I'm here also as your friend. In my first role,

163

I have to admit that our side would benefit even if a coup attempt fails. The mere effort would shake up the Kabaka government and make it moderate its position. At least, that's the calculation of some on our side. As your friend, I want to assure you that we would do whatever it took to get you out if things went sour."

"How about others associated with me?"

"To tell the truth," Erikson replied, "the discussions I've had on this matter centered only on you, but I'd go out on a limb here and say that the assurance would also cover those closely associated with you." Erikson took a bite on the cheese sandwich. "This is pretty good; a bit hot though."

"I should have warned you," Rambarran said, "they tend to grind in some *wiri-wiri* peppers in the cheese sandwiches."

"Some what?"

"*Wiri-wiri* peppers," Rambarran replied, smiling. "They're small round peppers that are very flavorful but also very hot."

Erikson nodded as he chewed. "You can say that again. Fortunately, I'm getting accustomed to hot peppers. Dinners at your uncle's house, you see. I'm actually beginning to enjoy hot dishes."

"In that case, I should share with you a local saying: 'What's sweet in a goat's mouth is bitter in its behind.'"

Steve Erikson laughed out loud. "I've discovered that." He took another bite of the sandwich. "Did I tell you I am resigning my commission in August?"

"That's when my contract ends as well," Andrew said.

"I know," Steve said. "Maybe we'll end up in graduate school together. I hear the University of Florida has a very good business school. That's where you're heading, isn't it?"

Andrew nodded and swallowed. "It'll be like old times."

"One other thing," Steve said. "We'd like advance notice of the date of the coup. That way we can bring in a team from the National Security Agency to help monitor the transmissions during the operation and offer timely advice."

"Is there more?" Andrew asked, taking another bite of his egg sandwich.

"No," Steve replied, "unless there are things you need."

"I'd like that offer kept open, but for the time being I'll entrust the safety of my uncle and cousin to you. They are the only close relatives I have in the city. My other concern would be the Spooners."

Steve nodded. "The first would be easier to handle than the second simply because of location. But we'll do everything we can."

"Would you have ever imagined we'd be having a conversation like this?" Andrew asked. "Seems like only yesterday we were pounding racquetballs after classes."

"But then we were mere boys in a sheltered environment. Now, it seems, we have to assume greater responsibilities in an increasingly menacing world."

"Sounds dire." Andrew laid the rest of the uneaten sandwich on the plate.

"Isn't it though?" Steve Erikson touched his mouth with a napkin and set it down. Rising, he extended his hand to Andrew. "You know how to reach me." They clasped hands. "Godspeed," Steve said, and Andrew nodded.

*   *   *

Andrew Rambarran sat under the *benab* outside of the Officers' Club mulling over the brief visit he had had from his friend. He had known that in the end he would side with Colonel Taylor and Ralph Spooner if they persisted in the quest. And they did. Odd though how Erikson had read his inclination and how easily they had reached an understanding. He couldn't recollect being asked directly by Erikson whether he would join the coup plotters; yet, when he and Steve parted company, each left with an understanding that a coup was in the making and that he was a part of it. He had no doubt that Colonel Taylor and Ralph Spooner were right that those who could, should try to end the tyranny the Kabaka Party had imposed. The confluence of interests with the Americans and their promise of aid to better the lives of people made the enterprise worthwhile. Still, he had reached a crossroad, and life for him was about to be changed forever. It was at once exhilarating and intensely intimidating.

The sounds of footsteps crunching the gravel on the diagonal driveway from the East-bank road to the Club made Andrew turn around to see Ralph Spooner change direction and traverse the wooded area in which the *benab* was located.

"What are you doing up here, squaddie?" Spooner asked.

"I had promised my friend, Steve Erikson, to show him the Club. He just left, as a matter of fact."

"My parents said he's a very nice fella. How come I haven't met him?"

"Well, you know how the spies are around here," Rambarran replied. "It's one thing for me to associate with the American officers. But if they see you doing it, they'll suspect something must be going on."

"Good thinking," Spooner said, taking a seat directly across from Andrew.

"And what are you doing up here?" Rambarran asked.

"Colonel Taylor and Colonel LaFleur are coming up with their wives. Taylor plans to slip out briefly so he and I can speak to Captain McGowan. As you know, McGowan is the Duty Officer at Camp Stevenson this weekend."

"You are rather open about this, Ralph," Rambarran observed.

"Only with you, Andrew. We're still hoping that you will join us. In fact, Colonel Taylor asked me to talk with you again." Ralph Spooner looked around as if checking to make sure there was no one nearby. "You know, you were the first person to ever talk with me about getting rid of this crowd of crooks. You and Alan Moore."

"Well, they pushed Alan out," Rambarran remarked.

"I know," Ralph Spooner replied, "but the conditions have worsened since, and the case for removing these people is far more compelling now."

Rambarran leaned forward, elbows resting on his thighs and the back of his hands supporting his chin. Ralph Spooner mirrored his companion's posture and, in a lowered but resolute voice, said, "Andrew, I'd like to tell the others you're with us. Please."

Andrew Rambarran nodded. They held each other's eyes for a few somber moments, and then Ralph Spooner rose. Colonel Taylor's car had just turned onto the gravel driveway.

NINETEEN

February 20, 1980
HQ, Internal Operations Command
Camp Ayanganna, Georgetown

Noting with a smirk that his Executive Officer was away on a Commission of Inquiry, Colonel Taylor began the briefing with his Company Commanders by reading from his notes. "As you all know," he began, "February 23rd this year falls on Saturday, and the official holiday for Republic Day is on Monday, the 25th. That's when the float parade will take place and that's when the President will be hosting a reception for the diplomatic community and top government and party officials. Light Colonels and up have been invited. However, the official Republic Day parade involving the Army, National Service, and Police would take place on Saturday, February 23rd. March off would be at 08:00 hours. The army units participating will be Captain Spooner's A-Company and the Headquarters Company from Camp Ayanganna, and, from Camp Stevenson, the WAC Company, Engineer Squadron, and a contingent from Agriculture Corps. All army personnel participating in the parade will re-deposit their weapons at the armories at Camp Ayanganna or Camp Stevenson, except for A-Company, which will be on security duty at Camp Ayanganna for the weekend. After the parade, Captain Spooner will assume duties as Duty Officer at Camp Ayanganna, and Lieutenant Beharry will be his Orderly Officer. Beharry's platoon will be the Standby Platoon for the weekend. At Camp Stevenson, Captain McGowan will be the Duty Officer and his C-Company will be responsible for security there.

"Officially, Captain Rambarran's F-Company will be on security duty in Berbice, and Captain Malcolm Felix's B-Company in West Demerara. However, the Chief of Staff and the Force Commander have agreed that B-Company should mass at Vreed-en-Hoop for the security of Georgetown. That's lucky for us.

"One platoon of B-Company will cross with the ferry on its final run to Georgetown. Once the passengers and vehicles have disembarked, the Captain and crew are to be detained. Since the ferry station normally closes at 21:30, no one outside of the ferry station would have reason to suspect anything. At 22:00, the ferry will return to Vreed-en-Hoop to transport the rest of the B-Company to Georgetown."

Colonel Taylor paused and looked up. "We agreed that our operation would begin at 23:00 on Saturday, February 23rd. In reality, it would begin when Captain Felix and B-Company reach Georgetown. Lieutenant Ian Morgan will take and secure the Maritime Base at South Ruimveldt and also hold the Vreed-en-Hoop ferry. Lieutenant Anil Rampersaud and Captain Felix will position themselves, as arranged, to help me arrest the President. Lieutenant Leonard McKenzie will take and hold the Police Headquarters at Brickdam. Task completions from those locations should be reported in by phone. That accounts for B-Company."

Colonel Taylor then reviewed the assignments of Captain Spooner's A-Company. Lieutenant Ramesh Beharry would secure Camp Ayanganna which meant disarming the MPs and placing them in the cell at the Guard House. All senior officers resident on the base would be placed on house detention and telephone wires to their houses severed.

Lieutenant Duncan Clark would be responsible for the detention of the Police Commissioner and senior police officers resident at Eve Leary. They will be transported to Camp Ayanganna. Senior government ministers and the leader of the Opposition People's Party would be arrested and brought to Camp Ayanganna. Lieutenant Alex Mitchell would secure the Ogle Airport and Telecoms on Hadfield Street. From this HQ, Internal Ops, Captain Spooner would oversee the operations of his company.

Captain Rambarran's F-Company would be responsible for demobilizing the entire police establishment in Berbice. Lieutenant Asad Shah would take Central Police Station, New Amsterdam and Captain Rambarran would use the Communication Center at Central Police Station as his command post. Lieutenant Shah would take control of the New Amsterdam-Rosignol ferry, the *MV Kurtuka*.

Lieutenant Michael DeFreitas would take the Springlands Police Station. Because F-Company would control communications at both ends of Berbice, the police stations in between would really be unaware of what was happening. Lieutenant Ron Peters would take the police station at Adventure. All members of the Police Tactical Service Unit should be incarcerated. In all cases, the police should be told this would be a temporary detention until the army completed its objectives.

"Captain Spooner and I went over with Captain McGowan his company's assignments," Colonel Taylor continued. "His C-Company will take and secure Camp Stevenson and The Air Wing simultaneously. They will then sweep the area, disarming the guards at the Motor Transport and the various sites outside of the base compound, including the ammunition dump at Timehri. All military personnel residing outside the base compound, especially any officers still in their quarters, would be rounded up and transported to the enclosed base at Camp Stevenson. There is another ammo dump at Camp Groomes on the Linden Highway, where the heavy weapons company is stationed. Since the entire company would be away for the weekend, that camp will be lightly guarded. It will be taken and the armory and ammo dump secured. All of this would be the responsibility of Captain McGowan, as well as securing access to the Timehri International Airport after it terminates its operations at 22:00."

"No roadblocks anywhere?" Captain Rambarran asked.

"No," Colonel Taylor replied. "We don't have the troops to carry out the necessary tasks and man roadblocks. Once we've taken over, we'll switch to a defensive mode."

"If that's the case, Captain McGowan's company is not as heavily tasked in the initial stage," Rambarran said. "As you've noted, the Timehri International Airport is closed from 22:00 hours. One squad to control access afterwards; one squad to hold Air Wing; one platoon to take Camp Stevenson."

"Don't forget the Officers' Quarters and the WAC compound," Colonel Taylor interjected.

"But they'll be unarmed," Rambarran pointed out. "The weapons would be at the armory. In any case, they won't find out what's happening until morning, and most would be away for the holiday."

"What's your real concern?" Colonel Taylor asked.

"I am concerned that you will be operating in Georgetown without really isolating the city. There'll be an open access from the east and from the south, and we won't have early warning of any development."

"Such as?"

"I don't know, Colonel," Rambarran replied. "That's why we plan for contingencies."

"We have limited troops," Colonel Taylor said, "we have to sequence the tasks. The risks you imagine are remote. Captain McGowan's in the south and there's nothing in between Timehri and Georgetown to threaten us."

"Admittedly, there'll be less of a risk from the east because Lieutenant Mitchell can monitor the East-Coast road, but the south side of Georgetown is a gaping hole. There's a police station at Providence, just seven miles out. We have army officers who don't live on post. What if they commanded a small police contingent. At the very least that could complicate things."

"Come on," Colonel Taylor said, "that's so far fetched. We have to take some calculated risks. I think those you identify are not significant, not in the first phase anyway." Colonel Taylor looked from left to right and back left. "Any other concerns?"

"Why fly the President out?" Rambarran asked. "Why not detain him while we consolidate our hold over the government?"

"Flying him out was the majority view," Colonel Taylor replied, adding "taken before you came on board."

"Then, why not fly him out of Ogle?" Rambarran asked. "It's just a few miles outside of Georgetown; it would be faster."

"We have no guarantee there'll be a plane there," Colonel Taylor replied. "The main hanger is at Timehri. As you know, only late flights overnight at Ogle. Besides, we have to deal with Captain McGowan in good faith. We can't make him feel we're trying to marginalize him."

An awkward silence followed. Colonel Taylor leaned back in his chair and looked at each of the three Company Commanders, then sat forward again. "Look, I can tell you all agree with Andrew about setting up roadblocks at various points and I know that was part of the original plan, but here is the problem. Several of the tasks which I have assigned to platoons can actually be carried out by individual squads. But the squads are commanded by Lance Corporals. What happens if one of them is confronted by a higher rank, army or police? Will he hold his ground? A Lieutenant with a platoon is less likely to be bullied. Once we've completed the initial tasks and are in charge, the soldiers will follow us to the stars, *but* in the initial stages, I want them carrying out the orders of their own officers, just as they've been trained to do. Everything will be fine, I assure you."

"Colonel, please," Rambarran asked, "just one roadblock on the south-side, by Rahaman Soda Factory."

"Oh, stop it, Andrew," Colonel Taylor responded sharply. "You're spooking the rest of us."

"Sorry, Colonel," Rambarran said quietly.

"Okay, I'll tell you what I'll do," Colonel Taylor said. "I'm going to ask Captain McGowan to arrange a patrol between Soesdyke and south Georgetown."

TWENTY

February 23, 1980
Georgetown, Guyana

At 21:15 hours, Station Chief Hitchcock left the listening post which the team from the National Security Agency had set up on Middle Street. There had been no transmissions on the frequency stipulated for use by the coup units. The NSA technicians, using the large living room of the safe house as the communications center, had probed other frequencies and intercepted routine end-of-day situation reports from interior locations to Camp Ayanganna. It was going to be a long evening. Colonel Stanford and Captain Erikson, for whom the ball game would not really begin until about 22:00, sat at the dining table playing gin rummy. Excusing himself, Hitchcock told Stanford and Erikson that he'd let them monitor the play-by-play execution of the coup, the outcome of which seemed certain to him. He was going to get himself a drink.

Hitchcock drove his Toyota Celica west on Middle Street and turned right onto Main, past the Embassy and skirting the western edge of the Kingston section of the city into the parking lot in front of the Pegasus Hotel. Locking the vehicle as he left, he walked into the hotel, veering right into the lounge and taking a seat at a table in the center rear from which he had a wide field of view, including of the lounge entrance, the bar, and the dart board against the front wall, between the bar and the lounge entrance. The waiter came over and took his order, then stopped at two tables closer to the bar, from which billows of cigar smoke arose to blanket the lounge. The occupants at those tables spoke Spanish and appeared to be Cuban trawler men. They seemed to show up everywhere in Georgetown, and their brashness was a constant source of irritation to Hitchcock. From the way the waiter looked back over, Hitchcock gathered that the Cubans had made some type of crude remark about him.

A mixed couple walked up to the dart board. When she turned

around, Hitchcock recognized the buxom black woman as a regular at the lounge. The European with her Hitchcock had not seen before, and he wondered whether the European's enthusiasm was for the dart game or the prospect of sampling a bit of the local fare. The waiter brought Hitchcock his rum-and-Coke, which he nursed disinterestedly as he followed the progression of the dart game and the flirtations of two people from different worlds, who, until minutes ago, had no idea the other existed and would probably part on the same terms. He cast occasional glances at the Cubans too, internally amused that, after tomorrow, theirs would be a rare presence in Georgetown.

At about 21:40, one of the Cubans walking out to the lounge entrance bumped Hitchcock's table. He apologized, but Hitchcock thought it was a deliberate act. Fearing repetitions from inebriated Cubans, whose loud voices and repetitively raucous laughter permeated the lounge, Hitchcock abandoned his unfinished second drink and headed out to his car. He took the Seawall Road, lowering his window to imbibe the refreshing salt air. As he approached the bandstand at the head of Camp Street, an army officer and a soldier with a sub-machine gun flagged him down.

"What's the problem, Officer?" Hitchcock asked, observing the two pips on the officer's shoulders.

"You need to come with us," the Lieutenant said.

"I'm sorry, but I am a member of the U.S. diplomatic staff here."

"Please follow our instructions," the Lieutenant insisted, signaling with a tilt of his head for the soldier to get into Hitchcock's car.

"Look, I don't think you fully understand—"

"Please," the officer insisted.

The soldier opened the passenger door, tilted the front seat forward and took a seat behind Hitchcock. The Lieutenant took the passenger seat in front.

"Now, take Camp Street," the Lieutenant said. "I'll tell you where to turn."

As he drove off, Hitchcock saw a jeep on the side of the road with soldiers in it, pulling up behind him.

"Where are we going?" Hitchcock asked.

"I'll tell you where to turn. Don't worry, we won't harm you."

"Well, what's the point of all of this?"

"I have no idea myself," the officer replied, "but please no more questions."

Within about fifteen minutes, they were on the outskirts of Georgetown passing by Rahaman's Soda Factory on the East-bank road to Timehri. The Lieutenant refused to be drawn into conversation in spite of numerous attempts by Hitchcock in the twenty-five minute drive to Timehri. Here, the officer directed Hitchcock to turn onto the gravel driveway to the Officers' Club and to park in the open sandy clearing at the southern edge of the building, just past the main stairway. The jeep also came in and parked beside them.

The Lieutenant escorted Hitchcock up the main stairs, leaving the soldiers with the vehicles. The door opened into the dining area, unoccupied and dark. The Lieutenant guided Hitchcock to the left into the huge lounge, where the music from behind the bar gave the impression that the celebration of Republic Day was still in swing, except that the sole reveler sat on a stool at the bar and glanced up from his bottle of Pepsi with a somber face.

"Make yourself comfortable," the seated officer, with three pips on each epaulette, said. "You are going to be here until morning."

"You don't seem to realize what you're doing," Hitchcock protested. "I am a member of the U.S. Embassy staff. I demand to speak to my ambassador."

"I am Captain McGowan," the officer said, "A. C. McGowan. Please make yourself comfortable. We may need to have you call your embassy, only not quite yet. Now, we can offer you something to drink, if you like."

"I protest this detention, Captain," Hitchcock said. "I would like to call my ambassador."

Captain McGowan ignored him, walking over and whispering some instructions to the Lieutenant. The Lieutenant left and, moments later, two soldiers stepped into the lounge with sub-machine guns, standing guard at the front and rear entrances to the lounge. McGowan picked up a set of darts at the bar and tossed them at the dartboard against the back wall, stepping over occasionally to take a sip of Coke.

Hitchcock finally seated himself on the sofa near the center of the lounge, facing the bar. He leafed through the newspapers on the coffee table in front, got up and paced for a while, then sat down again. Except for the Captain's admonition that he would be there for the evening, he felt no sense of real threat, only the anxiety of waiting out the night. "Captain, may I speak to you in private?" Hitchcock finally asked.

"Sure," Captain McGowan replied, walking over to the screened windows at the side of the lounge facing the East-bank road and looking in the direction of the parked vehicles and the soldiers below. "We can use the game room." He led Hitchcock through a door at the rear of the lounge into a room with a ping pong table and several card tables. He then invited Hitchcock to sit across from him at one of the card tables.

*   *   *

Headquarters, Internal Operations Command

At 22:55, the phone rang. Colonel Taylor nodded to Captain Spooner, who picked up. "Duty Officer, Captain Spooner," he answered.

"Captain Felix reporting. All objectives secured. Escort platoon in place. I am moving to that location. Estimated time of arrival 23:05."

Ralph Spooner repeated each portion of Captain Felix's report to Colonel Taylor before responding to Captain Felix. "Thank you, Malcolm. *Operation New Leaf* is underway. Good luck."

At 23:10, the phone rang again. This time, it was Captain Rambarran. "All objectives secured, Ralph. Good luck at your end. It's likely to be much trickier there."

"Thank you, Andrew," Spooner replied.

Colonel Taylor stood up. "Okay, Ralph, make the call. Bypass the Presidential Guard House; use the President's direct line."

Captain Spooner dialed the number to the President's residence. He counted five rings before the phone was picked up and the President in a deep throaty voice answered, "Yes?"

"Comrade President, this is the Duty Officer at Camp Ayanganna. Sorry to wake you up; but the Chief of Staff instructed me to notify you that there is a fire at Party headquarters on Camp Street."

"What's your name?"

"Captain Spooner, Comrade President. I'm the Duty Officer at Camp Ayanganna."

"What time is it, Spooner?"

"23:15, Comrade President."

"Have you all notified the Fire Brigade?"

"Yes, Comrade President. They are already at the scene. We've also notified the Party Chairman, the General Secretary, the Vice President, the Interior Minister. The Police Commissioner and the Chief of Staff are on the scene. They believe it was arson."

"You're calling from Ayanganna?"

"Yes, Comrade President."

"Do you know if the fire has been contained?"

"They're battling it right now, but they're also trying to save the buildings around it."

"I see."

"Comrade President, the Chief of Staff thought that if you are planning to go to the scene, we should reinforce your escort. We have two jeeps loaded up on standby."

"Very well, Spooner. Have the additional escort outside the Residence as soon as possible."

"Yes, Comrade President. They should be there in about ten minutes."

"Are you going to be with them, Spooner?"

"No, Comrade President. We're on alert; I need to remain at this post. I was planning to send one of my lieutenants."

"Huh," the President grunted, evidently mulling over the information.

"If you prefer, Comrade President," Spooner said, trying to sound reassuring, "Colonel Taylor has stopped by the base. He's heading over to Camp Street. I could ask him to take over the escort detail."

"Why don't you do that, Spooner?"

"Yes, Comrade President."

Re-cradling the phone, Spooner turned to Colonel Taylor. "Well, Colonel, this is it. Good luck. As Brutus said to Cassius, 'if we meet again, we will smile.'"

"Don't worry, we'll be smiling in a couple of hours," Colonel Taylor said and left.

*   *   *

The Presidential Residence, Vlissingen Road

The black Rolls Royce came through the gate, followed by a 3/4-ton jeep from the Police Tactical Squad, stopping in the entrance way adjoining Vlissingen Road. Colonel Taylor walked up to the Rolls, saluted and spoke to the President through the lowered window.

"Comrade President, if your car and the Police jeep would insert themselves between the two army jeeps, we will pick up North Road and then turn on to Camp Street."

The President nodded.

Taylor's 3/4-ton jeep, with two soldiers in the rear, led the way north on Vlissingen; the second army jeep, a quarter-ton, with a corporal and five soldiers brought up the rear of the four-vehicle convoy. Within a couple of minutes, they turned left onto North Road, then Taylor's jeep slowed down and stopped at the army roadblock by the entrance to the grounds of the Georgetown Cricket club. Taylor stepped out of his vehicle and spoke to the corporal at the roadblock looking behind him as the corporal and five soldiers from the last jeep in his convoy got out and surrounded the President's Police detail. Walking back to his own jeep, he ordered the two soldiers out, sub-machine guns at the ready, then proceeded to the black Rolls Royce.

"What's going on here, Colonel?" the President asked.

"I'd like you to step out of the car," Taylor replied.

"And if I refuse?"

"You'll be shot," Colonel Taylor replied, resting his right hand on his service revolver.

The President accompanied Taylor to the roadblock, which was being dismantled. He ordered the President into the back of his jeep. A quarter-ton jeep, parked on the bridge to the North Road entrance of the Georgetown Cricket Club, pulled up the embankment, and a three-ton truck on New Garden Street moved up to North Road from its previously concealed position behind the Cricket Club pavilion. Captain Felix got out of the quarter-ton and joined the President behind Colonel Taylor's jeep. Taylor then ordered the two soldiers into the back with Captain Felix and the President.

"Lieutenant Rampersaud!" Colonel Taylor called out in the direction of the three-ton truck. Lieutenant Rampersaud descended from the cab of the truck and approached Taylor. "Okay, Anil, transfer the police and the President's driver to the truck and assign two of your people to drive the Rolls Royce and the Police jeep. Come on, on the double."

Colonel Taylor watched as Lieutenant Rampersaud ran back and herded the police and the Rolls Royce driver into the parked truck. The task completed, he reported back to Colonel Taylor. "Okay, Anil, take Captain Felix's jeep, your platoon sergeant, and the two soldiers and return to Camp Ayanganna," Colonel Taylor said. "Captain Spooner should have the Chief of Staff and Colonel LaFleur in custody by now. You are to transport them to Timehri. They are leaving with the President. The company sergeant-major will command the three-ton and bring up the rear. Okay, off you go." Lieutenant Rampersaud saluted.

Colonel Taylor watched the vehicles load up, then entered his jeep. He ordered his driver to proceed slowly to allow the other vehicles to line up properly. His jeep was followed by the Rolls, the Police jeep, the three-ton truck, and the quarter-ton, whose soldiers had disarmed the President's police detail. Satisfied with the alignment of the vehicles, Taylor ordered his driver to accelerate. The other vehicles did likewise, maintaining a fifty-feet distance between vehicles. When they reached the intersection with Camp Street, the convoy turned left. Soon they were in South Ruimveldt and, very shortly thereafter, they had passed Rahaman's Soda Factory, heading for Timehri.

"What did I ever do to you, Captain Felix?" the President asked.

"Shut up!" Captain Felix ordered.

"What's the problem, didn't you always get promoted on time?"

"This is your last warning," Captain Felix said. "You will not be man-handled, and your life will be spared. But you are to keep your mouth shut. If you speak again, I will shoot you. Do you understand?"

The President did not speak again.

TWENTY-ONE

February 23rd, 1980
Officers' Club, Timehri

"Mr. President, I protest my detention by your soldiers!" Hitchcock shouted, when he saw the President entering the lounge.

"Mr. Hitchcock, I have also protested my detention," the President replied.

"You mean—?"

"Yes, Mr. Hitchcock, these soldiers seem to be in charge." The President pointed to Colonel Taylor, Captain Felix and the four soldiers armed with SMGs.

"Well, I'll be damned," Hitchcock said.

"Captain McGowan, what's this fellow doing here?" Colonel Taylor asked, not masking his irritation as he pointed to Hitchcock.

"He got in our way, Colonel," McGowan replied. "I thought we'd hold him until the President leaves."

"Very well," Colonel Taylor said. "Let's talk at the back. Captain Felix, keep an eye in here."

Colonel Taylor and Captain McGowan went through the door at the back of the lounge and sat at a card table in the game room. "Okay," Colonel Taylor began, "what's the situation with the plane?"

"The twin-engine Islander is at the Air Wing hanger, ready to depart for Trinidad. We have a pilot: Lieutenant Gomes."

"Good," Colonel Taylor said. "The Chief of Staff should arrive at any moment, along with Colonel LaFleur. In the meantime, we'll just have to wait."

"I assume things went well in Georgetown," McGowan said.

"Without a hitch," Colonel Taylor replied. He sighed heavily. "Of course, I'll feel better when that clown is on the plane out of here."

"How is Ralph Spooner holding up?" McGowan asked.

"Spooner is fine. His Lieutenants have performed splendidly. Lieutenants Beharry and Clark are with him at Ayanganna. Lieutenant

Alex Mitchell is holding Telecoms. Captain Felix's company is more scattered. Lieutenant Ian Morgan is at the Maritime base in South Ruimveldt; Leonard MacKenzie is holding Police Headquarters; and Anil Rampersaud is on his way here."

"Very well done, Colonel," McGowan said.

"Well, it's not over yet," Colonel Taylor pointed out.

*   *   *

"Mr. President," Hitchcock said, leaning forward on the sofa across from where the President sat, "I've been held here for about an hour. I believe from the talk they plan to turn over the government to Donald Nelson and the Workers' Party."

"There's not much I can do about that now," the President replied.

"I don't know," Hitchcock said, looking directly at the President. "I don't think Captain McGowan is fully committed to this caper. I believe I could turn him." The President sat up; the despair seemed to have vanished from his face. "Of course, there'll be conditions," Hitchcock continued.

"Such as?" the President asked.

"Pardon for McGowan, to begin with."

"I would promote him on the spot," the President declared.

"Then there is Donald Nelson," Hitchcock said. "He's been a thorn in your side, but we have our concerns about him too. We would not like to have a socialist extremist running this government."

"I'll take care of him," the President said, adding, "I should have taken care of him a long time ago."

"Also, we don't care for all the socialist bullshit you and your party are spouting. Tone it down. Stop the talks with the Opposition about a national front government."

The President nodded. "Okay."

"One other thing, if you mess with our interests, we will respond—hard." The President said nothing. "Shall I indicate to Captain McGowan you are in agreement?"

"What's your connection with Captain McGowan?" the President asked.

"None, actually."

"His brother, Joe Henry, then? And the Public service Union?"

Hitchcock laughed. "Surely you remember from your days in the opposition back in the 60's that we have friends in the trade union movement. It worked to your advantage back then. For the present, look at things this way: if you are good to McGowan, you'll win points with his brother, who controls the Public Service Union, and you'll have a key ally in the army, one to whom you'll owe your retention of power. Do we have an understanding?"

The President nodded enthusiastically.

"Of course, I myself will have to follow through with what I promised him," Hitchcock said, "but be sure to do as McGowan says."

The President nodded again.

Hitchcock rose from the sofa. "There's one other small point."

"Yes?" the President responded.

"It relates to Captain Rambarran, a minor and apparently reluctant player in all of this. He has applied for a visa to study in the U.S. when his contract with the army ends in August. Let him go."

"Very well, if Rambarran ceases and desists when ordered to."

The arrival of Lieutenant Anil Rampersaud with the Chief of Staff and Colonel LaFleur brought Colonel Taylor and Captain McGowan back into the lounge.

"Comrade President," Colonel Taylor said, "please come with us."

The President got up and walked over to where Colonel Taylor and Captain McGowan were standing. "Better arrange an escort back to Georgetown for Mr. Hitchcock," Colonel Taylor said to Captain McGowan. "We don't want the Americans on our back over a simple misunderstanding." Flanked by the armed soldiers and Captain Felix, Colonel Taylor pushed the President ahead toward the lounge entrance. "Let's go," he said.

Captain McGowan then turned to Hitchcock. "Mr. Hitchcock, I'm sorry we had to detain you. You are now free to go. However, it's late, and I'd like to offer you an escort back to the city. Will you accept the offer?"

"Thank you," Hitchcock replied. "I hope we still understand each other."

"We do," Captain McGowan said. "Now, if you'd wait a moment, the officer who brought you here will provide you an escort back." With that, Captain McGowan left to join Colonel Taylor in the parking area below.

Hearing several vehicles start up, Hitchcock walked over to the screened windows facing the road and saw three army jeeps lining up along the southern driveway. They seemed to be waiting on Captain McGowan. The Rolls Royce and the Police jeep remained parked by the rear stairway, as was Hitchcock's car and the 3-ton truck, all of which were guarded by soldiers. Within a few minutes, the Lieutenant came into the lounge to escort Hitchcock to his car. Hitchcock was to drive himself back to the city, with the army jeep following behind. It was 23:45 on February 23rd.

*   *   *

When Captain McGowan's jeep joined the line of vehicles, Colonel Taylor signaled his driver forward. The convoy moved slowly, skirting the Motor Transport compound, up the hill past the Timehri International Airport, then slowed to a stop when the lead vehicle reached the gate at the Air Wing. The sentry saluted, slung his rifle over his shoulder, and pulled the gate wide open. Colonel Taylor's jeep went past the southern end of the Admin Building, coming to a stop on the concrete apron far forward of the building to allow the other vehicles room to clear the gate. About a hundred feet ahead on the tarmac sat the twin-engine Islander Captain McGowan had arranged. For several feet ahead of Colonel Taylor's jeep and, on both sides of it, were two rows of soldiers from McGowan's company. The rows extended back to the edge of the Admin Building, suggesting platoon strength. Most of the soldiers held their standard-issue SLR rifles at port arms, though the ones at the front and rear were cradling sub-machine guns. The jeep carrying Lieutenant Rampersaud and his prisoners, the Chief of Staff and Colonel LaFleur, pulled up behind Colonel Taylor's, with the third jeep carrying soldiers from Rampersaud's platoon close to it. Captain McGowan directed his driver around this line of vehicles to the breeze-way below the Admin Building, where the pilot and one of McGowan's lieutenants were awaiting instructions.

Colonel Taylor got out of the cab of the jeep and stood by as Captain Felix lowered the tail gate for the two guards and the President, whom he led to Colonel Taylor. From the second jeep, Lieutenant Rampersaud and his two guards brought the Chief of Staff and Colonel LaFleur, both of whom advanced with their hands bound behind their backs and their mouths taped, a precaution Colonel Taylor had insisted on to prevent them from using their rank and authority to confuse the soldiers.

"We're ready," Colonel Taylor called out to Captain McGowan. "Let's get this over with."

Captain McGowan began walking toward the group with his Lieutenant and the pilot. Just then, Lieutenant Rampersaud turned in the direction of the last jeep from where he had heard someone call his name. One of his soldiers signaled with his hand for the Lieutenant to come back. Irritated that an enlisted rank would summon him this way, Lieutenant Rampersaud walked to the back of the last jeep where the four soldiers from his platoon stood with their sub-machine guns. Several feet back, McGowan's two rows of guards had looped around to close the space that existed between them and Rampersaud's soldiers. Before Rampersaud could speak, one of his soldiers whispered, "Lieutenant, one of those guards asked another if now was the time to rush us."

"Are you sure?" Lieutenant Rampersaud whispered urgently. Two of his other soldiers nodded. "Let me have that SMG," he said, grasping it from the hands of the nearest soldier. Weapon in hand, he walked briskly on the left side of the stopped vehicles to where Colonel Taylor stood with the prisoners. The two rows of McGowan's soldiers ahead had also merged into an arc, and out of the corner of his eye, Rampersaud saw Captain McGowan reaching for his service revolver. "Colonel, it's a trap!" Rampersaud shouted, as he leveled the SMG at the soldiers ahead. But a single shot rang out striking Rampersaud in his right temple, and he slumped first to the side, then backward, dropping the SMG onto the concrete apron. Revolver in hand, Captain McGowan said, "Colonel, you are under arrest. Order your soldiers to drop their weapons or they will be shot."

"What?" Colonel Taylor was incredulous. "McGowan, we've achieved all of our objectives, man. The government is ours!"

Captain McGowan was unmoved. "Order your soldiers to drop their weapons, Colonel, or I'll shoot Captain Felix first, then you."

"Are you out of your mind?" Taylor asked. "You can have anything you want."

"No, Colonel," Captain McGowan replied. "Comrade President, Chief of Staff, Colonel LaFleur, step over here."

Colonel Taylor stood speechless. The President stepped out of the encircled group, as did the Chief of Staff, and Colonel LaFleur.

"Soldiers," the President said, addressing the soldiers in the rear who had come with Colonel Taylor, "I am the President of the Republic. You followed the orders of your officers. I understand that. You will not be punished, but you must put down your weapons *now.*"

Like firecrackers, the clatter of weapons, hitting the concrete apron in front of the Admin Building, again shattered the stillness of the morning. McGowan and his Lieutenant took the service revolvers of Colonel Taylor and Captain Felix.

"Thank you, Major McGowan," the President said.

"Captain, Mr. President," McGowan reminded the President.

"Not anymore. You've just been promoted. From now on, you can expect great things."

Colonel Taylor walked over to where Lieutenant Rampersaud's still body lay. Picking up the body by the shoulders, Colonel Taylor wept.

"I don't have time for this ridiculous display of sentimentality!" the President's voice boomed. "Those men are all traitors. Bind the officers and throw them in the back of one of those jeeps."

The Chief of Staff and Colonel LaFleur were unbound and the same cords were used to bind the wrists of Colonel Taylor and Captain Felix. "Let's go back to the Officers' Club," the President said. "We need to figure out our next steps."

*   *   *

At 00:25 on February 24th, the Officers' Club acquired a restive air. The bar was opened for the President and the senior officers. Meanwhile, Major McGowan had called the Guard Room at Camp Stevenson with a request for handcuffs. With their hands bound behind their backs, Colonel Taylor and Captain Felix lay next to each other on their stomachs on the lounge floor, their heads facing the bar. A large rum-and-Coke in hand, the President paced and gulped. Twice he stepped over to where the two officers lay and spat on them.

184

When the MPs arrived with the handcuffs, the President ordered them to cut off the epaulets on the three officers before securing the handcuffs on them. "These dogs are traitors," he said. "I don't want to see them with any type of rank." Then he stepped over to the bar to have the soldier behind the counter refill his glass. "I want Captain Spooner dead," the President continued. "I don't care how. I don't want that man to see another day." He paced in front of the bar. "'Comrade President, this is the Duty Officer at Camp Ayanganna. There is a fire at Party Headquarters'," he said, imitating Captain Spooner. "I'm going to put a fire up his ass when I get a hold of him."

"This isn't over yet, Comrade President," Major McGowan said. "We need to get Spooner and Rambarran to surrender."

"Alright, how do we do that?" the President asked.

"Have Taylor call on them to give up, then you speak to them," Colonel LaFleur suggested.

"Very well, get the dog up," the President said.

"With respect, Comrade President, I think we should delay that call," Major McGowan said.

"Why?"

"Comrade President, one of Captain Spooner's platoons under Lieutenant Mitchell is holding Telecoms. If Mitchell is unaware of what has happened, I could re-take Telecoms and arrest him."

"How long would that take?" the President asked.

"I have units moving in on Telecoms and Police Headquarters right now," McGowan replied. "Colonel Taylor here left the southern side of Georgetown open, so I sent in those units yesterday evening."

"How does this help us dislodge Spooner?"

"Without Mitchell and his platoon, Spooner will have only two platoons at Ayanganna. He can't hold out; he'll be easily surrounded. Add to that the demoralization of knowing that we have Taylor and Felix. A call at that point will force him to surrender or make a run for it."

"Very good thinking," the President said, pacing slowly and nodding. "Very impressive."

The phone rang. Major McGowan rushed to it. Covering the mouthpiece, he said, "Comrade President, we have control of Telecoms.

Lieutenant Mitchell has been arrested. We should hear anytime from Police Headquarters."

"Explain to me how you managed this," the President said.

"My officer was to tell Lieutenant Mitchell that he was there to relieve him. Mitchell, I am sure, would have tried to contact Spooner for confirmation, during which time, my troops were to use their weapons to overwhelm them. As far as Mitchell knew, we were on the same side. Let's hope it works at Police Headquarters as well."

The phone rang again. This time, McGowan received confirmation that Police Headquarters had been re-taken.

Major McGowan positioned the radio on the bar while the two MPs helped Taylor to his feet and walked him over. McGowan held up the mouthpiece to Taylor's mouth.

"Alright, Taylor," the President said, "contact those two Company Commanders and call off this thing. I will make sure you and Felix don't suffer."

McGowan pressed the button on the microphone to allow the Colonel to speak. "Captain Spooner, Captain Rambarran, this is Colonel Taylor. Acknowledge, over." Taylor repeated the call.

"Spooner here, over."

"Rambarran here, over."

"The President is free. I say again, the President is free. We were betrayed. Lieutenant Rampersaud is dead. Save yourselves."

"Give me that damn microphone!" the President said, snatching it from Taylor. "Listen here, Spooner; you too, Rambarran. This is the President. I know you can hear me. I have with me the Chief of Staff and the Force Commander. Taylor and Felix are under arrest. This exercise is over. Surrender now and you will be treated leniently."

There was no response.

"What do you think they will do?" the President asked, looking at the Chief of Staff, Colonel LaFleur, and Major McGowan.

"They will discuss it with their platoon commanders," McGowan replied. "Spooner is cornered; he has little choice. I am not sure about Rambarran."

"Why not?" the President asked. "My understanding was that he joined reluctantly."

"But he joined," McGowan said.

"Meaning what?"

"You never quite know about Rambarran," McGowan replied. "There are issues about honor."

"Honor, you said? These men are all traitors."

"Not from their point of view," McGowan said. The President stopped his pacing and looked sternly at McGowan. "I'm sorry, Comrade President, but to anticipate their moves, we have to try to see things from their point of view."

The radio came alive. "Comrade President, this is Captain Spooner. I am prepared to surrender my command if you would assure me of a pardon for all the officers and men. I alone am responsible. They followed my orders."

"You have my word, Captain," the President replied. "The officers and men will be pardoned, but you must surrender yourself to the Force Commander when he arrives within the hour. Do you understand?"

"Yes, Comrade President," Ralph Spooner replied.

The President clapped his hands. "One down, one to go." Walking back to the bar, he said, "Fill me up." He raised his glass and took a double swallow from the rum-and-Coke, then glanced at Major McGowan, who stood looking at the President with his brows furrowed. "You don't seem pleased, Major."

"I believe, Comrade President, that Captain Spooner is playing for time."

Before the President could react to McGowan, the radio belched again. This time, it was Captain Rambarran. "Comrade President, my officers and I are prepared to stand down if you would grant a blanket amnesty to all the officers and men who participated in this exercise. This means releasing Colonel Taylor and Captain Felix, whom you have in custody. The officers will then turn over their commands and resign their commissions."

"And if I refuse, Captain?"

"Comrade President, I believe you share our desire to avert any further loss of life and destruction of property. Please think on it. I will give you one hour." Rambarran went off the radio.

"Do you believe this?" the President screamed. "That rice-farming, little bastard gave me an ultimatum? I said I was going to let him leave the army. Not so anymore. He wants to hold out? He wants to give ultimatums? I want him dead, along with Spooner! Is everybody hearing me?" He gulped the rest of the drink and walked up to the bar, slamming his glass down. Noticing Colonel Taylor still standing there, he said, "Get this dog back on the floor." The two MPs walked Colonel Taylor back to where Captain Felix was lying and helped him first to a kneeling, then a lying position. "Bind their ankles," the President said, "and have the guards wait outside. Give them something to drink out there."

When the guards and the MPs left, the President sat down on the sofa where he had earlier been a prisoner. Major McGowan, the Chief of Staff, and Colonel LaFleur took seats facing him. "I would like you all to tell me what kind of cards Captain Rambarran is holding. Why does he think he can give me an ultimatum?"

"I believe the ultimatum is a bluff, Comrade President," Major McGowan said. "I am sure Captain Rambarran would like to save Colonel Taylor and Captain Felix, but he really has no way to do it. So, he decided, as they say, to bowl you that ball." The President did not take his eyes away from McGowan. "On the other hand, if Captain Rambarran holds out, we would have a very serious problem."

"How so?" the President asked. "Exactly what kind of cards is he holding?"

"Comrade President, with the police there neutralized, Captain Rambarran is effectively in control of Berbice, one-third of the country, with a natural defensive line behind the Berbice River. That region, as you know, is predominantly Indian, and the sugar workers there are on strike. If Captain Rambarran does not surrender and we try to re-take Berbice, Indians might get killed. If that happens, many young men might join Rambarran, and we could face a full-fledged insurgency aimed at secession. Berbice is one of the two bread baskets of the country. They could hold out indefinitely."

"Christ!" the President hissed, rising from his seat. He paced in front of the bar. "Okay," he finally said, "I'll settle with the sugar workers; I'll give them a sizable wage increase. The Opposition Leader will like that: they're his people. Colonel LaFleur, get me the Opposition Leader on the telephone; call him at his house."

"He's not there," McGowan said. The President stopped and looked quizzically at McGowan. "Colonel Taylor's plan called for the detention of the Opposition Leader," McGowan explained. "He's most likely at Camp Ayanganna."

The President laughed out loud. He walked in the direction of the two prisoners on their stomachs, laughing still. Retracing his steps, he stopped in front of his three officers and, with his face still brightly lit up, said, "The Opposition Leader is a Marxist-Leninist and, man, do they hate military take-overs. *Putschists*, he calls them! And they detained him? He is going to be so mad. He will never let an adventurer like Rambarran take over his support base in Berbice. We have to free the Opposition Leader, which means we have to get Spooner to abandon Camp Ayanganna. Get Spooner on the telephone."

"Don't you mean the radio?" McGowan asked.

"No," the President answered. "I don't want the Americans to hear what I want to say. I have a good feeling they are monitoring radio transmissions."

Colonel LaFleur dialed the direct line to Headquarters, Internal Operations. When Captain Spooner picked up, Colonel LaFleur said, "Hold for the President, Spooner."

The President walked up to the bar and took the phone from LaFleur. "Captain Spooner, I just received an ultimatum from Captain Rambarran. Now I have an ultimatum for you and Rambarran. You and Rambarran are holding soldiers who belong to me. I'll give you both ten minutes to release them unconditionally and answer for your crime. I have contacted the Corentyne branch of the Kabaka Youth Movement. They are going to occupy your family farm at Philippi. Some of the KYM boys are socialist ideologues, but many, as you know, are ruffians, ex-convicts. I understand your sister is very attractive, and, your mother, she is young-looking, they say."

"You ugly bastard!" Spooner screamed, causing the President to pull the phone momentarily away from his ear.

"Now, you tell Rambarran you both have ten minutes." The President slammed the phone down and walked back to his chair, dropping himself into it. "It's only a matter of time before Spooner abandons Camp Ayanganna." No one spoke for a while. The President looked at his watch. "LaFleur, fix me a drink." Colonel LaFleur rose quickly and went behind the bar. When he returned with the rum-and-Coke, the President took two swallows. "I don't want word of this coup attempt to get out," he said. "I want those dogs on the floor to disappear, some kind of accident. I want Spooner and Rambarran pursued and eliminated. Understood?" Everyone nodded. "Colonel LaFleur, I want you to let all the troops know that they were involved in a training exercise. You and the Chief of Staff are both to visit the list of installations McGowan will provide. This is Sunday morning. I want normal operations by 08:00 Monday morning. *The Guardian* will carry accounts supporting what you are doing."

"How about the Opposition Leader and the soldiers who freed you?" the Chief of Staff asked. "Wouldn't they give a different account?"

"The Opposition Leader will cooperate on this one, I am sure. I've played this harp before. The silence of the soldiers I will leave to McGowan; they are under his command. It wouldn't matter after a while anyway. Once the official propaganda machine goes to work, anything else that comes out will be rumor." He paused and studied the three officers sitting in front of him. "Now, I want you to give me a plan to eliminate those dogs lying on their bellies."

The three officers looked at each other, but it was McGowan who spoke. "One of my assignments in the coup was to take the ammo dump at Camp Groomes on the Linden Highway. We could place Taylor, Felix, and Rampersaud there." The President's eyes did not leave McGowan. "If the ammo dump explodes, it could be reported as an accident."

The President smiled and nodded. He took another swallow of rum. "I like how you think, Major. Now, help me with this one. Donald Nelson, he is popular with the mine workers at Linden, yes?" The officers nodded. "Bribe someone to draw him out to Linden on some urgent matter. Pick him up on the Linden Highway and put him with the others. He said in a public speech that he wants to remove this government by any means necessary. Did he not?" The officers nodded again. "*The Guardian* will speculate that he might have been conspiring to get ammunition and incendiaries from Camp Groomes, and the plan went bad." The President rose, tilted his head backward and emptied the rest of the drink into his mouth. "I want to get back to the Residence; I need an escort."

Major McGowan left the lounge. In a few minutes, he came back with the President's chauffeur. "The escort is ready," he announced.

"Major McGowan, you've saved my government," the President said. "Get rid of those scoundrels with the same type of efficiency you've demonstrated and I will appoint you Force Commander with the rank of Colonel."

"What about me?" Colonel LaFleur asked.

"Colonel LaFleur, you've been the acting Force Commander since last August and, under your very nose, those officers planned to overthrow this government. You were too damned dependent on Taylor. No, you can remain as CO, Border Operations, or retire. But until this thing is over, I need you to continue as the acting Force Commander."

*   *   *

February 24th, 1980
NSA Listening Post, Middle Street

Erikson jumped out of his chair and rushed into the living room. "Did I hear that right? Did Colonel Taylor ask the other officers to save themselves?" He turned to Colonel Stanford, who had followed him out. Stanford shrugged. The next transmission made things clear.

> *Listen here, Spooner; you too, Rambarran. This is the President. I know you can hear me. I have with me the Chief of Staff and the Force Commander. Taylor and Felix are under arrest. This exercise is over. Surrender now and you will be treated leniently.*

"Oh my God!" Erikson felt the blood drain from his temples. He leaned forward, resting both hands on the back of a sofa. "How? What could have gone so terribly wrong?"

"I don't know," Colonel Stanford said quietly.

"They seemed to have everything in place. What happened at the airport? Why the double cross?"

"Maybe they didn't have everyone on board," Colonel Stanford said. "You know what Yogi Berra said: 'it ain't over till it's over.'"

"No, I don't believe it's that simple," Erikson said. "I believe Hitchcock had something to do with this."

"Why do you think that?" Colonel Stanford asked.

"Well he seemed keenest on the coup. Look at the pressure he put on Captain Rambarran. Yet, he wasn't the least interested in monitoring the coup."

"Maybe he thought it was a done deal," Colonel Stanford suggested.

"You mean he's never heard of Yogi Berra?" Erikson asked.

"Are we getting sarcastic?"

"I think there's a lot of room here for skepticism, Tom," Erikson replied. "Hitchcock wanted a coup so badly he was prepared to hold up Rambarran's visa. The question is: did Hitchcock really want the coup to succeed?"

"You heard the man. A brief period of military rule would give us one less thing to worry about while we dealt with Iran and Central America."

"True, but he could also accomplish the same thing by scaring the bejesus out of this government. Couldn't he?" Erikson paced behind the sofa. "Let's see. Hitchcock has the head of the Public Service Union in his pocket. This fellow's brother is a Captain in the army, and Hitchcock has been well up on developments in the army. Haven't you noticed? Now, to put the pieces together: Hitchcock encourages a coup against the government, then saves the government to make the President indebted to him. Tell me I am wrong, Colonel." Colonel Stanford did not respond. "Did you know anything about this?" Erikson asked.

"No," Colonel Stanford replied, "but I think this is all speculation on your part. In the final analysis, the question is: are we better off vis-a-vis this government than we were before the coup attempt? I think we are."

"Is that all that matters here, Tom?" Erikson asked. "God, we betrayed a whole bunch of fine officers. And, tonight, what's left of it, might be the night of the long knives."

"Let's hope not," Colonel Stanford said. "In any event, it's an internal matter, isn't it?"

"Do you hear yourself?" Erikson asked. "You were with Hitchcock in encouraging the damn coup! We pushed them, Colonel! We have some responsibility here."

"I'll concede we have some responsibility to Andrew Rambarran," Colonel Stanford said, "and I'd be prepared to ask the Ambassador to intercede on his behalf. I am sure we can get him out of the country."

"And the others?" Erikson asked.

"That's as far as I think we'd be able to go without implicating ourselves."

"Christ!"

"Don't worry, Steve. It might turn out okay. They'll be tried, and who knows? The Comrade President might pardon them in the interest of unity."

"Tried? You know who controls the courts in this country. The same fellow who rigs elections and kills Catholic priests. You think he'll spare any of those officers? My God, what have we done?" Erikson walked off toward the main entrance.

"Where are you going?" Colonel Stanford asked.

"To get Anita and her father to my place, then I'm going to find Hitchcock."

TWENTY-TWO

February 24, 1980
Headquarters, Internal Operations Command
Camp Ayanganna

Captain Spooner sat behind Colonel Taylor's desk, shell-shocked by the change of fortune and unable to find words of comfort for his two lieutenants slumped in the chairs on the other side, their faces haggard from sleep deprivation. He tried to figure out what signals from Captain McGowan he had failed to recognize in their months of association and planning. True, Andrew Rambarran had warned against McGowan, but that was based on mere suspicion. Other forces, which Spooner could not grasp, must surely have been at work but it seemed pointless to try to figure that out now; he had graver responsibilities. He realized that his fate and those of his officers rested on a slender reed. Reaching for the phone, he dialed Central Police Station, New Amsterdam. Lieutenant Asad Shah answered and passed the phone to Andrew Rambarran.

"Yes, Ralph," Rambarran said.

"Andrew, have you discussed our situation with your officers?" Spooner asked.

"Only to tell them to hold their positions," Rambarran replied. "I need a rough idea of what we're going to do first. Surrendering is simply not an option open to us."

"What if a majority of the officers choose to do that?" Spooner asked.

"They're smarter than that," Rambarran replied. "I'm sure Colonel Taylor was asked to call on us to surrender. He didn't. He said Lieutenant Anil Rampersaud was dead and he told us to save ourselves. He must have known something they're planning for us."

"I agree with you," Ralph Spooner said. "I just wanted to hear you confirm what I picked up from that call."

"You can't hold Camp Ayanganna, Ralph."

"I know, Andrew. I'm just trying to digest the losses. They picked up Lieutenant Mitchell at Telecoms and Lieutenant MacKenzie at Police Headquarters. You were right about the roadblocks, and about McGowan."

"Well, now's not the time for that, Ralph. You need to move to a more defensible position."

"Of course," Spooner replied.

"Have you briefed Lieutenant Morgan about our situation?" Rambarran asked.

"Yes," Spooner replied, "after we heard from Colonel Taylor. Lieutenant Morgan is standing by with the patrol boat, *Parakeet*, and he's still holding the Vreed-en-Hoop ferry."

"He'll have to abandon the ferry and haul ass out of there."

"Can we run through a checklist for this withdrawal?" Spooner asked.

"Okay."

When Captain Spooner ended his call, he dispatched Lieutenant Beharry to the Officers' Club to release the Opposition Leader and to load up whatever food supplies he could get from the Mess, then he called Lieutenant Ian Morgan at the Maritime Base in South Ruimveldt.

"Ian," Spooner said, "I want you to disable the Vreed-en-Hoop ferry. Use bats or whatever is available and work over the engine room. Make sure the patrol boat is topped up, but bring additional gas and drinking water."

"Right, Captain," Lieutenant Morgan responded.

"Assemble your platoon at the wharf and have them turn in their weapons. Tell them the exercise is over. Load the weapons in the boat and drop them in the Demerara River on your way over here. Retain the machine gun, a couple of the SLR's, and all of the SMGs. You might need to bring a couple of soldiers with you. Salvage what you think might be usable from the stores—flare guns, an inflatable raft. Then torch the building. Hurry, and contact me on the VHF when you depart South Ruimveldt."

"Yes, Captain," Lieutenant Morgan replied, ending the conversation.

Two sets of footsteps coming up the external stairway announced the return of Lieutenant Beharry with the Opposition Leader. When Lieutenant Beharry showed the Opposition Leader in, Spooner rose to greet him. "Comrade," Captain Spooner said, "Time is of the essence to us, so I'll dispense with the formalities. I'm sorry we had to detain you. We, in the military, made an attempt to restore democracy to this country, something you've fought for, for a long time. Our effort failed. The corporal downstairs will take you back to your home."

"Thank you, Captain," the Opposition Leader said. "I can't say I approve of your method, but I understand your motivation. I also appreciate your hospitality. If I were a drinking man, I would have greatly enjoyed the bar in your Club." Spooner managed a smile as the Opposition Leader reached forward and shook his extended hand. No one spoke until the Opposition Leader had descended the stairway.

"This is it for us here, isn't it?" Lieutenant Clark asked, rising from the chair in front of Spooner's desk.

"Yes, Duncan, this is it," Spooner replied. "Disable the helicopter on the drill square, then you and Lieutenant Beharry have the men turn in their weapons and assemble them outside the armory."

Ralph Spooner waited by the radio and, at 02:15 hours, Lieutenant Morgan called to report that the *Parakeet* was sitting a few hundred feet from the seawall. Spooner left the Headquarters building and walked over to the armory where Lieutenants Beharry and Clark had assembled their platoons. Standing at attention in front of the formation, Spooner requested a report. Both Lieutenants reported their platoons fully present.

"This exercise is over," Spooner declared. "When you're dismissed, you are to go home. You will not be incarcerated or harmed in any way. But you must leave the base quickly or you could be fired upon. Those are the terms we agreed to. Company, dismissed!"

The officers watched the soldiers race to the main gate. When the last of them had turned onto Thomas Road, Captain Spooner climbed into the driver's side of his jeep and started the engine. He drove slowly toward the main gate as Lieutenants Beharry and Clark poured gasoline outside the armory and set it alight, before jumping into the moving vehicle. Out of the main gate and along the short stretch of Vlissingen Road, the jeep sped. Spooner and Beharry looked across at Camp Ayanganna on their left. Flames had covered the entrance to the armory, and the fire seemed to be following the wind direction toward the southern side of the building. Officers on the base, who had earlier been under house arrest, were scurrying around presumably to contain the fire.

At the seawall, Spooner used his patrol flashlight to locate the approaching rubber raft, undulating with the swells. When the two soldiers in the raft finally tossed out the mooring rope, Beharry caught it. Spooner was the first to wade into the water carrying the machine gun and steadying himself by holding on to the rope. Once he had settled into the raft, Spooner sent the two soldiers to the seawall to bring back the sacks of food from the jeep, then he ordered them to go home and to lie low. Carrying two SMGs, Duncan Clark used the rope to guide himself to the raft. Last came Beharry still holding the rope and pulling himself to the raft. Once he was in, Spooner pulled the cord starting the small engine, and the raft struggled forward against the incoming tide. About a third of the way to the waiting patrol boat, the officers were startled by the boom from Camp Ayanganna. Huge, shooting flames illuminated thick, black smoke billowing aloft, but the seawall blocked any view of the buildings or personnel on the ground.

"They're going to be really mad," Duncan Clark observed.

"I'm afraid so," Ralph Spooner replied, "but it'll slow them down. Let's hope it's long enough for us."

"Captain, why doesn't the patrol boat try to approach us?" Ramesh Beharry asked.

"It's dark," Spooner replied, "and my guess is that Lieutenant Morgan can't see where the submerged jetties are. He doesn't want to damage the propeller."

When the raft reached the patrol boat, the officers disengaged the engine which they passed onto willing hands on the patrol boat. They unloaded their weapons and climbed aboard before joining the effort to haul the raft onto the deck. Then, Lieutenant Morgan ordered the boat operator, a corporal from the Maritime Command, to take them to New Amsterdam.

*   *   *

Central Police Station, New Amsterdam

"Asad," Rambarran said to Lieutenant Shah, "why don't you get a few hours of sleep in the office next door? I'll call Ron Peters and

Michael DeFreitas and tell them to do the same. We have a long day ahead. And, don't worry, I'll make the next round of inspections."

After Rambarran put through the calls to his other two platoon leaders, he left with McCurchin. The encampment at Esplanade Park was the first stop. The camp was still: two squads were asleep in the tents, but the sentries were alert. He walked down to the edge of the Berbice River to check on the machine gun emplacements, ordering one team to relocate further up the mouth of the river directly across from Crabb Island. Then, he left for Palmyra to check on the squad he had positioned there to avoid being outflanked. The defense was thinly spread out, he realized, but there was only so much he could do with just one company. A massive attack, and it could be all over. But it would be at least one day before the other side could mount a serious attack. For one thing, they didn't have enough troops on the coast. They'd have to extract some of the platoons from the interior and, with only limited airlift capacity, they would not have enough of them out by the end of the day. One day, of that, he was sure.

At Palmyra, on the extended river mouth, one team was manning the observation post, while the other slept. The soldiers on duty were pleased to see their company commander, especially since he had brought a container of coffee, which McCurchin extracted from the back of the jeep. However, Rambarran kept the visit very short partly because of tiredness but largely because he wanted to avoid responding to questions from the soldiers. Promising the soldiers they would be rotated out at breakfast, Rambarran left with McCurchin for the New Amsterdam ferry station. When the jeep stopped in front of the gate at the ferry station, Rambarran remained seated with his eyes closed.

"Captain?" McCurchin said. Rambarran opened his eyes and instinctively wiped his mouth. Stepping down from the jeep, he walked through the gate which the sentry opened for him. Smoke from several zinc buckets on the ground swirled around the covered section of the wharf, but the sentries still swatted mosquitoes which occasionally penetrated the smoke barrier. Rambarran walked down the gangplank onto the lower deck of the *Kurtuka* and looked across at sentries on the pontoon and tugboat, which were moored on the other side of the *Kurtuka*. Using the stern stairway of the *Kurtuka*, he made his way to the bridge, where the ferry skipper, who had been sleeping in his chair, groggily returned his "good morning" greeting.

"We won't be operating the ferry or the pontoon today, Skipper," Rambarran said. "It's Sunday, so it shouldn't affect too many people."

"It's your show," the ferry skipper replied. "How about breakfast for my crew?"

"Don't worry," Rambarran replied. "I'll see that you get scrambled eggs, toast, and coffee. Maybe cheese as well; I'll check with the supply sergeant."

"Thanks," the ferry skipper said. "It'll be good to have real bread again."

"I am sorry about your detention, Skipper," Rambarran said. "No harm will come to you or your crew. But you might walk out there and reassure them. I don't want anyone to do anything stupid."

"I understand," the ferry skipper said. "Things have been fine on the boat, you know. The soldiers have not pushed anyone around."

"Glad to hear that," Rambarran said; "they're a good lot. They follow orders." Rambarran turned to leave the bridge. "I'll see you get breakfast, don't worry," he shouted back at the ferry skipper.

When they had returned to Central Police Station, Rambarran directed McCurchin to rest on the hallway sofa. He himself sat wearily on the chair behind the desk, set his beret down on the desk, and lowered his head on his arms, resting crosswise on the desk. When the radio crackled, he checked his watch. It was 05:35 on Sunday, February 24th. Sunlight was already pouring in through the windows.

"Fox Trot One, this is Alpha One, over," Ralph Spooner said.

"Come in, Alpha One," Rambarran responded, "this is Fox Trot One. Over."

"Entering river mouth, over."

"Proceed to the wharf, Alpha One," Rambarran instructed. "Will see you there. Out."

Rambarran shook McCurchin awake and off to the wharf they went, arriving a few minutes before the *Parakeet* pulled alongside the pontoon and was moored to it. The four officers and the boat operator on the *Parakeet* walked across the pontoon to the lower deck of the *Kurtuka* and then up the ramp to the wharf, where Rambarran received them. Detailing two soldiers from the wharf to guard the *Parakeet*, Rambarran left with his guests in the back of the jeep for Esplanade Park. Off-duty soldiers at the Esplanade encampment were at breakfast, and the Supply Sergeant's voice issued loudly from the mess tent. Captain Rambarran left the officers and the jeep at the bandstand and walked over to the mess tent with McCurchin and the *Parakeet* operator.

"Sergeant Duffy," Rambarran said, after returning his Supply Sergeant's salute, "see that the skipper and crew of the *Kurtuka* are served a full breakfast, would you?"

"Yes, Captain," the Supply Sergeant replied. "How about you and the officers I see over at the bandstand?"

"Yes, I think we're ready," Rambarran said. "The corporal here is the boat operator for the *Parakeet*. See that he and McCurchin are fed. The boat operator is restricted to camp."

"Yes, Captain," the Supply Sergeant responded.

Captain Rambarran returned his salute and walked back to the bandstand. Coffee followed quickly, then came breakfast, served by the Supply Sergeant's two assistants. Over a breakfast of scrambled eggs, toast, and cheese, the officers seated at the bandstand reflected on their situation.

"I'm sorry I got you into this mess," Ralph Spooner said. "I can't believe I could have been so blindsided by what McGowan was doing."

"This isn't the time," Rambarran said. "We have more pressing matters right now. But I am really sorry about the way things have turned out. God only knows what will happen to Colonel Taylor and the other officers they're holding."

"I've been thinking on the way over here," Ralph Spooner said, "we could hold on to Berbice and carry on the struggle. We know this region; we'd be well supplied with food. The people would be sympathetic. We could fight the Kabaka government to a standstill."

"That'll be the bluff we will present to the government," Rambarran responded, "but we'll have to come up with an alternate plan."

"What's wrong with holding out here?" Lieutenant Beharry asked. "We could take a third of the country away from that clown."

"Believe me," Rambarran replied, "I'd like to hit the government hard, but we're playing a losing hand."

The other officers appeared tired, but it was clear from the way they were pushing the food around on their plates instead of eating that they were not pleased with Rambarran's position.

"Captain, we're holding one of the six rifle companies in the Brigade," Lieutenant Duncan Clark said. "The government has to man the borders and it will have to keep a company in Georgetown. The odds favor us."

"That's how it appears at first blush, Duncan," Rambarran said, "but here's the problem. To get the soldiers to support the coup, we told them that the army was taking over. It will soon become clear that not only was the army as a whole not involved but that the effort failed. We will soon be faced with desertions if we continue a confrontational stance with the government. Secondly, Berbice is predominantly Indian, and F-Company is eighty-five percent black. Do you really expect black soldiers to support the secession of an Indian region of the country. It won't be long before the Kabaka Party begins to make its racial appeals and then we could have more desertions or worse." The officers listened and ate slowly. Rambarran could tell the truth of what he had said was sinking in, but he worried about making them feel too dejected. "Look," he resumed, "we're safe here for a while. It'll give us time to work out a plan. After breakfast, I'd like all of you to get some sleep. Lieutenant Shah will be up shortly. He'll have a late breakfast and oversee things for a while. Then, we'll regroup and make a plan."

The officers nodded their agreement and eating resumed. After breakfast, Lieutenants Beharry, Clark, and Morgan left, with their weapons, to the tents the Supply Sergeant had designated as their sleeping quarters.

"Do you really think we're playing that weak a hand?" Ralph Spooner asked.

"Yes," Rambarran replied. "To hold Berbice, you're making an assumption that the people in Berbice are prepared to secede. I don't think they are. In any case, they'll take their cue from the Leader of the Opposition, and he'll be opposed to secession."

"But he can only get access to Berbice with our permission," Spooner insisted.

"No, he'll get on national radio. Besides, look at it from a military point of view. Berbice has a long coastline which we can't secure. They can land troops at various points and cut off some of our units. Airlift capacity is only limited, true, but they can safely fly in troops, a little at a time, behind our defensive line."

"What then are our options?" Spooner asked.

"To tell the truth, not good, Ralph; not good."

"Lay them out as you see them," Spooner said.

"We'll posture as though we will hold Berbice indefinitely, but in reality we can't."

"I still don't see why not," Spooner asserted.

"Ralph, quite apart from the fact that the other side has more forces, there is the question of police units in Berbice."

"We can neutralize them."

"Come on, Ralph. We can't kill them. These are police officers we know; we've worked with them over the years. In any case, I plan to ship them to Georgetown this afternoon. And, here's something I didn't want to discuss when the others were here, Ralph. The President wants us to relinquish control of Berbice, so he will apply the pressure at your family farm at Philippi. He will make this personal! You and I have an interest in defending your family, but it will be hard to use F-Company just for that purpose. We could bring your family to New Amsterdam, but that would implicate them, and if things go badly, they could be tried for treason."

"So what do you propose we do with them?" Spooner asked.

"You'll pick them up with the *Parakeet* and bring them aboard the *Kurtuka*. In two days or so, we could reach Florida."

"How about going to Suriname?"

"Out of the question. The President will get the Surinamese government to apprehend us all and turn us over. The best chance for us is to head out to open sea. Your family holds US passports. The rest, myself included, would seek political asylum."

"What if they intercept us?"

"We will leave in the dark, tonight."

The sun was above the horizon and the air was still. Andrew Rambarran felt his fatigues sticking to his skin. It was going to be a hot, humid morning.

"Why don't you get some sleep, Ralph? You can take the hammock here or come back to the police station with me."

"I'll stay here, but I'll come up to take a shower. I also need a change of uniform. Can you spare a set?" Rambarran nodded, then left.

Back at Central Police Station, Lieutenant Shah was up. Rambarran put through two calls to Lieutenants Peters and DeFreitas summoning them to a meeting at 12:00 hours; then he pulled a cushion from one of the chairs in the office and, using it as a headrest, laid himself out on the floor.

*   *   *

Embassy of the United States
Main Street, Georgetown

Colonel Stanford's office door was partially closed when Steve Erikson walked by; Stanford appeared to be on the telephone. It was just as well: there wasn't much Erikson wanted to say to him just then. He himself had barely managed to get a couple hours of sleep. Anita's father wasn't too pleased to be awakened at 04:00. He was even more exasperated to learn that the deal he had secured on the sale of his business might fall through when word got out that his nephew had been involved in an attempt to overthrow the government. He couldn't understand why "that boy," as he referred to Andrew, had to do a thing like that when he was just months away from leaving the army and the country. It took a while for Erikson to convince him that much more was at stake if he did not vacate the premises. In the end, with some cajoling from Anita, he got dressed and drove the family car, following close behind Erikson to Bel Air Park. There, Anita's worry about her cousin's fate became infectious and they sat drinking tea while Erikson tried, without any real basis, to reassure them that Andrew would come out just fine.

Erikson felt listless. Sitting in his chair, he reached for a pencil and scratched on the blotter on the desk. Other than detecting changes in Colonel Stanford's intonation next door, the place was quiet. Then, he heard the rattle of keys and a door being opened at the end of the hallway. Hitchcock had come to his office.

Pushing his chair back, Steve Erikson jumped to his feet and strode into the hallway to find Colonel Stanford in his way.

"Take it easy, Steve," Colonel Stanford said.

"I just want to find out what he knows," Erikson responded.

"He doesn't have to tell you a thing, you know."

"Oh yes, he does," Erikson asserted. "He used me and he used Andrew Rambarran. Officially he may not be obligated to tell me anything but, when I put a bullet through his head, any distinction between official and unofficial will immediately cease. And he knows that."

With Stanford in tow, Erikson walked into the Station Chief's office without knocking. Hitchcock, who had just set his briefcase down was sitting in his chair facing away from the door. He looked over warily as Erikson lowered his tall, muscular frame over the desk resting his palms at the edge.

"Tell me why, Hitchcock. Why did you turn McGowan against the others?"

Hitchcock breathed heavily. He crinkled his nose and moustache as if the movement would push his glasses further up on his nose. "Because Colonel Taylor was going to turn the government over to Donald Nelson and the Workers' Party."

"How do you know that?" Erikson asked.

"He had several meetings with Nelson."

"Why didn't you stop the coup from going forward? You could have let us know. We would have warned Rambarran and Spooner."

"You're right; maybe I should have."

"That's it? Maybe you should have? Why did you step in to save this corrupt egomaniac, who has just made himself president-for-life?"

"First off, we couldn't have a government under a diehard Marxist like Donald Nelson. Even you know that. And we weren't about to invade this country. So, how else could we produce a change of course here? Scare the daylights out of this egomaniac, as you call him, then make him indebted to us, again."

"And you didn't care whom you sacrificed in the process?"

"I once told you, Captain, that you should concern yourself with American interests," Hitchcock replied, "but, yes, I do care about our allies. I should remind you that Colonel Taylor was involved in this enterprise for reasons of his own. Nevertheless, I hope he and the others survive."

"Does this mean that you will support a strong intercession effort?" Erikson asked.

"No," Hitchcock replied. "Such an effort would suggest to the President that we were behind it all the time. For Captain Rambarran only, but he would have to come in to us."

"Are you kidding me?" Erikson screamed. "You expect him to drop his weapon and just taxi in to Georgetown?"

"We can't very well go to him," Hitchcock said flatly.

"You'd better think of another way, Hitchcock, because if he dies, you die."

"You should consider your career, Captain. Such threats won't serve you well."

"My career is over, Hitchcock. I'll be resigning my commission. But Colonel Stanford here will tell you that I was the captain of the Academy's pistol team. If Andrew Rambarran dies, I will shoot you as a matter of honor." Erikson walked out of Hitchcock's office and, as he walked down the hallway, he heard Colonel Stanford telling the Station Chief, "He's upset, Fred. Andrew Rambarran was his roommate. Let's see how we can help to extricate him from this mess."

"Making threats won't help Rambarran," Hitchcock asserted.

"Maybe not," Colonel Stanford said, "but I think he means it."

TWENTY-THREE

February 24, 1980
Central Police Station, New Amsterdam

Andrew Rambarran felt his body jerk. When his eyes opened, he closed them back to avoid the brightness of the room. His joints felt stiff, and his entire frame ached with fatigue. He heard Lieutenant Shah's voice and boots on the wooden central stairway and reluctantly brought himself to a sitting position, pulling his legs to a bent position and noticing he had slept with his boots on. Reaching for the edge of the desk, he pulled himself up and walked around to lower himself in the chair. There was a knock at the door, and McCurchin popped his head in.

"Captain Spooner would like to borrow one of your uniforms."

Rambarran nodded and waved him away. "Give him a set and get me a change of uniform as well."

"Right, Captain," McCurchin said and stepped away from the door to allow Lieutenant Shah in.

"I've just returned from inspecting our positions," Shah reported. "Everything is fine. Some of the soldiers wanted to know whether we were in control yet. Evidently, nothing's been said on the two radio stations."

"Have the police officers been fed?"

"Yes, Captain. They wanted to know when we'll let them go. I was afraid they'd crowd you when you go over to the Police Officers' Quarters to shower so I posted two guards to clear a path for you."

"Thanks, Asad," Rambarran said, still slumped in the chair. "Get word to the Assistant Commissioner that they will all be allowed to leave after lunch. Any word from Ron Peters and Michael DeFreitas?"

"Peters left Springlands about half an hour ago. He should have picked up DeFreitas already. I expect they'll be here within twenty minutes or so."

"In that case," Rambarran said, "I'd better get cleaned up. You stay here and keep an eye on things."

*　　　*　　　*

At 12:00, in the Police conference room, Captain Rambarran addressed the three platoon leaders of F-Company, Captain Spooner, and the officers who came with him.

"Let's take a look at our situation, shall we? As we speak, the other side is probably rapidly reconsolidating its hold over Camp Ayanganna and reducing its presence at some of the border locations to build up strength before confronting us. My estimate, which I believe Captain Spooner agrees with, is that they will have sufficient strength within twenty-four hours to start selective aerial insertions of troops in Berbice. Capture of the Maritime Base at South Ruimveldt yielded one of the two smaller patrol boats, the *Parakeet*. The two larger Vosper Patrol boats, *Peccari I* and *Peccari II*, are still out there. Our own capture of the Maritime Base at Crabb Island yielded nothing except two inflatable rafts and some flare guns, which have been placed on the *Kurtuka*. My guess is that once the opposition has platoon strength at any location behind our lines, they would begin to move to reassert control over some of the more distant villages in Berbice. The larger patrol boats will then be employed against us while aerial insertions of troops continue. The *Peccaris*, as you know, have 20-millimeter cannons but they have limited stores of ammunition because of impoverishment of the government. On the other hand, they can be used in amphibious operations, and Berbice has over a hundred miles of Atlantic coastline, which we can't monitor.

"What are our options? One obvious one is to engage in an act of bravado and hold Berbice. The preponderance of forces favors the government. Can we resort to guerrilla warfare? Consider the following: the bulk of the population is coastal. To elude capture, we would have to go further inland and that's where the army has bases. We'd be caught between advancing troops from the coast and troops in secure bases further inland. Secondly, it won't be long before our soldiers learn that the coup did not succeed. I have a feeling they might have already guessed. In time, we will face desertions if we try to keep the company together. After all, we told them the overthrow was an army effort; they will soon learn that only a portion of the army was actually involved. Even in the current circumstances, these soldiers, out of habit and loyalty to their officers, will carry out orders for a while, but only for a while. I would not like to test the time limit on this one.

"The other option follows from what I have said regarding the first. My guess is that the Comrade Leader wants to eliminate the officers involved in the coup. My basis for this is Colonel Taylor's admonition that we try to save ourselves. I intend, toward the end of this day, to have all of the soldiers lay down their arms. They will be transported by the pontoon to Rosignol for eventual pick up by the army. They followed orders and will be spared, at least that is my hope. The officers must choose what to do. I would recommend we try to escape by open sea and put into Florida, where we'd seek political asylum. Suriname is not an option simply because the Kabaka government will lean on the Surinamese government to arrest us and turn us over. Anyone who chooses to may stay, but I'd caution you to consider what you risk by doing so. In any event, that decision must be made now."

"Can we make it to Florida on the *Kurtuka*?" Lieutenant Peters asked.

"Less sea-worthy boats have put out from Cuba and made it. I spoke with the Captain of the *Kurtuka*. He believes the *Kurtuka* should perform splendidly if we don't attempt to circumnavigate the world. This is not hurricane season, so the waters in the Caribbean shouldn't be too bad."

"I was thinking of the two larger Vosper Patrol Boats," Peters said. "They are faster and more maneuverable than the *Kurtuka* and, as you've just reminded us, they have 20-millimeter cannons."

"We will leave at dusk; I am hoping the darkness would help us. In addition, we'll have some defenses afforded by machine guns. But you are correct: it is a risky undertaking."

There was a loud knock on the door and McCurchin entered. "Captain?"

"Yes, McCurchin," Rambarran replied. McCurchin seemed tongue-tied. "Oh, come on, McCurchin, spit it out!"

"Colonel Taylor," McCurchin said softly.

"What about him, McCurchin?"

"Captain, Radio Demerara reported that Colonel Taylor is dead."

"My God!" Rambarran uttered, steadying himself. "Did they say how?"

McCurchin nodded. "They said there was an accident at Camp Groomes, some kind of explosion. Colonel Taylor, Captain Felix, and two other officers were killed."

All of the officers were on their feet, pacing and uttering expressions of disbelief. "Look," Rambarran said, "we have to continue with our planning. McCurchin, let us know if you hear anything else." McCurchin remained standing in place. "You can go, McCurchin," Rambarran said.

"Captain, they also said that Dr. Nelson was killed."

"Donald Nelson? Leader of the Workers' Party?"

"Yes, Captain. They said that the Police are investigating why Dr. Nelson was in the vicinity of the camp. His car blew up somewhere along the access road from the Linden Highway."

"Oh my God!" Rambarran exclaimed. "That maniac intends to kill every one of his opponents."

"Personally, I think we should stay and do as much damage as we can," Lieutenant Beharry declared. "What bothers me is that we are considering escaping without having struck a blow." Several officers murmured support.

"Look," Rambarran said, "don't you think I'd like to strike at that murdering bastard? But, here's the thing. If we stay and fight, we won't be hurting him. The soldiers we kill would be soldiers you've worked with before. The Comrade Leader wouldn't care. All he'll be interested in would be getting us. And in the end, he will. Also, you have no guarantee the soldiers we have will stay and fight in the current circumstances. My only goal now is to save as many lives as I can. And time is not on our side."

"Lieutenant Alex Mitchell, who commanded my third platoon was one of the officers killed at Camp Groomes," Captain Spooner said. "I, too, would like to get some revenge against this government, but Andrew is right. Attempting that now would be like pissing upwind. So, I agree with Andrew. We've already lost several lives. Let's try to save those we can."

Captain Rambarran watched as, one by one, the officers raised their hands, declaring in favor of flight by sea.

"Okay," Rambarran said, "here's the chain of command. Captain Spooner will be the second in command, then in order of date of appointment, Lieutenant Shah, Lieutenant Peters, Lieutenant Beharry. Decision-making hereafter will be by simple majority." Rambarran turned and noticed McCurchin had not left the door. "Get on the radio, McCurchin. Send the following message every five minutes: 'How are they all?'"

"'How are they all?'" McCurchin repeated, cringing his forehead.

"Yes, McCurchin, please. Just that: 'How are they all?'"

When McCurchin closed the door behind him, Lieutenant Peters asked, "Can you tell us what that's about?"

"Yes," Rambarran replied. "I have a friend at the U.S. Embassy who would recognize that code. I am hoping he can help us at the Florida end." Rambarran then outlined the evacuation plan before inviting them for lunch at the Esplanade Park encampment.

*　　*　　*

Georgetown

At 13:00, Erikson decided to walk up Main Street to get something to eat. At *Perreias's Snackette*, he ordered a tennis roll with a slab of cheese sandwiched in, and a peanut punch, a bottled blend of peanut butter and milk. Halfway into the tennis roll, Erikson glanced over his left shoulder at an attractive black woman and her male companion taking two of the vacant stools and, in what appeared to be a continuing conversation, the woman said, "What was Dr. Nelson doing out there?"

"That's the strange part," her companion replied. "It's an army camp."

"Gosh, he was such a brilliant man," she said, adding, "and so young."

"The radio said the Police are investigating," the man said, "but everybody knows how the government used the Police to harass that man."

"I still don't understand how an army camp can just blow up," the woman said. "You can't tell me that a Colonel didn't know what he was doing."

"The radio said that they stored ammunition and explosives there."

Mr. Perreia, the proprietor came over to the couple to take their order, and Erikson who had been eating slowly as he listened, took a final swig of his peanut punch and left for the Embassy.

Turning into the hallway where his office was located, Erikson saw Colonel Stanford and Station Chief Hitchcock talking.

"Colonel, do you know who just got blown up?" Erikson asked. "I heard some people talking about some radio report."

Colonel Stanford looked at Hitchcock then replied, "They're reporting that Colonel Taylor, Captain Felix, and several other officers were killed in an accidental explosion at Camp Groomes."

"My God!" Erikson exclaimed. "And what's this about Dr. Nelson?"

"His car evidently blew up somewhere along the access road from the Linden Highway to the camp."

Erikson's eyes riveted on Hitchcock, who instinctively turned to walk away. But Erikson grabbed him by his shoulders and slammed him against the wall. "You son-of-a-bitch! This is all your doing. You cut a deal with that devil, didn't you? You surrendered those officers to get Nelson, didn't you?"

Hitchcock said nothing nor did he attempt to tear himself away. Rather, it was Colonel Stanford who separated Erikson from Hitchcock, saying, "Take it easy, Steve. What's wrong with you?"

"What's wrong with me? Why don't you ask that sicko what's wrong with him? If we didn't want this government out, we could have discouraged the coup. But, no, that would not have achieved the ends of this fat rat. He wanted Nelson out; the Comrade Leader wanted Nelson out. Now everybody is happy. You used those officers and you used me. Take a good look at me, Hitchcock; you're looking at your executioner."

Erikson walked off to his office. Seating himself in his swivel chair, he slowly swung from side to side, unsure of what to do next. He thought about his house guests and what assurance he could now provide that Andrew Rambarran might survive. Erikson ignored Colonel Stanford when he walked into the office and sat down. For a couple of minutes Stanford said nothing as if waiting for Erikson to cool off; then, he broke the silence in a quiet, steady tone. "Steve, Andrew Rambarran's been trying to contact you."

Erikson stopped swinging. "When? How?"

"The NSA Listening Post reported monitoring the question, 'How are they all?' They said it was being sent every five minutes or so. No question it's him."

"We have to respond," Erikson said. "Christ! We have no plan."

"Look," Colonel Stanford said, "we'll need Hitchcock's help to get him out, so you'll have to tone it down."

"We? Did I hear you say 'we'?"

"Yes," Colonel Stanford replied. "I'll help as much as I can."

"Okay," Erikson said. "First, we let him know we heard him. Let's send the response he's waiting for."

"We can't do that openly," Stanford cautioned, "the government would know we're involved."

"Then how?" Erikson asked.

"We have to talk to Hitchcock," Stanford replied.

"Shit!"

"Come on, Steve, there isn't much time to lose."

Reluctantly, Steve Erikson elevated himself out of his chair and followed Stanford to Hitchcock's office. Hitchcock seemed to be expecting them. Colonel Stanford sat and signaled with a tilt of his head for Erikson to do the same. When they were both seated, Stanford spoke. "Fred, Steve wants to send a message to Rambarran."

"What's the message?" Hitchcock asked.

"They are all fickle but one," Erikson replied.

"Is this some kind of joke?" Hitchcock asked.

"No, no," Stanford interjected, leaning forward. "It's a bit of information the Plebes at West Point learn. It is the only answer that Rambarran would recognize as authentic. Trust me."

"Okay," Hitchcock said, "but we can't transmit in the open. I have an agent with a transmitter in New Amsterdam. He'll convey the message to Rambarran."

"That's only a tiny part of this," Erikson said. "How do we get him out of the country?"

"We have two trawlers operating off the Corentyne coast," Hitchcock replied. "They're armed to the teeth. They will pick up Rambarran and the others, but they will have to get out of Guyana's territorial waters."

"How will he locate the trawlers?" Erikson asked.

"He must use his VHF and transmit 'Wild Geese in flight,' a few times. The trawlers will triangulate his position."

"How soon can your agent contact Rambarran?" Erikson asked.

"Ten minutes," Hitchcock replied. "He's been standing by."

"Okay," Erikson said, standing up. Then as he walked toward the door, he turned around and very quietly said, "thank you."

Hitchcock glanced at Colonel Stanford and smiled broadly.

*   *   *

Central Police Station, New Amsterdam

"Captain," McCurchin said, standing at the door, "there is a man outside insisting on talking to you."

"Soldier?" Rambarran asked.

"No, Captain, a civilian."

"McCurchin, I don't have the time. We're leaving here in a couple of hours, so send him away."

"Captain, he says it's urgent."

"I don't have any dealings with civilians here, so get rid of him."

"He told me to tell you, 'They are all fickle but one.'"

"Oh, thank God!" Rambarran exclaimed. "Get him up here quickly."

"Who's he?" Lieutenant Shah asked.

"I don't know him, Asad; he's just a messenger, I'm sure. Let's hope the message he brings promises us deliverance."

In a couple of minutes, McCurchin was back with a slender, black man of medium height. He had a scraggy beard, but his hair appeared well tended. "Are you Captain Rambarran?" he asked. Rambarran nodded. The man reached into the right pocket of his cream shirtjac and handed Rambarran an envelope. "I copied the message verbatim," the man said. "You'll have to destroy that note, Captain, so they don't trace it back to me."

"What's it say, Captain?" Lieutenant Shah asked.

"It says we will be picked up outside the 12-mile territorial limit."

Lieutenant Shah smiled. "At last, some hope of deliverance."

"We still have a lot to do, Asad. And, make no mistake, twelve miles

213

could prove to be quite a challenge. McCurchin, show this gentleman out." When the man turned to go, Rambarran said, "thanks."

Rambarran stood thinking as he heard McCurchin's boots descending the wooden stairway. "Asad," he said to Lieutenant Shah, "start pulling the troops in from their defensive positions. You'll have to go to each location. Start with Palmyra."

Before Lieutenant Shah took leave to go, McCurchin returned, knocked, and stepped into the office.

"Yes," Rambarran said.

"Captain," McCurchin said, "I'd like to go with you."

"You can't, McCurchin," Rambarran replied. "Your best chance of staying alive is to be with the rest of the soldiers. It's hard enough to carry responsibility for the lives of the Officers; I can't add yours to that list."

"Captain, what chance would I have if I stay behind? I was Captain Moore's driver. When he was pushed out of the way, I became your driver. Can you guarantee this government would let me live after I've driven for two of their enemies?"

Rambarran looked from McCurchin to Lieutenant Shah, then turned his back and looked outside. Turning around again, he leaned forward on the desk. "McCurchin, you didn't do anything. You carry no blame. Now, what we are attempting could end in disaster. The best thing I can do for you is to provide you a sure way of living. Go with the other soldiers."

"They killed Colonel Taylor and Captain Felix. Who's to say I won't meet with some type of accident soon? Please, give me the choice to go with you or remain with the soldiers."

"I can't, McCurchin. Every officer here chose to be involved in the coup. You did not. Every officer knows he can die before we get out of territorial waters. Out of loyalty to you, I want to provide you a way to stay alive."

"I, too, have been loyal, Captain; first, to Captain Moore, your friend, and then to you. And all I ask in return is the chance to go with you. I am very good with the rifle and I can use the machine gun. And I am prepared to take full responsibility for whatever happens to me. Just give me the chance to get out of here."

Andrew Rambarran hoped Asad Shah would have supported

his position but the look in Asad Shah's face showed sympathy for McCurchin's plea. "Okay, McCurchin. You will continue to carry out all of your duties. However, you will not get on the pontoon with the soldiers of F-Company when they are ordered to."

"Yes, Captain," McCurchin saluted with the brightest smile Rambarran could remember in months.

"I wonder whether I've just signed his death warrant," Rambarran said to Asad Shah, after McCurchin had left.

"I don't think so," Shah replied. "I'd say you've just improved our chances of getting out."

"I hope you are right, Asad," Rambarran said. "I hope you are right."

TWENTY-FOUR

February 24, 1980
Ferry Station, New Amsterdam

At 16:00 hours, Captain Rambarran ordered all police personnel aboard the pontoon moored on the port side of the *Kurtuka*. Because of the narrowness of the gangplank to the *Kurtuka*, the policemen walked three abreast onto the Kurtuka's lower deck, and the column led back to the wharf, where Lieutenant Shah's platoon stood guard. The rest of F-Company's soldiers watched from the vicinity of the trucks which had brought them to New Amsterdam. All of the officers on the wharf were armed with SMGs, in addition to their service revolvers. On orders from Captain Rambarran, Lieutenant Morgan and the Maritime corporal had moved the *Parakeet* upstream to allow the pontoon and tugboat to be separated from the *Kurtuka* at the appropriate time. When the last of the police were aboard the pontoon, Captain Rambarran positioned himself, with Captain Spooner and his two Lieutenants behind him, at the center of the wharf.

"Sergeant Major!" Captain Rambarran's voice rang out. "Fall in the company!"

At the Sergeant Major's order, the soldiers arranged themselves in three platoons. Lieutenants Shah, Peters, and DeFreitas took positions in front of their respective platoons.

"Open ranks!" Rambarran ordered.

One after the other, each platoon leader yelled, "Open ranks, march!"

The front ranks of three platoons took one step forward, the rear ranks one step backward, and the center ranks remained in place.

"By sections, stack arms!" Captain Rambarran ordered.

In the open spaces created between the ranks, the soldiers stacked their weapons in groups of five, then resumed their place in ranks.

"Company, atten-tion!" Rambarran ordered and, in unison, the soldiers pounded their right heals into the concrete. "Stand-at-ease!"

Clasping their hands behind their backs, the soldiers of F-Company separated their feet shoulder-width apart.

"Brigade Officers, including the Officers of F-Company, were involved in an army attempt to overthrow the government," Rambarran said. "That attempt has failed, and I'm sorry to report that several officers lost their lives. You did nothing wrong; you merely followed the orders of your officers. As such, you will not be punished. However, you must surrender to the forces of the government, which means that you cannot report back to Camp Ayanganna bearing arms.

"When I dismiss you, you are to board the pontoon, which will take you to Rosignol. From there, the army will transport you back to Georgetown. It is absolutely important that you have no arms or ammunition on you or you could be shot. Remember too that you are not a rabble but a military unit, subject to military discipline. Once on board the pontoon, the Sergeant Major will be in command." Rambarran paused, looking from the left flank to the right, and then back to the center of the formation. "On behalf of myself and the other officers, I thank you for the privilege of serving with you. I wish you all a long life." Rambarran's voice fractured. He took a deep breath. "Company, atten-tion! Company will retire; about face! Company, dismissed!"

The armed officers watched the soldiers walk down the gangplank onto the *Kurtuka* and then into the pontoon. When they were all aboard, Captain Rambarran signaled to the sailors on the *Kurtuka* to release the moorings. The tugboat skipper revved up the engine and gradually separated the pontoon from the *Kurtuka*, pointing its bow toward Rosignol. Rambarran ordered the sailors from the *Kurtuka* to load the stacked weapons onto the ferry. In the meantime, the *Parakeet* had been repositioned on the port side of the *Kurtuka* for Captain Spooner to board with Lieutenants Beharry and Clark. As the tugboat and pontoon turned to dock at Rosignol on the other side of the river, Spooner waved to Rambarran and ordered Lieutenant Morgan to head out to the mouth of the Berbice River.

Aboard the *Kurtuka* with McCurchin and the remaining officers, Captain Rambarran watched the progress of the *Parakeet* until he was sure its course was hidden from Rosignol by the curvature of the river bank. He ordered the *Kurtuka* skipper to proceed to the middle of the river and to move slowly toward the river's mouth. He continued to monitor the *Parakeet* through his field glasses and, as agreed, the patrol boat turned northward as if heading to Georgetown but arced around and settled on a course due east for Adventure Village. The soldiers and police had long disembarked from the pontoon, and Rambarran felt satisfied they could not be sure of the true course of the *Parakeet*. It was the same course he ordered the ferry skipper to follow, when, at 16:25 hours, the *Kurtuka* emerged out of the Berbice River.

*   *   *

The Lesbeholden Channel

At 18:15, the *Parakeet* turned into the Lesbeholden canal separating Adventure from Hog Sty, moving past multicolored fishing boats moored on both sides and coming to a stop close to the Lesbeholden sluice. Lieutenant Morgan attached a rope to a fishing boat moored to the left bank, allowing Captain Spooner and Lieutenants Beharry and Clark, each carrying an SMG, to walk over to the bank. Galloping to the highway, Spooner flagged down a taxi, ordered the passengers out, and climbed into the front while his Lieutenants jumped into the rear.

"Philippi!" Spooner ordered the frightened driver. "And step on it!"

In less than ten minutes, the taxi pulled into the front entrance of the Spooner farm. The gate watchman was gone and, a couple of hundred feet in, a police jeep sat across the access road. Rifle shots discharged from somewhere ahead of the jeep were striking the Spooner residence. The taxi advanced, the report from the gunfire masking the crunching sounds it made on the gravel road. Spooner ordered the driver to stop about thirty feet from the jeep, and the officers quickly exited, rushing toward the jeep. Just then, a Police Inspector, who was evidently directing the rifle fire, came around the jeep, service revolver in hand. A quick burst from Spooner's SMG, and the Inspector fell dead. From their vantage point behind the jeep, the officers saw four police constables at staggered distances along the side of the road, lying in a low crawl position with their weapons pointed toward the house. The burst of gunfire had halted their forward movement. They turned to re-aim their .303 Enfield rifles in the direction of the jeep, but short bursts from Lieutenants Beharry and Clark took out the closest ones, while Spooner hit one of the further constables. The last constable tossed his rifle and was attempting to rise when nine millimeter rounds from Beharry and Clark struck him. There appeared to be no other armed elements in the front of the property, so Spooner and his Lieutenants rushed toward the house. Once on the concrete apron, Spooner signaled Beharry and Clark around the eastern and western sides of the house respectively and, entering the ground level garage, he approached the door leading upstairs to the living room, where his mother unbolted the door to let him in.

"What's happening, Ralph?" Susan Spooner asked.

"I can't explain it all right now, Mother, but we attempted to overthrow the government. We have to get out now. We have a boat waiting."

"We can't leave," Susan Spooner said.

"What? Why not?"

"Lena," Susan Spooner replied, "she's not here. She went for her afternoon ride to the back of the farm before all of this started. There are Party people with guns out there. Do you think they have her?"

"No, Mother," Ralph replied. "If they did, they would have used her to get you and Dad to give up. Lena is a smart girl. I bet she's hiding out back there."

Ralph led the way up the stairs to the second floor and then up the winding stairs to the Observatory, where Dr. Spooner sat with his hunting rifle pointed to the rear. Ralph greeted his father briefly and related his involvement with the failed coup attempt as he moved around the southern half of the octagon with the binoculars. He saw several figures in military-type fatigues carrying guns, but they appeared to be keeping out of range.

"Dad, I think those Party people were backstopping for the police. They are between us and Lena, and my guess is that they don't know she's out there. Try to pick them off with the rifle while we advance on them. Don't worry, I have two other officers with me."

Ralph Spooner picked up his SMG and rushed down to the ground level and out to the eastern side of the house, where Beharry had taken up his position. Extending his head around the edge of the building, he called out to Lieutenant Clark. "Duncan, we'll have to rush them. Follow me, and keep low."

The rifle in the Observatory went off, and someone in the distance screamed out. Ralph Spooner seized on that moment to rush forward, keeping his body bent fully forward. The other two officers followed, hitting the dirt in a prone position every time he did. With Ralph Spooner at the apex of a triangular formation, the three officers ran and stopped, aided by covering fire from the Observatory. As they neared the back canal, Ralph Spooner fired short bursts into the fruit orchard. Apart from the one man writhing in pain from the Dr. Spooner's rifle shot, the other Party men were fleeing.

"Prone position!" Spooner ordered, and Lieutenants Beharry and Clark lay flat on the grass with their weapons pointing out. "We need to wait a while. My sister is out there with her horse."

*　　　*　　　*

Aboard the *Kurtuka*

Andrew Rambarran stood outside the pilothouse observing the helicopter above the northern horizon, flying toward the shore. As the helicopter neared the coastline, it turned and began trailing the *Kurtuka*, staying out of range of small arms fire. When Lieutenant Shah joined him, Rambarran passed the binoculars to him. "Well," Rambarran said, "they have our location. The question is how fast can they get a gunboat out here."

"What if they can't," Asad Shah asked. "Do you think that helicopter is going to close in?"

"No," Rambarran replied. "This boat has a steel hull and that helicopter doesn't have the munitions to disable it. Besides, they know that we can bring down that plane."

"So, what do you think they'll do?"

"My guess is that they'll enlist the help of the Surinamese government. They have four of those old Dutch patrol boats. They are not very fast but each carries two 40-millimeter Bofors cannons. If this tub runs into one of those patrol boats, they'll blow us to bits."

"Why is the helicopter staying with us?" Shah asked.

"Partly to confirm our course," Rambarran replied, reaching back for the binoculars. "They have soldiers with SLRs on board. I believe they are planning to insert them somewhere."

At the back of Cromarty Village, the helicopter turned south, heading inland.

"Looks like they might be heading for the Spooner farm," Lieutenant Shah said.

"I'm afraid you might be right," Rambarran responded. "I hope to God the Spooners are out of there."

At 18:40, the *Kurtuka* stopped outside of the Lesbeholden channel. From the upper deck, Rambarran could see the *Parakeet* moored near the sluice. With the engines of the ferry shut down, he could hear the report from gunfire. "Spooner is tied down at the farm," he said passing the binoculars to Lieutenant Shah. "Stay here with Lieutenant DeFreitas; I'll take a couple of people out there." He ordered the sailors to lower the rubber raft. "McCurchin," Rambarran called out, "here's your chance. Bring the machine gun and tripod."

"Captain, you'll need someone to feed the ammo belt," Lieutenant Peters said.

"Okay, if you want to volunteer," Rambarran replied, stepping into the rubber raft with an SMG. McCurchin climbed in with the machine gun, and Lieutenant Peters followed carrying an SMG and an ammunition canister. Rambarran pulled the starter cord, and a sailor tossed the mooring rope into the raft. Slowly, the raft edged away from the ferry before Rambarran opened the throttle propelling the raft along the channel toward the Lesbeholden sluice. As they approached the moored fishing boats, Rambarran eased down on the throttle and brought the raft next to the *Parakeet*, where Lieutenant Morgan secured the raft to the patrol boat. Once on the bank, Rambarran and his two companions dashed up to the main road where he commandeered a passing taxi for the trip to Philippi.

*   *   *

The Spooner Farm

As the taxi pulled into the main entrance of the Spooner farm, Rambarran saw in the distance beyond the house a slow-moving helicopter, flying eastward. The taxi stopped by the police jeep blocking the road, and the occupants got out, freeing the taxi driver to reverse rapidly back to the main road. Rambarran and his companions were moving around the police jeep when they heard the sounds of a second helicopter coming in toward them from the west.

"Take cover!" Rambarran ordered, still watching the first helicopter in the distance behind the house.

McCurchin set the machine gun on the ground, just by the edge of the jeep, and opened the breach for Lieutenant Peters to feed in the ammo belt. They waited. The first helicopter behind the house had turned around and was now flying westward. Rambarran surmised that the two choppers were coordinating their movements and he expected both to land, one at the front and the other at the rear. Soon the loud sputtering sounds from the front chopper announced its arrival at the western edge of the property, where it hovered over the flamboyant tree, spewing its red flowers like so many butterflies above the western pasture.

"McCurchin, aim that weapon at the engine!" Rambarran ordered. McCurchin and Peters repositioned themselves away from the jeep to get a wider field of view and to allow for a wider sweep of the gun. The tripod now rested on the beveled side of the road, the muzzle of the gun pointing upward, directly at the chopper.

"Okay, McCurchin, let's see what you can do," Rambarran said, and, for several minutes, the machine gun spitted 7.62 millimeter rounds into the hovering chopper. The pilot slumped forward before the chopper exploded, and Rambarran felt sure Ralph Spooner would know that assistance had arrived.

"Let's go!" Rambarran said, advancing ahead, with McCurchin carrying the machine gun and Lieutenant Peters the ammo canister and his SMG. At the house, he motioned the other two around the eastern side as he reconnoitered the western side. The sounds of the rear helicopter suggested it had not landed, but seeing no immediate threat around the house, Rambarran rushed to the ground level and knocked at the door. Susan Spooner opened for him.

"Susan, where's Ralph?"

"He's near the back canal with two other officers," she replied. "They're waiting for Lena, who's out there somewhere."

"Oh, my God!" Rambarran said. "Listen, Susan, you need to get your passports and any valuables you can lay your hands on. We're leaving as soon as they get in." Before Susan Spooner could say anything, Rambarran dashed out of the garage, only turning to say, "Get that Land Rover started and ready to go."

Keeping a low profile, Rambarran began running to the back of the property, McCurchin and Lieutenant Peters lagging behind on account of the weight of the load they were carrying. The helicopter ahead was hovering above the rice fields out of range of the SMGs of Spooner and his two officers, who had risen to kneeling positions to see over the back dam. Rambarran stopped in his tracks when he heard Lieutenant Beharry yelled out, "Ralph, ten o'clock!" and saw the figure of Lena Spooner on her horse galloping on one of the causeways separating the fields and passing under the rear of the helicopter. The pilot swung the chopper around to give the riflemen aboard a better position from which to aim, but Lena and the horse had not been struck. Seeing her predicament, McCurchin attempted firing from the hip with Peters assisting, but McCurchin could not control the rapidly firing weapon, and they did nothing more than to alert the pilot to the danger the machine gun posed. The pilot brought the chopper down in the rice field, where it remained, hidden behind the back dam. Lena Spooner was advancing rapidly toward the bridge over the back canal and, from the Observatory, Dr. Spooner fired into the rice fields, reloaded, and fired.

Lena was now over the back canal bridge, riding past Ralph Spooner's position. Just then, there were staggered bursts of rifle fire from concealed positions behind the back dam. The galloping horse buckled under, throwing its rider into the air. The officers watched helplessly as Lena Spooner's body somersaulted forward and bounced off the edge of the east-side canal into the water. Lieutenant Beharry leapt into the canal and, moments later, reached up to the bank, pulling Lena Spooner behind him. With Ralph Spooner and Duncan Clark firing short bursts and Dr. Spooner in the Observatory firing selective shots, Beharry picked up Lena Spooner across his shoulder in a fireman's carry and commenced running toward the house.

"How bad is she?" Rambarran asked, when Beharry reached his position.

"Badly bruised," Beharry replied. "I think her left shoulder might be dislocated."

Lena Spooner teared-up when Andrew Rambarran stroked her face. Relieved that his fiancé was not more seriously hurt, Rambarran said, "Get her to Dr. Spooner, Ramesh, and tell him we're leaving in a hurry." Rambarran signaled Ralph Spooner to withdraw, pointing to McCurchin and Peters beside the machine gun on the western side of the road. McCurchin fired, scalping the top of the back dam, daring the opposition to show their heads. Keeping a low profile, Ralph Spooner and Duncan Clark ran toward the house, stopping at intervals and checking behind to make sure it was safe to move again. When they had passed the machine gun emplacement, they took up positions behind Rambarran to allow McCurchin and Peters to retreat. As they approached the house, they saw widely dispersed, uniformed soldiers, who had crawled over the back dam, advancing by short runs and low crawling. Rambarran decided it was time for them to leave the property.

Dr. Spooner had the three-quarter ton Land Rover pointed toward the front entrance, with Susan and Lena Spooner sitting beside him. Rambarran rushed in front to check on Lena and learned that Dr. Spooner had re-set her shoulder. Her face was cleaned up, and she seemed shaken but relieved. She smiled when Rambarran winked at her before returning to the back of the jeep. Lieutenants Beharry and Clark were already seated. Ralph Spooner preceded Rambarran, and McCurchin and Peters entered last, positioning the machine gun on the tail gate. The Land Rover sped off, but was stopped by the police jeep obstructing the road. Dr. Spooner attempted to move around the eastern side but backed up on account of the softness of the canal bank.

"We've got to move that bloody jeep," Rambarran said.

"I'll do it," Spooner said, jumping out of the Land Rover and moving to the right side of the jeep where the steering wheel was located. The key was still in the ignition. He started it, set it on neutral, then came to the back where Rambarran helped him push the jeep into the canal. They quickly ran around to the back of the Land Rover, where Ralph Spooner stood aside to let Rambarran enter first. Then came an explosion from a grenade, and those at the back of the Land Rover saw the area of the Observatory hollowed out, with splintered wood and other debris raining down. Two other grenades followed in rapid succession and, except for the front facade, the rest of the edifice was gone. Ralph Spooner's fists went up and he screamed.

"Come on, Ralph!" Rambarran yelled, but Ralph Spooner fell to his knees before they heard the report of a rifle. Out of the Land Rover came Rambarran and Clark. They picked up Spooner by his shoulders and dragged him into the vehicle, laying him flat on his back. The Land Rover sped out to the property entrance while McCurchin and Peters fired the machine gun. Dr. Spooner did not slow down to make the left turn onto the coastal road and, with very little traffic on the road, sped along the highway. The machine gun was pulled in but the tailgate remained down to accommodate Ralph Spooner's extended legs. His head rested on a couple of berets and he was sweating profusely. While Duncan Clark sopped the perspiration, Andrew Rambarran undid a couple of buttons on Spooner's shirt to examine the wound. There was surprisingly little blood on the shirt and the spot where the bullet had entered was tiny and noticeable only by the blood stain.

At the Lesbeholden sluice, the Spooners rushed to the *Parakeet*. With Ron Peters and McCurchin providing rearguard cover, Andrew Rambarran and Lieutenants Beharry and Clark carried Ralph Spooner. As they approached the *Parakeet*, screams issued from the patrol boat when Susan and Lena Spooner realized that it was Ralph the other officers were carrying. Ralph was laid at the stern, his head resting on a life vest, and the patrol boat began moving, pulling the rubber raft behind it. With his wife beside him, Dr. Spooner gave Ralph the shot of morphine Lieutenant Morgan had retrieved from the first aid kit, and bandaged his wound.

"How bad is it?" Andrew asked, kneeling with Lena beside the Spooners.

"Bad," Dr. Spooner said grimly. "His pulse is weak, and his heart rate is very fast."

"But he hasn't lost much blood," Rambarran remarked.

"You can't see it," Dr. Spooner replied. "The blood is filling up the abdominal cavity. That's why his stomach is getting distended. Only serious medical attention can save him."

"Maybe the trawler we're going to will be equipped to handle this," Andrew said.

"I hope so," Dr. Spooner replied, "but I am worried we might not arrive in time." That declaration caused Lena Spooner to utter choking sounds as she tightened her arms around Andrew Rambarran. Susan Spooner wept while she sopped perspiration from the face and forehead of her son, and the officers looked on helplessly. It was 19:30 hours; the sun was down, but there was still some daylight.

"Captain Rambarran!" The call came from Lieutenant Morgan at the bridge of the patrol boat.

Kissing Lena on her temple, Andrew went to the bridge. The *Kurtuka* was gone. With the binoculars, Rambarran scanned ahead, then eastward. What appeared in his view was the stern of one of the *Peccaris*.

"Goodness," he said. "They're chasing the *Kurtuka*." Rambarran found himself flanked by the other officers, who had rushed up to the bridge and were looking at him for a decision. "Okay, here's what we'll do," he said. "Lieutenant Morgan will take the *Parakeet* out to the trawler. I'll remain here with the rubber raft in the event the *Kurtuka* returns."

"What if they catch the *Kurtuka*?" Lieutenant Morgan asked.

"Until I know that as a fact, I have to assume they'll return, and I have a responsibility to those officers." No one said anything. "Look, if they don't return, I'll try to make it out on the rubber raft."

"Twelve miles out?" Morgan asked.

"It'll be dark soon. Maybe the trawler can fudge the twelve-mile limit. I'll fire flares."

"I'll remain with you," Lieutenant Peters said. Lieutenant DeFreitas made the same offer, as did McCurchin.

"Just Ron Peters, no one else," Rambarran replied. "Remember, you are to broadcast 'Wild Geese in Flight,' to get the trawler to pick you up."

Andrew Rambarran went to the stern to let the Spooners know what the situation was. Lena remonstrated, but Andrew insisted he had to carry on with his obligations, assuring her he was going to be fine. Then he climbed into the rubber raft with his SMG and flare gun, followed by Peters and, to everyone's surprise, McCurchin. Rambarran did not protest; instead, he gave the signal and the mooring rope was tossed over. The three on the raft waved and watched the patrol boat head out to sea. The *Parakeet* was still in sight when the men in the boat heard the sound of a helicopter. When it came in sight, it was maintaining a high altitude and heading in the direction of the patrol boat.

It was getting darker. The three in the raft had drifted closer to shore where they waited. Hardly half an hour had elapsed when they saw an elegantly lit vessel traversing the horizon in a northwesterly direction as if to intercept the escaping patrol boat. The vessel's searchlights were sweeping ahead as it moved purposefully at a steady clip.

"That's the same *Peccari*," Rambarran said. "They must think the *Kurtuka* is just a decoy."

The three watched the lights of the *Peccari* grow dimmer with distance until it faded altogether.

"Captain," Lieutenant Peters said, "what if the *Kurtuka* is still intact and heads out to sea on the assumption that we left in the patrol boat?"

"We'll have to risk going out in the raft," Rambarran replied. "We should find out within the hour, but I know Lieutenant Shah. His orders were to wait and pick us up. He will return to this area before he puts out to sea."

It seemed like an interminable wait, though it was only three-quarters of an hour by their watches when they caught sight of a vessel whose lights outlined the profile of the *Kurtuka*. It was heading west. Captain Rambarran pulled the starter cord, and throttled up to get the raft out to deeper waters. As the *Kurtuka* neared their location; he fired a flare. Soon the *Kurtuka* slowed to a stop, and Rambarran maneuvered the raft toward the waiting boat.

TWENTY-FIVE

February 24, 1980
Aboard the *Kurtuka*

At the lower deck of the *Kurtuka*, Lieutenants Shah and DeFreitas welcomed Rambarran, Peters, and McCurchin aboard and assisted in pulling in the rubber raft.

"I don't know why," Shah said, "but the *Peccari* turned away from us."

"My guess is that they thought the *Kurtuka* was a decoy," Rambarran responded. "The helicopter tailing us out here must have radioed back that the *Parakeet* was racing out to open sea. Let's hope the *Parakeet* outruns them."

"What now?" Shah asked.

"We head out as planned," Rambarran replied. "I'll have the skipper take a more northeasterly course."

"I believe we were spotted by one of the Surinamese patrol boats," Lieutenant Shah reported.

"Where?" Rambarran asked.

"We were outside of No. 63 Village," Shah replied. "We saw it through the binoculars. I'd say it was in the mouth of the Corentyne River, about six miles due east of Springlands."

"Well, we won't go that far east," Rambarran said, walking off with Lieutenant Shah in the direction of the stern stairway. At the door to the pilothouse, he was struck by how much like an excursion boat the lights on the *Kurtuka* made the ferry appear.

"Set a course 10 degrees east of north," he said to the ferry skipper, "and turn off the lights on the boat."

"I'm following navigation codes," the skipper replied, "and that requires lights on the starboard and port sides, as well as at the stern."

"Look, skipper," Rambarran said, "right now, we're a bunch of outlaws. So, don't tell me about navigation codes, or any other codes for that matter. I don't want to advertise our position."

"You're the boss," the ferry skipper said. "Now, I have a question for you." Rambarran looked at him and shrugged. "My crew would like to know if political asylum would be open to them."

"Skipper," Rambarran replied, "the truth is that I don't know how all of this would be handled. I am hoping that my officers would be covered. If you and your crew continue to cooperate as you have, the argument could be made that your lives would be in danger were you to return home. I would be prepared to make that case."

"That's good enough for me," the ferry skipper said.

"In the meantime," Rambarran said, "remember that all of the officers on this boat can read a compass."

"You seem to be on edge, Captain," the skipper said. "You should get some rest." Rambarran remained silent. "Did something happen back there?" the skipper asked.

"My best friend got shot," Rambarran replied.

"Dead?" the skipper asked.

"We don't know as yet, but it's a gut wound."

"Sorry to hear that," the skipper said.

"Ralph Spooner?" Lieutenant Shah asked. Rambarran nodded. "Oh my God!" Shah uttered. "How bad is it?"

"Bad," Rambarran replied. "Dr. Spooner said he was spilling blood into his abdomen. It'll take an hour for the *Parakeet* to get to the trawlers, and I don't know how well equipped they are to deal with this type of wound."

"I'm sorry, Andrew," Shah said, "I really hope he makes it."

"So do I Asad; so do I."

The night grew darker, and the wind picked up. The waves crashed against the bow, casting over sheets of water, which rolled along the lower deck and drained out at the sides. Even the sailors retreated to the passenger deck above where the officers were opening up the food stores. Dinner consisted of dry bread, slabs of cheese, bananas, and un-iced Cokes.

At about 21:00, Lieutenant Peters came into the pilothouse with food for Rambarran, Shah, and the ferry skipper. Rambarran passed on the food but took a bottle of lukewarm Coca-Cola.

"Why don't you and Asad get some rest, Captain?" Peters suggested. "I'll take over here."

"Thanks, Ron," Rambarran replied, "but I'm too wound up to fall asleep right now. Besides, we should be out of territorial waters in about an hour. How are the other officers doing?"

"A bit gloomy over Ralph Spooner's prospects," Peters replied. "I'm sure they'd be glad when this is over."

"I know the feeling," Rambarran said. "And McCurchin, how's he?"

Lieutenant Peters laughed. "Just being McCurchin. He's fitting in very nicely, I think you should give him a field commission."

Andrew Rambarran laughed. "That's right. I can do anything out here. How about if we make him a Field Marshal?" They both laughed. "You know, I'm glad he came along," Rambarran said calmly. "Odd as it may seem, his presence and his antics are quite reassuring to me. I've been so accustomed to having him around. I hope for his sake we make it out okay."

In the pilothouse, they heard yelling from the passenger deck.

"Better go and check on that kuffufle down there," Rambarran said to Ron Peters, but there was no need. Gesticulations from the open end of the passenger deck made Rambarran and the ferry skipper look over to the rapidly moving, brightly lit profile of the *Peccari* on the rear port side. With its searchlight sweeping ahead, the *Peccari* was moving eastward to intercept.

"Couldn't we elude them by going west, then north?" Lieutenant Shah asked.

"No, I don't think you can hide this elephant in a paper bag," Rambarran replied. "The *Peccari* is equipped with radar. We'll have to gamble that they won't risk going into Surinamese waters." Turning to the ferry skipper, he said, "Turn this boat due east."

Thus began the chase. The *Kurtuka* was moving at 17 knots heading for Suriname; the *Peccari* maintained a parallel course due east, narrowing the distance separating them.

"What's your estimate of the distance separating us?" Rambarran asked the ferry skipper.

"I'd say two miles, north, two to three miles back," the ferry skipper replied.

"Let's see," Rambarran said, figuring.

"At 25 knots, the *Peccari* can intercept us in less than twenty minutes."

"That's about right," the ferry skipper said.

"But in fifteen minutes, we could be in the mouth of the Corentyne River. That's Surinamese territory. We'll have to take the chance that the border dispute will work to our advantage."

"What do you want me to do, Captain?" the ferry skipper asked.

"Make for the Corentyne River."

The skipper gave the wheel a gentle turn to the right, nudging the *Kurtuka* away from due east onto a course which brought it closer to the Guyana coastline. The *Peccari*, on the other hand, maintained its straight line course.

"Don't you think that's odd?" Shah asked.

"Yes," Rambarran replied. "It's like they're only interested in keeping us hemmed in." Then, turning to the *Kurtuka* skipper, Rambarran asked, "Any ideas?"

"Sorry, I'm not Horatio Nelson; I'm just a ferry skipper."

"Well, I know this coast," Rambarran said, "and at the current speed, we should be in the mouth of the Corentyne River before they intercept us."

Andrew Rambarran walked out of the pilothouse with Asad Shah and Ron Peters. "Lieutenant Shah," he said officiously, "assemble the Officers on the lower deck; McCurchin too." Rambarran remained outside the pilothouse, leaning against the rail and watching the *Peccari*, its course still unaltered. On the starboard side was the Corentyne coastline with clusters of light in what he estimated to be No. 64 Village. He took a deep breath, then went down the stern stairway to the lower deck.

"Gentlemen, here is the situation as I see it," Rambarran began. "That *Peccari* appears to be trying to keep us from heading out to open sea, but it is doing so rather gingerly. Which makes me believe they might be maneuvering us toward a second boat. My guess is that they've worked something out with the Surinamese. If we stay on this tub, they'll blow us out of the water. So, we will turn into the Corentyne River and get behind the Papegaaien Island. It's the largest one in the river mouth. We'll get off in the rafts, allow the sailors off, and blow the boat."

"Why can't we get off now?" Lieutenant Shah asked.

"Because the *Peccari* or some other gunboat will keep tracking the ferry and fire on it," Rambarran replied.

"But that's not our responsibility," Shah asserted.

"The safety of the skipper and crew became our responsibility from the time we took over the ferry. Look, we don't have time. Put food and water in the rubber rafts. Grab all the flares you can get. Also be sure you have one VHF radio per raft. Take only the SMGs and extra ammo, and stay on the lower deck."

"Why, Captain?" McCurchin asked.

"Because if the *Peccari* fires its cannons, it will likely, given the closeness of the range, strike the upper deck."

As the *Kurtuka* passed outside of Springlands, a sailor walked up to the group. "Captain Rambarran, the skipper wants you on the bridge right away. There's another boat ahead."

"Get moving!" Rambarran said to his officers, as he rushed up the stern stairway to the pilothouse. "Put on life vests and get the sailors to lower the side ramps," he added before he disappeared into the upper deck.

From the pilothouse, Rambarran saw the approaching vessel. It was still some ways northeast of Nickerie, moving parallel to the Surinamese coastline but directly toward the *Kurtuka*. It sat much higher in the water than coastal fishing boats, and its searchlight shone brightly ahead. There was no question in Rambarran's mind that this was a Surinamese gunboat. More trouble, Rambarran thought when he looked to the port side and saw that the *Peccari* had changed course and was also moving directly toward the *Kurtuka*.

"Okay, skipper," Rambarran said. "Take us into the Corentyne River. When we get around the first island, pull the boat in close."

"We could be grounded," the skipper warned.

"It doesn't matter," Rambarran responded. "We need to get you and the crew off. They're going to blow this mother out of the water."

The *Peccari* was closing in faster than the Surinamese gunboat.

"Can't this thing move faster?" Rambarran asked.

"The tide is going out," the skipper replied. "This is the best we can do."

Both the *Peccari* and the Surinamese patrol boat were in the mouth of the Corentyne River and, in a matter of minutes, the searchlight beam from the *Peccari* would strike the *Kurtuka*.

"Which side of the island do you want me to take?" the skipper asked, as the ferry approached Papegaaien Island.

"Take the passage on the Surinamese side," Rambarran replied.

The passage was wide enough, and the shadows from trees on the bank and on the island rendered it pitch black. The *Kurtuka* came into the passage at the end of the same arc it had begun from Springlands. It had just rounded the northeastern end of the island when Rambarran saw the bright flash from near the river bank and heard the impact of shell striking the bow of the *Kurtuka*, shearing off one portion and warping what remained. Everyone and everything on the lower deck had been thrust over the starboard side. The searchlight of the hidden gunboat flashed again, directly at the pilothouse blinding the two occupants. Then came a second round striking the steel scaffold supporting the pilothouse. The impact slammed Rambarran and the skipper against the rear, shattering the glass windows, then propelled them forward against the control panel before they fell on the floor. With blood streaming down the back of his neck, Rambarran crawled to the door which had flung open. The pilothouse was now a collapsed compartment resting on the stern gunwale of a boat that was now sinking. Reaching for the dazed skipper, Rambarran placed a doughnut float over him, and helped him crawl out to the gunwale, from which they jumped.

The coldness of the water revived Rambarran somewhat; the skipper too seemed more alert and was wading himself away from the wreckage. When the beam from the searchlight fanned in his direction, Rambarran went underwater, swimming toward the bank on the Surinamese side. He resurfaced some distance from the bank and paused to catch his breath since the searchlight continued to focus on the area where several of the ferry sailors were treading water. Diving again, he moved even closer to the bank, emerging in the shallows. Standing erect and taking advantage of the distraction of those on the Surinamese patrol boat, he thrust himself forward through the *moko-moko*, gasping each time the nettle ripped into the skin of his forearms. Finally, he reached the grassy bank and lowered himself down, feeling secure behind the tall elephant ears of the *moko-moko*.

He told himself he'd stay put until the commotion nearby diminished, then he'd figure out his next move. He pulled out the wet handkerchief from his hip pocket, pressed it against the sore spot at the back of his head, then wiped the scratches on his forearms. Soon, the patrol boat would move on, and it would be safe to pick his ground. He lay on his back and stretched out. The tall, untended grass cushioned his body like nothing he had experienced over the past two days. For a while, he listened to the voices on the river, but they seemed to get fainter and fainter.

Andrew Rambarran awoke from someone kicking against his boot. Several figures were standing around him when his eyes opened. He tried to scramble to his feet, but his body seemed reluctant to act, and he found himself sitting up and flailing his arms. He stopped and hung his head toward his chest, fatigued and disoriented.

Two people picked him up by the arms, walked him up to the back of a jeep and helped him in. Three policemen entered the back with him, pulling the tailgate behind them. When he could focus clearly, he recognized the Surinamese uniforms. He wanted to sleep some more, but the jeep bounced around on the dam. From his seat on the right side, he could see they were following the bank of the river. Soon there were no more *moko-moko* or mangrove, but a seawall like the one around Georgetown. They passed a few houses before the jeep turned right onto an asphalt road and sped along. It made a couple of turns until it passed by what appeared to be a municipal market where it turned toward an imposing cream-colored building, not unlike the police station at Albion or Springlands. They lowered the tailgate and led him into the office on the ground floor where the Creole Inspector, who had ridden in the cab of the jeep, offered him a seat.

"Would you like something to eat?" the Inspector asked. Rambarran shook his head. "How about something to drink? Some hot coffee?" Rambarran nodded. The Inspector said something to a Hindustani constable in Dutch and, shortly after, the constable came back with a hot cup of instant coffee. Sipping the strong blend of coffee lifted Rambarran's spirits.

"We're going to place you in a holding cell until morning," the Inspector said. "Then, we'll transfer you back to Guyana. Those are the orders. You don't have to, but you might want to get out of those wet clothes. You'll get them back in the morning before you leave. No hurry, you can do that before you retire."

"Thank you, Inspector," Rambarran said. "I appreciate the consideration."

"No problem," the Inspector said. "You are not an ordinary prisoner, Captain. Besides, you committed no crime in this country. The sergeant here will see you to your cell after you're through with the coffee. Let him know if you have any special needs. Otherwise, I will see you tomorrow morning."

"Thanks again, Inspector," Rambarran said, and as he left, the Inspector reached up with his fingers, touched his forehead in a simulated salute.

Rambarran had not asked about his officers, fearing that such a question might alert the Inspector to the others still on the loose. Instead, he continued sipping the coffee under the watchful eye of a Hindustani sergeant seated at the desk. When the cup was empty, Rambarran placed it on the sergeant's desk and rose to follow the sergeant. It was 23:45 hours on February 24th.

Twenty-six

February 25th, 1980
Regional Police Headquarters, Nickerie, Suriname

The Hindustani constable, who came to open the cell doors, left the door to the reception room ajar, and through it came a cacophony of agitated voices. Rambarran felt sure they were not prisoners because they were speaking too freely, mostly over the voices of one another.

"What's going on out there, constable?" Rambarran asked.

"Big problems," the constable replied. "The military has taken over the government."

"In Guyana?"

"No, right here in Suriname."

"When did this happen?" Rambarran asked.

"This morning," the constable replied, "and it's going on right now."

"How did you find out?"

"I heard it on *Radio Radika*," the constable replied. "A bunch of sergeants. They wanted to form a union in the army, but the government jailed a few of them. That's what set them off."

"Sergeants?" Rambarran asked.

"Yes. They don't like the police. That's what they're talking about outside. The sergeants blew up the Police Headquarters on the Waterkant in Paramaribo."

"What's the Waterkant?"

"That's the name of a stretch of road in Paramaribo along the western bank of the Suriname River."

"So, what about me?" Rambarran asked. "What will happen?"

"I don't know," the constable replied. "We'll have to see what the new government wants."

"What are the possibilities here? Can I leave? I've committed no crimes in Suriname."

"You're on the prisoner manifest," the corporal replied, "you can't leave. They'll either send you back to Guyana or transfer you to the Central Penitentiary in Santo Boma, outside of Paramaribo."

*   *   *

February 25th, 1980
Embassy of the United States, Georgetown

Steve Erikson came to the Embassy to take refuge. He had been up most of the evening with Anita and her father speculating about the whereabouts of Andrew. He left home while they were still asleep, hoping to get the answers before returning there. The coffee pot was on when he passed by the lounge, so he fixed himself a cup and sat in his office with the newspapers. The headline in *The Guardian* read, "*Donald Nelson killed in Explosion.*"

The article recounted what the two government-run radio stations had been reporting. An explosion at Camp Groomes, off the Linden Highway, had taken the lives of several army officers. Donald Nelson and an operative from the Workers' Party had also been killed, but on the access road from the highway to Camp Groomes. The Police were investigating. It was thought at first that the explosion had been an accident, but a similar explosion at the Camp Ayanganna armory had raised the possibility of sabotage as well as speculation that Donald Nelson and the Workers' Party might have been involved in both.

The article went on to lament the death of Colonel Franchette Taylor, Captain Malcolm Felix, and Lieutenants Anil Rampersaud, Alex Mitchell, and Leonard MacKenzie. The article did not attempt to explain why no enlisted ranks had died in the explosions but went on to say that Colonel Taylor was slated to become the new Force Commander and, in an effort to ferret out the saboteurs within the army, the President had decided to appoint Anthony Cassius McGowan as the new Force Commander with the rank of Colonel.

"My God!" Erikson sat up. "What a crock!" The Comrade Leader now had an excuse to persecute the Workers' Party, and Hitchcock had secured McGowan's appointment as Force Commander. But, was McGowan Hitchcock's man or the Comrade Leader's?

The telephone rang, and Ambassador Hales invited Erikson to the Conference Room. Colonel Stanford, Station Chief Hitchcock, and the Political Officer were already seated when Erikson arrived. He took a chair across from Hitchcock, who nodded perfunctorily, then looked away. Ambassador Hales did not keep them waiting. He walked in moments after Erikson, placing his large, ceramic coffee cup down on the table and began the meeting.

"Today is an official holiday here, and we need to show our respect as is appropriate. But I suspect the President is huddling with his advisors to assess what has happened and how to move forward, which, of course, brings us to why I asked for this meeting.

"I assume you've all seen the newspapers. The government claims sabotage at Camp Groomes and Camp Ayanganna, and a Donald Nelson connection. There's been no acknowledgment of a coup attempt. We do have a new Force Commander—Anthony Cassius McGowan. A curious name, I must say. What do we know about him?"

"Commissioned after being locally trained," Colonel Stanford replied. "Only overseas travel includes a short course in Cuba. Brother of the head of the Public Service Union. His accelerated promotion is the reward for betraying the coup."

"So, has the President successfully neutered the army?" Ambassador Hales asked.

"I think so," Colonel Stanford replied. "The dissatisfaction that exists will be repressed. They have a police officer as Chief of Staff and now a pliant Force Commander. Even McGowan has to be seen as a temporary stand in, likely to be removed in the next purge. And the President would probably beef up the National Service and the People's Militia as counterweights to the army."

"Does anyone believe the Kabaka government will change course?" the Ambassador asked.

"No," the Political Officer replied. "The political landscape has not fundamentally changed. The principal opposition is socialist; the Kabaka Party is socialist. To outbid the opposition, the Kabaka Party will continue with the socialist rhetoric. Their fundamental problem remains how to feed the population. They have no hard currency for imports so they have to continue with the barter trade. This is the angle we can exploit; use food aid to wean them away from the Eastern bloc."

"I tend to agree with the Political Officer," Station Chief Hitchcock said, "except that I think we don't have to worry much about further radicalization of the type the Workers' Party offers. This, I think, is good. I believe the President will be consumed with his own survival. In this regard, I believe what has happened in Suriname will add considerable pressure on him. I agree with Colonel Stanford that we'll see more purges in the army and a beefing up of the National Service and the Militia, but I also believe that the President will tone down the anti-American rhetoric and might accept food aid."

Suriname? Erikson was puzzled. What the heck are they talking about? We just had a coup attempt here!

"Colonel Stanford, can you explain how a handful of sergeants could have taken over the government of Suriname?" Ambassador Hales asked.

"Excuse me, Ambassador," Erikson interjected, "did I understand you to say that the government of Suriname has been overthrown?"

"Yes, Steve," Ambassador Hales replied. "While we were all asleep this morning, a handful of sergeants toppled the Surinamese government. I was notified by phone around 06:15 today."

"Ambassador," Colonel Stanford said, "I've been in touch with Colonel Wesfall in Paramaribo. It seems that the Surinamese Prime Minister was too bogged down in parliamentary politics to take serious notice of his own army. His government ignored the complaints of the sergeants regarding disparities in pay, lengthy deployments, and the formation of a union. But, to answer your question more directly, that's a small army and the sergeants and other non-commissioned officers greatly outnumbered the officers. In other words, the non-commissioned officers were the center of gravity in the command structure, a fact which eluded the government and the small cadre of army officers."

"Well," Ambassador Hales said, "we'll have to keep a close eye on what's happening there; I'm sure the Kabaka government will." Ambassador Hales pushed back his chair. "Thank you all for coming in. Enjoy the rest of the holiday." Everyone but the Ambassador rose to leave. "Colonel Stanford, Station Chief, would you remain for a few minutes, please?" he asked, as the others filed past.

Erikson left the meeting troubled that the Embassy preoccupation with developments in Suriname had diminished their interest in the fate of the surviving officers of the Guyana coup attempt. He sat swiveling from side to side, waiting for Hitchcock and Stanford to return to their offices. When finally he heard their voices down the hall, he jumped out of his chair and rushed out toward them. "What's the word?" he asked. "Did they make it out to the trawler?"

"All but two," Hitchcock replied. "Spooner made it out but died of a gut wound. Andrew Rambarran is missing."

"Missing, as in?"

"Not dead," Hitchcock replied. "I'll let Tom fill you in while I work the phone and the teletype."

In his office, Tom Stanford outlined what they had learned. *Parakeet*, the small patrol boat carrying the Spooners and Lieutenants Beharry, Morgan, and Clark, made it out. However, Captain Spooner died of a serious gut wound. The ferry with Captain Rambarran and the second group was destroyed by a Surinamese patrol boat in an ambush in the passage between the Papegaaien Island and the Surinamese eastern bank of the Corentyne River. The three officers and Rambarran's driver floated out of the Corentyne River with the tide, holding on to the tow rope and sides of two inflatable rafts which were on the lower deck of the ferry and had been jolted off the deck when the first rounds hit the bow of the ferry. Further out from the wreckage, the officers eventually got into the rafts, started the engines and made it out, using flares to signal the trawler. Those officers did report seeing Rambarran jumping into the river with the ferry skipper.

"Where do you suppose he is?" Erikson asked.

"Best guess? Suriname."

"Why do you think so?" Erikson asked.

"The ferry was in the passage between the Papegaaien Island and the eastern bank of the Corentyne River. He most likely made for that bank. The west bank, on the Guyana side, would have been too far for him to swim without avoiding some notice, even at night."

"Which, of course, brings us to the question: Has he been captured or is he at large?"

"If he was injured in the blast," Stanford replied, "he'll probably get captured. Otherwise, he's at large. Hitchcock should find out before the day is out." Erikson sat quietly, dispirited by the lack of good news and fatigued by worry and too little sleep. "Why don't you go home and get some rest," Stanford suggested. "I'll stop by and see you later today."

"What did the big guy have to say?" Erikson asked, pointing upstairs.

"He wanted a briefing on the status of the surviving officers," Stanford replied. "Once we locate Rambarran, he'll decide what to do." Erikson nodded. "Go on, get some rest," Stanford said. "I'll stop by, don't worry."

"Thanks, Tom."

*   *   *

February 25, 1980
Bel Air Park, Greater Georgetown

It was starting to darken outside when Colonel Stanford arrived at Erikson's, joining Steve, Anita, and her father on the balcony looking out to the seawall. He accepted a cup of coffee to neutralize the vat of rum he said he must have imbibed at two separate receptions. His attempt at humor did not assuage the anxiety he sensed in Anita and her father so, without waiting to be asked, he proceeded to disclose what he had learned about the whereabouts of Andrew Rambarran.

"First off," Stanford said, "Andrew is alive. He's being held at the Regional Police Headquarters in Nickerie. Things in Suriname are a bit of a mess right now, but our police contacts believe he will be transferred to Paramaribo very shortly."

"Can anything be done to get him released?" Anita's father asked.

"We don't know," Stanford replied. "A new government hasn't been formed as yet. It could be that the new government doesn't want to hold him, in which case they might be persuaded to release him to a neutral country like Brazil."

"What would happen then?" Anita's father asked.

"We could arrange for him to be picked up and flown out," Stanford replied. "That's the scenario we think is most likely, but I have to tell you that the sergeant who led the coup in Suriname is said to be a sort of quirky fella."

"Is there anything we can do?" Anita's father asked.

"I don't think so," Stanford replied. "And that's just as well. We're better positioned to monitor things. You'll need to be patient; it might take a while and, please don't discuss this with anyone."

"Thank you," Anita's father said, "we won't."

The news he had brought was not uplifting enough to change the atmosphere he had found on arrival and, unable to offer additional words of comfort, Stanford took a sip of coffee. The silence was interrupted when they heard the telephone ringing inside the house. Erikson went in to answer it but returned shortly to get Anita's father. "There's someone on the phone for you," Steve said.

Perplexed, Anita's father walked into the house to take the call. On the balcony, they heard him ask the person at the other end "When did it happen?" Anita rose quickly and went to her father. Hanging up the phone, he said, "I have to go; someone fire-bombed the store."

"I'll drive you over," Stanford offered, and they hurried down with him to the car parked on the street in front of the house.

The area on Regent Street where the store stood was crowded with onlookers. Three fire trucks and two police jeeps had formed a U separating the onlookers from the blaze. Colonel Stanford drove slowly past until he found a space to park, a couple hundred feet from where the store stood. When they made their way back to the store front, the night watchman came up to Anita's father, telling him he had seen a car pull up and someone throw a bottle with a lighted wick. He himself ran out to the road as the fire broke out by the right store front. This was also what he had told the police.

"Are you the owner?" an approaching police officer asked Anita's father.

"Yes," he replied.

"Come with me," the officer said. They walked over to one of the police jeeps where a police sergeant told Anita's father to get in. Seeing her father climbing into the jeep, Anita rushed to it, with Erikson and Stanford following.

"Where are you taking him?" Anita asked.

"This doesn't concern you," the sergeant said.

"He's my father," Anita asserted.

"Well, you can come to the police station," the sergeant said, and signaled the driver on.

Stanford drove Anita and Erikson over to the Brickdam Police Station, where they learned that Anita's father was being charged with arson.

"Look here," Colonel Stanford said to the booking corporal, "Mr. Rambarran was with us when that fire was started."

"Have a seat," the corporal said, "I'll take your statements later, but this man is not leaving tonight. He is being charged with arson. Too many business people want to set fires and collect insurance money."

"I think I get what's going on here," Stanford said loudly. "Stay here," he told Erikson and Anita, and left the police station.

When Stanford returned half an hour later, Erikson was waiting at the entrance of the Police Station, with Anita and her father. Once they had seated themselves in the car, he drove off in the direction of Vlissengen Road.

"What'd you do?" Erikson asked.

"I spoke to Ambassador Hales," Stanford replied, "and he called the President at the Residence. He told the President that Mr. Rambarran was with us at your home, and we would vouch for him. He said that if Mr. Rambarran was not released, he would issue a public statement tomorrow declaring what he knew about recent events. And he wanted the President to have his people back off."

"Well, it worked," Erikson said.

"I should also mention that Ambassador Hales called this a clear case of arson and said he wanted no impediments to Mr. Rambarran's insurance claim."

"Thank you very much, Colonel, for what you did," Mr. Rambarran said, "and please also thank the Ambassador for me."

"I will," Stanford replied, as he turned onto Vlissengen Road, heading toward the seawall.

When they arrived at Erikson's, Stanford accompanied the party into the house. "Look at the bright side," he said, "now you don't have to worry about selling the business." Mr. Rambarran's laughter assured everyone he had shaken off the ordeal, and Stanford decided to take his leave. Erikson excused himself from his guests to walk Stanford out. They stopped by the gate.

"Steve, if we decided to apply pressure on this government, Anita and her father could be in the way," Stanford said quietly.

"I've thought of that," Erikson said.

"Mr. Rambarran is a resident of Canada, isn't he?" Stanford asked.

Erikson nodded. "Once he has filed for insurance, he can leave. Anita is a different matter. I assume you're planning to get married?"

"Yes," Erikson said.

"I'd suggest you get her to the U.S. until the big event. We can arrange a visa for her."

"I'll discuss this with them," Erikson said. "And now I have a question for you." Stanford nodded. "Look, Andrew is in a holding cell in Nickerie, and his officers are still on that CIA trawler. Why can't they mount a rescue effort?"

"If it fails, it will make the new government mad," Stanford replied, "and it would complicate our efforts to use diplomacy to get him out. Besides, we don't know how soon he will be moved to Paramaribo. What if they mount a raid in Nickerie and he's not there?"

"Tom, if this goes badly, meaning that if this becomes a protracted incarceration, I'll mount such a raid."

"Let's hope it doesn't come to that."

"Do you think you can spare me for a few days?" Erikson asked. "I'd like to get acquainted with Suriname, just in case."

"I'd recommend you hold off for a while," Stanford replied. "You have house guests who could still come to harm. Maybe after you've seen them off. Hopefully, Andrew Rambarran will be free by then."

Twenty-seven

April 25, 1980
Ferry Station, Springlands

The crunching sounds of the tires on the gravel road finally opened Erikson's eyes fully to the ferry station ahead, and Anita, whose head rested against his left shoulder, began to sit upright. The ferry was moored against the wharf, and parts of it were visible between the uprights that supported the metal roof covering the wharf. The wharf itself appeared crowded with people. Colonel Stanford had said that the larger ferry to Nickerie had a capacity of two hundred passengers in addition to the crew, which meant that even in that circumstance many people who were at the station were likely to be disappointed. The situation would be worse if the smaller ferry ran.

The line to the ticket office led back away from the wharf to the access road. Fortunately, Colonel Stanford had secured two return tickets, sparing Erikson the challenge of queuing up and the possibility of being turned away. Stanford had also told him that the ticket clerk and other wharf employees were notoriously corrupt, which was not really news to Erikson, given the way official business was being conducted in the country as a whole.

The car drove slowly along the line of prospective passengers and stopped just shy of the wharf entrance. The chauffeur bounded out of the Embassy car and retrieved Erikson's overnight bag and Anita's suitcase from the trunk. Erikson slung the long strap of his bag over his right shoulder, lowered his sunglasses from his forehead and, carrying Anita's suitcase in his left hand, led the way in. The center of activity on the wharf was the ticket office, a rectangular enclosure framed by solid wood below waist level and wire mesh above, with a wooden counter at the intersection of the mesh and the wood siding. The ticket clerk sat on a stool, dispensing tickets through a semicircular aperture in the wire mesh just above the counter. The ticket office was surrounded on the other three sides by people pleading that they had been waiting for days to buy their tickets; some said three days, others five. They clearly had the price of the ticket in hand, leading Erikson to surmise that these people did not have the bribe money. What surprised Erikson was that the ticket clerk denied a ticket to a woman at the counter, pointing to the people around the ticket office begging for a ticket and telling the woman that those people had been waiting for days and that she had only just arrived — not that the ticket seller had any intention of selling a ticket to those people who had been waiting for days. It was simply that the newcomer had to be socialized into the practice of offering up enough bribe money for the privilege of buying a ticket. The newcomer pleaded to no avail, and the ticket clerk unashamedly called out "Next!" The next customer proffered a wad of bills covered under his left palm and holding the ticket fare folded in his open right hand. The transaction was quick. Ticket in hand, the man waved jubilantly to awaiting acquaintances, seemingly undisturbed by the loss of the bribe money.

A line was also beginning to form in front of the ticket collector at the head of the ramp leading to the boat. To get there, Erikson had to traverse the full breadth of the waiting area, where all of the benches were fully occupied. People, with blankets and other spreads, also sat on the flooring with their backs against the walls of the enclosed waiting area. Erikson even noticed people camped outside of the sheltered area, people whom he had not seen from the access road at the front. Wending his way through the huddled mass, Erikson heard people talking about the three or five days they had camped out waiting to buy a ticket. In all cases, they had the passage money, it seemed. They simply continued to wait, hoping that at the time of departure, there would still be space on the ferry for which the ticket seller might accept less than the top bribe rate. It was now clear that the wharf and its surrounds had become a refugee encampment for people desperately seeking to flee the punishing conditions of life created by the mismanagement and corruption of a self-perpetuating clique. And Erikson felt ashamed. Ashamed, because he had been a part of the conspiracy which had forestalled what would have been a successful surgical excise of a regime which sat suffocatingly on its people. Now that suffering would continue, and every low-level official would exact, with impunity, bribes and other favors from people too destitute to pay but too powerless to resist.

When Erikson and Anita came aboard the ferry, they chose to sit on the last bench on the starboard side, directly under the pilothouse of a boat, which was about sixty feet long and twelve feet wide and was one of the smaller ones plying that route. A narrow walkway from bow to stern separated the benches on the starboard and port sides, but the available seating amounted to little more than eighty. A curved corrugated zinc covering extended out from the base of the pilothouse, providing partial shelter from overhead sun and rain. Salt water had leached the paint on the sides of the vessel, but the name *Nickerie Queen* was still clearly discernible on both sides of the bow, just below the gunwale.

The boat engines revved up above the hum of a few minutes earlier, clearly signaling imminent shove off. The mooring ropes having been released from the wharf, the captain was slowly orienting the bow north to head into the channel when commotion on the wharf drew everyone's attention to two police jeeps which had stopped at the upper end of the ramp. An Inspector, with his swagger stick, was flagging down the captain, and the grating chimes of reverse engines indicated compliance.

"Oh no," Anita said.

"What?" Erikson asked.

"I think they're going to do a currency search," Anita replied. "They do it often at the Timehri International Airport."

"How much are people allowed to take out?"

"A measly fifteen dollars," Anita replied. "The sad thing is that most of these people are fleeing. They'll never return. That's why they are camped out there for a ferry ticket. It makes me so mad."

"Okay," Erikson said. "Let's stay calm. We have other things to attend to."

Word spread very quickly on the covered deck that people might be searched for currencies above the official fifteen-dollar limit. Passengers rushed to the port side of the boat away from the dock and began emptying their pockets and purses into the Corentyne River, and soon the water around the boat was papered over in a colorful assortment of currencies. Waves of left-behinds were jumping into the river, seemingly in unison, and grasping at the American and Canadian currencies, Surinamese Guilders, and Guyana dollars, while dejected passengers

247

on the boat looked on, perhaps relieved they would not be taken off the boat but lamenting the loss of the money they had scrounged to give them a new start in Suriname. Laughing loudly as he entered the boat, the Police Inspector said they were checking for drugs. None was found in the ten-minute stay of the police aboard the *Nickerie Queen,* an exercise Erikson saw more as a demonstration of power than a serious search. Hardly anyone spoke as the bow swung out again and headed out to the center of the river.

The *Nickerie Queen* moved up the mouth of the Corentyne River at a slow crawl of about ten knots, leaving a wake of white floating bubbles on top of the muddy brown river water. The low water level bared the white, stringy roots of the mangroves along the banks. There was no breeze and no current; ebbtide had probably spent itself, and anytime now the Atlantic Ocean would swell the river again. At 14:15 in the afternoon, the sun's reach had extended under the zinc shelter to much of the seating on the starboard side. The high humidity compounded the discomfort of passengers, some of whom used newspapers to fan themselves. Nearer the mouth, the river widened considerably, and the horizon was framed by the Atlantic Ocean ahead. The boat maintained its course up the channel into the ocean where the waves became higher. The *Nickerie Queen* pitched badly, and sheets of salt water scaled the bow to drench passengers seated up front. Many moved to the stern, and Erikson and Anita found themselves pushed closer together because of additional passengers on their bench.

At about mid-course, the boat began to turn in a northeasterly direction to proceed into the mouth of the Nickerie River. It was a long, slow turn, and the boat rolled like a swaying cradle provoking screams from passengers, several of whom grasped the port and starboard gunwales and vomited over the side. Because neither Erikson nor Anita had eaten since breakfast, their empty stomachs were not as seriously challenged. Nevertheless, Anita grasped Erikson's upper arm and tucked her face against him to avoid looking at the vomiting. Once the boat had completed the arc and was heading into the mouth of the Nickerie River, the rolling subsided, and the ride became smoother.

Anita straightened up on the bench. "Gosh, I'm glad that's over," she said, smiling. "I don't think I could stand it much longer."

Erikson patted her arm. "Not to worry," he said, "looks like we're almost there."

On the starboard side sat the promontory separating the mouths of the Corentyne and Nickerie Rivers and, extending from the promontory along the western bank of the Nickerie River, was the seawall, which was to be their constant companion until the boat docked on the outskirts of the Niew Nickerie. In anticipation of disembarking, many passengers moved closer to the exit ramp leaving Erikson and Anita room to make a more leisurely exit.

They were spared queuing up before the two main immigration checkpoints when they were signaled to come up to the Javanese immigration officer on the right side. The Hindustani man in his late forties, who had signaled them, turned out to be the driver of the Embassy Jeep, parked outside the wharf. The immigration officer quickly stamped Erikson's diplomatic passport but studied Anita's. He leafed through the Guyana passport, pausing at the page with the U.S. visa. "What is the purpose of your visit?" he asked.

"This is my fiancé," Erikson interjected. "She is visiting with me before flying out to Miami."

Anita produced her KLM ticket to Miami, which the immigration officer eyed suspiciously. "Why are you flying out of Zanderij?" he asked.

"The alternative is Carib Air," Anita replied. "You know their reputation for losing luggage?"

The immigration officer laughed out loud, nodding his head and stamping the passport. As they walked past the immigration officer, the Embassy driver took Anita's suitcase and repeated what Erikson had already known, which was that they could not travel up to Paramaribo that day because they would have to take ferries across the Nickerie, Coppename, and Saramacca rivers. Given the ferry schedules and the fact that it was almost 16:00 in the afternoon, it seemed pointless to attempt the trek to Paramaribo that afternoon.

"How do you feel about driving around Nickerie before checking in at the hotel?" Erikson asked.

"That's fine with me," Anita replied. "I wouldn't want to do that later because of the dusk-to-dawn curfew."

The wharf was just off on the right of G. G. Maynard Street which ran roughly north-south along the western bank of the Nickerie River, on the inside of the promontory separating the Nickerie and Corentyne Rivers. Just up from the wharf was the municipal market where Hindustani and Javanese vendors shuffled behind their stands to cater to a predominantly female stream of shoppers. Through the two palm trees directly across from the market and just less than a football field away, stood the Regional Police Headquarters, a three-storied bungalow, painted cream, except for some green trim around the windows.

The jeep proceeded eastward on G. G. Maynard to the edge of town and turned right on Waterloo Street, the eastern boundary of Nickerie, before taking A. K. Doerga Street for the return to the city center. A. K. Doerga ran through the entire mid-section of the city, changing its name to Graderweg as it traversed the Courantijn Polder to its termination point at an unpaved, water-logged road at the base of the seawall along the eastern bank of Corentyne River. At the top of the seawall, a short, pot-bellied Hindustani man was conducting a lively banter with several young men around him and, on the other side of the seawall, according to the Embassy driver, was a stone jetty for mooring the back-track boats, which plied illegally between Nickerie and Springlands.

It took some persuasion to get the driver to negotiate the unpaved road running along the seawall and curving at the base of the promontory back to G. G. Maynard. The four-wheel drive feature of the jeep was in active use as the jeep dipped into large watery cavities that challenged any serious claim to this being a road. The jeep stopped at the base of the promontory and Erikson and Anita scaled the gentle grassy slope to the top. On the left, the mouth of the Corentyne River stretched out to Guyana's eastern coastline; on the right, the mouth of the Nickerie River, not quite as wide but equally majestic, and straight ahead the boundless expanse of the Atlantic pushing its huge waves into the mouths of the two rivers and swelling them into high tide. The Atlantic breeze brought a soothing chill, a welcome respite from the oppressive heat and humidity they had experienced that afternoon but one which forced Anita to keep pressing down on her cotton skirt. The driver, standing by his muddied jeep, did not seem to share their appreciation for the scenery, and Erikson felt obliged to shorten their stay on the promontory. Back on the road, the jeep dipped and rose and splashed muddy water until they reconnected with the paved section of G. G. Maynard by the wharf, passing by a sawmill and a handful of boarding houses and restaurants on both sides of the street before reaching the municipal market.

The hotel was on West Kanaal Street directly across from the Nickerie Regional Police Headquarters but, because West Kanaal was one-way from South to North, the jeep turned into East Kanaal Street passing close by the Police Headquarters, where a handful of men and women stood outside the door at the street level evidently waiting to see friends or relations imprisoned in the holding cells. The wide canal separating East and West Kanaal Streets was covered with large, deep-green lily pads, many of which held up pink lotus flowers on long stems. The jeep eventually made a U-turn onto West Kanaal Street, but Erikson kept his eyes on the lily-laden canal and the Police Headquarters until they turned into the parking lot of the three-storied *Lotus Lily Hotel*.

Their room on the second floor was modestly furnished with a dresser and mirror, a morris chair, and a queen-sized bed. The window unit air conditioner directly across from the bed hummed intolerably but assured Erikson that he and Anita would be spared the heat and humidity that can afflict the Nickerie region at night. Reaching up, he turned up the thermostat to moderate the polar condition in which he had found the room before adjusting the mini-blind on one of the two windows facing West Kanaal Street and the Police Station. The holding cells appeared to be on the first floor where a police constable controlled entry and egress of individuals and small groups. The other entrance into the Police Station was by an external stairway, which had a landing by the door on the second level and one on the third floor. Most of the police officers walking in and out of the building carried a revolver on their hips.

After Anita had freshened up, they walked over to the *Pink Lily Restaurant*, which they had passed earlier on G. G. Maynard Street. Seated on the outside balcony, Erikson could not help observing the ghost-like appearance the streets were acquiring. The market had long since shut down. There was no pedestrian traffic; those still on the road were on bicycles or *bromfiets*, as mopeds were called there. Even in the restaurant, the alacrity of service reflected a cultivated awareness that the curfew would begin in just over an hour.

Sipping a Parbo beer, Erikson ordered curried *yarabakka*, after the waiter explained to Anita that it was the same fish the Guyanese called *gilbakka*, a sweet-tasting fish with the texture of swordfish. Unlike Anita, Erikson passed on the rice, electing instead to have hot *roti*, catering to a culinary addiction he had developed in Guyana. For dessert, they took back a couple of currant rolls, which they could have with coffee within the safety of the hotel lobby after the now rapidly approaching curfew.

Twenty-eight

April 26, 1980
Nickerie, Suriname

After a breakfast of toast and Dutch gouda cheese, washed down with a Brazilian blend of Nescafe instant coffee, Erikson and Anita were ready to leave. The driver, who was waiting in the lobby, came up the central stairway, relieving Erikson of Anita's suitcase and leading them out to a clean jeep in the parking lot. The jeep took West Kanaal Street to G. G. Maynard, then Waterloo Street on the eastern edge of town and onto the highway to Paramaribo. About five minutes on the highway, they reached the pier on the Nickerie River where crossing was by a pontoon pushed by a tugboat. The operation at the pier showed extended practice: fifteen minutes of loading, ten across the river, and then the vehicles were let out.

The jeep traveled due east with the Atlantic coastline on the left and rice fields on the right, all the way past the Waginingen junction to the outskirts of Coronie District. On each side of the road through Nickerie and Coronie Districts, a wide drainage canal with light brown water hugged the course of the road, and the frequent, loud splashes in the canals bore evidence of an abundance of freshwater fish. The embankment on each side of the road was an untended hedge of tall razor grass, *busy-busy*, and carrion-crow bush, the overflow from which was sheared off by passing vehicles. At various intervals along the road, anglers were positioned at clearings along banks, their *bromfiets*, cars, or minivans parked in the hedge.

From Coronie District all the way to the outskirts of Paramaribo, villages occurred with greater frequency and, with them, *drempels* or speed bumps across the highway to compel slower speed in their vicinity. Bare patches on this two-lane asphalt road and large pot holes, occurring without much warning, caused frequent and sharp swerves of the jeep and calamitously close shaves with oncoming vehicles. At about 14:15 in the afternoon, the jeep was driving through Kwatta on the outskirts of Paramaribo, and twenty minutes or so later, it pulled up to the front entrance of the Hotel Torarica.

The hotel attendant opened the right half of the large glass door to unleash a gush of cold musty air. Moisture from the Suriname River, on whose western bank the Torarica sat, had suffused the carpets and everything else to create mold in areas not visible to the naked eye but which imparted a noxious heaviness to the cold air generated by an air conditioning system operating at full bore. The desk attendant was very polite, greeting Erikson and Anita and guiding them through the requisite forms before sending them off to find Room 314.

The way to the elevators led past the entrance to the twenty-four-hour casino, directly across from which was a large fish pond on the outside of the building but with a part of it intruding into the lobby. The most visible pieces of art in the lobby were two large wooden carvings of Amerindian women in semi-recumbent positions, their pronounced hind quarters rendered more sensuous by the highly lacquered finish applied to them. The bar and café entrances rounded out the lobby.

Erikson's meeting with Colonel Wesfall was not until 17:00 hours, so after he and Anita had freshened up and had a light snack at the café, they left the hotel on a brief walking tour. They took the concrete sidewalk along Kleine Comb Weg past Fort Zeelandia, the headquarters of the post-coup Military High Command, onto the Waterkant from which the Suriname River was in clear view on their left. Between the sidewalk and the seawall hugging the river, snackettes dispensing hot and cold dishes, soft drinks and alcohol, were doing a thriving business before curfew. The fast-food business area ended where the concrete walkway gave way to a sandy embankment just before Platte Brug, the center of small-boat life in Paramaribo.

Platte Brug, or Flat Bridge, was a concrete ramp descending from the embankment into the Suriname River. A barn-like roof provided shelter for about twenty feet of the descending ramp. Multi-colored boats ferrying passengers between Paramaribo and Commewijne District on the other side of the river were tethered parallel to one another on the left side of the ramp with the one closest to the ramp departing when filled. The ferry boats themselves were simply wide canoes powered by outboard motors, the passengers aboard being sheltered from the elements by a wooden roof above the boat and rolled up canvas on each side, to be lowered in the event of rain. A wooden strip along the top of the boat bore the name of the boat and its registration number. The one closest to the ramp that afternoon read VS09 GOSLAR. It was being rapidly filled from the long line of people trying to get out of Paramaribo before curfew time.

On the right side of the ramp, a fishing boat was tethered and its catch was being unloaded for ready sale to fishmongers on the ramp. Other fishing boats attached to wooden pylons lay at rest in the vicinity. Fishermen were evidently allowed to berth in the river after curfew time. Erikson and Anita lingered on the ramp, with Erikson feigning interest in the fish being unloaded, but studying the fishing boat whose near duplicate cousins were moored nearby. Anita took her cue from Erikson, completely unaware he was planning to rescue Andrew Rambarran and that the rescue plan he had in mind would employ such a boat.

The fishing vessel before Erikson was a thirty-foot, flat-bottomed boat with an outboard motor, tilted forward out of the water. The bow end was covered with decking for about eight feet to provide sleeping quarters for the crew. The covered section ended in a foot-wide vertical overhang to which was attached two sections of canvas to provide shelter from the elements. The most conspicuous part of the boat was the eight-foot high icebox occupying six feet of boat length at the mid section of the boat. The space between the icebox and the sleeping quarters served as the galley. A two-burner kerosene stove rested on the floor boards and cooking utensils hung from large rails in the ribs on both sides. A bench across the width of the boat butted against the icebox and served as both cooking platform and seating. A walkway on both sides of the icebox allowed movement from bow to stern. The stern gunwale had a U-shaped notch for the engine mount and a boat-wide seat for the operator. Gasoline drums and large plastic water containers were lashed against a solid vertical wall behind which was the cavity housing the drift seine. The space between the seine housing and the icebox was the area where fish were decapitated and gutted for storage in the icebox.

The large icebox troubled Erikson. It was fine for a fishing boat trekking along the coast but should the escape he was planning require greater maneuverability of the boat, the icebox would not only be a visual obstacle but would add unduly to the weight of the boat. Clearly, that would need to be modified on his boat. Since the boat would also be used as a firing platform, other modifications would be necessary, but those would require more thought.

Erikson led Anita back up the ramp onto the sandy pathway along the side of Waterkant and paused briefly by the landmark Banyan tree where people were piling into buses. Directly across the street, the charred remains of white concrete columns of what used to be Suriname's Police Headquarters were the most prominent reminders of the violence used to bring down the elected civilian government on February 25th. The story was that the coup plotters' gunboat came down the Suriname River and, from a stationary position directly across from the building, had delivered one, then another, round from the 40-millimeter Bofors cannon into the mid-section of the Police Headquarters, persuading the Police Chief to surrender. After that, the government was defenseless. The debris from the building's collapse had been cleared away, but the new "revolutionary" government had announced plans to use the site to create a monument to the *revolutie,* as the military junta referred to their coup.

Further up from Platte Brug was the ferry station, where the *Maratakka* transported vehicles and passengers between Paramaribo and Meerzorg. The wharf was filling up with new passengers and vehicles even though the *Maratakka* had just departed and was just about mid-course to Meerzorg in what was at most a fifteen-minute trip. Perhaps this was an everyday occurrence, but the fact of a dusk-to-dawn curfew added urgency to all travel arrangements. The Waterkant changed to Saramacca Street as it traversed the market before joining Van't Hogerhuys Street, leading out of the city, and delineating one possible route to the Santo Boma Penitentiary.

Colonel Wesfall was waiting in the lobby when they arrived back at the hotel, and he introduced himself and another gentleman, Tom McGinnis, to Erikson and Anita.

"It's a pleasure to meet you gentlemen," Anita said. "I'm sure you have business to attend to; so, if you'll excuse me, we've had a bit of a long trip." Both gentlemen gave her a gentle nod before she departed the lobby for her room.

Colonel Wesfall led the way out to the terrace where they took seats at a table under a thatched umbrella in the south-western-most corner, affording them a complete view of the terrace, the swimming pool, and the rear entrance to the hotel. Colonel Wesfall ordered a Heineken while Erikson and Tom McGinnis, who turned out to be the new CIA Station Chief at the Paramaribo Embassy, ordered Parbo beers.

Wanting to provide Colonel Wesfall the ability to deny knowledge of the operation he was mounting, Erikson talked as if he was present in his capacity as Assistant Military Attaché. "How are things here?" he asked.

"Well, with three counter-coup attempts, the military junta is extremely nervous," Colonel Wesfall replied. "The Hindustani Lieutenant, who led the last counter-coup attempt, has already been tried and sentenced to twelve years in prison. He's actually serving that sentence at the Santo Boma Penitentiary, where Captain Rambarran is being held."

"Why has the military junta kept Rambarran for so long when the Guyana government is so eager to get its hands on him?" Erikson asked, aware that Station Chief McGinnis had been studying him since he sat down.

"My guess," Colonel Wesfall began, "is that since the coup attempt in Guyana had taken place just over twenty-four hours before the sergeants here overthrew the Surinamese government, there might have been some sympathy toward Rambarran; initially, anyway. They probably felt that he would be killed if he were sent back and they didn't want to share the blame, especially when they learned of his background. They also probably thought we had an interest in Rambarran's welfare. But the recent episode with the Hindustani Lieutenant really shook up those fellas, and they might be ready now to get rid of Rambarran, if the price from the Guyana government is high enough."

"What type of military assets do they have?" Erikson asked, taking a sip of Parbo. "And how are they deployed?"

"They've beefed up the military since the February takeover," Wesfall replied. "They now have about 2,000 soldiers; no significant air capabilities—two helicopters and two Cessnas. I presume the helicopters will have a machine gun each on board. They have concentrated their military assets around Paramaribo and are monitoring Albina on the French Guiana side for possible foreign involvement with the Bush Negro population there. They don't seem to be as concerned with Nickerie because the Guyana government is so anti-Western."

"How about maritime assets? Patrol boats?"

"They have two World War II vintage Dutch patrol boats with bow-mounted 40mm Bofors cannons plus, of course, a couple of machine guns and individual arms carried by personnel on board. They also have a few speed boats, used mostly for ferrying the officers around, a sort of status symbol. Then, of course, the Police have some small patrol boats. Those don't carry any armaments, except those borne by individuals."

"How safe is it to walk around Paramaribo?" Erikson asked.

"Quite safe in the daytime," Wesfall replied. "The Surinamese are accustomed to Dutch tourists. Look at the pool over there, for instance. They won't be able to tell you from a Dutchman until you open your mouth. Walk around like a tourist, and you'll be okay. Buy some local craft and burden yourself with a plastic bag or two. You have a woman with you, don't you?" Erikson nodded. "Take her on a tour."

"Well, that's not why she's here," Erikson said.

"But she's here, isn't she?" Wesfall asked, and Erikson shrugged acknowledgment. "Well, take her on a tour. And walk leisurely, like a tourist; like a Dutchman who has come to see where his wife grew up. It's a good cover; use it."

Station Chief McGinnis drained the last of his Parbo and tapped the glass down on the table. "Look, fella, your fiancé is flying out of Zanderij, isn't she?" he asked. Erikson nodded. "The road to Zanderij passes by the Santo Boma Pen. The highway is called Pad van Wanica, and the access road to the Pen is Welgedact A. It's your chance to give the place a once over." McGinnis signaled another round to the waiter, and Erikson realized from his declaration that the two gentlemen in his company were aware of what he was contemplating.

Apart from Dutch tourists in and around the swimming pool, all of the locals had departed the terrace, no doubt because of the approaching curfew. As a consequence, the service was prompt, and there seemed to be an understanding at the table to defer conversation until the waiter had poured the beers. "This is a bit awkward for me," Erikson began, after the waiter had left, "but I have the impression you're aware of what I'd like to do."

"I have a sense of why you're here," Colonel Wesfall responded, "and Tom Stanford asked me to assist you getting around. But, if I were to advise you, I'd say, forget it. First, you're risking a court-martial and possible prison sentence, if you attempt this as a serving officer. Second, the main prison is a rectangular enclosure within a larger rectangular enclosure. The only viable method of extraction, as I'm sure you've figured out, is by air, and you don't have a chopper."

"Well, since we're here shooting the breeze, why don't we assume I could lay my hands on a chopper?"

"That's fine with me," Station Chief McGinnis said. "I don't have anything else to do for an hour and a half before curfew."

"Do you know the prisoner delivery routine for the Santo Boma Pen?" Erikson asked.

"The Police Station at Nieuwe Havenlaan is responsible for transporting sentenced prisoners from the greater Paramaribo area," Station Chief McGinnis replied. "That's done every Thursday. They use an old, cream-colored VW van to make the rounds at the police stations with those prisoners. Typically, that includes the stations at Kwatta, Meerzorg, Duisburglaan, and Keizer Street, which is now the police headquarters. You'll need to intercept that van and use it to get into the Santo Boma Pen."

"Is there a place I could overnight with a team?" Erikson asked.

"We can find you a safe-house in Nieuw Amsterdam, on the other side of the river," Station Chief McGinnis replied. "Because it's relatively remote, it won't be as closely watched as Paramaribo. You can come in through the mouth of the Suriname River on a fishing boat and pull in at the Nieuw Amsterdam pier. If you time it close to the curfew, there won't be anyone there but a car designated to take you to the safe house. This is all theoretical, of course."

"That would mean re-crossing the river to get into Paramaribo, won't it?" Erikson asked.

"Yes," McGinnis replied, "but that would actually help to keep suspicion away from you."

"How so?"

"If you cross with the *Maratakka* at rush hour in the morning, no one would single out your group. I assume that white face of yours would be camouflaged?"

Erikson nodded. "May I ask about an obvious need in such a scenario?"

"Sure," McGinnis replied.

"It has to do with transporting a team from Nieuw Amsterdam."

"You could be picked up by a VW van almost identical to the police van. The driver and his assistant could come in from French Guiana through Albina and exit the same way. You could use the vehicle to intercept the police van and swap yourselves for the prisoners being transported."

"What if the numbers don't square?" Erikson asked.

"Simple," McGinnis replied. "Discard one or more of the warrants. The prison warden, we are told, matches the number of prisoners with the number of warrants."

"Here's a big fly in the ointment, Steve," Colonel Wesfall said. "There are any number of routes the police van could take to get to Santo Boma Pen. If it simply transports prisoners from the Buro Keizerstraat, which is the official name of the Keizer Street Police Station, it will go via Waterkant, Saramaca Street, Van't Hogerhuys, Latourweg, and then Pad van Wanica. If the Kwatta Police Station is the last pickup point, it would go by Leiding 9A, Commisaris Weytinghweg, and on to Welgedact A. You get the picture?"

"Yes, but either way, they'll have to come into Welgedact A, isn't that right?" Erikson asked.

"True, but from different directions," Wesfall asserted. "When you are planning an ambush, you don't want the quarry coming in from a direction that allows it to bypass you."

Erikson was stumped. He felt the eyes of Tom McGinnis on him, even though the Station Chief was sipping his beer. Were they testing him? He felt like a Plebe in the company of Upperclassmen at the Academy. "Is there a way to constrain the movement of the van to a predictable route?" he asked.

Colonel Wesfall looked over to Station Chief McGinnis, who smiled. "Yes, there is," McGinnis replied. "It'll cost a few dollars, but it can be done."

Erikson felt relieved. He also felt that maybe he had won over McGinnis. He decided to push his luck. "Is it possible to get an actual layout of the Santo Boma Pen so that we can build a model for training purposes?" he asked.

"Yes, again," McGinnis said. "I could get that to Fred Hitchcock in a day or so."

"This is quite a bit," Erikson said. "Thank you very much."

"Now all you have to do," Colonel Wesfall said, rising, "is to find yourself a helicopter. And *we* need to get out of here before we have a confrontation with overzealous patrols carrying Uzis."

*   *   *

April 27, 1980
Paramaribo, Suriname

At 09:00, Erikson left with Anita by taxi to the Leonsberg pier, a seven-minute drive on Cornelis Jongbaw Street, the eastern extension of the Waterkant. The pier was virtually deserted except for a few boatmen sitting with their feet hanging down the side of the pier, their boats tethered to one another. Most of their morning business, bringing workers and school children to Paramaribo from Nieuw Amsterdam, had long since been over. Lunchtime, when schools let out, would provide passengers for the return trip to Nieuw Amsterdam. The young Javanese man who got up and offered to take Erikson turned out to be the operator of the closest boat, the one actually tied to the pier. The fare, he said, was five guilders if they have a full load, but the man offered a private charter for twenty dollars, which Erikson accepted.

The boat operator helped Anita and Erikson onto the boat, seated himself at the back and started the engine. One of his comrades on the pier released the rope, tossing it into the bow. The operator reversed the boat and then pointed it northeast to Niew Amsterdam. The boat was of a similar type to the ones they had seen at Platte Brug, and how grateful they were that the roof above provided shelter from the sun on what was a bright, warm day. The boat rode low in the light brown water of the Suriname River, allowing Anita to reach over the side and lower her hand into the water. Closer to the river mouth, the soothing breeze from the Atlantic high tide fanned across the width of the boat, making Erikson, with his arm around Anita, regret the end of the ten-minute ride. They were helped off the boat at the Nieuw Amsterdam pier by the boat operator and were fortunate to find a few parked taxis, the drivers of which were playing dominoes at a nearby snackette. Erikson explained to the driver who approached them that he wanted to tour the fort at Nieuw Amsterdam but he also wanted to make the noon crossing from Meerzorg back to Paramaribo.

The taxi ride to the town of Nieuw Amsterdam was a smooth one on an asphalt road. However, the access road to the colonial fort was badly pitted and waterlogged, and the trek became an effort to dodge one pothole after another. Fortunately, there was hardly any oncoming vehicular traffic, and the zigs and zags on the two-lane, unpaved road posed little risk to anyone.

"This is like the ferry ride from Springlands," Anita said.

Erikson laughed. "Yeah, and we just ate breakfast!"

Part of the old fort had been converted into a military encampment and was therefore off limits; the rest of it was simply a built-up embankment buttressing the sea walls. There was a police post by the sea walls and old cannons with cannonballs heaped on the ground next to them. The best part of the tour for Erikson was just holding Anita close to him as they stood on top of the seawall, enjoying the breeze and the view presented by the wide expanse of water in front, and listening to the water lapping against the seawall. However, time constraints and a waiting taxi abbreviated their stay.

While the taxi driver negotiated the potholes back to the asphalt road, Erikson explained to Anita that Nieuw Amsterdam was located at the confluence of the Suriname and the Commewijne Rivers. "If you like," Erikson said, "we could take the drive along the western bank of the Commewijne River."

"Where would it take us?" Anita asked.

"I'm not sure of all the villages," Erikson replied, "but, according to the tourist map, if we turn south at Alkmaar, we could pick up the East-West Connection at Tamanredjo and head back to Meerzorg for the ferry. Isn't that right, driver?" The driver nodded.

"Do we have time?" Anita asked.

"Oh, yes," Erikson replied. "We're good."

Once they reached the asphalt road, the driver settled on a cruising speed of sixty kilometers per hour, taking them though villages with names but not many houses. At Alkmaar, the taxi turned southward and, about twenty minutes later, reached the Tamanredjo, where they took the East-West Connection to the Meerzorg ferry station. Erikson secured their tickets for the *Maratakka*, then they snacked on plantain chips and Cokes while they waited.

At 11:45 hours, the *Maratakka* docked and, shortly thereafter, passengers for Paramaribo were allowed to board. Like the *Kurtuka* in Guyana, the *Maratakka* had an upper deck for passengers and an open lower deck for vehicles, though passengers could move between decks by stairs located at the bow and stern. The boat arrived full but, when it shoved off back to Paramaribo, there were just a handful of military jeeps and cars with markings of various ministries, suggesting that they were also government owned. The passenger deck appeared deserted.

At about 12:30, the *Maratakka* docked at the Paramaribo ferry station near the Waterkant, and Erikson and Anita descended the scaffolded steps, which butted against the upper deck. The Paramaribo ferry station presented a very crowded appearance. Both the passenger and the vehicle sides of the wharf appeared full, with the passenger side dominated by uniformed school children, returning home after their truncated school day. Walking out of the ferry station compound onto Waterkant, Erikson decided they should take Keizer Street to the city center. The Police Station, officially called Buro Keizerstraat, was only half a football field in, on the left, though it was not visible from the Waterkant. It had the characteristic cream color with green trim, but the building itself was much larger than the Regional Police Headquarters in Nickerie. If Station Chief McGinnis could insure that the prisoner van made its last stop at Buro Keizerstraat, Erikson thought, that would make tracking the prisoner van considerably easier for him in the operation he was contemplating. They stopped in some of the craft shops on Dominie Street. Not wanting to add to the luggage she was taking later on her flight, Anita bought some postcards by which to remember her Suriname visit. Erikson bought a black-and-white photo of the pre-revolution Police Headquarters on the Waterkant, the one which had been destroyed during the February coup. For their return trip to the Hotel Torarica, they took an alternate route, passing by the Presidential Palace, before rejoining Kleine Comb Weg to the hotel.

At 14:00, Erikson and Anita took a hotel taxi for the Zanderij International Airport for her 17:00 hours KLM flight to Miami, from where she would travel on American Airlines to Atlanta. The taxi took Kleine Comb Weg to the Waterkant, through the market on Saramacca Street and onto Van't Hogerhuys Street, then turned on Latourweg. Soon after, they were on Pad van Wanica for the thirty minute drive to the airport.

At the Zanderij International Airport, Erikson helped Anita with the check-in at the KLM desk and walked with her to the Immigration checkpoint, where he kissed her goodbye. "Mother will be there at the Atlanta Airport," he assured her, "but call her during the layover in Miami."

She wiped the tears from her face. "Be careful," she said.

"I will," he said, and kissed her again. He waited until she had passed through Immigration, waving to her as she glanced back before disappearing into the waiting area on the other side of the terminal building.

Erikson left the airport at about 16:10, traveling back with the same taxi. After about twenty minutes on Pad van Wanica, they reached Welgedact A, where he asked the driver to turn so that he could see the famous Santo Boma Prison. Welgedact A was an unpaved road, with hardly enough space to warrant it being a two-lane. So deeply pitted was the road, and so waterlogged, the taxi had to stop at various points to allow bicyclists and riders on *bromfiets* to zig-zag around deep, water-filled potholes. There were houses on both sides, but their scattered nature suggested that the owners might have begun as squatters. A desolate area about a half-mile into the road suggested itself as a perfect ambush site because vehicular traffic would have to slow down to negotiate the potholes and because there was no one living directly on either side. A further half-mile or so up the road was the prison. Above the main entrance in a semicircular metal arch was the name, *CENTRALE PENITENTIARE INRICHTING*. The taxi driver explained that because it was located in the Santo Boma Polder, it was commonly called the Santo Boma Prison. The right half of the main gate was open, as it was visiting period, and Erikson and the driver entered to take a look. The first checkpoint beyond the entrance was the Guardroom, on the right side, but one had a clear view of the wall ahead behind which was the main part of the prison. In front of the wall, in the open area past the Guardroom, were offices and living quarters. Not wanting to draw undue notice to himself, Erikson did not venture too close to the Guardroom, where the prison officials inside seemed busy attending to the line of waiting visitors, as well as keeping an eye on those visitors who had been allowed beyond the Guardroom to visit with inmates.

Satisfied that the prison was generally laid out as Colonel Wesfall had indicated and reassured that he would later obtain a more precise layout, Erikson rejoined the taxi for Paramaribo. At about 16:40 when they reached the outskirts of Paramaribo, the car slowed and inched forward in bumper-to-bumper traffic in a city, where citizen behavior had become conditioned by dusk-to-dawn curfews. At 17:15, when Erikson arrived at the Torarica, he stepped into the café for an early dinner, washing down a club sandwich with a bottle of Parbo beer before retiring to his room. Having been cautioned that in order to make the ferry from Nickerie back to Springlands he had to leave Paramaribo by 04:00 hours the next day, Erikson called his mother to tell her he had seen Anita off; then, he went to bed.

TWENTY-NINE

April 28, 1980
Bel Air Park, Greater Georgetown

Steve Erikson set down the *Teach Yourself Dutch* primer and looked out to the Atlantic. Waves were crashing against the seawall, casting sheets of water across the East-coast road. The power of the waves on the coastline worried him. The *Nickerie Queen,* on a fairly tranquil sea, had rolled badly. Now, the waves pounding against the seawall raised a terrifying specter of the difficulties an un-harassed coastal fishing boat could experience negotiating twelve miles of open sea, which was what he knew the rescue plan contemplated.

It had been two weeks since Anita's father had left for Canada. Mr. Rambarran was persuaded that all of the paperwork regarding his insurance claim had been filed and was satisfied with the arrangements Steve had made for Anita. Now that Anita had left, he felt the sense of relief he needed to concentrate on planning the liberation of Andrew Rambarran without fearing for her safety. At home and at the Embassy, Erikson listened to Dutch cassette tapes, which came with the *Teach Yourself* book, and had now acquired proficiency with quite a handful of everyday Dutch expressions. In Suriname, he learned that most Surinamese spoke some English, but in a clutch, a bit of Dutch could make a difference. The doorbell announced the arrival of his company, and down the central stairway he went to bring them up. With Colonel Stanford and Station Chief Hitchcock were the Military Attaché and CIA Station Chief from the U.S. Embassy in Suriname, Colonel John Wesfall and Tom McGinnis. After a perfunctory greeting, he led them up and seated them at the kitchen table.

"Okay," Stanford said, "let's get started. Officially, we're here for lunch; the rest of this meeting simply didn't happen." Stanford paused; Erikson nodded.

"Hold it," Hitchcock interrupted. "Don't you have anything to drink in the house?"

"Sure," Erikson replied. "What would you gentlemen like? I have beer — Heineken and Banks. If you prefer something stronger, I have Scotch and rum. Also, I picked up lunch from *Shanta's*, if you wanted to work on that as well."

"Lunch later, I'll have a Heineken," Hitchcock said; "Same here," the others added.

Erikson poured bottles of Heineken in glasses for his guests, and opened a couple of packets of plantain chips. He chose coffee for himself and took the seat between Colonels Stanford and Wesfall but across from Hitchcock, who was sitting beside Chief Tom McGinnis.

"This is an off-the-shelf operation for which you will carry full responsibility," Stanford said. "If anything goes wrong and you're picked up, I have no doubt you'll rot in a Surinamese jail. For what it's worth, I wish Andrew Rambarran were free, but we are where we are."

"I just couldn't rest until he's free," Erikson declared.

"Well, it's your annual leave," Stanford responded. "Some people spend theirs at Myrtle Beach; you want to invade Suriname. Okay, here goes. Fred?"

Fingers interlaced over his protruding stomach, Station Chief Hitchcock crinkled his nose and mustache. "I'll invite Station Chief McGinnis to say a few things about the new head of state in Suriname."

"The head of the military junta in Suriname is a paranoid fella," McGinnis began. "Can't say that I blame him; he's already faced down three counter-coup attempts. By the way, he has promoted himself to Major and, in Suriname, he is known as the *Bevelhebber* or Commander. He is very thin-skinned." McGinnis took a sip of beer. "Can't stand criticism. His people fire-bombed a Hindustani radio station that was criticizing him. Some of his sharpest critics have fled the country. He believes they're in Guyana, and he wants them. He might be holding Rambarran to effect a swap."

"Well, Erikson," Hitchcock said, "you want to break him out? Colonel Stanford has a plan, which we can tweak with your input."

Laying out a map of Guyana and one of the Paramaribo area on the dining table Colonel Stanford began the briefing. "Let's start at the top," Stanford began.

The Prison

The Central Penitentiary at Santo Boma is a rectangular complex of concrete walls topped by barbed wire, with sixteen-foot metal gates at the entrance. To the inside right is the admitting guardroom and armory, as well as the office of the warden, a Senior Inspector. Beyond the guardroom is an open courtyard, at the perimeter of which in clockwise order are the women's prison, apartments, and offices. The apartments and offices butt against a solid wall separating this administrative section from the main prison, which occupies the greater proportion of the entire rectangular complex.

Entry into the main prison is through one large metal gate, opened by a guard inside of that prison compound on orders from superiors there or from the guardroom. There are no towers, and the prison guards carry no shoulder weapons — only .38 service revolvers for which they receive no regular target practice, according to our sources. Like the anterior compartment, the prison area has a large open area but is crisscrossed by footpaths and ringed by one-storied and three-storied buildings. From the large metal gate to the back wall of the prison, an unpaved road runs through, dividing the prison into an eastern and a western wing. On the western side, next to the gate is the Guard House and canteen, then a wide open space before the buildings housing prisoners. That open plane would be a perfect landing site for a helicopter. On the eastern side nearest the gate are the infirmary and the Central Guardroom, where the largest concentration of guards are. That's the nerve center of the prison. You will need to control that for the duration of the extraction or to neutralize guard personnel, if you deem that expedient.

The prison was built some time in the colonial era and has undergone no serious upgrade. In particular, no provision currently exists for the possibility of a highly organized break-in. However, given that the prison is located near to population centers and very far from international waters, escape by overland routes is likely to be very costly in lives and the obstacles will favor pursuing forces, raising the specter of failure. Extraction should be secured by helicopter, coordinated by radio to land in the inner prison compound, just about the time when the penetration team has secured Andrew Rambarran.

The Aerial Plan

The helicopter will be a Bell 206L, Long Ranger, on loan from a Brazilian Air Force Colonel in Bon Fin, in the northwest of Brazil across from Lethem on the Guyana side. Let's say, the loan involves an exchange of favors. The Brazilian pilot will be accompanied by a gunner operating a 38-caliber machine gun. The helicopter markings will be temporarily camouflaged with a water-based, poster paint. The pilot's call sign will be "Dom Pedro."

Because prisoners are transported from holding cells at various police stations on Thursdays, the extraction should occur on a Thursday when the extracting team can enter the prison from the main entrance. The helicopter, however, will depart Bon Fin at 17:00 hours on the preceding Wednesday. It will fly northeast across the mid-section of Guyana, passing due south of Kurupukari and will put down in a clearing at Molson Creek, eight miles south of Springlands on the western bank of the Corentyne River, where it will overnight. It will be refueled there from pre-positioned aviation fuel, transported in by a fishing boat, whose crew will serve as night guards. Note that, in both Guyana and Suriname, there are no aerial defense systems or aerial surveillance.

At 06:30 on Thursday, the helicopter will fly out, staying about five miles inside of Suriname's northern Atlantic coastline, parallel to the highway linking Nickerie to Paramaribo, and will put down at Peperpot, an abandoned coffee plantation on the bank of the Suriname River across from Paramaribo and about ten minutes from Santo Boma. Estimated time of arrival at Peperpot 09:00 hours. The helicopter will be refueled while on the ground.

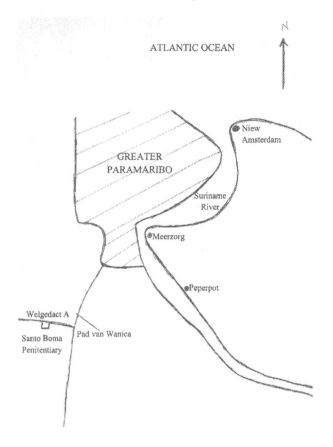

The Extraction

The extraction team will shadow the police van transporting prisoners to Santa Boma. I would recommend you carry UZIs. The team leader, that's you, will decide on where and how to intercept and commandeer that van to gain access into the prison. Once that has been accomplished, the team leader will make contact by radio to the helicopter. Your call sign will be "Trojan Horse."

Just before the extraction team enters the main prison compound, the helicopter will be contacted again, and Operation Eagle Claws will commence. The helicopter will be in flight while the extraction team disarms the guards and secures Rambarran. On arrival, the helicopter will hover and serve as a spotter, firing only if necessary. Once the helicopter puts down, the extraction team will use smoke grenades around its perimeter and proceed to board. The team plus Rambarran will be flown back and deposited at Molson Creek, and will help to refuel the chopper for immediate departure to Bon Fin. The team will then make its way out of the Corentyne River in the fishing boat, on the assumption that the Surinamese military will be searching for a helicopter.

"This is the general plan," Colonel Stanford concluded. "I'd like to know what modifications you'd like to make."

"I've found an ambush site on Welgedact A," Erikson said, "and, of course, you know that Station Chief McGinnis will arrange a safe-house in Niew Amsterdam and a VW van. How about personnel?"

"The officers who escaped will be made available to you," Stanford replied. "I would recommend you take Rambarran's three platoon leaders, Shah, Peters, and DeFreitas, as the members of the extraction team. Others might volunteer, but there's a limit to the number of people you can put on that fishing boat. Ian Morgan seems to have acquired some boat experience; you might consider him as an extra." Erikson nodded agreement. "You can train with those platoon leaders on the trawler for a week in mid-ocean," Stanford continued. "That will also let them familiarize themselves with some of our weapons. Fred Hitchcock will arrange for you to get onto the trawler from Miami."

"Just remember," Hitchcock warned, "once the Brazilian chopper takes off, you and your party must make it out of the twelve-mile territorial limit to be picked up. No if's, and's or but's. Understand?"

"We're assuming that the fishing boat would go out unchallenged," Erikson said. "What if, at some late stage perhaps, it is challenged? Will it have the means to at least provide convincing resistance?"

"Such as?" Hitchcock asked.

"I'd like a 50-caliber machine gun," Erikson replied.

"Are you nuts?" Stanford asked. "The vibrations from that gun will tear apart the flooring of the boat!"

"I need it as a contingency weapon," Erikson asserted. "I don't anticipate using it for sustained fire."

"How would you mount it?" Stanford asked.

"I'd like a steel plate bolted on to the flooring to support a steel pedestal," Erikson replied. "When in use, the gun can be secured to the pedestal by a pin."

"How about the steel pedestal?" Hitchcock asked. "It will protrude up like your dick. Any patrol boat will detect that yours is not a regular fishing boat."

"It depends on the installation," Erikson replied calmly. "The seine compartment has a wall separating it from the rest of the stern. If the pedestal came up at the center of that wall, just high enough to allow for maneuverability, no one outside the boat would notice it, especially if we draped a piece of old canvas or a towel over it."

Colonel Stanford looked over at Hitchcock with raised eyebrows and nodded slowly.

"Also," Erikson continued, "I'd like to have the two halves of that back wall made of plywood so that we can kick them in once we decide to use the 50-caliber."

"That's a long gun, Steve," Colonel Stanford observed. "Where will you store it when it's not in use?"

"Under the covered bow of the boat," Erikson replied.

"It seems like you've thought this through," Stanford said, "but I got to tell you, I'm concerned about what the vibrations from a 50-caliber might do to the flooring of that boat."

"Noted, Colonel," Erikson responded. "Hopefully, we'll not have to use it at all. But here's the thing: The Guyana Maritime Command has two 105-foot patrol boats, *Peccari One* and *Peccari Two*, each carrying two 20-millimeter cannons, and the Surinamese patrol boats have 40-millimeter Bofors cannons. I need some kind of enhanced defense. For close quarters, I'd like a stash of M-72 Light Anti-Tank Weapons; for distance, I'd like a 50-caliber machine gun."

"What type of ammunition for the 50-cal?" Stanford asked.

"High Explosive Incendiary and tracer rounds," Erikson replied.

"Steve, have you considered the fact that you'll have an eight-foot high ice box blocking your field of fire?" Stanford asked.

"Ah, yes, the ice box," Erikson replied. "The icebox on that boat typically rises to eight feet. Now I am not a navy man, but that raises the center of gravity of the boat. If we have to maneuver to elude pursuit, that could cause the boat to tip over in open sea. The weight could also slow us down." Hitchcock and Stanford were listening intently and, by the glances they cast each other, seemed to agree with the analysis. "What I'd like," Erikson continued, "is a detachable icebox, hinged at the level of the gunwale to an open cavity below. The sides of the cavity would need to be reinforced to support the weight; the cavity itself would be used as an arms cache."

"I see you've done your homework," Hitchcock said, smiling. "I'll see what I can do. Now, let's see what you picked up for lunch."

Erikson put out bowls of curried shrimp and curried chicken on the table, as well as the *dal puris* he had picked up from *Shanta's*. Refilling their beer glasses, he watched Hitchcock fix his favorite roll-up of *dal puri* and curried shrimp. When Erikson sat down, he took sips of beer but did not fix himself a plate.

"Is there something else on your mind?" Hitchcock asked from across the table.

"Yes, as a matter of fact," Erikson replied, leaning forward with his elbows on the table and looking directly at Station Chief Hitchcock. "Look, I know this is a long shot, but here it is. Negotiating twelve miles of sea in a boat that can manage 15 knots in tranquil coastal waters means about an hour of exposure to possible strafing from one helicopter, maybe more. We could try to manage if it came to that, but there is no optimistic outcome for us in a scenario of combined attack from air and patrol boat pursuit."

"What exactly are you asking for?" Stanford asked.

"Well, could we count on a Brazilian helicopter outfitted with Hydra-70 rockets to take care of aerial harassment?"

"No." Stanford had been shaking his head before Erikson finished the question. "Look, Steve, it's one thing to ask a Brazilian base commander to allow a chopper on a recon mission to go off-course. We can compensate them for the fuel in many ways. It's quite another thing to have them engage in active combat. Think of the international repercussions if Brazilian involvement becomes known?"

"How would it?" Erikson asked. "I mean, a helicopter so outfitted could take out a Surinamese or Guyanese chopper and be on its way back in no time."

"No," Hitchcock said. "This is an off-the-shelf operation. You are getting assistance because we feel a moral responsibility for Rambarran, but don't overvalue your friend. You'll get the weapons and supplies from surplus we have. But minimal assistance otherwise ..."

"Even assuming that Brazilian involvement can go undetected, there is the practical issues of inventory and cost," Stanford added. "No Brazilian Colonel is going to survive signing off on such a mission."

"What if they didn't have to deplete their inventory?" Erikson asked.

"Where the hell would you get the rockets?" Stanford asked.

Erikson tossed his head in Hitchcock's direction. "The guys in the CIA have everything, don't they? Just a couple of rocket pods to even up the odds."

Hitchcock ignored the request and took another bite of his roll-up. Erikson looked over at Colonel Stanford, but the Colonel's countenance suggested no forthcoming support. He took another sip from his glass. "Can I ask you something, Hitchcock?"

"You don't want to go nuclear now, do you?" Hitchcock asked, and Stanford laughed out loud.

"No, nothing like that," Erikson replied.

"Well, what is it?" Hitchcock asked.

"What's your angle, Hitchcock?" Erikson asked.

"What do you mean?" Hitchcock sounded irritated. "You want to rescue your friend, don't you? I'm trying to help."

"But why?" Erikson got up and paced, deep in thought. "You called this an off-the-shelf operation, which it is. But you had to get clearance from Operations at Langley. So, why is the CIA interested in the rescue of Andrew Rambarran?"

"Okay," Hitchcock began, "members of the ruling military junta in Suriname are calling what they pulled off a revolution. They've established connections with Sandinistas in Nicaragua and may have even traveled to Cuba. A scheme like yours, which plucks a prisoner out of their grasp, would really shake up that junta. They'll have to wonder what might be next. So, yes, we're banking on your success, and we'll help. As the saying in this country goes 'hand wash hand make hand come clean' or, if you like, we'll scratch your back, you'll scratch ours."

"Exactly," Erikson said. "If we fail, you and the CIA boys will look like a collection of incompetent assholes." Hitchcock grimaced and began chewing more slowly. "So, how about it, Hitchcock? Just a couple of rocket pods?"

Hitchcock looked across at Colonel Stanford but remained non-committal.

"The Brazilians don't have the Hydra-70 rockets," Colonel Wesfall asserted calmly. "As far as I know, only US attack helicopters have them."

"There you go," Stanford said, "it's out of the question. Ain't no way you'll get a US chopper out here with that kind of firepower."

"That's not exactly true," Colonel Wesfall interjected.

"What do you mean?" Stanford asked.

"I'm sure you'll be informed about it," Wesfall replied, "but US forces will be conducting joint exercises with the French next door in French Guiana. You and I will be invited as observers. It's fair to say there are multiple goals to the exercises. One is to scare the military junta in Suriname, but drug interdiction and jungle warfare training for our troops are also a part of it. What I'm trying to say is that AH-1 Cobras will be involved in those exercises and they carry Hydra-70 rockets."

"Oh come on, John, why are you giving this guy false hope?" Stanford asked.

"Well, to tell the truth," Wesfall replied, laughing, "this is one of the most exciting things to happen in these parts for a while."

"I don't believe this!" Stanford exclaimed. "This is really getting out of hand."

"Okay," Wesfall said, "it seems to me that this little caper to get Andrew Rambarran out dovetails with one of the missions of the joint-exercises, namely, to scare the bejesus out of the *Bevelhebber* in Suriname. I'm sure that our choppers will take advantage of the absence of aerial surveillance over Suriname to overfly Surinamese airspace, especially across the southern part of the country where drugs enter for transshipment to the Netherlands. That would put those choppers darned close to where Erikson would be operating."

"It doesn't mean they are available for use in some off-the-shelf operation!" Stanford insisted.

"You're right," Wesfall conceded, "but I got to tell you, I know several of those chopper pilots who'd love to fire on a couple of live targets instead of those make-believe ones in the jungle."

"What would it take to draw one of them into the fight?" Erikson asked.

"Some credible individual making the case that the targets in question are involved in the drug business," Station Chief McGinnis replied with a wink. There was silence around at the table. "If that Cobra returns safely to base, believe me, no one will give a fig about searching the ocean for the destroyed targets."

"Well," Colonel Stanford said, "this has been an interesting discussion. The operational plan, as it stands, calls for an escape by fishing boat."

THIRTY

May 8, 1980
Nieuw Amsterdam, Suriname

"The VW van's here, Captain," Peters announced from his lookout position beside the front window of the safe-house.

"Just last names, Peters, no rank," Erikson whispered sharply from the breakfast table.

"Sorry, Captain, I mean, Erikson. Habit, sorry."

"Probably nerves too," Erikson added. "Let's all calm down. We have a long day ahead." He swallowed the last bit of coffee and walked to the bathroom, where he checked the tan camouflage on his face in the small mirror mounted over the sink. When he reemerged into the kitchen area, his three companions were standing, each by a bag on the floor.

"Okay, listen up," Erikson said. "We're aiming to cross with the 07:15 ferry, which will put us in Paramaribo by 07:40. That means we'll have at least an hour-long wait. We'll hang out by the Waterkant. Do *not* eat anything on sale; I don't want anyone having diarrhea. Drink only water or coffee to kill the time. We'll go down to the van by two's," Erikson said. "Peters, left rear seat in the van. Take the satchel with the grenades. DeFreitas, the Uzis and magazines; sit next to Peters. Okay, off you go." Erikson and Shah waited a few minutes for the others to settle into the van. "Take the rucksack with the snack bars and the water canteens," Erikson said to Shah. "I'll bring out the radio."

The assistant driver, who was standing by the door when Erikson and Shah came out, offered to help. Erikson allowed Shah to precede him to the seat behind the driver, then asked the assistant to sit beside Shah, before closing the door. Setting the radio on the floor in front of the van, Erikson took the seat by the driver. He glanced back to locate the grenade satchel and laundry sack with the guns, both of which rested on the floor in front of DeFreitas and Peters and felt uncomfortable with the way the sacks appeared. "Driver, did you bring the pieces of tarp?" he asked.

The driver nodded and went to the back of the van to get them. Erikson covered the radio and passed rectangular sections of the soiled and faded tarp to DeFreitas to cover the grenade satchel and the laundry sack with the Uzis and magazines. "Please keep your feet off the grenades. If one pin slips off a percussion grenade, we can kiss our asses goodbye." He checked his watch. "Let's synchronize watches; it's 05:30 hours. Okay, driver."

The sun was not up, but it was quite light, and most of the traffic on the highway appeared bound for Meerzorg. After twenty-five minutes or so, they turned onto the East-West Connection, passing multicolored buses, which reminded Erikson of Guadalajara, Mexico. Shortly afterwards, the driver was pulling into the ferry station at Meerzorg and joining the vehicle line for the next crossing. The *Maratakka* was still moored to the Paramaribo wharf. It was 06:15 hours. The driver went over to the ticket office and secured tickets for the van and passengers.

"Okay, we have a thirty to forty-five minute wait here," Erikson said, looking over his shoulder to the back of the van. "Try to rest your eyes." He slid the window open and stretched out and rested his head back. He knew he couldn't sleep: too much to think about. He hoped they had considered all the possibilities and planned for every contingency. They'd know soon enough, when the mess hit the fan.

This was his last mission. He was leaving the service in August when his five-year contract ended. He thought of Hitchcock's attempt to recruit him into the CIA; he would have told Hitchcock what he thought of him and the CIA, but Stanford had advised against it. It didn't make sense, Stanford had said, pissing off a man on whom the success of this operation depended, but he was sure Hitchcock was calculating he might change his mind if they pulled this one off.

He wondered what he'd do when his discharge papers came through in August. He had always pushed away this question, but he would soon have to face it. Marriage to Anita would necessitate having a source of income, especially since she would not be able to work for a while, but selling furniture at his father's store in Cartersville, Georgia, didn't seem too exciting. Still he knew the business, having worked in it on weekends and during summers during high school. It could also pay for his MBA studies. Anita would probably want to get legal certification in the US eventually, though she didn't seem as concerned about that as she was about having children. He missed her awfully. The failed coup had had one unanticipated consequence: it had lodged Anita at his house for over two months. What a wonderful tour of duty that became!

The sounds of the *Maratakka*'s engines refocused Erikson's attention to the approaching ferry. It passed by the wharf and executed a wide left turn to re-orient the bow northward. Next came the grating sounds of the reverse engines slowing the boat as it drifted in sideways against the pylons fronting the wharf. Sailors from the lower deck tossed out the loops of thick rope for wharf workers to wrap around the iron cleats on the wharf. Securely moored, the boat disgorged its light cargo of passengers and a handful of cars and trucks, confirming what Erikson had been told about the heavy one-way traffic to Paramaribo until 12:00 hours, when the traffic turned the other way.

The truck ahead cranked up and began moving down the ramp into the ferry. The driver of the VW followed suit, stopping to give the tickets to the ticket collector. The sailor managing the vehicular boarding directed the van next to the truck in a corner on the starboard side. From there, the van occupants watched the rest of the boarding. When the vehicle deck was filled to capacity, the metal ramp was winched up, the moorings unhitched, and the bow oriented northwest toward Paramaribo. It was 07:20 hours.

"Okay," Erikson said, "this is a ten-minute cruise, so why don't you go ahead and use the toilets. Go in pairs, DeFreitas and Peters, then the drivers. Shah and I will go last."

By the time Erikson and Shah had returned to the van, the *Maratakka* was executing a wide turn to present its port side to the Paramaribo wharf. When the moorings were securely fastened to the metal cleats on the dock, the ramp was lowered and the disembarkation began with the last in, first out. At 07:40, the VW van rolled up the ramp onto the Waterkant and, on Erikson's instruction, the driver pulled off the road and parked close to the seawall, behind the food shops.

"We can't just sit here in the van for the next hour or so," Erikson said, "it might draw suspicion. Peters, DeFreitas and the assistant driver: why don't you go out and get some coffee? Let the assistant driver do the ordering. Take about half an hour. When you return, the rest of us will go."

On the seawall side of the van, the Suriname River displayed the bustle of river commerce. Fishing boats, which had entered the river's mouth were making their way to Platte Brug to unload their catch, and multicolored ferry boats were crossing paths between Commewijne and Platte Brug. At the sidewalk food shops, business was brisk. Pedestrians on the Waterkant bee-lined to the ordering-windows, and vehicles pulled over to the curb for their occupants to make food purchases. What emanated from the ordering-windows and from people seated at the picnic tables nearby sounded to Erikson like an assortment of babble. Some spoke Dutch; many spoke *Sranang*, the local dialect; and still others spoke Hindustani. On the Waterkant, army trucks and jeeps drifted by intermittently, the occupants in their rear holding Uzis.

At 08:05 hours, Peters, DeFreitas, and the assistant driver returned to the van, and Erikson and the others decided to stretch their legs. As they walked along one of the alleys between the food shops, a scrappily dressed Creole man approached them. Wanting to shield Erikson from the potential panhandler, the VW driver said something in *Sranang*, but the Creole man ignored him and went over to Erikson, "A cup of coffee, please." Erikson signaled with a tilt of his head for the driver to buy the man a cup of coffee. When the driver put his arm around the man's waist to lead him away to the coffee shop, the man pushed him away, saying, "I want the tall one to buy me a cup of coffee."

Not wanting a scene, Erikson responded, "Okay," and continued walking, with the man slightly ahead of them. Then, the man pointed to a coffee shop, which required them taking a transverse alley. Since it seemed safe enough, no one objected. Mid-way in the alley, the Creole man stopped and faced them. "The van will go to Duisburglaan first, then to Buro Keizerstraat. Do you understand?" Erikson nodded. "When the van is about to leave Buro Keizerstraat, I'll return to let you know." He winked and left.

"Let's get that coffee," Erikson said, smirking. "That fellow sure made a convincing case."

At the coffee shop, the driver ordered and paid for three cups of coffee. The Creole woman behind the counter transmitted the order to her helper who poured hot water in three styrofoam cups and added instant coffee, milk, and sugar. Erikson took a sip and led the way back to the van, where he asked his companions to give him a ten-foot protective perimeter around the van while he tried the radio. While they set up outside, he uncovered the radio on the floor and turned it on.

"Dom Pedro, Dom Pedro, this is Trojan Horse. How do you read me? Over." He released the button on the mouthpiece and waited. He heard the squelch from the radio but no response. He repeated the call.

"Trojan Horse, this is Dom Pedro," came the response. "I read you loud and clear. Over."

"Roger, Dom Pedro," Erikson said. "Wheels about to roll. Over."

"Eagle in flight, Trojan Horse. Estimated time of arrival, 09:00 hours. Over."

"Roger, Dom Pedro. Out." Erikson turned off the radio, covered it with the tarp, and sipped his coffee.

At 09:15, the scrappily dressed Creole man approached gesticulating and yelling that the VW was blocking his view of the river. The driver rushed back to the van and started up. Erikson signaled the others in and the van moved off slowly, while the Creole man continued his act. The driver idled the van on the curb, waiting to join the flow of traffic out of town. Almost directly ahead of them was the cream-colored, VW police van executing a right turn from Keizer Street onto the Waterkant. Accelerating from the curb onto the road amid honking horns from the vehicles which had just averted hitting his VW, Erikson's driver joined the traffic, a few vehicles behind the police van. The chase had begun.

The adrenaline flow was quickly checked a hundred feet from Platte Brug by the vehicular and pedestrian traffic at the Central Market. Erikson's VW van drifted through, stopping and moving with a slow monotonous regularity. He consoled himself by the thought that the police van was also having to negotiate the market and couldn't be too far ahead. Once through the market, the VW moved with the flow of traffic onto Van't Hogerhuys Street, shortly thereafter taking Latourweg. On Pad van Wanica, the VW opened up and they soon discovered that the police van was far more respectful of whatever speed limit there was. It was moving at a leisurely crawl, and Erikson instructed his driver to overtake it and to maintain his speed.

When he figured they had attained a sizable lead on the police van,

Erikson began to look for a spot to pull over. There wasn't much traffic on the road; the cars and trucks on the road were mostly moving in the direction of Paramaribo, at staggered distances from one another. "That looks like a good spot ahead," Erikson said to the driver, pointing to a wide patch of red sand on the left, where there were no houses on either side. Erikson had the driver angle the nose of the van at forty-five degrees to the road to block the view from any coming traffic. He got out with the radio and rushed to place it at the back of the van, whose rear doors the driver had already opened. DeFreitas brought the weapons bag to the back, taking out the four Uzis, which he placed side by side on the floor and covered with a piece of canvas. He set the bag with the extra magazines in one corner, while Peters stowed the grenade satchel in another.

One truck passed by in the direction of Paramaribo, but neither it, nor a car from the Paramaribo direction, slowed down. The driver and passengers in the car looked over, but vehicles on the sides of roads in Suriname were a common enough occurrence. Once Erikson and the others had retaken their seats, the VW pulled back onto the road and sped on. Ten minutes later, they took the right turn onto Welgedact A, and came to a stop after a half of a mile, at the spot Erikson had identified on his earlier trip to Santo Boma. He had the driver park close to the drainage ditch on the left side of the unpaved road. There was a large pothole ahead of them and one behind them. The one-storied shacks on either side of the road were at least a hundred feet up. Erikson slid the door open and moved quickly around, followed by Shah, DeFreitas, and Peters. The driver had opened the rear doors, and Erikson picked up the Uzis, keeping the canvas wrap over them and set them on the grass beside the van. The driver propped open the hood and stood in front with his assistant, both appearing to be diagnosing a problem.

DeFreitas sat on the grass, his back resting on the left rear of the van, Peters kneeling in front of him, appearing to be tending a wound. Erikson and Shah stood behind Peters, trying to appear concerned, while looking intently at the intersection. Javanese young men on *bromfiets* passed by from both directions giving protracted stares but not slowing down. The wait seemed interminable. Then the cream-colored police van turned onto Welgedact A.

"Okay, they're here, folks," Erikson said. "Time to rock and roll."

The VW driver stepped away from the front of the van into the path of the oncoming police van, waving his hands into the air, his assistant moving next to Erikson. The police van slowed down, then stopped on the right front of the parked VW.

"Translate!" Erikson whispered to the assistant driver.

"The driver told the Inspector we have a problem," the assistant driver said, "and that our van struck that man. He thinks the man's hip might be broken. He said the man came out of nowhere, and he couldn't stop in time. The Inspectors are talking to one another. I can't hear them."

The police van pulled over to the left side of the road, slightly ahead of the parked vehicle. The right front door opened and the Hindustani Inspector, whose name tag bore the name, Sardjoe, stepped out. The VW driver led him along the road to the back of the van. Once he was behind the van and out of view of the police vehicle, Erikson pointed the Uzi at him.

"Just stand against the van, Inspector, you won't be harmed. Understand? *Verstaat u?*" The Inspector nodded. "Take his revolver," Erikson said to DeFreitas, who was now on his feet, Uzi in hand. "And keep him here."

Erikson rushed over to the police van where Shah and Peters stood, leaning into the right front door and the open side door respectively, their weapons pointing at the driver and Sub-Inspector Geffrey, sitting behind the driver. Standing in front of the open side door, Uzi tucked into his own stomach, Erikson said, "Inspector Geffrey, you'll be okay, just don't do anything stupid. First, let me have that revolver." Then, looking directly at the four prisoners in the back seats, he said, "When I say go, the four of you step out and rush over to the van behind you. Understand?" They nodded. "Do anything else," he warned, "and you're dead. Okay? Go."

The first pair of handcuffed prisoners stepped out and ran into the rear van, followed by the second pair. Erikson's VW driver ordered the prisoners to crouch down on the floor and to remain there. DeFreitas brought Inspector Sardjoe back to the police van, where Erikson ordered him to retake his seat next to the driver. Peters and DeFreitas rushed back to the VW to pick up the radio, the grenade satchel, and the food and water rucksack. The exercise lasted only three minutes. The driver of the rear van reversed and executed a right turn, heading out of Welgedacht A for Pad van Wanica, to take the long trek back to French Guiana.

In the police van, Erikson and Shah sat behind Sub-Inspector Geffrey, and Peters and DeFreitas were assigned the rear seats. Erikson ordered the van forward.

"*Spreekt u engels?*" Erikson asked.

"Yes, we speak English," Inspector Sardjoe replied.

"Now, listen, both of you," Erikson, "we're going to the Central Penitentiary. We want a particular prisoner, that's all. We don't want to hurt you or anyone else. But if you don't cooperate, we will shoot you. Understand?" Both police officers nodded.

"Good," Erikson said. "Now you are going to get us into the prison compound. We will act like your prisoners. Remember, I understand Dutch. *Verstaat u?*"

"We understand," Inspector Sardjoe replied.

"Inspector, we know the prison routines," Erikson said. "So just follow instructions." He paused. "Remain in the van when you register us at the entrance. When we get inside to the Central Guard House of the main prison compound, you will translate my orders."

"Which prisoner do you want?" Inspector Sardjoe asked.

"The Guyanese army Captain," Erikson replied. "Do you know him?"

"I know of him," the Inspector said, "but there are other army prisoners here. Surinamers."

"Oh? Who are they?"

"Some of the very people who helped overthrow the government of Suriname."

"I thought they were being held at Fort Zeelandia," Erikson said.

"They were moved here," the Inspector replied.

"Good to know," Erikson said, thinking this should not materially affect the task at hand.

The police van slowed to execute the left turn into the *CENTRALE PENITENTIARE INRICHTING*, entering the right half of the metal gate, which was open, and coming to a stop by the entrance to the registration office. The Prison Warden, a Senior Inspector, appeared in

The February 23rd Coup

the upper half of the Dutch door and greeted Sardjoe, who handed over the warrants. The Prison Warden leafed through the pages, peered into the van, visually reconciling the number of prisoners with the warrants, then walked back to the sergeant seated at a desk to have him log the prisoners. The Prison Warden returned to the half-opened door and spoke to Sardjoe. Erikson could not follow any of what was being said, but from the intermittent laughter, he gathered it was just a light banter. The sergeant then came out, handed the warrants back to Sardjoe, and walked around the van, looking over the prisoners. He returned to the entrance and stood beside the Prison Warden and joined the banter. They spoke in Dutch and Hindustani, occasionally inserting a *Sranang* expression.

Christ, these people are such talkers, Erikson thought, wanting to nudge Sardjoe to move on. Then he heard the Prison Warden, in a serious tone, mention the *Politie Militaire*. Sardjoe seemed to tense up, and his Sub-Inspector turned and looked at Erikson.

"*Accha*," Sardjoe finally said in Hindustani, and signaled for the driver to proceed.

"What did he say about the Military Police?" Erikson asked.

"They're here," the Sub-Inspector answered, preempting Sardjoe.

"How many?" Erikson asked.

"He didn't say," Inspector Sardjoe replied.

"Okay, it doesn't change anything," Erikson said. "Do exactly as I tell you, and you will be fine." Then turning to Shah and the others, he said, "We may have to take out the Military Police. If they get in the way, shoot them." Erikson then bent forward and turned on the radio. "Sardjoe, have the driver turn the van toward the Women's prison."

"That would be irregular," Sardjoe said.

"Well, I need a few minutes," Erikson asserted. "Stop the van. See that prison guard over on the left, Sardjoe, the one flirting with the female inmates? Go on out and talk to him. Shah, keep the weapon on him."

"You're making a mistake," Sardjoe said. "Look ahead, they've already opened the gate for us. They'll think something is wrong."

"We'll take that chance. Just call out to the fellow and find something to talk about. Now, out!"

Inspector Sardjoe got out of the van and, standing near the left front, called out to the prison guard, who was flirting with the female prisoners. The man, clearly junior in rank, walked briskly over and saluted. Sardjoe greeted him in Dutch and then took on a more conversational tone. In the meantime, Erikson bent over and spoke into the mouthpiece. "Dom Pedro, Dom Pedro, this is Trojan Horse. How do you read me? Over." No response; Erikson repeated his call.

"This is Dom Pedro," came the response. "I read you loud and clear, Trojan Horse. Over."

"Commence Operation Eagle Claws. I say again, commence Operation Eagle Claws. Over."

"Operation Eagle Claws underway. I say again, Operation Eagle Claws underway. Acknowledge, over."

"Roger, Dom Pedro. Operation Eagle Claws underway. Out."

Erikson ordered the Sub-Inspector Geffrey to get Sardjoe back into the vehicle. Geffrey complied. "*Inspector, kom hier, alstublieft,*" he said, and Sardjoe reentered the van and took his seat beside the driver.

"Drive slowly," Erikson said to the driver, and to his squad, "Lock and load!"

The van passed through the gate into the main prison compound, Sardjoe waving to the guard in the gatehouse as they passed. The unpaved road went all the way to the back wall, as Colonel Stanford had said, parting the compound almost evenly. On the right, beyond the guard hut and the canteen was a large, open space, beyond which were rows of two-storied buildings. On the left was the infirmary and the Central Guard House. Rows of prisoner housing mirrored those on the right side. The van turned off the road to the left onto the open space in front of the Central Guard House, where there was an army jeep parked at the entrance and guarded by two soldiers with Uzis. On Erikson's instruction, the van driver went past the jeep and stopped closer to the infirmary.

"Why are they here?" Erikson asked Sardjoe.

"There are four army sergeants imprisoned here for an attempted coup. The *Bevelhebber*, the Commander, sends for them from time to time."

"Very well, let's wait here until you absolutely must get out."

An MP sergeant came out of the Guard House, entering the cab of the army jeep while the soldiers entered the back. The jeep reversed, then turned around and moved onto the unpaved dividing road, traveling toward the rear of the prison compound. Erikson ordered the van driver to reposition the vehicle in front of the Guard House. Inspector Sardjoe stepped out and slid open the van's side door. A burly Hindustani prison sergeant stepped into the open entrance of the Guard House and waved Sardjoe in. Sardjoe and Sub-Inspector Geffrey walked ahead of Erikson, Peters, and DeFreitas, all of whom held their Uzis tightly tucked in a port-arms position. Shah came through the entrance last with the driver. The prison sergeant was backing the entrance and talking with two juniors sitting at desks. When the two junior guards jumped to their feet, staring at the entrants, the sergeant turned around to see the four Uzis pointing at them.

"Tell them they won't be harmed if they cooperate," Erikson said to Sardjoe.

"They understand English," Sardjoe replied. Addressing the sergeant, Sardjoe said, "they've come for the Guyanese officer."

"Hey, I'll do the talking, okay?!" Erikson said, sternly. "DeFreitas, take the revolvers from these guards and toss them in the van. DeFreitas walked over to each of the prison guards, took the revolvers, and rushed out to the van.

Observing that the windows on the left allowed a clear view into the office, Erikson ordered his companions to kneel on the concrete floor. He sat on a chair facing the guards whom he instructed to sit at their desks. The sergeant complied.

"Okay, where is Captain Rambarran?" Erikson asked.

"He's not here," the sergeant said, "they moved him out this morning."

"You're lying," Erikson asserted.

The sergeant replied, "the *Bevelhebber* wanted to talk with him."

"Where did they move him to?" Erikson asked.

"Fort Zeelandia," the sergeant replied.

"What now?" Shah asked.

"Let me think," Erikson replied. Then pointing to the corporal seated to their right, he said to Shah winking, "shoot that one."

"Please, no," said the corporal, jumping to his feet. "They took him to Nickerie. They left at 09:00 this morning."

"Why Nickerie?" Erikson asked.

"They are going to turn him over to the Guyanese government," the corporal replied.

"Last chance for you," Erikson said to the burly Hindustani sergeant. "Don't fuck with me or I'll drop you. You got it?" He stared at the sergeant, who nodded. "Which station in Nickerie are they taking him to?"

"*Oost Kanaal Straat*," the sergeant replied, adding, "sorry, East Kanaal Street."

"Then what?" Erikson asked. "How will they turn him over to the Guyanese authorities?"

"They will take him across by the back-track and turn him over to the Springlands police."

"When?" Erikson asked.

"Sometime today; that's all we know," the sergeant replied.

"Peters, DeFreitas, tie those two corporals to their chairs and tip them over. Inspector Geffrey, on the floor. Shah, tie him up." Turning to the Hindustani sergeant, "Show me on the prisoner manifest where Andrew Rambarran was held and get the keys for that cell."

The sergeant retrieved the roster from his desk and showed Erikson that Andrew Rambarran's name was next to cell 217 Building C. Erikson signaled with a tilt of his head for the sergeant to stand by Inspector Sardjoe. He watched Shah bind the ankles and wrists of Inspector Geffrey behind his back with a piece of telephone wire Peters tossed him. "Sorry about the discomfort," Erikson said, "I'm sure you'll be released shortly. Remember, you don't have to lose your lives over this. Alright, use your handkerchiefs to gag them."

When the gagging was completed, Erikson turned to the sergeant. "Come on you, take us to Building C." He followed the sergeant out and seated him at the front of the van, next to the driver, who was escorted out by Peters. Inspector Sardjoe was escorted out by Shah and DeFreitas and made to sit next to Erikson. When everyone was in the van, Erikson said, "Alright, sergeant, tell the driver where to go."

The van reversed, then turned around and picked up the unpaved road toward the rear of the prison. At the second cross street on the right, it turned and stopped at about the mid-section of the two-storied building there.

"Shah, stay here with DeFreitas and keep an eye out for that army jeep," Erikson said. "Peters, come with me. Okay, sergeant, you and the Inspector can show us the cell."

The sergeant led Erikson, Peters, and Inspector Sardjoe up one flight of stairs and walked along a narrow veranda to cell 217, which he opened. Empty. "Fuck!" Erikson exclaimed, pacing the small cell. The cot had been stripped bare to just the sheet of foam resting on a bed spring. He looked at the walls for signs Rambarran had been there. There weren't any. He pulled out the cot from the wall. Just below the level of the bed spring was a hand-written calendar, with headings, "February," "March," "April," and "May." Each day was individually marked, beginning under February with the number "26," coincidentally the day Rambarran was transferred from Nickerie to Santo Boma. The numbers inked on the wall were in a tiny font, but carefully and compactly etched, and painstakingly accurate. The last entry under "May" was "8." There was no question Rambarran had been there.

"Okay, you two will stay in this cell," Erikson said to Inspector Sardjoe and the sergeant. "Don't worry, you'll be safe here; probably safer than being outside." Just then, Erikson heard the faint buzzing sound of the helicopter. He rushed out with DeFreitas, locked the door and tossed the key over the veranda rail as they continued down the stairway to the van, which had already been turned around.

"Get in!" Erikson said to Shah and Peters, who entered through the van's sliding right door and were joined moments later by DeFreitas, then Erikson. With the side door closed, the driver accelerated to the junction with the unpaved central road. However, the buzzing of the helicopter had brought the two soldiers and their MP sergeant out. The MP sergeant shouted at the van to stop and, when the van turned onto the unpaved road ignoring the sergeant, the soldiers began firing their weapons.

"Everyone down," Erikson yelled, as shells hit the back of the van. "We'll have to take those soldiers out."

The van went past the first building, and Erikson ordered the driver to pull off the road onto the outer edge of the wide, open area between the building and the canteen.

"Driver," Erikson yelled, "spin the van around, then run the hell away." The van was spun around so that its width provided cover as the officers exited the sliding door on its right side. "I'll provide cover here," Erikson said. "Take up positions on the perimeter."

Erikson fired in the direction of the MP sergeant and the two soldiers, while his three companions took positions at the other three compass corners about forty paces from each other. A burst of machine-gun fire from the helicopter, which was hovering just beyond the western wall, kept the MP and the soldiers from advancing. The helicopter swooped down, settling on the grassy quadrangle framed by Erikson's team. Shah and Peters tossed their smoke grenades and raced to the helicopter, as did Erikson and DeFreitas. The helicopter lifted off and ascended at an angle like a flying saucer, over the western wall and behind the first building, sheltering it from ground fire as it then climbed to higher altitude on a westerly course.

"I just don't believe this!" Erikson declared, strapped to his seat beside DeFreitas and across from Shah and Peters. "All the bloody planning. Christ!" None of his crest-fallen companions seemed to be in a mood to speak. He couldn't blame them. They had risked their lives and had done everything as planned, only to come away empty-handed. Yet he realized that he needed to build up their spirits in order to get them committed to another attempt in Nickerie. He asked DeFreitas to pass out the candy bars, which they washed down with water from two canteens.

"How do you think the *Bevelhebber* will react?" Shah finally asked.

"He'll first have to figure out who initiated the raid," Erikson replied. "If it's true that he was about to hand over Rambarran to the Guyana government, he'll likely rule them out as the source of the operation. Also, because he's had to fend off three counter-coup attempts, he might see this breakout attempt as the start of something else against him, which means that he might keep most of his assets around Paramaribo."

"Does that mean we're not going to be pursued?"

"No, we are, but without the *Bevelhebber* having full consolidation over either army or the country, the effort will be limited. Besides, as you know, they have very limited aerial capabilities."

"Where are the risks than?"

"Well, they can visually monitor the Atlantic coast and will quickly rule that out. No helicopter, no enemy. The French Guiana side will be one possibility, Brazil the other."

"How would they deal with a Brazilian destination?"

"The only way they can: by notifying the Brazilian military authorities and asking that they take action against the plane. However, they'll soon be getting reports from their southern interior locations negating any sighting of a chopper. Same on the side with French Guiana."

"So you think they'll throw their limited assets westward, behind us?"

"Yes. I wouldn't be surprised if they don't already have a couple of Cessnas in the air for observation, one heading this way."

At 12:10 hours, the chopper was over the Saramacca River, further in from the Atlantic coastline than on the earlier trip, the pilot taking care to fly over densely forested areas, where there were no police or military installations. The next landmark would be the Coppename River, about thirty minutes away. The Brazilian pilot called their attention to a Cessna flying on their left in the direction of Paramaribo. Erikson looked out of the window and, after a few moments, saw the Cessna in the distance. Shah leaned over to have a look as well.

"Probably a charter from the bauxite company," Shah said. "They have some operations in the Wasjabo-Apoera area, on the Surinamese side of the Corentyne River."

"They'll probably radio in our location," Erikson said.

At 12:47 hours, the chopper was flying over the Coppename River, just over a third of the distance they needed to cover and about an hour from the Corentyne River. The pilot warned that a pursuing helicopter with a lighter load would likely be closing in on them over this leg.

"Would the Surinamese fly into Guyana airspace?" Erikson asked Shah.

"Yes," Shah replied. "Out here, national airspace doesn't mean much because neither side can police it. Besides, they can always claim hot pursuit."

"Alright, listen up everybody," Erikson said above the chatter of the helicopter. "Once the pilot radios in his approach to Ian Morgan on the fishing boat, Morgan will get ready to refuel the chopper. We'll give them a hand, then we'll get the hell out of there."

"How about if a pursuing Surinamese chopper catches up with us?" Peters asked.

"In the air, it'll still be up to the Brazilian pilot and his machine gunner," Erikson replied. "If it happens while we're on the ground, we'll have to take the Surinamese chopper out. We'll use the 50-caliber machine gun. You'll assist me, Peters; Shah will organize ground fire from the bank."

"How about Andrew?" Shah asked. "Surely we're not heading out without him?"

"No," Erikson responded, relieved that another member of the team was suggesting a rescue effort. "Once we've seen the helicopter safely off, we're heading for Nickerie. We need information. But, I'm with you: if they're taking Andrew out by boat, we're going to snatch him away. Agreed?" Everyone nodded. "Well, get some rest; we're not quite half-way yet."

At 14:00 hours, the chopper had reached the eastern bank of the Corentyne River. There was still no evidence of aerial pursuit. "Homing Pigeon, this is Dom Pedro," the pilot was saying into the radio. "How do you read me? Over."

"Loud and clear, Dom Pedro," came the response, the voice recognizable as that of Ian Morgan. "We also have you in sight."

"This is Dom Pedro. Give me a long count so that I can home in on you. Over."

"Roger, Dom Pedro. Commencing long count." And Ian Morgan began slowly counting from one to twenty.

Mid-river, the pilot banked and headed north-westerly, hugging the Guyana bank of the river, just above tree-level. The elephant-eared leaves of the *moko-moko* at the river's edge swayed violently, and the branches of the *cookrit* and *awara* palms behind them on the inside bank, shimmied. Still seeking the point from which the long count was coming, the chopper followed the river bank to a spot where large clumps of bamboo interrupted the *moko-moko* monopoly. In one of the inlets formed between two bamboo clumps sat the *Lakshmi*, a forty-foot fishing boat, under a camouflage of brush, part of which had been removed to reveal the boat to the approaching helicopter. The chopper banked and descended over the *cookrit* and *awara* palms to settle onto the clearing, where it had overnighted the evening before, about two hundred feet down river from the boat. Ian Morgan had already left the *Lakshmi* and was moving the portable scaffold next to the chopper.

Erikson led the way out of the helicopter. Detailing Shah and DeFreitas to help Ian Morgan with the refueling of the chopper, he and Peters carried their radio, the grenade satchel, and the knapsacks to the fishing boat. He adjusted some of the camouflage over the boat, then returned to the refueling site.

"How're we coming?" Erikson asked the pilot.

"Another ten minutes," the pilot replied.

The refueling complete, Shah and DeFreitas were moving the scaffold away from the chopper when Erikson heard the shout from the direction of the boat. "Captain, we got company," Peters yelled from his position on the bank, near the fishing boat.

Erikson ran back to join Peters and saw the helicopter approaching from the east. It was keeping a high altitude and had not yet reached the river bank. When it did so, it changed direction, flying upriver along the Suriname side of the river. Erikson rushed over to the pilot. "I think that helicopter will cross over at some point and come up along the Guyana side."

"I think so, too," the pilot said.

"You need to maneuver the chopper to give us a chance to take it down," Erikson advised. "Okay?" The pilot nodded. "Shah, organize the ground fire from the bank," Erikson said. "I'm going to get the 50-caliber out."

Erikson ran to the boat, accompanied by Peters, and, from under the bow, he secured the 50-caliber machine gun, which he mounted on the steel pedestal protruding up from a steel plate bolted down on the reinforced ribs running across the width of the boat at the stern end, beyond the seine compartment. On his instructions, the boat skipper started the engine and moved the boat out of the inlet and began slowly drifting down river, away from the refueling spot. From the stern, he observed the flight of the Surinamese helicopter through a pair of field glasses and, sure enough, the helicopter began flying across the river. It went over the western bank of the river into Guyana and out of sight, suggesting to Erikson that the pilot of the Surinamese helicopter intended to come around and cut off the Brazilian from westward flight.

The refueling complete, the Brazilian pilot revved up his engine and took off due west into Guyana, over the thickly forested area.

Erikson could not see the bank closest to the refueling spot, but he assumed Shah had his people under cover. "Turn the boat around," he said to the skipper. "Go slowly back and, when I tell you to, bring the boat perpendicular to the bank. I'll need an unobstructed field of view."

At mid-river, Erikson had a better view of the flight of the Brazilian chopper, which seemed to be hovering over the densely forested area. A few minutes later, the Brazilian helicopter turned and began heading directly back to the refueling area. In hot pursuit was the Surinamese chopper. The Brazilian chopper dropped low and skimmed over the refueling area then lifted up over the *cookrit* and *awara* palms, before dropping again gliding across the surface of the river, hardly fifty feet ahead of the *Lakshmi*. Behind it came the Surinamese chopper in dogged pursuit, imitating the trajectory of its prey but maintaining a higher altitude. Small-arms fire from the river bank had not affected the pursuing chopper. Just above the *cookrit* and *awara* palms, the Surinamese pilot banked the chopper to give his machine gunner an opportunity to fire. With Peters handling the ammo feed, Erikson knelt behind the 50-caliber and, aiming upward, fired at the exposed body of the Surinamese chopper. The high-explosive rounds from the 50-caliber slammed into the chopper, cutting down its machine gunner and exploding the engine. Burning sections of the chopper fell on the tops of the *cookrit* and *awara* palms, the tail section flipping over before bursting into flames on the elephant ears of the *moko-moko*.

"Everyone into the boat," Erikson yelled at his comrades on the bank, as the skipper angled the boat in their direction. Shah, DeFreitas, and Morgan ran, Uzis in hand, past the area of the burning wreckage to the cove between the bamboo clumps and climbed into the boat. Erikson removed the anchoring pin from the 50-caliber and lifted the weapon off of the pedestal to stow it under the covered bow. The others followed suit with their Uzis. As the boat moved back to mid-river, the Brazilian helicopter had turned and was hovering ahead for a look at the wreckage, then the pilot came down for a final salute before the chopper sped away.

THIRTY-ONE

May 8, 1980
On the Corentyne River

The fishing boat, *Lakshmi*, headed toward the mouth of the river. In the galley, Erikson traded his cream shirtjac for a faded, long-sleeved, cotton shirt, which he allowed to hang loosely over his trousers. His other companions also changed into an assortment of hole-ridden, cotton shirts and tee-shirts, befitting fishermen, and retired to the small galley to help themselves to the freshly prepared *cook-up*, a melange of rice, black-eyed peas, vegetables, chicken, and salted beef. Bypassing the chow line, Erikson decided to inspect the boat, beginning at the bow, to insure it had the modifications he had requested. The pedestal mount for the 50-caliber had already proven invaluable.

Lakshmi was typical of the fishing boats on the Corentyne River and those that plied the coastal waters of the Guianas. Forty feet in length, it was driven by a 75 horse-power Yamaha engine and, if actually loaded with fish and ice, it could move at a maximum speed of about twelve knots, depending on the current. The tapered bow was tightly covered with the same type of hardwood which was used to strengthen the sides of the boat. This sheltered area extended from the painted nose back to about twelve feet or so of boat space and ended in a two-foot overhang to which had been tacked a canvas curtain. On a regular fishing boat, this entire arrangement facilitated day-round shift sleeping, and the large sheet of foam resting on the flooring served as the communal bed. On this foam, Erikson had decided to stow the 50-caliber gun and the Uzis for quick use, should the need arise. Shelves built into the sides of the bow provided storage space for personal items and, from large nails partially driven into the ribs at the bow end, hung bags of vegetables, flour, sugar, salt, split peas, and rice. In the narrow nose of the bow rested extra cans of water and gasoline.

Like other fishing boats, the most prominent part of this boat was the rectangular icebox, which, from its seated base at the center of the boat, rose to about eight feet and was topped by a wooden pallette with a zinc underlay. The icebox was built to fit all of the width of the boat except for a narrow ledge along the two sides, and, from front to back, occupied four feet of boat length. At Erikson's request, the icebox on *Lakshmi* was configured as three separate compartments, hinged to each other. The top compartment below the top lid was only two feet deep and had ice and fish, which the boat skipper had purchased the previous day. The lower compartment was empty, except for a layer of sand for stability. The lowest compartment, which rested directly on the flooring, was an arms cache, with access doors on two sides. Eight M-72 rockets, stacked on one side, shared this space with 50-caliber ammunition, magazines for the Uzis, and grenades in satchels.

Behind the ice box, a couple miles of drift seine lay in a cigarette roll in a rectangular compartment, whose sides rose to about four feet from the bottom of the boat, the compartment itself extending about eight feet from front to rear. Between the icebox and the seine compartment was a deep cavity, two feet wide, where fish caught by the seine would be tossed during normal fishing operations, for temporary storage.

Erikson walked on the ledge on the side of the seine compartment to the rear of the boat. Strapped against the back wall of the seine compartment would normally be found large cans of gasoline and water. On the *Lakshmi*, the steel pedestal for the 50-caliber machine gun bat-winged the back wall of the seine compartment and was covered by a piece of old canvas. At the stern, a ten-inch wide seat across the boat allowed the boat skipper to handle the engine, which sat on an elevated platform abutting the stern gunwale of the boat, where a two-foot wide V had been notched out to accommodate the engine.

Erikson notified the skipper that the plans had been changed; they were heading for Nickerie. "Do you think you can find mooring for one or a couple of nights, if needed?"

"Yes," the skipper replied. "I know the area very well and, with fish in the icebox, we can buy mooring space."

"Good," Erikson said, turning to pick his way back to the bow. In the galley area, Shah, DeFreitas, and Peters were re-living some of mid-ocean training for the rescue effort, Coke bottles in hand. Peters passed Erikson a heaping plate of the *cook-up*, which he rested on the covered bow and ate with a tablespoon, while considering the next moves. For sure, he'd have to notify the trawler to defer pick up, but how to get Rambarran out of the clutches of the Surinamese police? Well, that was a different matter. What he needed was more information, and he hoped the contact he had been provided would be able to help out.

The vegetation along the river bank was changing. *Moko-moko* still predominated at the water's edge, but mangroves were more in evidence, their stringy roots reaching up above the shallow water. The movement of the boat created some breeze, through hardly enough to mitigate the riveting heat of the sun.

"Okay, listen up," Erikson said, turning to face his team. "We're heading for Nickerie. Shah and I will go into town to see what we can find out about when they'll transfer Rambarran. The rest of you will remain here. Peters will be in charge. And from here on out, Morgan, you are the assistant skipper of this boat." Erikson took no questions; instead, he pulled the radio out from the sleeping area and turned it on. "Mother Goose, Mother Goose, this is Trojan Horse. How do you read me? Over." He repeated this two more times before he received a response.

"Trojan Horse, this is Mother Goose. We read you loud and clear. Over."

"This is Trojan Horse," Erikson said. "Defer pick up, quarry has been moved. I say again: defer pick up, quarry has been moved. Acknowledge, over."

"This is Mother Goose. Defer pick up confirmed. Defer pick up confirmed. Good luck, Trojan Horse. Over."

"Thanks, Mother Goose. Out." Erikson secured the radio and reclined on the foam in the sleeping area, partly to elude the sun and partly out of a desire to rest for a while. He jerked awake at the sound of his name. "Erikson, we got company!" he heard someone say. Unsure who had said it, he scrambled out of the sleeping area and looked over the covered bow. The small boat about half of a mile ahead was advancing rapidly. He retrieved his binoculars, which he covered with a piece of canvas. "Police," he said to the others. "Guyanese police. Two officers in khakis, someone operating the engine."

Erikson ordered the skipper to keep up the speed but to follow police instructions. Ian Morgan and the boat skipper, who were least likely to be recognized by Springlands police officers were to do the talking;

the others were to get under the bow and take a weapon. Morgan lit a cigarette and sat on the galley bench. At the skipper's suggestion, he turned up the volume on the transistor radio, which had been set on a Nickerie radio station, putting out Indian film music.

A couple of minutes later, a loud voice from the police boat called over to them to stop. The boat slowed to a crawl before the skipper cut off the engine and, against the current, the boat came to a stop. The police boat eased over butting the bow of the fishing boat.

"Oi, cut off the radio!" a police officer ordered. "You all see any planes around here?"

"Yes, officer," Morgan replied. "As a matter of fact, two helicopters passed over a little while ago."

"Which way they heading?" the police officer asked.

"They flew across the river into Guyana, then we lost sight, you know."

"Did you notice anything strange about them?" the police officer asked.

"No, officer," Morgan replied. "But we did hear a loud noise way back and we saw some black smoke."

"Did you go back and take a look?"

"No, officer. It sounded like it was way out in the bush, and we got to get we fish to the market."

"What kind of fish you got?" the police officer asked.

"Mostly *basha*," Morgan replied.

"How much?" the police officer asked.

"You got to ask the boss," Morgan said, tossing his head in the direction of the skipper.

"What you say, comrade?" the police officer asked.

"Three for fifty Guyana dollars," the Skipper answered.

"You crazy?" the police officer exclaimed. "How about thirty?"

"Alright," the skipper said. "Just for you."

Ian Morgan lifted the icebox cover and pulled out three fish, two large and one small.

"Oi man, swap out that little one," the police officer said.

Morgan tossed back the small one and got a larger *basha*. Walking over to the side of the boat, he handed them to the police officer who wanted them and accepted the payment.

"Better let me have three as well," the other police officer said.

Ian Morgan returned to the icebox and took out three large *bashas*, which he turned over to the officer. "Where you heading?" the officer asked, counting out the money to pay for the fish.

"Nickerie," the skipper replied.

"What's your name?" the police officer asked.

"Kandasammy," the skipper replied. "Vincent Kandasammy."

"Where you from, Kandasammy?"

"Enmore on the East Coast, but the other fellas from Stanleytown."

"Where are the other fellas?" the police officer asked.

"Sleeping," the skipper replied. "You know what is like to fish all night?"

"Alright, move along, Kandasammy." The police boat moved laterally away from the fishing boat; its engines were revved up, and it sped off, up river.

"Good work, fellas," Erikson said, crawling out from under the bow, with the others following. "Very good acting back there, Morgan."

They passed on the western side of Lange Island, and the boat ride became bumpier. Waves slapping into the bow confirmed that the Atlantic tide was coming in. There was hardly any *moko-moko* in the shallows along the Guyana bank, only mangrove, whose lower branches rested on top of the water, waving harmoniously with the crests and troughs of the waves pushing upriver.

Estimating that they were just shy of Molson Creek on the Guyana side, Erikson instructed the skipper to get over to the Surinamese bank and maintain course to Nickerie. The *Lakshmi* took a long diagonal trajectory, passing on the eastern side of tiny Vossen Island, then straightened up and hugged the eastern bank of the Corentyne River. A few minutes later, it was passing on the eastern side of Papegaaien Island into the upper throat of the river. On the left, at a distance, was Springlands and, on the right, the western edge of Nickerie. From the bow, Erikson paused to appreciate the full majesty of the Corentyne River, revealed by its expansive mouth, blurring the divide between the river and the ocean. The waves were more robust, cresting higher and over longer distances, and the fresh ocean breeze provided a mildly chilling tingle in the hot afternoon sun.

As they approached the base of the promontory formed by the Corentyne and Nickerie rivers, the mangroves thickened, then ended abruptly. The seawall, emerging past the mangroves, skirted the western edge of Nickerie like a stone fortification, obscuring everything from view, except the red-painted, zinc roof tops of the houses. From the base of the seawall, and continuing into the river on an incline pattern, were large chunks of stone which had been piled to reduce the force of approaching waves. A back-track speed boat, on the last quarter of a mile of its trek from Springlands to Nickerie, was heading for the stone jetty that thrust out from one point of the seawall. Pylons on both sides of the jetty served as tethering points for the bobbing boats moored there, and likely for the approaching boat as well.

Assembled at the top of the seawall, from where the stone jetty arose, was a group of boat operators and customers seeking passage to Springlands. The loud conversations of a few moments earlier quieted down as the *Lakshmi* approached the lower end of the jetty. Not wanting to be among the first faces presented to the onlookers, Erikson moved to the rear of the boat, where the skipper was maneuvering to point the bow at right angles to the jetty. Just then, Asad Shah, who was still at the bow but looking across the river, called back. "Erikson, take a look in the direction of Springlands."

Erikson turned around. The boat in the distance seemed small, but its profile, as it rounded Springlands was unmistakable: a patrol boat. Hastening to the bow, Erikson picked up the binoculars and, from a crouching position behind the icebox, looked across the mouth of the river. "Guyanese patrol boat," he said. "A Vosper craft, one of their two *Peccaris*."

The skipper slowly eased the boat parallel to the partially submerged jetty, then guided it toward the seawall, skirting around the boats already moored. Taking the rope tied to the bow, Ian Morgan climbed onto the jetty and secured it to one of the free pylons. Erikson and Shah climbed out and waited on the skipper, who cut the engine and joined them on the jetty. Leading the way up to the top of the seawall, the skipper hailed a dark complexioned, pot-bellied, Hindustani man, wearing an open shirt and displaying a thick gold necklace, from which hung a golden pendant. He sported a couple of wide gold bracelets on his right hand, a gold-plated watch on his left, and gold rings on several fingers. The young men around him called him Soeresh.

"You think we can tie up here?" the skipper asked Soeresh. "We ran out of supplies."

"Where you heading?" Soeresh asked.

"Back up the river for another night of fishing," the skipper replied.

"How long you staying?"

"Well, we sold most of the fish we had, so the boys might want to get a few beers and sport a little."

"What kind of fish you got?" Soeresh asked.

"We still have a few *basha*."

"How you selling them?"

"Three large ones for ten guilders."

"Lemme have six," Soeresh said, counting out the money to the skipper. Then he told one of his hands to go down and get the fish.

"Oi," the skipper called out to Ian Morgan, "give him six. Pick out big ones."

"Better finish your sporting early," Soeresh advised. "You know we have a curfew from 7 p.m."

"You're right," the skipper said. "I think I'll just send those two comrades to bring back some stuff to the boat."

Erikson and Shah had already walked away from the group and were heading down the stone stairway on the other side of the seawall toward the taxis, parked in the open area adjacent to the snack bar. Vehicles, traversing the softened ground around the snack bar, had created huge indentations, which had been filled by water splashing over the seawall. Navigating around the puddles, a taxi driver rushed to Erikson and Shah and led them to his vehicle. Out of the parking area, he took Graderweg, a well-maintained asphalt road, which divided Nickerie into its northern and southern sections.

Houses on stilts, some painted but faded from unrelenting salt air, and others unpainted, formed the outermost fringe of the Courantijn Polder of the Nickerie District. Further west along Graderweg, the houses improved in brightness, but not in size. East of the intersection with Margarethenberg Street, Graderweg became A. K. Doerga Street. The car turned left onto West Kanaal Street and, at its intersection with

G. G. Maynard Street, made a right turn to take its passengers to the municipal market.

Erikson paid the driver, requesting a few one-guilder coins in change, which he used at the public telephone to dial the number of the safe house. Station Chief McGinnis' Nickerie agent, who had been expecting the contact, assured Erikson he could meet him right away and provided Erikson directions. Detailing Asad Shah to check out the seawall road and to get some take-out food from the restaurant, Erikson left for the safe house. He walked past the Regional Police Headquarters on East Kanaal, where there appeared to be nothing unusual occurring, then took a right turn onto Hendrik Street and counted off the houses to the one-storied house with an unpainted picket fence. The agent, an elderly Creole man, readily opened the back door for him and assured him they were alone in the house.

At the kitchen table where they sat, Erikson explained that Captain Rambarran had been moved to Nickerie and would likely be transferred to Guyana that evening. The agent indicated he had suspected such a development. "The *Bevelhebber* has been keen on a swap for a journalist by the name of Van Booren," the agent said. "Van Booren had been very critical of the Commander and had gone into hiding in Guyana."

"Why didn't they do the swap?" Erikson asked.

"The word was that Van Booren couldn't be found."

"So, he's now been found?" Erikson asked.

"Yes," the agent replied. "Dead."

"Any idea who killed him?"

"Probably the *Bevelhebber's* people."

"Or the Guyana government, maybe?" Erikson suggested.

"Possibly," the agent conceded. "Either way, it doesn't look good for your Captain."

"Why do you think so?" Erikson asked.

"Well, let's see," the elderly Creole man said. "The journalist whom the *Bevelhebber* hated was killed in Guyana. He could have been swapped for Rambarran, but that would have entailed an arrest by the Guyana government, and the killing would have been left to the *Bevelhebber*. The elimination of Van Booren under confused and probably unresolvable circumstances spared both parties some difficulties. Now, the Guyana government wants Captain Rambarran, the only major coup player remaining. Several coup leaders have already been reported as accidentally killed in the explosion at Camp Groomes. The Guyana government has never publicly acknowledged the coup attempt. So, why do they want Rambarran? A Camp Groomes solution, perhaps?"

Erikson pondered the agent's analysis. The *Bevelhebber* had never publicly acknowledged holding Rambarran. Returning the Captain to his home country freed the *Bevelhebber* of any responsibility but created a dilemma for the Guyana government. What would they do with him? Eliminate him where no one would notice? Of course; and what better place than the mouth of the Corentyne River at ebb tide? The body would be pulled out into the Atlantic, and no one would notice. Yes, that was what they planned to do, Erikson was sure. They were going to kill Andrew Rambarran during the transfer. That's what the Guyanese patrol boat off the coast of Springlands was going to be used for. The agent was staring intently at Erikson. "I believe they're going to kill him tonight," Erikson declared.

"I believe you are right," the agent said.

"When is the transfer likely?" Erikson asked.

"If they plan to kill him, it'll be under the cover of darkness. The curfew goes into force from 19:00, but it's not very dark at that hour, so I'd say, 20:00 hours, the earliest."

"Can you find out?"

"I'll try," the agent replied, "but our police source might not know in time for us."

"Can you confirm his presence at the East Kanaal Street station?"

"Yes, that would be easier," the agent replied. "Anything else?"

Erikson thought for a moment. "If we rescue Rambarran and have to stay in the river overnight, we may need to change a few things on the boat. Can you get us some blue paint, a brush, and a stencil?"

"I can do the paint and the brush," the agent said, "but even on a good day, it would take some doing to find you a stencil. This is Suriname, you know."

"Okay," Erikson said smiling, "I'll settle for the paint and brush, a narrow brush, mind you." Erikson walked across the small kitchen to the back door, where he stopped and turned around. "If they're taking

Rambarran from the Police Station at East Kanaal Street, which way are they likely to go to effect the transfer?"

"They can use the seawall road, but it would be difficult, especially at night because of the huge potholes. Graderweg would be my bet. No reason why not, since a curfew would be in effect, and that's a perfect asphalt road."

"Thanks, I'll call before the curfew," Erikson said, noting by a glance at his watch that it was already 17:00 hours.

*   *   *

Asad Shah was waiting for Erikson outside the *Pink Lily Restaurant.* Together they ascended the outside stairs and took seats at a table on the second-story veranda overlooking G. G. Maynard Street. From where they sat, they both had a diagonal view of the Nickerie Regional Police Headquarters, and what surprised them and became a source of doubt that Rambarran could be lodged there, was the sheer calm in the police compound. There seemed to be no unusual movement of vehicles or personnel. Shah ordered for both of them—fried rice and chow mein, both with chicken, and Cokes.

"What's the seawall road like?" Erikson asked.

"Difficult," Shah replied, confirming what the agent had told Erikson. "The potholes are huge and waterlogged."

The waiter served the Cokes and, as they sipped, Shah asked, "What if they bypass Nickerie?"

Erikson had not spent much thought on that possibility. He pondered it for a few moments. "Not likely," he replied.

"Why not?"

"Well, the Police are like the military. They have standard operating procedures. Even here; especially here."

"How so?"

"The police and the military hate each other," Erikson replied. "During the February coup, the *Bevelhebber* shelled the Police Headquarters in Paramaribo, and after the takeover, the police had to turn in their weapons. Anyway, I just think the police are likely to rigidly follow SOP, just to be able to cover themselves in case anything goes wrong."

Erikson then related what he had learned about the fate of the

Surinamese journalist, who had fled to Guyana and had been the candidate for a possible swap. He also expressed his sense of what might be in the offing for Andrew Rambarran.

"Another Camp Groomes scenario," Shah declared.

"Exactly," Erikson added. "And here's the thing, I don't think the Surinamese police are aware of the plan. The *Bevelhebber* wouldn't care if a couple of them got waxed in the process."

Their food arrived. In front of Erikson was a heaping plate of rice, colored brown by soy sauce, with pieces of lettuce, green onions, and tomatoes scattered in between. Leaning against the mound of rice were a couple of pieces of baked chicken in matching brown color. Shah's plate resembled Erikson's, except for brownish noodles instead of rice. Erikson ate a mix of chicken and rice until all the chicken was gone, leaving a crescent-shaped mound on the plate. Shah applied himself more diligently to the task, leaving only the few pieces of chicken bones resting on the bare plate.

Erikson left Shah at the restaurant to order take-outs for their companions at the boat and went over to use the public phone outside the municipal market. When he called the agent, he learned that Andrew Rambarran was due in at the station at any time. He was going to be fed, and his transfer by the back-track would be done later that evening using one of the boats operated by Soeresh, the gold-laden man Erikson had left at the seawall. The agent could offer no additional information.

It was 18:05 when the call ended. Erikson retained a taxi in front of the market and returned to the restaurant. Shah had settled the bill but was waiting at the table with five large brown-paper bags containing the take-outs. They brought the bags down to the taxi and, the driver, who hoped he would be able to get passengers from the last back-track boat from Springlands sped to the seawall. Soeresh, owner of the fast-track fleet was still standing at the top of the seawall, surrounded by some of his workers. When he saw Shah and Erikson unloading the trunk, he sent over a couple of young men to help, but Shah declined in order to avoid having any of those young men get too close to the *Lakshmi*. Once on the boat, Erikson learned that the crew had spotted a Surinamese patrol boat at the mouth of the Nickerie River.

The take-out food was quickly distributed, the boat skipper and

Ian Morgan sitting on the covered bow, DeFreitas and Peters in the food preparation area. They were finishing up when the last back-track boat from Springlands arrived, the passengers anxious to get off and get home before the curfew. Most of them walked from the seawall to their homes nearby in the Courantijn Polder; the rest taking taxis by the snack bar. The crew on the *Lakshmi* looked on as the back-track boat operator lifted the engine out of the water and, with the help of Soeresh's other workers, took the engine off the boat, up the jetty, and over the seawall into Soeresh's truck.

"Watch yourselves," Soeresh cautioned before he left. "Stay in the river after 7 p.m."

"We're heading upriver in a little while," *Lakshmi*'s skipper shouted back, and waved at the departing boat magnate, whom Erikson felt sure was as yet unaware that the Police planned to hire one of his boats.

The area around the seawall had become desolate. The sounds of the waves splashing against the stone chunks and of nearby boats butting each other and against the pylons reinforced the feeling of those on the boat that they were completely alone. Their voices in simple conversations, as they finished up their meal, sounded louder than when the seawall had more inhabitants. Nevertheless, the *Peccari* sitting off of Springlands, and the feeling that the Surinamese patrol boat was still nearby, inspired a sense of dread. A shout came from the top of the seawall, where a young Hindustani man was pointing to two brown paper bags he had set down.

"Peters," Erikson said, "get those, would you please? It's paint, I believe." Erikson watched Peters walk up the stone jetty to the top of the seawall and pick up the bags. When he returned to the boat, Erikson inspected the bags. One contained a gallon of blue paint and a wide brush, the other a gallon of white paint and a narrow brush. With Asad Shah heating some water on the stove for coffee, Erikson instructed the skipper to start the engine and take them slowly upriver. Once they entered the passage between the Papegaaien Island and the eastern bank, the skipper turned the boat around and eased the boat closer to the bank where the mangroves were thick, and the boat could be concealed. Shah fixed himself and Erikson a cup of instant coffee and invited the others to help themselves. Then Erikson gathered his companions at the bow end of the fishing boat to outline his plan.

"The information I have," Erikson began, "is that the Surinamese police will move Andrew Rambarran from the Nickerie police post some time after 19:00, when the curfew takes effect. Rambarran will be transported back to Springlands by one of the back-track boats. My fear is that the boat transporting Rambarran will be destroyed during the crossing by that *Peccari*, sitting outside of Springlands. What we are going to do is to seize Rambarran from the Police, once they come over the seawall." Erikson paused and took a sip of coffee. "It is starting to get dark. The skipper will move the boat slowly along the bank to the end of the mangroves; that's where the seawall begins. Ian Morgan and Michael DeFreitas will scale the seawall and take concealed positions about fifty feet on either side of the snack bar. Ron Peters will conceal himself in one of the boats, moored to the stone jetty. Asad Shah and I will sit in wait at the top of the jetty, against the seawall. We will take the police from behind when they come over the wall; Peters will be our back up. We will all carry Uzis with silencers. Any questions?"

"Do you have any sense of how many guards might be escorting Rambarran?" Peters asked.

"No," Erikson replied. "We're gambling that there won't be many. After curfew, the security forces own the roads. That might give them a false sense of security. Secondly, the police generally behave very differently from the army in the sense that they tend to use fewer personnel. Also, the jetty is narrow and would not accommodate anything other than people walking in a single file, which makes them vulnerable to an ambush. I am hoping we won't have to fire on his escorts, once they are on this side of the seawall. However, should that happen, it will be up to Morgan and DeFreitas to make sure no one else comes over that seawall. Finish your coffee and get your weapons."

The skipper re-started the engine and began moving the boat alongside the bank. It was getting darker, and with no lights on the *Lakshmi*, it was unlikely they would be seen from the brightly lit *Peccari*, which sat elegantly in the water, off the Springlands coast. As they approached the end of the mangroves, the boat slowed to a stop to allow Ian Morgan and Michael DeFreitas to wade to the base of the seawall. The skipper then moved the *Lakshmi* closer to the upper end of the jetty, where it butted against the seawall. Erikson and Shah climbed onto the jetty and took positions, one on each side of it; Peters followed and selected a boat in which to hide. Slowly, the skipper turned the boat around and headed back to the edge of the mangroves, as instructed.

For Erikson, the wait seemed interminable. Not only had the *Peccari* begun to move northwesterly toward their position but, directly north, a trawler was advertizing its presence with its floodlights scanning southward. At 20:15 hours, a vehicle pulled up on the other side of the seawall. Erikson recognized Soeresh's voice directing his people to unload the boat engine from the vehicle. Several people came up to the seawall. With a Coleman gas lamp providing illumination, two young men were picking their way along the stone jetty carrying the boat engine. Soeresh used the flashlight beam to identify the boat he wanted them to use and held the beam on the rear of the boat while they seated the engine. One young man remained with the boat, the other returned to join Soeresh at the top of the seawall. Soeresh said something to the young man in Hindustani and sent him back to the boat before leaving the seawall. Soeresh started up his vehicle and drove off.

Ten minutes later, a jeep drove up to the seawall, its narrowly-spaced front beams illuminating the path up the seawall. The beams remained while three people walked up, one after the other, to the top of the seawall. The first shadow cast on Erikson's side was an elongated, slender profile; the two others appeared chubbier, one shorter than the other. Erikson surmised that the first figure was that of Rambarran; the others were of the police. Two flashlights were turned on and pointed down to the stone jetty. One of the policemen shouted back "okay" to the jeep, and the vehicle could be heard reversing and driving off. The same policeman instructed Rambarran to walk out to the boat and, with their flashlights illuminating the way, both policemen followed behind. At first, the policemen walked side by side, but as the jetty narrowed, one had to follow the other. Erikson got up from one side of the jetty, Shah from the other, and both rushed toward the policemen.

"Halt!" Erikson ordered. One policeman turned his flashlight around.

"Cut the light," Erikson ordered, "unless you want your head blown off."

Forward movement ceased. Shah walked up and retrieved the service revolvers from the policemen, a sergeant and a constable in the uniform of the Guyana Police Force, tossing them into the river. Peters emerged and pointed his Uzi at the young men in the boat.

"Okay, who has the keys to the handcuffs?" Erikson asked. One policeman said he did. "Shah, get them," Erikson said. Shah retrieved the keys and undid the handcuffs from Rambarran. "Now, handcuff the policemen together," Erikson ordered, quickly shaking hands with Rambarran and walking past to the boat. "Start the engine," he ordered the boatmen, and signaled Shah to bring the policemen forward. "You two, get out and hold the boat," Erikson said to the boatmen. The boatmen climbed onto the jetty and held the bow of the boat. "Get in," Erikson said to the policemen. "Now, here's the deal: you two are free to go back to Springlands. One of you take the throttle. If you turn back, you'll be shot. Do you understand?" The policemen nodded. "Now, shove that boat off!" Erikson ordered. Soeresh's two boatmen pushed the bow away from the jetty, and the policeman holding the tiller pointed the boat toward Springlands.

Leaving Rambarran and Shah to watch the progress of the departing boat, Erikson and Peters brought the two boatmen to the other side of the seawall, where Ian Morgan and Michael DeFreitas moved in from their concealed positions. "Tie them up against the seawall, and gag them," Erikson ordered. "Don't worry," Erikson said to the two frightened boatmen, "we won't harm you. You're going to get a bit cold sitting out here, but sooner or later you'll be picked up."

Returning to the jetty, Ian Morgan, Ron Peters, and Michael DeFreitas greeted Andrew Rambarran in hushed voices while Erikson used the flashlight to signal the *Lakshmi* skipper to bring the boat forward. In a few minutes, the fishing boat pulled up to the jetty, and they climbed in. Erikson directed the *Lakshmi* skipper to follow the departing policemen for a quarter of a mile before executing a left turn and heading slowly up the Corentyne River. From the *Lakshmi's* stern, Erikson watched the bobbing Coleman gas lamp on the fast-track boat. By this time, the *Peccari* had moved away from Springlands in the direction of Nickerie, and the trawler out in the Atlantic had also moved into the mouth of the Corentyne River.

As the *Lakshmi* neared the Papegaaien Island, Erikson asked the skipper to slow down, and they all looked in the direction of the bobbing Coleman lamp. Suddenly, the stillness of the evening was shattered by a short, crisp, cracking sound like a thunderclap one hears on a dry tropical evening. Flashes of light from the *Peccari* preceded a second, a third, and a fourth weapon discharge, very methodical and evenly spaced, and a small fire appeared at the mouth of the Corentyne River where the bobbing Coleman gas lamp had last been seen.

THIRTY-TWO

May 8, 1980
On the Corentyne River

Steve Erikson moved to the bow just in time to hear Andrew Rambarran say, "That could have been me getting blown up in that boat. Thank you, all; thank you very much."

Scanning Rambarran quickly with the flashlight before shaking his hand again, Erikson observed, "You look rather well. Looks like they were fattening you for the kill."

"Strange thing," Rambarran replied, "They took really good care of me. I spent a week shuttling from prison at Keizer Street to the hospital for abrasions on my neck and back. But while I was at Santo Boma, once, sometimes twice a week, I got restaurant food in the evening, compliments of the *Bevelhebber*." Erikson smiled. "What now?" Rambarran asked.

"Well, first things first," Erikson replied. "Let's celebrate your return."

"Don't tell me you have champagne on this luxury liner?" Rambarran asked.

"Sorry, pal, we're operational," Erikson replied. "DeFreitas, break out those candy bars. Do we have any Cokes left?" DeFreitas passed out the candy bars, Peters retrieved three bottles of Cokes from the icebox, which they shared. "We could make another run for it tonight," Erikson began, "we have a trawler waiting to pick us up just outside the twelve-mile territorial limit. The trawler might fudge it some, but not too much, I expect."

"They'll search the wreckage around the speedboat," Rambarran cautioned, "then they'll continue to patrol the river mouth."

"I've thought of that, but the mouth of the river is wide, and darkness affords us some protection," Erikson said.

"How many vessels do you think they have out there?" Rambarran asked.

"I'm not sure," Erikson replied. "We saw one *Peccari* on the Guyana side. That's the one that just finished off the speed boat. Then there's the Surinamese patrol boat at the mouth of the Nickerie River, and a trawler. Not sure who owns that one."

"The Guyana Maritime Command employs armed trawlers to patrol the coastal waters," Rambarran said, "mostly to prevent illegal fishing. You'd have to assume the one you sighted at the mouth of the river was one of theirs."

"Wouldn't the Surinamese object?" Erikson asked. "I thought the Surinamese were sensitive about Guyanese boats on the Corentyne River."

"Normally they would," Rambarran replied, "but it seems from what you all have been telling me that the *Bevelhebber* is cooperating with the Guyanese government on this one."

"Assuming all of this to be true," Erikson said, "how would it complicate a night run?"

"They'll be searching all boats coming out of, or traversing the river mouth. At this time of the night, there aren't many, and they've already taken one out. They've tasted blood."

The *Lakshmi* was rounding the western edge of Papegaaien Island when they heard a loud, cracking sound, much coarser than the ones they had heard earlier when the speed boat was destroyed. Another followed.

"That's the 40-millimeter cannon," Erikson said. "The Surinamese patrol boat was firing at something."

"Must have been one of the smugglers, operating between Nickerie and Springlands," Rambarran said. "He was probably unaware of what's been happening."

"Seems to make your point," Erikson said. "They'll probably shoot at any motorized sound at the mouth of the river. But if you're right that they'll search the river, we'd better hide this boat before those patrol boats come upriver."

Erikson picked his way to the stern to speak with the skipper. His eyes had adjusted to the darkness and, fortunately, the wide expanse of river water reflected enough moonlight to help him on the ledge around the icebox. The skipper had pointed the bow toward the western bank and, when Erikson reached him, he had straightened the boat and was hugging the western bank, looking for a mooring point.

"I don't want to go too far upriver," Erikson said. "We'll have to get out in a hurry."

"We have to go further up," the skipper said. "The only cover near the mouth is from mangroves. The problem with that is that when the water drops at ebb tide, you'll lose that cover because the mangroves become exposed all the way down to the roots. And the tide is going out right now."

"What do you have in mind?" Erikson asked.

"Further upriver, where the *moko-moko* is thicker, would be better. We'll be grounded when the water gets real low, but the *moko-moko* will hide the boat pretty good."

"Okay," Erikson said, "but not too far upriver. We'll have to double back when that time comes." Erikson turned to leave. "One other thing," he added. "Be sure to gas up; we'll have to ditch all of the gas containers for the trip out."

Soon after, the mangroves began to thin out, and *moko-moko* appeared, as did bamboo clumps. The skipper slowed the boat down past a cove formed by two bamboo clumps and aimed the bow into the tall *moko-moko* beyond the second bamboo clump. The skipper shut down the engine and tilted it forward to get the propeller end out of water, allowing the forward momentum of the boat to clear a path through the *moko-moko* until the boat stopped very close to the bank. The tall, thick, rounded trunks of the *moko-moko* and the overhang from the lower level mangroves concealed the boat from river view, while the elephant ears from the *moko-moko* cast a black shadow over the boat rendering visibility on and around the boat well nigh impossible.

"Light one side of the kerosene stove," Erikson said to DeFreitas, who groped around the cooking compartment for the plastic bag hanging on a nail. Securing the matches, he lit one and stooped down to light the stove. On low wick, the stove provided illumination for all six officers to see one another in the huddle at the bow end. Erikson stood up to check how far beyond the boat the light went and was pleased by the screening effect of the *moko-moko* and the mangroves. DeFreitas placed a pot of water on the stove, and this further suppressed the light from the wick.

"Okay, Andrew," Erikson began, leaning back against the bow overhang, "you don't think we should make an attempt out tonight. What's the alternative? We can't very well do it in broad daylight."

"Why not?" Rambarran replied. "That's what they'd least expect. Besides, they don't have a clue as to where this boat is headed."

"What happens when they see this fishing boat heading out into open sea?"

"If we have enough of a lead, we could make it to the trawler," Rambarran replied.

"Twelve miles is a far way to go when you're being pursued by patrol boats with superior fire power," Erikson observed. "They could blow us out of the water long before we get to the territorial limit."

"True," Rambarran replied, "but we do have a couple of advantages. First, we know what armaments the opposition has and, second, they don't know what we have. That 50-caliber you have can be immensely destructive if we use the element of surprise. The same for the M-72 rockets."

Erikson looked at Rambarran, and then at the others. "There's still the question of when we leave here. We can't very well sit here come daylight."

"I'd say first light for a few reasons," Rambarran responded. "First, they don't expect it, and they would have been on alert all night, which means they're likely to be more sloppy in the morning. Second, there'll be a lot more boat traffic then, including fishing boats along the coast, up to three or more miles out. And, with so many boats out, they're less likely to just shoot at boats. They'll stop them and inspect."

"That's true what he said about boat traffic in the morning," the skipper said. "Some boats are trying to get their fish to market; others are putting out to fish along the coast."

Erikson thought for a moment. "Maybe, we need a common understanding about what 'morning' is. I've been in this part of the world long enough to know that it starts getting light at 05:30. So what I want to know is when would it not be unusual for boat engines to be heard on the river and along the coast?"

"Starting from about 04:30 hours," the boat skipper replied.

"Okay, then," Erikson said. "Everyone up at 03:30 tomorrow. It's now 21:20 hours; we'll keep watch in two-hour shifts."

"Why don't you guys turn in," Rambarran interjected. "I'll take the first watch. I had a lot of rest in prison."

"When do you want to be relieved?" Erikson asked.

"How about 24:00 hours?"

"Okay, Morgan will relieve you at 24:00; that'll be the last watch."

"Were you going to rename the boat?" the *Lakshmi* skipper asked.

"Holy shit!" Erikson exclaimed. "We have to re-name the boat; they've seen *Lakshmi* at the stone jetty. What should we call it?"

"*Tulsi Das*," the skipper said. "I have another registration paper in that name."

Rambarran smiled. Erikson reached under the bow for the paint. With Rambarran holding the flashlight, Erikson leaned over the side of the bow and used the wide paint brush to white out the name, *Lakshmi*, on both sides of the boat. A half hour later, he followed up with blue paint and the narrower brush to form the letters for the new name, *Tulsi Das*, on the damp white background. It was a laborious task, requiring him to dip the brush into the paint, lean over the side and apply the strokes. In about ten minutes, Erikson was through with the right side. He took a breather before starting on the other side. When he was through, he set aside the brush and paint and took the radio out to the cooking compartment.

"Mother Goose, Mother Goose, this is Trojan Horse," Erikson said. "How do you read me, over?"

"Loud and clear, Trojan Horse," came the response. "Worried about you."

"In hibernation, Mother Goose. Will emerge with quarry at first light. Two patrol boats in operation. Suspect an armed trawler also at river's mouth. Over."

"Surinamese patrol boat at the month of the Nickerie River, around the promontory. Information based on shore report. Over."

"Thank you, Mother Goose. Out." Erikson turned off the radio and looked up at Rambarran. "You heard that, didn't you?" Rambarran nodded. "If the Surinamese patrol boat is berthing for the night, we could mount a raid and take that boat."

"I wouldn't recommend it," Rambarran said.

"Why not?" Erikson asked, looking intently at Rambarran. "They believe they have control over the river mouth. They'll probably shut down their engine and stay on listening watch. They too need to sleep; so, they'll post sentries on deck. We move to the promontory; swim to that patrol boat and take out the sentries with the Uzis."

"What would we do with the Surinamese patrol boat after that?" Rambarran asked.

"What do you mean? It would improve our chances of getting out. That patrol boat would cope better than this fishing boat with the swells from the Atlantic and it has 40-millimeter cannons. We could blow that *Peccari* away."

"Steve, the Surinamese patrol boats are old World War II vintages. They are too big and too slow, and no one on this boat is familiar with those deck guns. The *Peccari* is a newer Vosper craft. It is nimbler, and the crew is far better trained with its 20-millimeter cannons. They'll blow that tub out of the water. Now, this fishing boat has its risks, but it is small and it sits low in the water, which means that the deck guns on the *Peccari* and on the Surinamese Patrol boat will be ineffective against it at close ranges. The platforms from which those guns will be firing are much higher than the fishing boat; the guns are fixed on the decks and can't be depressed to fire at objects low in the water. That was one of the problems with the Spanish galleons in the Armada."

"Shouldn't you be in the Navy or something?" Erikson asked, laughing.

"Captain," the skipper whispered loudly from the engine end of the boat, where he had been gassing up.

"I heard," Erikson said, slowly stepping over to turn off the stove.

The hum of a powerful boat engine from the direction of the river mouth was getting louder. Five minutes later, it was in the area of the *Tulsi Das*, its searchlight scanning the width of the river, lingering on the bamboo cove nearby. Along with the others, Erikson crouched below the side of the boat. For a moment, he thought of using the element of surprise and taking out the patrol boat with an M-72 rocket, but he rejected the idea. The explosion, he thought, would draw in the other boats and force them to move further up river, where the river was narrower and the chances of detection greater. Even if the *Tulsi Das* found another hiding place upriver, getting out later would be immensely more difficult. He decided to take no action, and the patrol boat continued upriver.

"Why don't you fix me some?" Erikson asked Rambarran, who was making himself a cup of coffee with the hot water on the stove. "I just don't feel like sleeping right now."

Cups in hand, Erikson and Rambarran sat in the pitch dark galley. The elephant ears of the *moko-moko* provided great cover for the boat and its occupants but it also blocked any breeze. The humidity under its cover was monstrous, and Erikson was worried whether any of the others could really sleep in such close proximity under the covered bow.

"I noticed you smiled when the skipper gave me the name, *Tulsi Das*, for the boat," Erikson said to Rambarran. "I thought maybe it was because the skipper had multiple registrations for the boat."

"That too," Rambarran replied.

"And?"

"Well, Tulsi Das was the poet who wrote the Hindu epic, the *Ramayana*."

"Ah, hadn't thought of that," Erikson said. "Wasn't there a battle for virtue in the *Ramayana*?"

"Yes," Rambarran replied, "also in the *Mahabarata*."

"How appropriate," Erikson said. "That's what we stand for, isn't it? Virtue?"

"Of course."

"I remember reading the *Bhagwad Gita* in our senior philosophy class," Erikson noted. "As I recall, Krishna was counseling Arjuna to do his duty in the battle against the Kourus." Erikson sipped from his enamel cup. "Ever notice how the concept of duty always seem to come up in times of battle? Arjuna in the *Mahabarata*; Nelson at Trafalgar?"

"I suppose it's a way of focusing the mind away from the unpleasantness of war," Rambarran replied.

"I suppose so," Erikson said, and took another sip of coffee. "I must confess, I dread what tomorrow will bring. Despite what you said earlier, the odds seem insurmountable."

"I have deep anxiety as well," Rambarran admitted. "Keep in mind that the boat I was in a couple of months ago was blown out from under me. But the circumstances are different, and we have to play the hand we are dealt. Which reminds me: there are no life vests on this boat."

"I hadn't noticed," Erikson confessed.

"If things go badly for us, those things could save lives. They did when the *Kurtuka* was destroyed."

"I'm sorry, but it's kind of late for that, isn't it?" Erikson asked.

"Not really," Rambarran replied. "We have ponchos on board; we can make poncho rafts with them."

"What happens if it rains tomorrow?" Erikson asked.

"Fishermen in these parts don't shelter from rain under American ponchos; they use pieces of canvas."

"You're right," Erikson said. "Let's do it. What do we need?"

"We need something to roll up inside, something with some length and stiffness, and weight."

"Well, we don't have rifles," Erikson said, "and we'll need the Uzis we have. So, let's see what we have in the arms cache." Leading the way back to the icebox with the suppressed amber light from his patrol flashlight, Erikson opened the access panel to the lowest compartment of the icebox. Apart from the canisters of 50-caliber ammo, the largest pile was of M-72 rockets.

"Those M-72s are about two-feet long," Rambarran noted. "Why don't we take four and cigarette-roll them in four ponchos. We'll still need three more rafts to take care of everyone on the boat, but we could wrap three ponchos around boots, sacks of potatoes, whatever."

"Let's do it now," Erikson said.

"Steve, why don't you get some rest?" Rambarran suggested. "I'm on first watch. It'll give me something to do."

"I can't sleep right now," Erikson replied, "and I won't sleep until that patrol boat returns this way."

Erikson reached in and carefully pulled out the rockets, one at a time, passing them to Rambarran. With Erikson lighting his way, Rambarran carried the rockets bundled in his arms to the seine compartment, where he laid them on top of the seine. Then, from the bow area, they brought back all of the ponchos, plus sacks of potatoes and flour. They each rolled a rocket into a poncho, making the wrap as tight as possible, then tying the ends with double slip knots. The sacks of potato and flour were used in the last three rolls. The loud hum of the patrol boat made Erikson and Rambarran cease work and crouch low. When it passed their position heading down river, the patrol boat was moving at maximum speed, its searchlight illuminating the water directly ahead. Surmising that the patrol boat was heading for a berthing spot, Erikson retired to the sleeping area, leaving Rambarran to continue his watch.

THIRTY-THREE

May 9, 1980
On the Corentyne River

At 03:30 hours, the crew was awakened by Ian Morgan, the last watch. With long bamboo poles, Shah and the skipper pushed against the clump of *moko-moko* to move the boat away from the bank, the task made easier by the fact that the water had risen overnight, lifting the boat to the slender upper trunks of the *moko-moko*, over which it slid comfortably. Once clear of the vegetation in the shallows, the skipper lowered the propeller end of the engine into the water, started the engine and moved the boat slowly along the bank in search of a breakfast spot, settling on a cove between two large bamboo clumps. While Rambarran helped Erikson apply brown camouflage to his face, the rest of the team entered the galley area by two's and helped themselves to a breakfast of instant coffee, toast made on a heated *tawa*, cheese and marmalade.

At 04:15 hours, Ian Morgan and Ron Peters removed the hinges from the uppermost compartment of the icebox and, with the help of Erikson and Rambarran, pushed it over into the river. The two remaining compartments now rose only about three feet above the gunwale, sufficiently high to convince a serious onlooker that the boat had an icebox like other fishing boats, but conveniently placing the crew one step closer to being rid of the icebox altogether. The entire seine, except for a small section to be used as a facade, was dumped overboard. The poncho rafts were replaced in the seine compartment, as were the 50-caliber machine gun and canisters of 50-caliber ammo, all of which were covered by the seine remnant and a section of old canvas. At 04:20 hours, Erikson instructed the skipper to take the *Tulsi Das* out.

The skipper restarted the engine and guided the boat toward the middle of the Corentyne River then straightened up and opened the throttle. About twenty minutes on the river, the boat was coming up against larger waves which made the ride bumpier, especially at the bow end. All of the crew had gravitated to the area between the icebox and the seine compartment, where the boat was lower in the water and the ride smoother. Erikson directed the skipper to take the boat across to the eastern side of the river and to hug the Surinamese land mass.

At 04:50 hours, they entered the passage east of Papegaaien Island, emerging a few minutes later into the upper throat of the river. The hum of other boat engines in the distance was more audible and the sweep of searchlight beams visible. The skipper eased up on the throttle, slowing the boat to a drift to allow Erikson and Rambarran time to assess the situation ahead. Branches from the mangroves rubbed against the right side of the boat as the skipper picked his way along the bank, stopping the boat where the line of mangroves ended abruptly at the commencement of the stone-laden sea defenses around Nickerie.

"Do we submit to inspection?" the skipper asked.

"Yes," Erikson answered. "Ian Morgan will act as the assistant skipper. Ian, talk to them the way you did to the Guyanese police yesterday." A sharp thunderclap interrupted Erikson. "What the hell was that?" A flash of lightning illuminating the breadth of the river followed. "What now?" Erikson asked.

"We can use strips of canvas," Rambarran replied, tilting his head toward the skipper, who had taken the rectangular piece of canvas on which he was sitting and, through a hole in the center, lowered it over his head.

"Okay, let's get to it everybody," Erikson said. "Get small strips of canvas from the bow and cut a hole. Remember, you need to have your hands free to use a weapon."

After the next lightning flash, the sky opened up, and the rain came in torrents. Except for Ian Morgan and the skipper, most of the crew remained under the bow. From the galley where Erikson and Rambarran stood, draped in old canvas and wearing baseball hats, Erikson called out to the skipper to proceed as though heading toward Paramaribo; and so, the *Tulsi Das* passed by the stone jetty, then rounded the promontory. At the mouth of the Nickerie River, a Surinamese patrol boat sat at anchor, its crew engaged in loud banter during breakfast. To the west, off the coast of Springlands, the lights on the water outlined the profile of the patrol boat they had seen the evening before but it appeared to have moved to about a third of the back-track route between Springlands and Nickerie. Directly ahead of the *Tulsi Das*, a fishing trawler was shining its floodlights southwards, but in their immediate vicinity, two police speed boats were crossing paths with each other as they inspected fishing boats in the area.

When the *Tulsi Das* entered the mouth of the Nickerie River, one of the two police boats pulled up to it. "Cut the engine," the officer in the raincoat shouted through the megaphone.

"We not gon be able to keep the boat steady," Morgan shouted back.

"Cut the damn engine!" the police officer said. "We're coming aboard." When the small speed boat butted the stern of the *Tulsi Das*, the officer stepped over. "Where are you heading?" he asked.

"Paramaribo," Morgan replied. "We need ice and supplies."

"Why can't you get them here in Nickerie?"

"It gon slow we down," Morgan replied. "We going to fish off Marowijne."

"Let me see your Suriname license."

The skipper handed the officer his Suriname certificate of registration and his fishing license. "Where in Paramaribo are you heading?" the officer asked.

"Platte Brug," the skipper replied. "We get ice and supplies at good prices. And the merchant does give we credit."

The police officer moved the flashlight beam toward the front of the boat. "Where are the rest of your crew?"

"Sheltering from the rain," the skipper answered.

"Get them out," the officer ordered.

The skipper placed his thumb and forefinger in his mouth and whistled. Out came Asad Shah, Mike DeFreitas, and Ron Peters, draped in sections of old canvas and wearing old baseball hats. The officer flashed the light into each of the faces, as the rain sliced into them. The *Tulsi Das*, which had separated from the police boat, had been turned by the incoming tide, and its broadside was being slapped by the waves. The boat rocked and, when the police officer tried to take a step in the direction of the seine compartment, he lost his balance and would have fallen over into the river if Ian Morgan had not reached forward and steadied him. "Okay, you can go," the officer said, and signaled with his flashlight for the police boat to pick him up.

The skipper restarted the boat and oriented its bow in a northwesterly direction, traversing the mouth of the Nickerie River, passing on the outside of the Surinamese Patrol boat before hugging the Surinamese coast. As the Surinamese patrol boat faded from rearview, the skipper, on Erikson's instruction, began to shift course northward. It was 05:15 hours. The sun had not yet appeared above the horizon, but it was getting lighter. Andrew Rambarran was monitoring the radio, changing frequencies in the hope of intercepting transmissions from the patrol boats in the mouths of the rivers. On the emergency frequency he picked up a transmission from the Surinamese patrol boat to its Guyanese counterpart. "*Peccari One*, this is Captain Mijnals. Police at Coronie are reporting a fishing boat heading northwest."

"Captain Mijnals, this is Lieutenant Commander Pilgrim on the *Peccari One*. We need to inspect that boat."

"Steve," Rambarran yelled, "they are talking about us. I think they are getting ready for a chase."

"I think we have other problems right now," Erikson responded.

The *Tulsi Das* was in difficulty. The crests were lifting the boat and slapping it onto the troughs. The skipper maneuvered the boat from the wave crests by angling the descent down the waves to prevent a direct plunge into the troughs. Some of the crests came faster and the ridges were too steep to allow gentle descent. The waves picked the boat aloft and slapped it into the troughs, causing everyone to hold on for balance and safety. In the troughs, the boat rolled violently.

"Sweet Jesus!" Erikson exclaimed. "If they come after us in this weather, we're finished."

Surviving the rough sea became the preoccupation of everyone on the *Tulsi Das*. The skipper's efforts to negotiate the crests and troughs slowed progress away from the Surinamese shoreline.

"How far do you think we are from the shore?" Erikson asked.

"About a mile," the skipper replied, adding, "the sea should be calmer further out from the shore."

"I hope you are right," Erikson said. "In the meantime, all of you assume that this is what we will have to deal with and try to man your weapons."

Over the next half-mile, the rain continued unabated, but the skipper's prediction seemed to be validated by the heaving of the sea. Wiping rainwater continually from his face, the skipper opened the throttle and finessed the swells. However, even with limited visibility, they noticed the Surinamese patrol boat ploughing headlong toward them and, from the southwest, came *Peccari One*. The radio squelched, and the voices became audible.

"I believe they have radio capability," Captain Mijnals was telling Commander Pilgrim of the *Peccari One*.

"Captain Rambarran, this is Lieutenant Commander Pilgrim of the Guyana Maritime Command. You have no chance in this rough sea. I don't want to blast you out of the water. Surrender, and I'll see that you are treated well."

"Commander Pilgrim, this is Captain Mijnals. That fishing boat is in Surinamese territorial waters. We'll make the arrest."

"That's fine," Commander Pilgrim responded. "We'll provide back up."

The waves were still cresting high, but the troughs were longer and gentler. The skipper seemed to be ignoring the radio chatter and concentrating on forward progress. Despite his best efforts, however, the fishing boat was losing ground to its pursuers. Directly behind, and to the southwest, the pursuing vessels were closing in.

"That Surinamese patrol boat is too close to use its deck guns," Rambarran said. "The *Peccari* might still be able to hit us though."

"Okay, Andrew," Erikson said, "we have the element of surprise and can take out the Surinamese patrol boat. What then?"

"If we maneuver to get the Surinamese patrol boat between us and the *Peccari*, we could take them out in sequence. The *Peccari* won't fire on us as long as any significant part of the Surinamese boat is in its line of fire."

"Okay, let's do it," Erikson said. "When Mijnals gets back on the radio, offer to surrender but stall as much as you can." Turning to the rest of his team, Erikson issued their assignments. "Morgan, stay with the skipper; make sure he does what I say. Peters and DeFreitas, use the hammer and chisel and loosen the hinges on the upper compartment of the icebox. When I say so, push that sucker over the side. Shah, get an M-72; you and I are going to take out that patrol boat."

The radio crackled. "Captain Rambarran, this is Captain Mijnals. Stop forward motion or we'll fire on you."

"He's bluffing," Rambarran said to his companions.

"Play along," Erikson said.

"What are your terms?" Rambarran asked on the radio.

"Surrender or we'll blast you out of the water," Mijnals responded.

"I need some time to consult with the people on this boat," Rambarran said.

"You have three minutes," Mijnals responded.

In the three minutes, Peters and DeFreitas had partially removed the bolts from the hinges on the icebox. Both Erikson and Shah had secured an M-72 rocket each and taken positions behind the icebox. The radio came alive again. "Captain Rambarran, your time is up. Stop forward motion and surrender or we will fire on you."

Rambarran did not reply for another minute, and the *Tulsi Das* continued moving forward. "Captain Mijnals," Rambarran said on the emergency frequency, "This is Captain Rambarran. I am prepared to surrender to the Republic of Suriname, but I want your assurance that all personnel on this boat will be humanely treated."

"You have my assurance," Mijnals replied. "Now cut that engine!" Rambarran did not reply right away.

"Okay, skipper," Erikson said, "make a wide turn to starboard and bring us parallel to that patrol boat."

The *Tulsi Das* turned away from its northerly course and began tracing a half-moon, on the eastern side of the Surinamese patrol boat.

"Captain Rambarran, cut the engine or we will fire," Mijnals shouted.

"Captain Mijnals," Rambarran responded, "these waters are rough and, if we cut the engine, the boat might capsize. We will surrender to you, but we want to get out of the line of fire of the *Peccari*."

Under the watch of personnel on the Surinamese patrol boat, who were manning machine guns and rifles, the *Tulsi Das* looped around and then the skipper reoriented the bow due north. The *Tulsi Das* was now parallel to the Surinamese boat and less than fifty meters away. The skipper slowed to a stop but kept the engine idling. Erikson and Shah, from their concealed positions at the left and right corners of the icebox, extended the inner tube of the weapons backward.

"Now," Erikson whispered. Everyone, except Erikson and Shah, took cover. With their weapons shouldered, Erikson and Shah quickly slipped out of hiding and fired at the patrol boat. The warhead from the left exploded against the deck gun, penetrating the protective shield around the gunners, unhinging the gun mount and rolling it over. The missile from Erikson's M-72 struck just below the bridge, cratering the patrol boat. Bodies were flung off the boat; debris rained on and around the patrol boat; and there was a fire at mid-ship. The *Peccari*, which had been speeding to the area, was now a few hundred meters away.

On the *Tulsi Das*, Peters and DeFreitas unhinged the upper compartment of the icebox and, with the help of Rambarran, pushed it over the side. What remained was a two-foot high cavity in which the arms and ammunition had been placed. From the seine compartment, Erikson picked up the 50-caliber machine gun which he and Peters mounted on the steel pedestal. Peters fed in the magazine belt; Erikson drew back the bolt and slammed it forward, chambering the first round. Through the hollowed out patrol boat, Erikson observed the advancing *Peccari*. He ordered the skipper to move the *Tulsi Das* further east of the deserted Surinamese boat and away from the advancing *Peccari*. When he estimated the *Peccari* to be about two hundred meters away, Erikson opened fire. The first few shells struck the mast of the advancing boat, which swerved shoreward to facilitate the use of its deck guns. The abandoned Surinamese patrol boat now posed a hindrance to Erikson. He opened fire, sweeping the boat from bow to stern with high-explosive rounds. The explosion from the engine room unleashed a fireball and fractured the hull of the vessel. Black smoke billowed up as the patrol boat sank in sections. Taking advantage of the shelter provided by the smoke from the exploding patrol boat, Erikson continued firing in the direction of the *Peccari*. The *Peccari* responded with its 20-millimeter cannons, but because of the proximity of the *Tulsi Das* and its low profile in the water, the shells passed overhead, allowing Erikson to fire again. This time, with sustained fire, he cleared the *Peccari's* deck of all personnel. Those who did not fall off the deck were jumping into the Atlantic under a hail of high-explosive rounds.

"Move the boat forward!" Erikson yelled at the skipper as he continued to pummel the *Peccari* with the 50-caliber. The explosion below the *Peccari's* deck halted its firing. The deck was ripped open, and a ball of fire, much bigger than from the Surinamese patrol boat, shot upward. The stern tipped backward and sank quickly. The bow soon followed. Smoke arose; debris rained down; and the *Tulsi Das* turned north to hurry out to open sea. Behind them, were patches of fire on the ocean surface and on pieces of the floating wreckage.

The icebox now gone, Erikson had a wider field of fire but, with the covered bow ahead and the skipper behind, he realized that, in the future, he could only fire from the broadside and he worried that exposing the entire width of the boat to the undulating swells would render that option dangerous. He stood pondering the predicament when Rambarran came back to congratulate him. Reaching forward with his hand, Rambarran stepped into some water. "Holy shit!" he exclaimed. "I think we've sprung a leak."

That declaration brought the other officers to the stern. Erikson knelt and cleared away the spent 50-caliber casings from the water. The seal between the timbers below the steel plate supporting the 50-caliber had loosened along two parallel lines and water was oozing in.

"Get some strips of cloth, canvas, anything," Erikson said. "Let's caulk this thing up."

Peters bailed water with an enamel cup; Shah and DeFreitas tore strips of canvas; and Erikson and Rambarran stuffed the strips into the cracks. The strips became wet but slowed the water seepage.

In the euphoria following the destruction of the two patrol boats and in the new preoccupation with the integrity of the *Tulsi Das*, everyone had forgotten about the trawler they had seen earlier at the mouth of the river. Now the trawler appeared to the northwest, moving eastward to intercept. The estimate on the *Tulsi Das* was that it was one mile due west and about two miles north.

"Remind me, Andrew, how is that trawler armed?" Erikson asked.

"Two British general purpose machine guns, SLR rifles, and SMGs," Rambarran replied.

"What caliber machine gun?"

"7.62 millimeter," Rambarran replied, "same as the M-60 machine gun. I think we can take out that trawler with the remaining rockets."

"No," Erikson asserted. "That trawler is moving, and it is out of range. If we allow them to use those machine guns, they could perforate the hull of this boat and we'll leak like a sieve. After that, they'll pick us off like fish in a barrel."

"Steve, the vibrations from the 50-caliber will rip the flooring wide open," Rambarran warned.

"It's a chance we'll have to take," Erikson responded. "I'd rather be floating in the ocean alive." He looked over at Rambarran's perplexed countenance. "Look, Andrew, I'll keep the firing to a minimum. I'll sweep the deck, then we'll get closer and you and Shah can finish it off with the rockets."

The trawler, which appeared to have overestimated the time to intercept, came to a stop while the *Tulsi Das* maintained its course, heading directly towards it. The rain had abated; the sun shone over the horizon; and the fishing boat made steady progress. When Erikson had estimated the distance separating the two vessels at about half a mile, he ordered the skipper to change course and head northwest. He kept his field glasses trained on the trawler, which had turned around and was now moving back westward to intercept.

"Okay, fellas," Erikson said, "time to rock and roll." With Peters kneeling beside him with the ammo feed, Erikson took control of the 50-caliber. Rambarran and Shah armed themselves with the M-72s.

Rifle shots from the trawler tapped the water in the vicinity of the *Tulsi Das*. As they drew closer, some of the rifle shots struck the bow of the *Tulsi Das*. Erikson opened fire, the recoil from the weapon shaking the *Tulsi Das* from side to side. The first burst from the 50-caliber demolished the pilothouse of the trawler. Erikson adjusted his aim downward, sweeping from bow to stern and stern to bow until there was no visible life on the trawler deck. Masts collapsed; sparks shot up where the rounds glanced off metal anvils; pieces of wooden boxes, scraps of canvas and other debris took a short flight into the air; and the topless trawler continued its westward course like a ghost ship. Continuing his firing, Erikson yelled, "Use the rockets!"

Rambarran and Shah fired the M-72 rockets, and everyone watched the projectiles explode close together at the bow end, just above the water, detaching a huge section of the vessel. The stern rocked backward and within a few minutes the trawler sank. Floating debris smoldered under the light drizzle.

The staccato sounds of the 50-caliber, the rattling of the spent shells against the wooden hull of the boat, and the explosion of the projectiles into the trawler had subdued the hum of an approaching helicopter.

When he had ceased firing, Erikson turned in the direction of the chopper, which was coming from Suriname directly toward them. Next to him, Morgan and DeFreitas were trying to stuff the cracks, which had widened from the vibrations of the 50-caliber. "Soak the cloth in the oil paint we have," Erikson said. "Let's see if that helps." Reaching for his field glasses, Erikson focused in on the approaching helicopter. It was an observation helicopter similar to the one they had shot down the day before. It had no exterior armaments, suggesting that it was only armed with a side machine gun.

Erikson was still observing the helicopter when Andrew Rambarran rejoined him. "What do you think?" Erikson asked, turning over the glasses to Peters.

"The odds appear to favor the chopper," Rambarran replied. "We could take it out but we'd have to change course to open up a field of fire for you. If you don't score, that chopper will reposition itself behind us. We can't very well zig-zag over this ocean without capsizing. Then there is the possibility of the flooring really coming apart when you use the 50-cal again."

"Well, we have to play the hand we're dealt," Erikson said. "Everyone, get yourself a poncho raft for flotation; I don't think the boat will survive this encounter."

"Funny," Rambarran quipped, "I always thought going down with the ship was a metaphor."

Erikson looked over sternly, but smirked.

"Captain," Peters said, looking through the field glasses, "there's another chopper coming from the west. It's armed with rockets."

"That's got to be a Hind," Rambarran said.

"What kind of rockets are those?" Erikson asked.

"Russian S-5, 57-millimeter flechette warheads," Rambarran replied. "They don't have many in their inventory."

"That's good to know," Erikson said, "but what are the weaknesses of that plane? Can we take it down with the 50-cal?"

"No," Rambarran replied. "The fuselage and cockpit are heavily armored. The rotor blades are made of titanium."

"So, how do we take it on?" Erikson asked.

"Evasion," Rambarran replied. "The Hind is fast but it can't maneuver; it swoops down like a regular attack plane. Also, because the rockets are so damned expensive, and there are so few of them in inventory, the pilots would be hesitant to use them unless they are sure they'll hit the target."

"We can't dodge them all day, Andrew," Erikson said. "We have a Hind with rockets on our left and a chopper with a machine gun on our rear. Unless we pull a rabbit out of a hat, they're going to buttfuck us. Okay, everybody, keep a low profile. Skipper, head this boat northwest."

The Surinamese helicopter from the southwest was now only a few hundred meters behind the *Tulsi Das.* The pilot banked to allow his side gunner to fire. The first burst from the machine gun made pecking sounds in the water beyond the fishing boat. Keenly aware of the danger the vibrations of the 50-caliber posed to his vessel, Erikson fired at the chopper. The tracers showed that the rounds went clear of the chopper, which pulled away and headed further north presumably to better position itself for the next opportunity to fire.

The cracks in the flooring had loosened, and Shah and DeFreitas stuffed canvas into them to stanch the seepage of water. Erikson was tempted to order the crew off the boat but delayed issuing that order until he had taken another try at the helicopter on his right. However, when that chopper turned around, it approached the *Tulsi Das* on a trajectory just above the ocean surface, a move which limited Erikson's firing options. On the crests of the waves, the *Tulsi Das'* bow rose too high to allow Erikson an unrestricted line of fire at the chopper. He ordered the skipper to maneuver westward. The chopper ahead hovered, its machine gun fired again, but the *Tulsi Das* was descending into a trough and the projectiles passed harmlessly overhead. The radio crackled. "Trojan Horse, Trojan Horse, this is Dom Pedro. Over."

"Captain, the radio," Peters shouted.

"I heard," Erikson said, "take the gun." Rushing forward to the radio under the bow and depressing the button on the microphone, Erikson said, "this is Trojan Horse; come in, Dom Pedro."

"The cavalry is here, Trojan Horse," the voice said with no trace of a Brazilian accent.

"And not a moment too soon," Erikson responded. "I have some hot shot in a Hind bearing down on me from the west."

"Not to worry, Trojan Horse," the voice responded, "my pilot assures me he can staple that mother-fucker into the back of his seat with a whiff of flechettes."

"Thank you, Don Pedro. Out."

"Who was that?" Rambarran asked.

"A mutual friend," Erikson replied, declining to identify Colonel Stanford to the crew. He returned to the 50-cal and recommenced firing at the Surinamese helicopter.

So intent was the Surinamese chopper pilot on the chase, he had not noticed the AH-1 Cobra, which had emerged out of the mouth of the Corentyne River and was just a few thousand meters away. The Cobra was maintaining the highest altitude of all of the helicopters in the area but was moving in very rapidly. So, too, was the Hind, which had begun its attack run. Then, the Cobra's minigun fired, its red stream of projectiles forming a parabola, which moved with the Cobra toward the Surinamese chopper and, for a brief moment before the Surinamese chopper exploded, it appeared as if a red hose connected the Cobra to the Surinamese chopper.

The Hind pilot had now recognized the danger and pulled up from its attack run, but it was too late. With the benefit of higher altitude, the Cobra's pilot delivered a pair folding fin aerial rockets, followed by another pair and, from the *Tulsi Das*, the crew observed a red conical dust cloud following the deployed flechettes from each rocket as they struck home. The Hind, which had been ascending, somersaulted after the initial impact, but exploded when blasted by the flechettes from the second pair of rockets. A huge fire ball appeared and dropped quickly into the ocean, and the crew on the *Tulsi Das* screamed in jubilation.

"Trojan Horse, Trojan Horse, this is Dom Pedro. Can we be of further assistance?"

"Thank you, Dom Pedro," Erikson responded. "Can you give us an estimate of the distance from shore?"

"Six miles, Trojan Horse," came the response. "Can we be of further help? This is borrowed equipment, and time is of the essence."

"Fishing boat rendered unseaworthy," Erikson said. "Repeat, fishing boat rendered unseaworthy. Might not make it to the finish line."

"Will see what we can do, Trojan Horse. Tally-ho! Dom Pedro, out."

The rain became heavier; visibility was poorer; and the *Tulsi Das* lumbered forward. Ian Morgan had relieved the skipper, and most of the crew had moved to the bow. Someone had mentioned Archimedes principle, and Rambarran thought shifting the weight on the boat would relieve upward pressure on the area of the cracks. The 50-caliber and ammo canisters had also been moved to the bow. The stuffing in the cracks slowed the water seepage but, with the rain, bailing had become absolutely necessary and was now on a rotation system.

Under the covered bow, Erikson, Rambarran, and the relief crew shared coffee from a thermos. "Shouldn't this be '*Miller* time?'" Rambarran asked, smiling.

"I'll say," Erikson responded. "We need to buy those fellas on that Cobra a beer when we see them."

"Do you think this boat will make it out in its present condition?" Asad Shah asked the skipper.

"I'm not sure," the skipper replied. "The wave crests are about forty feet apart. When we are riding the crests, the pressure on the cracks lessen. It's the descent into the troughs that worry me. We'll have to ease down slowly; that's the best we can do."

The rain continued, and the *Tulsi Das* made slow forward progress. The crew was apprehensive, but performed dutifully. When they had finished their coffee, Andrew Rambarran and Asad Shah went to the stern to relieve Peters and DeFreitas from bailing, and the skipper took back the tiller from Ian Morgan.

Erikson was lying on the foam mattress under the covered bow when the relieved officers joined him. He wished he had been spared the interruption of his thoughts which, for the first time in nearly forty-eight hours, had returned to Anita. With deliverance at hand, he tried to imagine what their reunion would be like. In the short time since the attaché assignment, life for him had changed in a way he could never have imagined.

The sound of gunfire startled Erikson. "It's the *Peccari Two*," he heard Rambarran say. Erikson rushed out of the sleeping area, carrying the 50-caliber. Even without the field glasses, he saw the *Peccari* to the west, moving leisurely on a parallel course. At the stern, Rambarran helped him secure the gun on the steel pedestal. "I'd swear," Rambarran said, "that decorated fellow on the *Peccari* is Colonel McGowan, the new Force Commander."

"He's keeping his distance," Erikson observing the *Peccari* though the field glasses.

"But they can use those 20-millimeter cannons from where they are," Rambarran said.

"How is this boat different from the one we sank earlier?"

"No difference," Rambarran replied. "They're both 105-foot Vosper crafts, which the Comrade Leader named after wild boars, hence *Peccari One* and *Peccari Two*. But they carry the same armaments."

The *Peccari* fired. The shells passed over the *Tulsi Das*. The *Peccari* fired again. The shells fell short. "They have us bracketed," Erikson said.

"Not necessarily," Rambarran responded. "Boats, as you know, are unstable firing platforms. It could be that our undulations are confounding their gunners."

"In that case," Erikson said, "let's give them a whiff of HE rounds." Erikson fired just as the *Tulsi Das* was descending a crest. The rounds went high above the *Peccari*.

"Captain," Shah shouted. "The cracks are widening. The stuffed material had popped out of one crack, and water issued up as from a geyser. Rambarran helped Shah stuff the crack; DeFreitas and Morgan bailed water. The stuffing seemed to be holding. Rambarran ordered the officers to the bow to lessen pressure at the stern.

Erikson fired again at the *Peccari*. The stuffed materials in both cracks flew out and water shot up. The *Tulsi Das* was now sitting on a crest. To prevent the boat from plunging into the trough below and aggravating the cracks, the skipper rode on the crest for a few moments. However, it appeared long enough for the gunners on the *Peccari*. Shells from the *Peccari* struck the tapered bow, shattering the timber and flinging wood splinters, one of which impaled itself in Rambarran's left shoulder, tossing him over the side. The boat went headlong into the trough, capsized and broke apart, scattering its former inhabitants, the poncho rafts, and sections of wood.

Grimacing from the searing pain in his shoulder and the sting from salt water, Rambarran propelled himself toward a poncho raft, which he secured under his right arm while keeping the left above his head. Closest to him was Asad Shah clinging to a curved piece of timber from the bow. Rambarran saw Erikson and the skipper swimming toward floating sections of the boat; the other members of the crew, however, had been carried further away by the waves. He waded closer to Asad Shah, who shifted his position on the timber section to allow Rambarran on. However, Rambarran did not let go of the poncho raft. The pain from his shoulder was intense. At times, he thought he'd pass out, then sprays of salt water assailed his wound and he yelled out. He draped his upper body over the floating timber and, with his right arm, tucked the poncho raft under his chest. Thus they drifted at the whims of the waves.

The relative quiet on the surface of the Atlantic was broken by the loud hum of boat engines. The *Peccari,* black for about six feet above the water and white everywhere else, had arrived at the scene of the wreckage. To Rambarran's horror, riflemen from the patrol boat were being directed to fire on the floating survivors closest to the vessel. The first scream sounded as if it came from DeFreitas. Others in the water were evidently going underwater necessitating repeated firing by the riflemen at the same targets.

"Asad," Rambarran said, "help me unwrap this poncho." Placing the poncho raft on the piece of timber, he urged Shah to undo the slip knot connecting the two ends of the cigarette roll he had made of the poncho around the M-72 rocket. Shah then went to the opposite side and began to slowly unwrap the poncho. When the rocket became visible, he grabbed it and held it up above water while he re-assumed his position on the same side of the piece of floating timber as Rambarran. "Climb on my shoulder," Rambarran said, but when Shah attempted to do so, Rambarran shouted out in pain, and Shah quickly abandoned the effort.

"Let me catch my breath," Rambarran said. After several deep breaths, he nodded to Shah to try again. "It's going to hurt," he conceded, "but we have to do this. Ignore my shouts but work as fast as you can, please."

The *Peccari* had repositioned itself closer to where Rambarran and Shah were, but the riflemen were focused on survivors on the opposite side of the boat. With Rambarran cradling the weapon in both arms, which were draped over the timber, Shah climbed on his shoulders. Uttering gasps of pain between breaths, Rambarran lifted the weapon up for Shah, who quickly extended the inner tube and fired at the exposed mid-section of the *Peccari*, quickly tossing the hollow residue and dropping himself forward into the water. Breathing hard and hoping the pain in his shoulder would pass, Rambarran watched the warhead impact mid-ship, just above the water line. The ensuing explosion shattered the hull of the vessel. Two secondary explosions followed, breaking the *Peccari* apart and creating a fiery indentation between the bow and stern, both of which keeled forward and sank, leaving simmering pieces of debris where only moments before the *Peccari* had recast itself as a vessel of death.

May 8, 2010
Kaieteur Restaurant, Queens, New York

I knew from the get-togethers at our house and at those of my father's friends that all seven from the *Tulsi Das* were eventually picked up by two rigid-hulled inflatable boats dispatched from the CIA trawler, which was waiting outside the territorial limits of Guyana and Suriname. The captain of that vessel had been persuaded by Colonel Stanford and Station Chiefs Hitchcock and McGinnis to fudge the international boundary lines and, for this, the rain provided perfect cover. Michael DeFreitas had suffered a shattered clavicle; Ron Peters had taken a bullet in his upper arm; and Ian Morgan had two badly bruised ribs, a consequence of a grazing from a rifle shot. They and Andrew Rambarran were initially treated on the trawler before being evacuated by helicopter to a Miami hospital for additional medical treatment.

From my mother, Lena Spooner, I learned of the reunion she and Anita Rambarran had with my father, Andrew Rambarran, and Steve Erikson at the Atlanta Airport on May 15, 1980. Great was her joy, my mother said, but she wept for her brother, Ralph, who had not made it. On Saturday, May 31st, 1980, in a double wedding in Cartersville, Georgia, my parents were married along with Steve Erikson and Anita Rambarran. All of the survivors of the February 23rd coup were present for the occasion.

This was the full story. I must confess that over the years I had heard almost all of the key elements. Perhaps, because I had processed it in bits and pieces, first as a child and later as a teenager who felt obliged to listen to the reminiscences of former soldiers, I had not digested the full import of it all. Today was different because the story was narrated from the very beginning, but it stopped with my father's description of their final encounter at sea and with the final shot in the conflict, which, of course, brought the focus back to the man who had delivered it and whose recent demise had provided the occasion for this reunion.

I look across the table at my friend, Altaf, in whose company I have been for much of the past few days. I have no doubt that in the privacy of his family he has been more unrestrained in venting his grief. However, in my presence, he appeared more stoic, even dutiful as he carried out the obligations his family had placed on him. This evening was different. Pride in his father and sorrow at his loss have overwhelmed him. His head is tossed back and his eyes tightly squeezed as tears, defying the swiftness of his hands, roll down his cheeks. Steve Erikson has placed his arm across Altaf's shoulder while Andrew Rambarran offers words of praise for their friend, Asad Shah, a brave man — a man who, like them, had risen against an oppressive regime and kept faith with his comrades when their fortunes seemed dim, and one to whom they owed their lives.

I know that I will hear this story again, in whole or in part. The episodes are now seared into my memory, but most memorable in all of the recountings of this story is the fact that on that fateful May morning when death loomed over seven defenseless souls, undulating on the ocean surface, Asad Shah's aim had proven true, and no one could ever be more grateful to him than me.

CHAITRAM SINGH is the author of The Flour Convoy. A West Point graduate and former officer in the Guyana Defense Force, he currently lives in Rome, Georgia, where he teaches international affairs at Berry College.